NAMELESS PASSION

Devlin's hands took Lauriette's shoulders, forcing her to look up at him. "I do not understand why! Why do you have to leave . . . to run?" he demanded angrily.

"Because," she blurted out. "Because you frighten me! You confuse and bewilder me! You appear in my life like a dark angel—as if you were Lucifer himself come to vex me!"

Devlin's face was so close, Lauriette could see her reflection in his misty brown eyes. She held her breath. He was going to kiss her. She knew it, but she was powerless to prevent it. . . .

Devlin embraced Lauriette, his lips finding hers. It was a gentle, yet urgent kiss. He did not demand a response from her, yet he was doing something to her senses, her control gradually ebbing away.

"Your name, cherub," he whispered huskily. "Tell me your name."

She was breathless, her lips soft and moist from his kiss. Gone were all her fears.

"Lauriette," she whispered back. "I am . . . Lauriette."

by
CYNDY
CARPENTER

ZEBRA BOOKS
KENSINGTON PUBLISHING CORP.

ZEBRA BOOKS

are published by

KENSINGTON PUBLISHING CORP.
475 Park Avenue South
New York, N.Y. 10016

Printed in the United States of America

To Karen and Vicki
who never stopped believing

One

The October wind madly whipped and snapped at the full sails of the *Intrepid*, a sleek well-built American frigate. She glided through the waves with ease on this her first voyage, and the crew felt a surge of pride. Dawn broke with a swift gush of crisp air, and the men silently watched as the sun began its climb from the sea.

The captain stood on deck, his keen eyes observing the crew. Eventually his face broke into a proud, satisfied smile. He would reach London by mid-afternoon—two full days ahead of schedule. This was a fine ship, indeed!

His eyes caught sight of a lone figure standing on the foredeck at the rail. The ever-brightening sun touched the woman's delicate features and a stab of regret ripped violently at his heart. It seemed as if she had blossomed into a woman overnight. Why, it was only yesterday he was drying her tears and tending skinned knees. . . .

The young lady's face held a serenely lovely expression, her blue eyes gazing out at the boundless sea. Her cheeks possessed a cherry pink hue from the wind, the hood of her green velvet cloak covering her mass of golden brown hair.

Sensing someone near, she turned and smiled at the captain, her eyes glistening at the wonder of the sunrise.

"Did you see it, Jamie, the magnificent sunrise?" she asked excitedly. "It was . . . breathtaking! Never have I witnessed anything like it in Philadelphia. I'll remember it forever!"

"Lauriette, you're an incurable romantic," Captain James Claymoor laughed, taking his sister's hands. "If only life was all that warm and wonderful . . . the right man for the right woman?"

"Jamie, this is not to be another lecture, is it?" she inquired impatiently. "How many times must we go through this?"

James lowered his eyes, staring sullenly at the deck. "Are you absolutely sure, pet?" his voice betrayed doubt. "It won't be easy living with Marie-Claire."

"There is just no way around this age-old argument, is there, brother!" she snapped.

"I wish to God this wasn't happening!" he argued hotly. "London is not for you, pet. Our relationship is very uneasy with England and most haven't forgotten the Revolution. They treat Americans the way they do the common folk—with contempt!"

"What about Marie-Claire?" she demanded.

"Marie-Claire has never been an American," he replied. "She may have been born there, but she has always maintained we were nothing but savages. Oh, no, Lauriette, Marie-Claire does nicely in the London society. She is a true-blooded English snob."

"Why don't you just face the truth," she declared, her blue eyes icy with anger. "You dislike Evan. If Elliott approves of him, why can't you?"

"Lauriette, my innocent, you've never given any

young man in Philadelphia an opportunity to approach you,'' he said softly, trying desperately to make her understand. ''I realize it was hard for you after Henry, but I do not think you've been fair to yourself. How can you marry a man you hardly know and how on earth can you live under the same roof with Henry and Marie-Claire?''

''As to Henry and Marie-Claire, I've gotten over my infatuation with him and the only thing I feel in my heart now is an affection I would give a brother-in-law,'' she explained tolerantly. ''And as for Evan, I know him well enough. He is all I want in a husband. He's good and kind—and I love him!''

James' boisterous laughter caught the ear of many of the crew. ''Love!'' he mocked. ''Pet, you've not yet felt the fiery touch of love! What you feel is a false sense of security with a man who hardly courted you before being whisked back to London without your having a chance to really know him. How can you say you love someone who you only saw approximately half a dozen times—while in the company of others? That brother of ours; if I had my hands on him right now . . .''

''You'd do nothing,'' Lauriette finished for him. ''Elliott only sought my happiness, nothing more!''

By now, most of the crew were secretly stealing glances at the battling Claymoors. This was not the first argument they had heard since leaving Philadelphia.

''Your happiness?'' he repeated with a slight sneer in his voice. ''Politician Claymoor, wishing to keep Sir Evan Brimley happy, subtlely throwing hints at you about the man's fine qualities and his blue blood? Bah! I know brother Elliott better than you think, little sister, and you are softheaded enough to think he was doing this little matchmaking for your welfare!''

''Evan asked and I accepted,'' she flung back at him. ''The only thing Elliott did was introduce us. He neither held a gun to my head nor threatened me with bodily injury if I did not accept Evan's proposal. And he gave us his blessings, which is more than I can say for you!'' She began pacing back and forth. ''You're only upset because you didn't have your hand in this. You'd sooner me wed one of those impossible boring friends who frequent Elliott's study.''

''To hell with all of them!'' he roared, his rugged face red with anger. '' 'Twould not matter if your man was but a common seaman, as long as you loved him. I don't trust The Honorable Evan Brimley and he's not my idea of a husband for you. What he is, is entirely different than what he appears.''

''You're being totally unfair, James Phillip!'' she accused, eyes narrowing.

Their eyes locked in silent battle.

''Fourteen months can change a man, pet.'' His voice softened.

''I accepted his proposal and I will go through with it,'' she vowed stubbornly.

''So, once again you'll have to learn the hard way, little sister,'' he answered coldly. ''I wonder which one of us is right? Care to place a small wager?''

Lauriette lay on her bunk staring at the ceiling. The argument with James had completely drained her. Why did she feel so guilty? After all, it was *he* who started it! This only made the hundredth time they argued about Evan, and no doubt before he left for the sea again, they would again. One thing about brother James—he was definitely persistent!

With a muffled groan, she rolled onto her stomach and pounded her fist into the pillow. *Damn James!* she cursed. He was continually making her think, making her examine her feelings.

There was a firm rap on the door and without waiting for Lauriette's response, James entered. Gone was any trace of anger from his face and he smiled affectionately at her. Though they quarreled often, their anger was always shortlived.

He gently placed his hands on her shoulders. "Am I forgiven, pet?" he asked in a half-whisper.

"There's nothing to forgive," she answered in the same tone. "You're my brother . . . and I'll always love you."

James fiercely hugged her, anxiety over her future encompassing him. "Together we've battled the world," he murmured sadly. "Ghosts, goblins, boogeymen under your bed—It's just so hard to let go. I've been your protector for so long . . ." his voice broke, then trailed off.

"Jamie," she breathed, tears rolling down her cheeks, "I'll miss you so!"

He lifted her chin and looked squarely into her eyes. "Lauriette, move cautiously into this marriage with Brimley. Look very deep into your heart and make sure—make *very* sure—it is what you want. Remember, once the deed is done it is too late."

Lauriette waited on deck watching James tend to the securing of his ship. She felt disappointment at the first sight of the London docks. This was not how she remembered it from four years ago, but then at seventeen a young woman sees things through different eyes.

"The Royal Coach Inn is not too far from here and is a most respectable establishment," James said, cutting into her thoughts. "I've arranged two rooms and a coach to take you there. I'm sure you would like a hot bath and a good night's sleep on a soft bed before facing the shrew."

"How long will you be?" she asked as he handed her into the coach.

"I'll arrive in time to dine with you," he replied, then looked at her sharply. "Lauriette, remember that you are in London now and not back in Philadelphia. No scampering about without a care in the world. The English idea of proper and ours are two different things. Be good." He shut the door and at a wave of his hand the coach lurched forward and Lauriette was on her way.

Leaning back, she drew a weary sigh. That James! Of course she knew that customs were different here than in Philadelphia. She was not exactly a nitwit no matter what brother James thought!

Her thoughts then ran to Evan. He knew she was to arrive some time this month. Would he be surprised and happy to see her? Of course he would! There would be so many plans to make, her time in Marie-Claire's home would race by. Thoughtfully, she frowned. It was true that she and Evan had not known each other very long, and if she were to stop and let herself dwell on it, she would have to admit that she did not know him well at all. But in Philadelphia he made her feel most comfortable in his company and did not try to presume or make any demands upon her. Did she love Evan? The answer was no. She liked and respected him very much, but the feelings she had for him were not like the ones she had had for Henry. She was certain, though, that after their marriage she would learn to love him. James had to be wrong, he just had to be!

The coach came to a gradual halt in front of the century-old inn, and within moments the coachman lifted Lauriette to the ground. She stood trying to familiarize herself with the many buildings while the driver took her trunk inside. Not much of this street had changed, yet many things had—so many lives had been turned around.

Her room was small but clean and very comfortable

looking. The sunlight filtered through the small window and made a pattern across the bed in the middle of the floor. She was too excited to take a long soak in the tub and a nap. An afternoon like this was meant for exploring, adventuring, not being cooped up in a stuffy room awaiting a brother who would no doubt be late!

She grinned impishly as she caught sight of herself in the oval mirror. Her face was flushed with excitement, her eyes were sparkling. *Do it!* her inner self urged. *Before you are penned in with custom and propriety. Before you have to become as they. One last jaunt as Philadelphia-born Lauriette Claymoor.*

With a sudden tilt of her chin, she checked the ribbons of her bonnet in the mirror and hurried out the door. She had three or four long hours before James would join her, and it seemed a fine idea to defy James just once more.

Lauriette strolled down the cobbled street oblivious to the curious stares she aroused in the passersby. She looked into this window and that and on impulse browsed through this store and that.

The smell of fresh baked goods filled the air and Lauriette's mouth watered. She turned into the small establishment and purchased hot bread from the baker. Turning out of the store she walked slowly, savoring the taste of it and the memories it brought on.

Her mind was filled with precious memories of summer picnics at Claymoor, of fresh baked bread and homemade jam and county fairs. It had been such a delightful summer—at least what she could remember of it. There had been lazy, breezy days, starlit nights, romantic balls, Henry . . .

She stopped suddenly, a frown creasing her brow. With a defiant shake of her head, Lauriette vowed not to think of the past any longer.

So preoccupied with her thoughts was she that she

did not realize how far she had walked until the squeaking sounds of a fiddle and loud, brawling laughter brought her back to the present. Her eyes scanned the area. Everything looked so unfamiliar. Panic began to mount and she nervously looked about. She seemed to remember turning a corner—or did she?

Lauriette turned to try and retrace her steps but was blocked by a tall, burly-looking seaman. His whole appearance was filthy, his clothes ragged and torn. He looked down at her and smiled, showing a mouthful of decaying teeth.

"Well now, girlie, an' who might ye be?"

"I—I was on my way home," she said, praying her voice was not trembling. "Let me pass, please."

The man threw back his head and laughed. "So! Ye wanna go home, eh, little lady?" he said in a sinister tone. "What's wrong then wi' me home?"

The panic Lauriette felt became almost uncontrollable. The man's eyes! Those terrifying black eyes! She began to back away from him, but he was expecting just that and in one quick movement his hand pulled at her wrist.

"Now, now, wench," he whispered, licking his lips, "yer wouldn't wan' ta run away from ol' Jake." In an instant, he loosened the ribbons of her bonnet and gave it a toss. He eyed her keenly in the waning sunlight and slowly let out a low whistle. "Ye be right comely wench. Ol' Jake's luck's a-turnin' ."

Oh, dear God! she breathed. "Please, let me go! There—there are people out looking for me and you'll have the devil to pay if I'm harmed. Now let me go!"

From behind them came the sound of a pistol cocking. The satisfied look on the man's face fell and slowly he turned to face the unknown enemy.

Night was quickly falling and whoever had cocked that pistol stood in the shadows of the alley. Lauriette's heart was pounding; it was a living nightmare and it was pulling her closer to something hidden in her mind. She was becoming dizzy and faltered against the man.

From out of the darkness came the sound of a deep, cooly controlled voice. "The lady—and as you can see by her dress she *is* a lady—does not care for your company."

"An' who just ye might be?" he asked arrogantly, a bit of his courage coming back.

"Just someone who does not like to see a lady molested," came the lazy reply. "Now, if you will release her."

The man glared down at the pale girl, then back to the shadows. "An' if I don't?"

"Then I guess I shall have to fire this pistol that's pointed at your belly." The deep voice was even and dangerously calm.

The man laughed nervously. "Well, now, there ain't no wench worth gettin' shot over."

"A fine decision," the voice agreed. "Now if you will just turn around and start walking toward the docks. . . . Aye, that's fine."

The burly man walked with a slow, steady gait for a few yards and then broke into a frantic run, disappearing into the oncoming darkness.

Lauriette went down on her knees trying to ease the dizziness away. She had been so childish and willful walking the streets of London alone. At the moment Philadelphia seemed so far away!

The flash of fear she had could not be recalled; it had been no more than an impression but it had left her weak with terror.

"Are you all right, mistress?" that same deep voice asked softly.

A pair of highly polished Hessian boots stood only a foot away. Lauriette looked up and found her eyes were irresistibly drawn to the man who had rescued her. His brown eyes were on her, they were soft and unreadable, yet she did not fear him. He was fashionably dressed and spoke with only a hint of an English accent. Wearing no powdered wig, his hair showed a curly brown reaching to his collar.

"I—I only needed a moment to—to collect myself," she answered weakly. "I'm fine now."

He offered his hand and she willingly took it. She could barely see in the dark but could make out the scowl on the man's face.

"Mistress, what the devil are you doing here by the docks without an escort?" he demanded. "Have you any idea what could have happened if I hadn't just come along?"

Lauriette was on the brink of tears but firmly refused to let this self-appointed protector see her cry. "Your London streets leave much to be desired!" she retorted angrily. "If you'll just point me in the direction of the Royal Coach Inn, I'll be on my way!" Without even bothering to look for her bonnet, she pulled the hood of her cloak up and waited for the man's reply.

"So it's the Royal Coach Inn, my little American friend." Without another word he roughly grabbed her arm and began marching her up the darkened street, her feet barely able to keep up with him. Lauriette was out of breath by the time they reached the inn.

"Thank you and good night," she said curtly.

His hand was still on her arm. "Oh, no, I'll see you to your door," he said harshly. "To make certain you aren't accosted by someone in the hall."

Before she could reply, the man ushered her into the inn. Brushing past several people, they mounted the stairs and entered the long, dimly lit corridor. Lauriette breathed a sigh of relief as they reached her door.

Automatically, she removed her hood and leaned

against the wall. "Thank you for seeing me to my—" She stopped short, looking up to see the man boldly staring at her.

"The pleasure is mine, mistress. Mistress?"

She lowered her eyes, blushing deeply. "There are no words to properly repay you for rescuing me," she said feeling a bit uneasy under the amused gleam in his brown eyes.

He placed an arm against the wall beside her shoulder. "Have supper with me tonight—downstairs."

She looked at him for a long moment, watching his eyes sparkle. "I'm sorry," she answered, "but I've already been engaged for this evening."

"Then perhaps payment can be made this way . . ."

Before Lauriette knew what was happening, his arms encircled her waist like a steel band and pulled her against him, kissing her full on her startled mouth. His tongue forced her lips apart and he gently plundered the sweetness of it. He was being forceful yet tender at the same time.

Using all her strength, Lauriette managed to pull away from his lips and immediately his arms released her. She was burning with anger at herself as well as this man who presumed to take liberties. She found herself trembling inside and was not at all sure of the cause of it. She lashed out, slapping him with a force that surprised him, the sound of it echoing down the empty hallway.

Lauriette glared at him contemptuously. "I believe, sir, you've now been paid—in full!" Presenting her back to him, she entered her room and with all her angry strength, slammed the door in his face.

He stood there for several minutes staring at the closed door and rubbing his reddened jaw. *Those bewitching eyes!* he mused. *Horizon blue is what they are . . . a sensuous mixture of blue and sea green. Quite a little spitfire.*

He mockingly bowed to the door and with a whistle on his lips, sauntered towards the stairs.

Lauriette stood beside her bed, her small hands rolled into fists. She was still trembling, an undefinable sensation pulsing through her blood. No one had ever kissed her like that before—neither Henry nor Evan ever caused such a tempest inside her that way. *It was the circumstances,* she told herself, *and him catching me so off guard.*

Absently, she traced the outline of her lips, which still burned from the pressure of his mouth. The sensation was pleasurable. She felt no fear of him. But this was insane! To have that kind of feeling . . . and with a stranger . . .

Lauriette sank to the bed, her eyes tightly closed. She was determined to blot out all memory of this evening . . . and of the dark stranger!

Two

The skies over London were dark. Rain was pouring down as the coach came to an abrupt halt in front of an impressive townhouse. With a whispered stream of oaths James alighted first and then assisted Lauriette, covering them both with his greatcoat.

Lauriette's laughter bubbled forth as James's boot carelessly found a puddle. He groaned aloud and looked to his sister, who was doing her best to control her mirth. By the time Jonas, the footman, opened the door they were both overcome with hearty laughter.

"Mr. James! Miss Lauriette!" the bondsman cried happily, relieving them of their wet garments.

They rudely stared at the man dressed in gold satin and sporting a powdered wig. James and Lauriette collapsed against each other as another fit of laughter shook them. Jonas stood wide-eyed, his mouth set grimly. He had known these two their entire lives, his affection for them deep and tender. Frantically, he tried to hush them, glancing towards the sitting room door.

"Oh, Jonas," Lauriette cried breathlessly. "Forgive our humor, but that *wig!*"

Jonas felt embarrassed. He despised the blasted thing, but his mistress insisted he wear it. "Part of being the help, missie."

Lauriette looked upon him with such warm affection. "It's been so long," she said softly, giving the old servant a brisk hug. "I can tell you, you're missed at home."

Jonas smiled sadly and replied, "I miss home. . . ."

"What in heaven's name is going—"

Lauriette turned to see her sister, Marie-Claire, staring at her as if she was some terrible apparition. Four years had done little to change her beauty. Her golden hair was piled high in the latest Parisian fashion, her pale blue eyes still beheld Lauriette with cold contempt while her full lips wore the smile of a polite hostess.

"Hello, James, Lauriette," she said, trying to compose herself. "I'm afraid we were not expecting you for several more days."

"Well, we're here, Marie-Claire, even though it is a few days ahead of schedule," he said flatly. There was no love lost between them, his voice showing no false affection. "Are you going to invite us in or do you plan to have us die of chill in this wretched foyer?"

The flicker of a frown tugged at the corners of her mouth, but remembering James's goading manner from childhood, Marie-Claire ignored this remark. "How remiss of me," she apologized sweetly. "Please, come and enjoy the warmth of my sitting room." She looked past her guests and barked, "Jonas! See to Miss Lauriette's trunks at once!"

The servant bowed curtly. "At once, milady."

James smiled reassuringly and took Lauriette's arm. She could not help but be nervous here in Marie-Claire's house. It was evident being separated from her for four years did not endear her to her sister. If she could only understand what she had ever done to antagonize her so.

Lauriette paused inside the door, her eyes eagerly taking in the richness of the room. Marie-Claire had excellent taste and the room was lavishly done in lavender and yellow, but even this room felt as cold and unwelcoming as Marie-Claire herself.

"Where is Henry on such a dastardly night?" James asked, warming himself by the fire.

"Henry and a few of his friends are spending the evening at their club," she answered simply. "As a matter of fact, Evan is with them at this very moment. You did not know that, did you Lauriette? Evan and Henry are such very good friends."

Marie-Claire moved around the sofa to where she could plainly see her sister. No, the only thing four years did to Lauriette was to make her lovelier. She despised this little milksop her brothers adored.

"I hope you'll be comfortable while you are here," she remarked evenly. "Henry took special care in choosing your room. He thought you might prefer one overlooking the garden."

A deep blush covered her face. "You and Henry are too kind."

Marie-Claire looked down at her rose satin gown and impatiently brushed away a bit of imagined lint. "I was not being kind at all," she whispered jealously. "Henry only sought to please you."

Lauriette felt James's hand on her shoulder. He was scowling at Marie-Claire, his blue eyes smoldering. She gave him a warning glance. "Marie, can we not forget the past?" Lauriette asked. "I have come here to marry Evan. You are Henry's wife. I could never forget that. I am no threat." Lauriette held her hands out imploringly. Could nothing at all change her sister's feelings? "I'll do my best to stay out of your way. Please, can we not try to become at least civil to one another?"

"Lauriette, you misunderstand." Marie-Claire's lip curled contemptuously. "The past *is* forgotten here. Henry is a very happy man with me as his wife—we love each other so! I did not mean to imply that I feel threatened by your presence, heavens no!" She turned to James. "Will you be spending time with us, James?"

"I wish I could," he said uneasily, "but I must sail on the morning tide."

"Then you will not be here for Lauriette's wedding."

James lowered his head. "Unfortunately, not," he replied.

"Come, James, I'll see you to the door."

James knew he had been defeated at last. Lauriette had refused to let him free her of her promise to a deceitful man, an ambitious brother, and from the clutches of an unfeeling sister.

He stood before Marie-Claire, loathing the sight of the beautiful woman. Always there was the undercurrent of contempt between the two. How could she be his flesh and blood, sired by the same parents? This woman was a total stranger.

"I bid you farewell, Marie," he said in a threatening tone. "Mind you treat our sister well. I'll be returning within six months and will settle any problems at that time."

Marie-Claire could feel the underlying threat in his calm voice. She smiled faintly. "To be sure, dear brother, I pray your journey will be a stormy one."

Lauriette was shocked by the vehemence in her voice and the distinct curse she laid upon him.

Under the carefully concealed eyes of the curious servants of Branscombe House, James hugged Lauriette tightly, as if not to let go. Tears welled up in her blue eyes and his image became blurred. She loved this man so! Suddenly, an overwhelming feeling of hopelessness rose and she had to fight down the urge to leave with him.

"I love you, pet," his voice sounded strained. "I'll return in six months to see how you fare." He looked past Lauriette at the sitting room. "Remember my words, little sister, look deep into your heart. Make very sure you do what is right for you."

"God speed, Jamie," she cried against his chest. "May He put a fair wind in your sails and a smooth sea to bring you safely back."

He cupped her small face in his hands and placed a lasting kiss upon her forehead. "Aye," he whispered, "I'll be back and there'll be hell to pay if you're the least bit unhappy!"

Three

Lauriette stood quietly, arms extended away from her sides and did her best to remain patient. Madame Charbeau turned her this way and that, snipping a piece of cloth here, pinning the pink satin fabric there.

Dolly sat back admiring her new mistress. It was the luckiest day of her life when Lady Marie-Claire assigned her to look after her sister. She smiled warmly and greeted her more as a friend rather than a lowly servant. From that moment on, she became devoted to her just as Jonas was.

Concern over her mistress's health caused a worried frown on the plump woman's face. Miss Lauriette appeared so pale and drawn, dark circles under those brilliant eyes.

"Miss Lauriette," she said softly, " 'Tis been over two hours ye've been a-standin'."

"Only a few moments longer, mademoiselle," Madame Charbeau said quickly, tossing an angry look toward Dolly. "This will be the final fitting. I beg of you, *cherie,* a few more moments."

Lauriette smiled weakly at Dolly, her blue eyes watering. "A few more moments won't make any difference."

Madame Charbeau stood back, arms akimbo, and appraised her work. This lovely thing would be the talk of London! Mademoiselle Claymoor did justice to her beautiful creations.

Dolly hastily helped Lauriette out of the ballgown and into a lavender street dress. " 'Tis disgraceful the way ye have to come here when her ladyship usually has the dressmaker come to her," she whispered angrily, "an' ye not feelin' well!"

"My, Dolly! You sound as fierce as Jamie!" she teased a smile from the woman.

"Aye, and well I should be," she retorted with a bit of her humor restored. "Ye've not slept well since ye entered Lord Branscombe's house and look at them dark circles under yer eyes."

Lauriette turned around, picking up her cloak. "Please, Dolly, don't carry on so," she pleaded.

Dolly said no more but assisted Lauriette into the green velvet cloak. No matter how the young woman protested, Dolly knew something was amiss. There were times when Miss Lauriette seemed beside herself, terror written on her face, and try as she may to hide it, the concerned maid could see through her facade.

The October wind rustled Lauriette's skirts as they left Madame Charbeau's. It was a lovely autumn day; red and gold leaves raced passed them like a small hurricane, coming to rest beneath a carriage.

"Dolly, the day is too lovely to spend it inside with a passel of cackling ladies," she laughed. "Come! Let us stroll a bit."

"But, Missey, are ye sure? I mean, ye don't—"

"Come along, Dolly," she cut in decisively, "the walk will do us both a world of good."

With a swish of her skirts, Lauriette left Dolly standing utterly speechless. The maid had to run to keep up with her.

Lauriette was deeply troubled as Dolly's keen eyes suspected. After James' return to sea, her sleep became anything but peaceful. There was nothing she could clearly define. When she awoke, all she knew was the the dreams were terrifying.

During her waking hours there were flashes of something—memory perhaps—that would tug at her consciousness then vanish. Tiny, minute bits that made no sense whatsoever. Even with Evan it would happen. This—this strange occurrence would take place and sometimes she would even be terrified of him!

What was happening? Was she going insane?

"Ye seem ta know this part o' town well, miss," Dolly cut into her thoughts.

She slowed her pace, waiting until the breathless maid caught up to her. They were now standing in front of an alleyway.

"My Uncle James was a country squire." She smiled faintly. "He lived on an estate, Claymoor, in Dorset. We came to spend the summer about four years ago—all of us. Has her ladyship never taken you there? It's such a lovely country home, away from the bustle of city life. In some ways it reminded me of our farm."

"Ah, I like th' country," Dolly mused.

"When our uncle died, he willed Claymoor to Elliott. He has been sending money to Marie-Claire for its upkeep. I'm surprised she hasn't taken the entire household out there. Seems a shame to stay cooped up in London when one has permission to reside at Claymoor." She sighed. "The house is so beautiful—particularly this time of year. The woods are an artist's delight. I loved staying there."

Dolly could see the pain upon the young woman's face. "Why then did ye leave, miss?"

"It was . . . only a holiday, Dolly," she murmured. "I became ill and my family thought it best for us to return home."

"Oh-h, miss!" Dolly breathed excitedly. "Look at that grand coach a-passin' by with those beautiful matching white horses!"

Suddenly, fragments flashed past her eyes as she stared in horror at the animals, the image so strong she covered her eyes. The horses! She could see blood streaking one side—fresh, human blood!

Lauriette swayed; Dolly screamed out, imploring someone to help. She had known something like this would happen—she had known it in her bones!

Strong arms embraced her as she began to slump forward and Lauriette felt herself being lifted up. The clean scent of soap and tobacco encompassed her. The images began to fade and blur as blackness finally brought her into nothingness.

"Oh, sir, sir!" Dolly cried, still wringing her hands. "God bless yer soul for helpin' us. I tried to talk her out o' takin' th' walk but the dear's so stubborn!"

The gentleman's dark eyes seemed to dance with a life of their own. He gazed at the young lady's calm face. She weighed a mere nothing in his arms and this thought brought a half-smile to his lips.

"Where is your carriage?"

"In front o' Madame Charbeau's," Dolly replied quickly.

"Best see to getting it here then," he said gently. "I'm afraid carrying your mistress through the street would cause quite a stir."

"Yer most certainly right, sir." She nodded and scurried towards the open street.

Taking the opportunity, he gazed at the girl in his arms for a long moment. It was the same young woman he rescued two weeks before. She was quite pretty, her skin a smooth, creamy color, not the deathly pale white of English ladies. Her nose was small, turning up at the end; her mouth full yet not to the point of being pouty. Long golden lashes shadowed her pale cheeks and he recalled those horizon blue eyes.

"Here it is," he heard Dolly's anxious voice. "She's over here, Mr. Clooney."

Mr. Clooney, the old livery, jumped down immediately from his seat, concern for his mistress's sister prompting him on.

"Now, what's all this?" he demanded of Dolly. She pointed toward the far end of the alley. "Oh, dear! The young missie!"

"She's fainted," she said anxiously. "Knew this would happen."

Mr. Clooney shook his head. "Rushin' her," he muttered. "Always a-wantin' somethin' from her. Poor, poor missie."

Lauriette began to stir, a soft moan escaping her lips. Presently her eyelids began to flutter and once again the scent of soap and tobacco filled her nostrils. She gradually opened them to find twinkling brown eyes staring back.

"Thank goodness, Mr. Clooney!" Dolly exclaimed. "She's comin' around."

Lauriette's cheeks blushed hotly to find herself being held in a man's arms. "Good gracious, sir, put me down!" she said indignantly. "I am in no way a cripple. Put me down!"

With little effort the gentleman placed her on her feet. Embarrassed, she glared at the man, her pert chin lifted a degree. This was the same man who had helped her on the docks!

"Now, missie," Dolly scolded, "this here gentleman kept ye from fallin'."

Guiltily, she lowered her eyes, a blush creeping upon

her again. "Forgive me, sir," she apologized softly.

His voice was deep and husky. "You are forgiven." With a slight tip of his hat, he turned and weaved in and out of traffic on the busy street.

Absently, Lauriette looked after him, her eyes darting back and forth but could find no trace of the man.

Dolly tenderly laid her hand upon the young woman's arm. "Come along, Miss Lauriette, time to get ye home."

She looked back one last time, not understanding her urge to see his face again.

"Do ye know him, missie?"

Lauriette nodded her head slowly. "I've seen him before, Dolly," came her soft reply.

Devlin Essex leaned back in the overstuffed chair, his tense muscles gradually relaxing. Contemplating, he stared down at his glass of brandy, a mysterious smile appearing.

Strange, he had hardly given that young woman a second thought since that night he had come to her aid. She was definitely not dreamlike today, he thought, remembering her startled cherub face when she opened those beautiful eyes.

"Horizon blue," he whispered aloud.

Frowning, he rose and freshened his drink. It was a sign that he must be getting too old for this cat-and-mouse game, when his thoughts begin to wander aimlessly over a wench with an unsavory disposition and a penchant for getting into trouble.

"Well, darling, I see you finally decided to keep our appointment."

Devlin lifted his glass in a toast. The woman was stunning, dressed in orchid satin, the neckline barely concealing her well-endowed charms. The blond hair was powdered and piled high, diamonds sparkling throughout the coiffure. Her soft brown eyes boldly showed her passionate nature, her voluptuous lips turning into a welcoming smile.

"I hope Gervis made you comfortable," she purred, lightly touching his arm.

"Comfortable indeed, Salene," he replied.

"How fortunate dear Oberly introduced us," she whispered. "I have long wanted to meet this close friend who is a living legend."

"My *acquaintance* thrives on listing my shortcomings," Devlin laughed.

"I do not think that they are shortcomings," Salene smiled. "I believe I could listen to you . . . forever!"

Devlin wearily shook his head, eyes lowered to his glass. This beautiful woman was no different from the rest he knew: shallow, spoiled, self-indulgent, marriage-hungry bitches with no other thought than of their own comfort. It was always this way—the flattery, the undivided attention. Then as the acquaintance blossomed into an affair, it would become endless whining and clinging.

Enjoy it, my man, he thought to himself. *Soon you'll be headed for the American frontier, leaving behind a bedful of broken hearts!*

Four

Marie-Claire paced back and forth across the sitting room, her finely arched brows drawn downward in a most unbecoming frown. The days were almost unbearable since the arrival of Lauriette. The simpering little chit seemed to have enchanted the entire household, each servant not being able to do enough for her!

"How can I go on like this?" she pouted. "The servants bow and scrape to her every command, listening attentively to every word she utters. And Henry! He is nothing but putty in her cunning hands!"

"I think your statement is greatly exaggerated, Marie."

Evan Brimley turned back to the window, watching Lauriette with pad in hand and Marie-Claire's husband, Henry, posing for her. A smile pulled at the corners of his mouth; in the time he had spent away from her, he had forgotten how lovely she was.

"I simply cannot give this ball!" she sniffed. "I shall be the laughingstock of London, announcing to all your betrothal to that—"

Evan turned, his cool blue eyes showing displeasure.

"She has to be properly introduced into society, Marie, you know that. I have been banished long enough and my peers need to see what I am doing to redeem myself."

"But the Winter Ball, Evan!"

"She is your sister, Marie, did you forget that?" he said impatiently. "Remember, it was actually you who first brought her to my attention."

"Had I known how taken you would become with her, I never would have suggested this alliance!"

Evan laughed, his lips barely brushing her ear. "We're alike, you and I. Your extravagance keeps dear Henry on his toes and my passion for gaming has me needing constantly. You said yourself the Claymoors are a rich lot—rich enough to keep both of us happy."

Sighing, she snuggled against him. "I love you so, Evan."

"I know you do, Marie," he answered absently. "I know."

"Tilt your chin just a little more," Lauriette quietly said, concentrating on the sketch of Henry. "Now, straighten your back . . . you're beginning to slouch like an old man."

"Old man!" he retorted. "I'll have you know I'm barely thirty, Mistress Claymoor."

Lauriette could not suppress her laughter any longer and momentarily Henry laughed too. She had secretly been afraid of the time when they would come face to face after four long years, but Henry sensed her misgivings and made it as easy for her as possible.

"Now let's get back to the job at hand," she tried to sound stern. "I dare say you're not cut out to be an artist's model."

As if she had delivered the ultimate insult, Henry stared straight ahead and sat erect. Four years had aged him more than she cared to admit. He was still one of the handsomest men she ever encountered, but now his light brown hair was beginning to gray prematurely at the temples, his blue eyes seemed to have lost a lot of the liveliness she remembered so well. Perhaps she looked at a face more closely than others—perhaps no one took the time to wonder about the deep frown lines around his mouth or the tiny creases at the eyes. Lauriette felt so much compassion for him!

"I've hardly had a chance to talk to you since your arrival," he finally said, sneaking a side-long glance.

She stopped abruptly and looked at him. "Yours is a very busy house, Henry, what with the ball only a week away and my wedding a fortnight after."

"Do you love him, Lauriette?"

She had mentally prepared herself for that question, but the sound of Henry actually voicing it startled her more than she thought it would. It would have been so easy to say yes and have done with it—to leave nary a doubt in Henry's mind, but she had always done her best to be honest with him from the beginning of their friendship.

"No, but I'm truly fond of him," she answered. "People have been known to marry for less."

Guiltily, he stared at the ground. "How well I know," his voice was almost a whisper. "Has Marie-Claire been civil to you? Knowing her, it would be the very best she would offer."

"I do my best to stay out of her way," she replied grimly.

Lauriette placed her pad and charcoal aside and quickly wiped her hands on a lace handkerchief. Proudly, she handed Henry his portrait and watched with pleasure as his face broke into a smile.

"Is that how you see me?"

"An artist sees much more than others, I think."

"Do you remember that summer at Claymoor, the day you talked me into letting you sketch me and you drew buckskins on me?"

Lauriette laughed, remembering the incident clearly. "As I recall you became furious and tore the picture into tiny pieces, calling me—what was that?"

" 'Rebel twit,' I believe," he grinned.

"Ah, yes! 'Rebel twit' and also, you included 'hussy' now and then." Lauriette could see it as if it were yesterday. "Then you had the audacity to call General Washington a pompous upstart—and you even added Mr. Franklin's good name!"

Henry was laughing heartily. "And then you jumped up calling me a 'redcoat jackass' and then you pushed me into the pond!"

Lauriette laughed till her sides ached. "Your poor coat," she cried, "and that terrible wig all wet and dripping!"

"I sneezed for days!" he guffawed. "That was the day I asked you—"

The laughter died out leaving them with an aching silence. Lauriette turned away, unable to endure the longing in his eyes.

"Lauriette, four years hasn't changed a thing," he whispered urgently. "I still love you."

"Henry, no!"

"Hear me out," he pleaded. "I was wrong—wrong to obey my father's wishes, wrong not to stand up to him. It should be you in that house, in my bed every night, not Marie-Claire!"

"Don't say another word, please!" she begged. "You are my sister's husband and you'll always be. I can't forget that—and neither can you!"

Footsteps neared the garden and both Henry and Lauriette said no more. Evan was walking towards them, his sure gait unmistakable.

"Well, I see today's sitting is at an end," he said slowly, observing the sober expression on Henry's face.

"Yes, Evan, we just finished," he said stiffly, and without so much as a farewell, he strode hastily to the house.

"Did Henry say something to offend you?" Evan's voice was stern.

Lauriette looked at him slowly, noticing the cold look on his face. "We simply had a disagreement . . . about my sketching of him," she lied.

"That is strange." He was staring at her with that cool indifferent way of his. "From yon window it looked as if you two were having a grand time."

Her eyes widened in surprise, unable to read the look on his face. Since arriving in London, Lauriette had seen a marked difference in Evan's attention to her. Gone was the undemanding gentleman she had been attracted to in Philadelphia and in his place was a stranger with a disturbing light in his eyes and an overpowering attitude towards her.

He began immediately by playing games with her; games Lauriette could only describe as cat-and-mouse. It seemed as if he knew every move she made, every breath she took. Even the smallest minute detail of an inconsequential moment he took pleasure in telling her all about.

The questions he threw at her were designed to startle her and they were always done so in a cool indifferent manner. It was grating on her fragile nerves and becoming increasingly difficult to control her temper.

"I need not account to you for my actions, sir, and I resent your spying on me as if I were some unfaithful wife!" she answered impatiently.

As if to apologize, Evan pulled her into his arms. This she allowed reluctantly.

"You cannot blame me, my dear, if I appear the

anxious bridegroom. As a matter of fact, you are the only woman I ever desired to marry. Does that help to soothe your injured feelings?"

"It is not an unpleasant thing to hear," she said shyly. When he was gentle like this Lauriette did not mind him holding her at all.

"I understand you fell ill at the dressmakers the other day," he said as he still held her tightly. Placing his hand under her chin he raised her face to look into his eyes. "You are still quite pale."

Lauriette disengaged herself and stood, pulling the cloak closely about her. Again he knew more than what she imagined.

"It has been the pace," she explained. "I came directly back and stayed abed the rest of the day."

He watched her expression closely, looking for any change in her sober demeanor. "Marie-Claire tells me a gentleman came to your aide."

Lauriette arched a brow. How had Marie-Claire found out about the man? She was positive neither Dolly or Mr. Clooney would breathe a word to her sister. Could it really be true that he was having her followed?

"That is true," her reply came slow. "He was kind enough to help me to the coach."

"Did you know him, Lauriette?" he asked bluntly.

Angrily, she lifted her chin. "Evan, why all these silly questions? My answer is no! I did not know that gentleman! Are you satisfied?"

He nodded, smiling that unusual smile of his. Before she could move away, his hands roughly grabbed her shoulders. "I don't care for the idea of any man laying a hand on you." His voice was so soft and calm it frightened her even more. "You're too lovely for your own good, Lauriette. I'm a jealous bastard and I'm the first to admit it. Remember that always!"

The look on his face was an intense, burning expression that caused panic to rise in her. She could not move, his hands firmly holding her still. Evan's mouth hurtfully claimed hers, one hand holding her tightly, the other moving to the inside of her cloak.

Trembling, Lauriette pulled away, bits of memory jolting her. This was not the gentle Evan who courted her in Philadelphia! This was someone she did not know!

"Don't pull away from me." His voice held suppressed anger.

The terrified look in her eyes cooled Evan's ire and he gradually released her. Nursing her bruised arms, she ran to the safety of the house.

Evan stood back and watched as she disappeared through the garden gate, feeling the oncoming of winter at his heels. Mistress Lauriette would indeed have a lot to learn after their marriage—and he smiled at the thought of teaching her!

Five

Salene Thompson, Lady Boling, lay back against the softness of her satin pillows, her full lips slightly parted and curving into a satisfied smile. She watched the meticulous movements of her lover as he dressed.

Salene's blue eyes devoured his features, raking over the slim, muscular body like a hungry she-cat. By heavens, he was a beautiful animal! The man was endowed with a certain grace and arrogance, reminding her of a magnificent Roman gladiator. His rugged tanned face was fringed by curly brown hair, his eyes a soft brown which turned black when angered. Oh! He was quite a catch, indeed!

It was time to put the final touches on her well thought out plan. Salene smiled, mentally patting herself on the back. After a night of love he would deny her nothing.

"So quiet, my dear?"

With deliberate slowness Salene pulled on her diaphanous robe, watching with secret delight as Devlin's eyes roamed freely over her supple body.

"Actually, I was thinking of Lord Charles Emory."

Devlin Essex laughed easily.

"Really, darling, you should curb your odd sense of humor." She angrily glared at him. "Lord Charles is a very rich and influential man."

His face sobered quickly, his eyes hard as granite. "Much to the dismay of many a poor soul."

Salene stood before him, one manicured nail tracing the outline of his firm jaw. "Charles has asked me to marry him."

Quietly, she moved to the window and waited. Any moment he would begin ranting and raving like a maniac. Her body trembled for Devlin to crush her to him, begging her to be his alone.

"Well," Devlin's tone was almost a sigh, "I wish you and that pompous jackass every happiness."

Salene whirled about, staring wildly, her mouth open in disbelief. This could not be happening! Where was his anger, his jealousy, his love for her?

Devlin grinned crookedly. "You've made the catch of the season," he added, enjoying her misery. "Charles will be able to keep you in the luxury you so dearly love."

"But—but I do not understand?" she stammered.

"Understand what, my dear?" he asked coldly.

Color rose in her cheeks as she turned from his scrutinizing stare. *Damn him!* she cursed silently. "Darling, naturally I assumed . . ."

"That I would marry you?" he finished.

"Devlin, I love you!" she desperately blurted out. "I—I give myself to you! I've been faithful to you!"

He gave out with an ugly laugh. "My dear, please! I detest women who pass themselves off as innocent maids." His eyes narrowed. "You knew from the very beginning where this would lead. I know the difference between a worldly woman and an innocent maid—and believe me, my dear, it has been quite a long time since you were a maid!''

''That was very cruel,'' Salene pouted. ''No woman can stay innocent in London for very long. Please, darling, don't do this to us—to what we have!''

Devlin eyed her warily. ''You will no doubt find a companion to keep you from becoming too bored after your marriage. I understand old Emory is very lenient with his ladies.''

''Why are you deliberately hurting me?'' she cried indignantly. ''After all we've meant to each other. I love you!''

''Love!'' he spat the word as if it offended him. ''There is no such thing as romantic, poetic, senseless love! What we shared was a mutual admiration of bodies. It was over, Salene, even before you played your devious hand.''

''Damn you!'' Salene cursed, lashing out at him with both fists flying.

With hardly any effort, Devlin caught hold of her arms and pinned them behind her back. Salene was caught in a trap of her own making and with a fury born of failure to succeed, she strained against him trying to get away.

''And now we play at being the outraged mistress,'' he mocked, eyes glistening black. ''I made you no promises, no commitments. I won't be trapped into a permanent situation by you—or anyone! Is that clear?''

''But you care, I know you do!'' Wildly, she flung her arms around him. ''It is different with you!''

''Stop deceiving yourself, Salene!'' he said angrily, giving her a good shake. ''You've become disgustingly possessive. You're desperate to grab onto someone—anyone! Well, I will not become your victim!''

Devlin roughly pulled her aside. He turned, picking up his coat at the bedroom door. He was sick to death of

London and its so-called beauties—selfish, mindless idiots, the lot of 'em!

Salene raced down the staircase, catching Devlin at the door. Frantically, she clutched his arm, halting his departure. He turned, jaw set firm, eyes blazing with anger.

"Someday, my darling, someday some woman will pierce that block of ice you so fondly call a heart!" she shouted, hatred and humiliation consuming her. "I want to be there when that happens and you are left with nothing—*nothing!* I'll even the score if it is the last thing I ever do!"

Without another word, Devlin tipped his hat and walked out, the cool morning sunlight touching his face.

Six

Lauriette stood under a barren oak, her slender arms outstretched as if embracing sunbeams. Gazing over her shoulder she grinned upon spying Dolly conversing with Mr. Bonnar, an enterprising older man with a modest coach business.

The country clearly showed the harsh markings of winter and she felt the icy touch of wind about her ankles. They were supposed to be at Lady Margaret Singleton's listening to a piano recital given by her daughter, Sarah.

On the way, Lauriette began to feel smothered by the society which she would soon become a part of. On a strong impulse she ordered Mr. Clooney to halt the carriage and giving instructions that he should meet them at the same place in a few hours, Lauriette and Dolly hurried to find Mr. Bonnar and his coach to carry them out of the city for at least part of the afternoon.

Her face glowed with happiness as she alighted the coach. It was not a Philadelphia countryside, but the mere thought of seeing endless land uncluttered by houses brought joy to her homesick heart. How she missed Claymoor farm and Jamie. If only she were home now!

She walked slowly, daydreaming of another time, and wandered aimlessly over the meadow. Lauriette walked a ways into the forest and then looked back to make certain Dolly and Mr. Bonnar were within her sight. Satisfied that all was well, she seated herself on a fallen log and then produced a blank pad and charcoal. When a sad and thoughtful mood possessed her, she found solace in creating her own little world.

Devlin spent part of his morning venting his anger upon any servant who came his way. His mood was black and his wise servants knew to tread softly. The more he thought of Salene, the blacker his mood became until the fury broke and Devlin, with one sweep of his arm, sent dishes flying from the breakfast table.

The maids stood back in horror as their master hurled a stream of oaths over their heads and stormed out to the stables. Waiting several minutes in silence, they eyed each other then breathed a sigh of relief.

Devlin leaned against the stall which housed his proud Arabian stallion, Nomad, and immediately ordered the spirited animal saddled. He had to get out—to cool his anger.

He raced the bay through the streets of London like a madman, his anger encompassing him. It was not until he was out of the limits of the city that he let up and Nomad slowed to a trot.

The confrontation with Salene caused him much concern. She was a scheming, calculating little bitch and he damned himself for becoming involved with an acquaintance of Oberly's.

The cold November air helped to clear his head a bit. If it had not been for Neville, he would have never returned to this dreaded place! How much longer would that brother of his be detained in India? How long could he avoid his father? To think he was playing watchdog over their title and inheritance until . . . *Damn Neville!* No doubt he was deliberately staying away, knowing Devlin's intense dislike for London and the nobility.

Devlin stopped, swinging one leg over the saddle horn. The forest was a good place to air out feelings. The sound of a woman's laugh caught his attention and he spied a lone coach, a man and a woman talking and laughing intimately.

The plump woman was waving to someone. A crooked smiled crossed his face as he saw a figure seated on a rock near the edge of the woods, wave back. From where he was, Devlin could only make out the profile of a pert, turned up nose and there was no mistaking the green velvet cloak.

"So we meet again, mistress," a husky voice whispered.

Lauriette looked up, her eyes widening at the sight of the gentleman who seemed continually to pop into her life. His gentle brown eyes were filled with amusement.

"I see you have a passion for drawing," he said as she silently tried to ignore him. "May I see?"

Before she could protest, he snatched several drawings from the rock beside her. One was of a young sea captain standing at the wheel, there was another of an elegantly dressed young gentleman with sad eyes, and last he looked upon a country scene, a large stone house in the foreground. Somehow it seemed familiar to him.

"May I have my drawings?"

Devlin looked down at the girl, her voice soft and whispery. Her round cherub face was haloed by a mass of golden brown curls beneath a fur bonnet. Those eyes he remembered well—horizon blue.

Embarrassed, Lauriette eyed Dolly, who was oblivious to her predicament. The dark eyes of this man seemed to take in her whole being.

"Forgive me, you were addressing me?"

"I—I would like to have my drawings."

Still holding them he placed a booted foot on the log beside her and leaned on his knee. "You are quite talented," he complimented. "I never met a young lady who could sketch so brilliantly."

"Do you have this talent, sir?"

"The talent, no," he replied, "but I thoroughly enjoy beautiful paintings."

She became immediately interested. "What do you enjoy the most? Landscapes? Still life? Do you have hundreds of portraits of your ancestors?" Suddenly she stopped, aware of her runaway words and how shocked brother Elliott would be at her unladylike chatter. Quickly, Lauriette lowered her eyes, blushing deeply.

Devlin smiled, obviously pleased with the becoming pink in her cheeks. He could not remember the last time he saw a woman blush.

"I appreciate anything beautiful whether 'tis landscape or portrait." He looked deeply into her eyes, holding her spellbound. "Beauty is pleasing to the eye."

With difficulty she pulled her gaze away from him. Lauriette felt so flustered in this stranger's company.

"Do—do you live close to these woods so that you may walk here whenever it pleases you?" she asked. Then an alarmed look crossed her face. "If—if we are trespassing—"

"Rest assured that everyone is welcomed in these woods," he quickly responded. "I do not own them. I arrived the usual way—on horseback. Come. Let me show you the pride of my stable."

Lauriette felt compelled to go with this man regardless of what would happen to her reputation if caught.

She felt no fear of him, no unease.

The huge animal stood not too far from them; Lauriette could still see Dolly. Her love of horses prompted her to have a closer look at this beautiful animal. Devlin walked behind her into the woods, an odd smile on his lips.

"He is magnificent!" she mused, stroking his mane affectionately. "An Arabian gray. What is his name?"

"Nomad."

She looked at him and smiled. "A proper name from the look of him."

Devlin moved closer and tilted her chin upward with his hand. "You seem much better since I last laid eyes on you." His eyes twinkled. "I see you've got color back in your cheeks. Quite becoming."

Lauriette could feel her pulse racing, her heart joining in. "I was very rude to you," she said quietly. "I—I do appreciate your—your—"

"Strong arms," he finished. "Perhaps you would have been wise to stay in America. Our London hostesses have been known to eat little girls like you at least twice a day."

Her blue eyes flashed an icy glare. "Sir! I am perfectly capable of taking care of myself. I grew up during the war and learned I have more spunk than you evidently give me credit for!" she declared hotly.

Absolutely lovely when angered, he thought with a grin. Somehow during the course of the minutes gone by, he had forgotten Salene and his black mood. Devlin found himself wishing he knew more about her.

He laughed out loud, surprising her. "Mistress, you are a treasure!"

Without a thought, Devlin reached out, taking her arm, his touch causing a tremor to sear through her. He was drawing her into his arms and her will quickly dwindled, caught in the spell of his bewitching dark eyes. His mouth sought hers with gentle urgency, the softness of her lips filling him with a want for more of this mysterious beauty.

"Please! I have to go!" she said quickly, her thoughts turning to Evan. "It's dangerous for me to stay longer."

"Tell me your name," he urged, reluctant to release her trembling hand. "At least tell me your Christian name."

"I . . . cannot!" she whispered. "It would be terribly wrong."

Before Devlin could stop her, the young woman ran to the coach some distance away.

"Wait!" he shouted, but it was too late.

He stood at the edge of the woods watching the coach speed away, his rugged face clouded by confusion. What was there about this strange girl that caused him to act like a schoolboy? He only talked with her a few moments and the desire to know all about her overwhelmed him. He felt as if he had made a fool of himself.

Devlin's eyes grew wide as he bent over. The young lady's drawings! In her eagerness to flee, she had forgotten them. Carefully he brushed a bit of dirt away and thumbed through them once again, looking for some clue to her identity.

Soberly he mounted Nomad and began the long trek homeward, the sketches tucked securely inside his greatcoat.

"My lady will be beside herself with anger!" Dolly fretted. " 'Tis my fault! If I hadn't talked ta Mr. Bonnar so long! Oh, miss, because o' me, ye'll have problems for sure!"

Lauriette smiled weakly and nervously patted Dolly's hand. "There's nothing for you to worry about. I was at fault for not going to Lady Margaret's."

"But it's my fault, too!" she protested. "I wanted ta be with Mr. Bonnar so much."

"Oh, no!" Lauriette exclaimed, anxiously looking about her. "My sketches! I've lost them!"

"Oh, missie, we'll go back and—"

"No!" she cried, then calmed herself. "No, Dolly, that would make us even later."

"Yer right, miss," Dolly agreed, "and if someone finds them—"

"I hope he enjoys them," she answered.

"He, miss?"

"I mean . . . whoever finds them," Lauriette quickly corrected.

Seven

The eve of the Winter Ball was ostentatiously greeted by a torrential downpour. The London streets glistened like tiny diamonds as far as the eye could see.

Lauriette, standing quietly at her bedroom window, viewed the bleak weather as a premonition—a feeling of impending doom. Involuntarily, she shuddered, moving away from the rain-streaked panes, her spirits thoroughly dampened. This was supposed to be her triumphant night, her official introduction into the wealthy society to which Evan belonged.

She picked up her sketchbook and charcoal and tried to draw from memory their farm outside Philadelphia.

After a time she shook her head. The stranger who seemed to be popping in and out of her life was most certainly unnerving. In her mind's eye she pictured his face. It was an artist's delight—brown, enigmatic eyes, a long slender nose, giving him an arrogant expression, thin masculine lips, even a tiny scar which curved down his left cheek. . . .

"Oh, no!" she gasped, staring down at the drawing. Over the light fluid lines of the farm, she had unconsciously drawn the stranger in bold black lines.

With an outraged cry, she ripped the picture from the book and tore it into tiny shreds, which fell like petals at her feet. Was she losing her mind?

What happened to all those beautiful dreams of marriage to Evan? In a fortnight she would be his wife. Wasn't that what she wanted? To become his wife?

Dejectedly, she plopped down on the bed. Those brief encounters with the man—Lucifer, she dubbed him—repeatedly haunted her mind night and day, those dark brooding eyes penetrating her thoughts, her dreams! The memory of his lips warm on hers . . .

Dolly entered the bedroom, a filmy chemise draped over her arm. The maid had been whistling but stopped upon seeing the bits of paper, and the expression on her mistress's face.

Lauriette stood as Dolly helped her to dress, the maid humming a merry tune.

"Dolly . . . Dolly, may I ask you a question?" the words came out slowly, as if she was unsure.

"Ask me, miss?" Dolly smiled. "Ye can ask me anythin'."

She sat down before her mirror and Dolly began dressing her hair.

"Have you ever . . . been in love?"

The maid stopped in the middle of brushing and stared for a long moment at the girl's reflection. "Well, miss, aye, I do believe I am right now."

"What is it like?" she encouraged. "Please, Dolly, I must know!"

"Well, miss, when I'm with Mr. Bonnar I feel like me and him's the only ones in the world. He—Mr. Bonnar makes me—oh—all mixed up inside, like I'm hot and cold at the same time. And when he looks at me? Ah'h, miss, it's—it's like he's a-looking straight through to me heart!"

Lauriette looked up and could not help but smile. Dolly had expertly styled her golden brown ringlets into a Grecian coiffure, tiny curls framing her small face. During their lapse in conversation, Dolly took the opportunity to place tiny pink rosebuds through her hair.

Moving to the bed, the maid carefully picked up the lovely white gown with an overlay of pink lace and held it out to Lauriette. The young lady's eyes were unreadable. Dolly quietly buttoned her, waiting to see where this unusual conversation would lead.

Putting the final touches on Lauriette's toilet, Dolly stepped back to drink in the loveliness of this lady. *She deserves more than what she's a-getting in Brimley,* Dolly thought bitterly.

Lauriette took Dolly's hands and held them tightly. "Dolly . . . Dolly, when Mr. Bonnar"—she was having a hard time asking—"when Mr. Bonnar kisses you, how do you feel?"

Dolly's plump face lit up with happiness. "Ah-h, miss, when Mr. Bonnar kisses me it's like—like me whole soul's afire! He causes me head to spin and me heart to pound so! He's all I can think of—he's in me mind all the time . . . even visits me dreams!"

Lauriette's eyes filled with tears as she slowly picked up her white gloves, hands shaking, her bottom lip quivering.

"Oh, miss! Did I say something wrong?" Dolly was beside herself with dismay.

Dabbing at the tears, Lauriette gave a weak smile. "It's just—it's just I've none of those feelings for Evan. Dolly, whatever am I to do?"

Sitting down on the bed, the story of the time at the inn, the day of her fainting spell, then the encounter in the country came pouring out. Dolly listened sympathetically, giving special attention to the stranger's effect on Lauriette.

"Forgive me," Lauriette whispered, drying her eyes. "I did not mean to go on like that. It's just this pace, this horrid pace, it's—"

A swift rapping came at the door, causing both women to jump. "Missie," Jonas' voice called through the closed door. "Sir Evan Brimley has arrived."

"Thank you, Jonas, tell him I'll be right there."

Beseechingly, she turned to Dolly for help with her tearstained face.

"Nothing that can't be repaired in a moment," the maid smiled.

The ball was being given at Halstead House, a huge monstrosity belonging to the Duchess of Wingreen, Lady Alice Halstead. As ugly and hideous as it was, the only room with tasteful elegance was the grand ballroom. So, as the years drifted by, each winter a London socialite was chosen to give the annual winter ball. This year Lady Marie-Claire Branscombe was selected.

There were already many elegantly dressed couples entering Halstead House as Evan and Lauriette alighted from the coach. The rain had stopped for a time and the night appeared less threatening.

Lauriette's heart was racing, pulse throbbing. This was to be the biggest ball of the season. As a servant took their cloaks, Evan stared in admiration at the enchanting creature soon to be his wife. At the beginning of this venture Lauriette had just been a means to an end, but now the thought of possessing her as well as her wealth had become almost an obsession with him. He gulped, nervously licking his lips, trying hard to keep his ardor under control.

Hell! The wench was a stunning beauty and it was all he could do to keep from slinging her over his shoulder and making for one of the bedrooms upstairs.

"The Honorable Evan Brimley and Mistress Lauriette Claymoor,'' the servant announced in ringing tones.

All eyes turned to the handsome couple on the stairs. There was a mixture of comments rising from the ballroom, some whispered loudly while others giggled, staring over their fans at Lauriette.

What was this world coming to when such common people could waltz right in and act as if they belonged! Such nerve could only come from a lower class of people. It did not matter how prestigious her family was in America—a commoner is still a commoner, and a Yankee at that!

Lauriette heard none of the wagging tongues or witnessed the open hostility and outrage on many of Marie-Claire's friends and acquaintances. She was too busy calming her nerves and fears. This was truly a grand ball—nothing at all like the cotillions given in Philadelphia.

At the bottom of the stairs Evan drew her into his arms and swung into the mainstream of whirling couples. It was as if she were in a fantastic dream—the music, the champagne, the beauty of the ballroom, and she was part of it all!

Dreamily, Lauriette gazed upward, becoming startled to find Evan staring at her with such intensity, she gasped. His look brought on a chilly sensation that frightened her.

''Evan, is—is anything the matter?''

He was half-smiling, his blue eyes boring into hers. ''Only that you are the loveliest woman here.'' His voice was low and husky. ''If only you would let me show you—show you now! I want to take you in my arms and teach you all you need to know to make me happy. You could make me so very happy, my dear. Your face, your love body—''

The waltz ended and she moved swiftly out of his

arms. He was saying things she did not want to hear. It sounded so lewd and vulgar—suddenly another flash coursed through her memory. A face! A bearded face!

Lauriette felt her legs tremble, but a hand supported her elbow. "Allow me the next dance, Evan," Henry said brightly. Before Evan could reply, he moved her out onto the dance floor and Lauriette sighed with relief.

It was raining and the drizzle did nothing more than put Devlin in an even blacker mood. He sensed a vague foreboding about going to the club but shrugged it off and went anyway. Damn!

Angrily, he slumped back in the seat and plopped a muddied boot on the velvet upholstery beside Judd. His black velvet superfine and breeches were mud splattered and wet. He shifted in the seat, then winced as a pain shot through his arm.

Sir William Fowley was quite an excellent shot when hunting, but dueling? Slowly a dark scowl covered his face and with a savage growl, he ran his fist against the wall.

"What is done, is done, Dev," Judd said quietly.

Damn Salene! Damn her to hell! The witch was a spiteful hellcat who gloriously thrived on revenge. The moment she walked in the club on the arm of Sir William, he knew something would happen.

Salene laughed and cooed and coquettishly displayed her charms to the young man. Poor Will! He was so besotted by her, he had no idea Salene was using him.

He had done his best to ignore her all evening, but she had subtlely made her way to his side at the gaming table. She gave him several sidelong glances, remembering the day he walked out of her life. He would pay, she had vowed, he would pay dearly!

She began to watch his every move, now and then

touching him, taunting him until he could hardly contain his annoyance. Gathering up his winnings, he moved away from the crowded game table and into the cold night air.

How on earth could he have ever been attracted to her? The thought of her now made him feel suffocated. Absently, he lit a cheroot and took a long, thoughtful puff.

"Are you leaving so soon?" Salene's pouty voice came from the darkened doorway. "The evening is still quite young."

Indifferently he turned towards her, a cynical gleam in his eyes. Salene emerged from the protection of the doorway and stood next to him, enjoying his nearness.

"By your leave, Lady Boling, it has been a rather trying day and at the moment it looks like rain."

Salene grabbed his arm as he started towards the courtyard. "Please, Devlin, you're being so unfair," she whispered fervently, her fingers digging into his arms.

His eyes held a cold, hard look; his face was a mask of contempt.

"Salene, must we go through this again?" he said through clenched teeth. "I'm sure young Will is searching everywhere for you."

"I need you! Can you not see that?" her trembling voice raised a degree. "And though you will not admit it, you need me, too!"

Devlin threw back his head and laughed cruelly. "Salene, why do you put yourself through this?" His voice was low and angry. "I don't need you—I never did—you or any other woman, for that matter."

William appeared from the same darkened doorway. "Salene, I've been looking all over for you."

Devlin turned to walk away.

"Don't turn your back on me!" she said vehemently.

"Salene, don't create a scene in front of your most recent admirer," he warned sarcastically. "Careful! You're beginning to show your true nature."

"How dare you!" she cried and before Devlin could step away, Salene's hand came down in a stinging slap.

Devlin was momentarily stunned, his mind dulled by drink, but the hate and cruelty in Salene's eyes penetrated through the haze.

By this time a large number of guests were crowding out the balcony doors, curious about the commotion.

Sir William was at Salene's side as she swooned. Supporting her in a most tender fashion, his eyes glared at Devlin.

"William! Oh, William!" she cried softly. "This—this *beast* has insulted my honor and the name of my dear departed husband!"

Sir William stiffened as he faced Devlin, his young face stricken with anger. From within his coat he produced a glove and threw it in Devlin's face. A shocked gasp came from the crowd and silence fell.

Devlin drew himself up to his full height of six feet, two inches, his common sense giving way to temper. "I am at your service, sir," he bowed curtly, ignoring the people who now crowded around them. "The appointed time?"

"Here and now!" he replied, his voice shaking with anger. "In the courtyard. Pistols?"

Devlin nodded silently.

"Henry Barrington will act as my second." he said. "Yours?"

"Judson Oakes."

"A duel!" someone in the crowd shouted. "Light torches! A duel with pistols!"

Various torches were lit, illuminating the courtyard. The two silently faced each other, their eyes locked in a cold war. On the appointed signal they turned, backs to one another. Sir Alfred Kingston began to count off the paces, both Devlin and Sir William began walking.

Before the count of ten, William turned and fired. The crowd gasped and a disapproving mumble rose from them. The ball grazed Devlin's arm and he became livid with anger and pain. Carefully, he leveled the pistol at Sir William's head and held it there for what seemed to the bewildered young man like an eternity. Then with an angry growl, he raised the pistol in the air and fired.

Shaking with relief, William fell to his knees crying hysterically. A stretcher was called for and Devlin watched, eyes dangerously narrowed, as they carted him off, a satisfied Salene at the young man's side.

Judd stood beside him, hands on hips. "Should have ended the snake's life, turning on you like that."

Numbly, Devlin shook his head. "Will's just a stripling, Judd," he said defeatedly. "To kill him would serve no useful purpose."

Salene's lust for his blood was sated at least for the moment. He could still see the triumphant expression on her face as he wearily moved to his own coach. That boy could have gotten himself killed becoming involved with such a sick, sick woman! How many more would she enlist for her revenge?

Hopelessly, Devlin bowed his head. As soon as Neville stepped foot in London, he would be bound for the sea for good!

Eight

Lauriette was completely entranced by the Winter Ball, the gaiety, the laughter, the very idea that she was part of it. She danced the night away, her world of dreams and fantasy coming true. Tonight she was only Lauriette, the young maid, and her thoughts of Evan and marriage were placed in the back of her mind.

She declined a waltz and strode toward the buffet, accepting a glass of champagne from one of the servants. She glanced across the table and was startled to find a pair of green eyes boldly staring at her. Blushing deeply, Lauriette acknowledged the gentleman with a curt nod and presented her back to him.

"I see your admirers finally gave you a moment to catch your breath," a soft, well-educated voice said.

Lauriette half turned, her eyes appraising the man beside her. He was tall, slender built, impeccably dressed. His eyes were a light green, his nose was short and stubby, his mouth rather on the thin side. It was impossible to tell the color of his hair underneath the elaborate powdered wig.

"Indeed?" she asked, one brow arched in annoyance.

Before Lauriette could move, the man grasped her gloved hand and pressed it to his lips.

"I am a good friend of Evan's," he informed her. "Sir Harry Oberly, your servant, Mistress Claymoor. I'm afraid Evan's description of you does not do you justice."

There was something unpleasant about this friend of Evan's, Lauriette felt immediately.

"I do apologize for not meeting you sooner," he ventured further. "I'm afraid Marie-Claire has been keeping you a secret. I'll have to scold her for that!"

Lauriette eyed him cooly. "If you will excuse me, I see Evan making his way to me." Without further comment, she turned and went to meet Evan halfway.

It was relief she felt upon seeing his face. He had been missing from the ball a long time and during her many dances, she was anxious to see his familiar face. Now Evan was here, standing before her but his face expressed displeasure. Taking her arm, he roughly guided her through the guests and out into the dimly lit corridor.

"Just what do you think you were doing?" he snapped, his fingers biting into her arms.

"I don't know what you mean."

"You know damn well what I mean!" he insisted, giving her a shake. "I saw the way your eyes were following Harry! You ply your trade well, Lauriette, but Harry would not give you the time of day were it not for me! Stay away from Harry Oberly!"

"Evan, you are hurting me!" she gasped, struggling to free her arm.

Gripping her other arm, Evan fiercely pulled her against him, the action wrenching a startled cry from Lauriette. She feared him now as never before, the look on his face pure rage.

"You belong to me, my dear," his voice was uncomfortably calm. "I'll not have you flaunting your charms to my many friends who may pass your way. Do you think me blind? You talked most intimately with Harry . . . most intimately. But it will not happen again, will it, Lauriette?" He looked down into her frightened eyes. "I will not have to remind you again, will I."

"No . . . no, Evan," she just barely choked out the words. "No."

Evan gradually released her arms then stood back and straightened his coat. His face was once again calm, revealing no trace of the anger Lauriette had just faced. Silently, she tried to blink back tears as she nursed her bruised arms.

"My dear, you are missing a great deal of the festivities." He smiled. "I see Henry there—perhaps he is looking for you."

Offering his arm, Evan escorted her back into the ballroom. His smile was as charming as ever and it was very hard for her to believe what had taken place.

"Henry," Evan greeted, "could I impose on you to keep Lauriette amused until I return?"

Henry nodded curtly. "Would you do me the honor, Lauriette?"

His arm encircled her waist while the other took her hand. They left Evan far behind as Henry whirled her out onto the dance floor. Lauriette focused her eyes on his handsome face, trying to banish the scene with Evan from her mind.

"You're trembling, Lauriette," Henry said gently.

She smiled weakly. "Just give me a moment to collect myself."

"I know something that will put that beautiful glow back in your cheeks," he whispered conspiratorially. "There is a guest that just arrived who claims to be an old acquaintance of your family."

"An old acquaintance?"

"According to him, he hasn't seen you in years."

Lauriette gazed up at Henry, her pretty face puzzled and brows drawn in contemplation. "I haven't any idea who."

"He's waiting in the alcove," he said, looking about for Evan. "I thought it best for you to see him alone first—then, if you wish, introduce him to Evan."

"*Bonsoir,* Lolly."

The man she had known from childhood—Jamie's dearest friend—smiled affectionately, his gray eyes taking in the graceful way Lauriette had matured.

"Jean! I can hardly believe my eyes!" she exclaimed, her lips breaking into a winsome smile. Long forgotten were her fears of Evan. "Six long years and not a single word!" He was more handsome than she remembered. He was the same height as Jamie, a good six feet, his sandy-colored hair covered by a powdered wig, but it was his gentle voice and irresistible smile she recalled most vividly.

Jean Bourget, second son of a wealthy landowner in Louisiana Territory, squeezed her hands affectionately. She was hardly what he expected, his mind's eye remembering a skinny moppet with a tangled mass of golden brown curls who loved to follow him and James about. Lauriette had outgrown childhood and emerged possessing a rare form of beauty, her personality equaling her loveliness.

"You have met Marie-Claire's husband, Henry?"

Jean acknowledged Henry with a nod of his head. "Your brother-in-law has been most cordial," he said easily. "James informed me you were here and I promised to look in on you."

"If you'll excuse me," Henry bowed, his smile most gracious, "as you are in very capable hands, I'll leave you two to reminisce." He turned and strode towards a group of men discussing politics.

"Marie-Claire's husband you say?" Jean asked. "Strange—his eyes held you most tenderly."

She looked away from Jean's direct gaze, a blush creeping over her cheeks. His questioning eyes were most disconcerting—as if he knew exactly what one was thinking.

"Henry is a very sensitive man," she answered quietly, then looked up and smiled brightly. "Let us talk of you. How long are you to be here, *mon ami?* And how is M'sieu Bourget and your brother, André?"

Jean held up his hands in appeal. "Please, Lolly, one question at a time!" he laughed. "I am here on my father's business and I will be here for only a few weeks. Papa and André are fine. Papa sends his love. I must tell you, I am a married man now."

"Married!"

"*Oui.*" He smiled. "She is a beautiful Creole from a very wealthy, influential family. Her name is Fleur and we have been married for two years now."

"My congratulations," she extended. "Knowing you, I am sure she is very beautiful. I imagine you miss her a great deal."

Jean nodded. "The first parting is always the hardest," he answered simply. "Your brother-in-law has extended his hospitality to me, but I will be staying with an old friend. I would like to see you during my visit."

" 'Twill be hard to catch up on so many years in so little time."

"Come, *cherie,*" Jean urged, "dance with an old friend?"

They joined the other dancers, setting tongues to wagging. It was utterly shameless the way Lady Marie-Claire's sister smiled so at that Frenchman!

"You have grown quite a bit, *ma petite.*" His voice was soft and melodious.

Lauriette smiled shyly, her round face shading pink. "A lot can take place in six years."

"So I have heard. James told me you are to marry before Christmas, *n'est-ce pas?*"

"Next week," she replied quietly. "I'm afraid Jamie has his reasons for being against our marriage—I'm sure he's told you that."

"*Oui.*" He nodded. "We talked of your coming marriage. He is still quite upset." He chuckled lightly. "You cannot blame him. I should be angry myself. *Mon Dieu!* Did you not pledge your love to me long ago?"

Lauriette's laughter was like the tinkling of chimes. "If you would have been wise, you would have scooped me up and fled—six years ago!"

Jean threw back his head and laughed heartily. "*Touché,* Lolly, what a fool I have been!"

"When did you see Jamie?" she asked anxiously. "How is he? When is he coming back to England?"

"I ran into him in New Orleans." He grinned wickedly. "It was at a questionable—"

"Wait," she cut in. "Let's retire to the library. I wish to hear all about my wayward brother's escapades in private!"

They weaved their way through the dancers and Lauriette hurried Jean to the open doors and down the corridor.

Her hand turned the doorknob. "I never realized how much I would miss—"

Lauriette was frozen to the spot, her hand gripping the doorknob. There were moans and sighs coming from the sofa. Evidently they had walked in on a liaison. She turned to motion Jean to tiptoe out, but a gasped recognition from the couple stopped her.

Evan had quickly composed himself, reaching for his discarded wig. Marie-Claire's face flushed hotly as she hurriedly pushed down her skirts. Lauriette's gaze shifted back and forth between the two, the scene slowly sinking in.

It was as if the past four years melted away and she was looking at Marie-Claire and Henry. All the hurt she had managed to get over, all the hate and humiliation she received at the hands of her sister came flooding back.

"Jean, you remember my sister, Marie-Claire," she said weakly.

Jean nodded stiffly.

"And this—this is my betrothed, the *Honorable* Evan Brimley!" she spat the words at him.

Marie-Claire smiled cooly. "Yes, I vaguely remember you, Jean."

"And I, you, Marie-Claire."

Evan was taken aback by the thought of being discovered and looked at Lauriette keenly. She had not gone into hysterics as he assumed she would, but her eyes! They were cold and hard, glistening like sapphires.

"I thought I knew you," she said evenly to Marie-Claire, her eyes boring a hole through her. She turned to Evan. "You and she deserve each other!"

"My dear—"

"How *dare* you, sir!" she raged. "Both of you are lower than the scum of London!"

Evan noted the murderous stare of Jean but ignored it, laughing cruelly. "It's too late, my dear. No matter what you've seen, you belong to me body and soul."

With an outraged cry, Lauriette lashed out catching his cheek with her open hand. "Never!" she flung at him, hot tears streaming down her cheeks. "I would sooner slit my own throat than to let you touch me!"

She ran from the room leaving a stunned Jean at the library door. Pushing through the dancers and spectators, she found herself at the bottom of the stairs. Her mind swimming, Lauriette ran out into the pouring rain.

Nine

Lauriette wandered aimlessly down the barely lit drive and out into the street. Without any destination in her dazed mind, she did not bother to look or even care what direction she was going. Her world had tumbled into ruins in a matter of moments and all the hurt, all the memories of that summer of four years before came falling in on her.

Jamie had been right all along. What had he said? Ah, yes! "What he is and what he appears to be are two different things." How he would laugh at this!

The cold rain was pouring down upon her beautiful pink gown. She stared straight ahead, trying to choke back the sobs. She did not hear the coach-and-four racing down the muddy street, she did not hear the driver yelling to warn her. She heard nothing but the sound of Evan's cruel laughter echoing in her ears.

Standing up, the driver used all his strength to pull back on the reins causing Fleet and Skylar, the two lead horses, to rear up. The girl gave out a startled cry and fell in a heap in front of the frightened horses.

"My God!" he exclaimed, jumping down from the

seat.

Judd Oakes was immediately out of the coach and was doing his best to soothe the frightened horses.

"Judd!" a man's deep angry growl came from the coach window. "What the devil's going on?"

"A young wench," he shouted back. "Ran in front of the team."

Devlin jumped out of the coach, drawing up the collar of his greatcoat against the rain. He hurried to where Judd knelt.

"It's a lady!" the driver exclaimed.

"It wasn't your fault, Perkins," Judd said quietly.

"I couldn't stop the team in time, sir," he said nervously. "She ran in front of it like she never heard them."

Through the rain Judd looked up at Devlin in confusion. "She doesn't seem to be hurt," he told him. "I can't find a mark on her person."

The light from the coach filtered through the rain, caressing the small cherub face. Devlin's heart gave an unexpected leap.

With an easy swiftness she was gathered in his arms and was being carried back to the coach. She was beginning to rouse and weakly protested the strong arms.

"Please let me down!"

"I warned you about London society and hostesses, little cherub."

Lauriette went rigid at the sound of the man's deep voice and in an instant knew in her heart who it was. Very gently, he placed her on the dry seat and covered her with his own coat.

Turning from her he walked back to Judd and the driver.

"She'll be just fine, Perkins," Devlin reassured him.

"Perhaps I should drive for a bit," Judd said, noting how distraught the driver was. "This rain will wake me up. Where should we take her?''

Devlin studied a moment before answering. ''Let's return to the townhouse and perhaps by then we'll know what to do with her. If she gives me a destination, I'll pound on top of the roof.'' He winced as he raised his arm. ''Damn! My arm is sore.''

''Home it is,'' Judd grinned, pulling himself up into the driver's seat.

''It's not home,'' Devlin grumbled, moving toward the coach door, ''never home.''

He swung himself up into the coach and as he shut the door the vehicle lurched forward.

''What in blazes are you doing out on a night like this?'' he demanded. ''Where is your escort?''

Lauriette could not force herself to look at him, but instead gazed down at her ruined ballgown. The lace was dirty and torn, the satin was saturated, revealing the shape of her legs quite nicely.

Silence. Did the girl never carry on an intelligent conversation? Impatiently he moved to the end of the opposite seat, stretching his long legs before him, and cradled his arm.

Tightly closing her eyes, Lauriette tried to force her tears back but the memory of Evan and Marie-Claire together became more vivid. *Fool!* she cursed herself. *Blind, blind fool! Jamie tried to warn me. Oh, Jamie! How I wish you were here!*

Crystal tears were falling, her shoulders began to quake uncontrollably. She had been used, humiliated, her faith had been betrayed cruelly.

Devlin closely watched her, his interest growing with each passing moment. She was so vulnerable, her wet hair glistening over one shoulder, a smudge of drying mud on her chin. . . .

''You're crying,'' he said gently, sitting up. ''Are you in pain somewhere?''

The gentleness in his voice caused the dam to burst and she could no longer hold back her sobs. He was at a loss; the girl's tears were absolutely genuine.

Forgotten was his own pain as instinct made him take her into his arms and hold her ever so tightly. Her small body shook with each sob and Devlin had an overwhelming sense of protection. Never before had he felt so helpless, so inept at what to do.

It was some time before she became calm and realizing where she was, disengaged herself from his arms.

"Where may I take you?" he asked, breaking into the silence.

Lauriette looked at him, a hopeless confused expression upon her tearstained face. "I—I have nowhere to go."

Devlin arched a brow and sat back in his seat, contemplating. "Then I shall offer you the hospitality of my townhouse."

"Oh, no, no," she declared. "It wouldn't be—"

"Mistress, I forbid you to sleep in my coach!"

She managed to recover some bit of her dignity as the coach came to a halt. She felt totally drained and old beyond her twenty years. Her rescuer climbed out, then against her protests, gathered her in his capable arms and made a dash for his front door.

The door swung open as Devlin mounted the steps and once inside, he carefully placed her on her feet. Candles lit the reception area, casting monstrous shadows against the walls.

"You'll have to excuse the condition of the room," he said casually, draping his greatcoat over a chair. "This place is rarely occupied."

Lauriette was freezing, the damp ballgown clinging to her body like a second skin. She was completely numb even to the fact that she was drenched, but this did not go unnoticed by Devlin.

"The fires have been lit," Judd's voice eachoed down the stairs. "I took the liberty of doing it rather than waking any of the servants."

Devlin looked toward the trembling girl. "Your room is ready, mistress—mistress—?"

She stared straight ahead, ignoring the man's inquisitiveness. She began to climb the mountainous stairway, dragging one foot up after the other. Finally, after a number of steps, she rested. Then with a strangled cry, Lauriette found herself being carried the rest of the way by this man who had caused her many troubled nights.

"At the pace you were going, cherub, you'd have made it to the top by daybreak," he said sharply.

Inside the spacious bedroom he placed her in front of the welcoming fire. How thoroughly comforting was the blaze after being chilled to the bone. She stiffly inched towards it, holding out her trembling hands. She stared tearfully into the leaping flames, a wrenching sigh escaping her lips.

"Here," Devlin broke into her thoughts. She looked confused as he shoved a goblet into her trembling hands. "It is brandy. It calms the nerves and will warm you."

Lauriette looked at it for a long moment before raising it to her lips. The first gulp burned down her throat as her eyes filled with tears and she began to cough.

Devlin grinned while slapping her on the back. "Brandy is supposed to be sipped . . . savored like a fine vintage wine," he advised, reaching for her goblet and taking a sip.

He nodded toward the huge canopied bed. "I've taken the liberty of laying out a nightshirt for you. Best get out of those wet garments or you'll catch your death."

"It really doesn't matter, " she announced quietly,

so final, placing the goblet on the table by the bed.

With an easy stride, Devlin whirled her around to face him. His face was angry, his eyes black as pitch.

"In my house you'll do as I say!" he snapped.

Lauriette was roughly turned back around and felt the man fumbling with the tiny buttons of her gown. After some time, he undid the last one, cursing under his breath.

"Now, when I return I expect to see you in that shirt and under those quilts!" he grunted, moving towards the door. "Is that clear?"

"Very clear," she returned coldly and turned back to the fire.

Lauriette flinched as the door slammed shut. She began to undress, neatly placing the ruined gown over the back of a chair to dry. The chemise crumpled to the floor, and absently, she stepped out of it. She stood close to the fire for a long moment, allowing the warmth to seep into her numb limbs before slipping the nightshirt over her head.

Refilling her goblet with more of the potent liquid, Lauriette collapsed into the overstuffed winged chair that faced the fireplace. She stared for a long time, her mind going over and over the scene in the library. Evan and Marie-Claire . . . Henry and Marie-Claire . . . Evan and Marie-Claire . . . Henry and Marie-Claire . . .

Again she wiped tears from her eyes, then took a small sip of the brandy. This time she did not choke and it went down much more smoothly. The second sip went easier than the first and by the time she finished it, she rather liked the taste of it.

"There is something wrong with me," she murmured aloud, tears filling her eyes once more. "Something very wrong. Am I not desirable? Am I defective in any way?"

Her wandering mind stopped suddenly, her hand flying to her mouth. Henry! Closing her eyes tightly, Lauriette sadly shook her head. Did Henry know of their sordid affair? How many honestly knew and were laughing all the while?

"No! He knows nothing of it, I'm sure!" she reassured herself. "Henry would've put a stop to it." A crystalline tear trickled down her nose. "I must protect him," she vowed in a whisper. "He must never know of this. I'll just tell him I've changed my mind about Evan. He need never know why."

There was a light rap on the door and without waiting for admittance, Devlin swung the door open and entered. He stopped suddenly, seeing the young woman as an enchanting vision sitting before the fire, her finger circling the rim of the now empty goblet.

What could have happened that would cause such unhappiness in her? Devlin's senses were racing, his emotions stirred as never before.

Lauriette wiped her eyes with the sleeve of the shirt and immediately felt someone watching her.

"I came to see if there was anything else you needed," he said slowly, coming towards her. "Why are you not abed?"

"I . . . perferred it here . . . by the fire." Her words were slurred and difficult to pronounce.

He picked up the decanter and found it almost empty. So the problem was serious enough for her to drink herself into a stupor.

She turned slowly to gaze at the dark man who once again seemed to appear from nowhere and rescue her. He was tall and broad of shoulder and to her he filled up the room. His compelling look caused her to hold her breath.

The fuzziness in her brain cleared a bit and her eyes widened at the sight of dried blood on his shirtsleeve.

"You are hurt," she whispered.

He looked down at his arm then back to her. " 'Tis nothing but a scratch."

"But it must be tended to or it will become infected," she insisted.

He grinned at her sluggish form. "You wish to tend this?"

Pushing back a stray curl from her face, she nodded dumbly. What kind of a lady did he think she was, to let him stand there in her presence and bleed!

"Of course I shall tend to it!" she said, flustered.

"Then I shall get what you will need to tend it." He made her a short bow and walked out of the room.

It required quite a bit of concentration for Lauriette to roll up the sleeves of the nightshirt. Faith, but she was feeling strange!

He returned quickly enough with a full tray of salves and bandages and a basin of water. Devlin stopped short at the sight she made standing before the fire, her figure most pleasantly outlined in the thin nightshirt.

"You will have to remove your shirt." Why did her mouth feel so dry?

Devlin grinned ruefully. "It will not offend your maidenly sensibilities?"

Her brow arched a trifle. "I am not English, sir," she replied indignantly. "It would take more than a mere chest to make me swoon!"

He eased the shirt slowly from his person, gritting his teeth when the shirt stuck to the wound.

As Devlin sat on the edge of the bed, Lauriette knelt beside him and with a most delicate touch that surprised him, examined his wound.

"It is superficial," she said quietly, using a light touch to cleanse the wound.

He watched her carefully as she cared for him. She was molded beautifully; the emotions crossing her face were easy to read. Evidently, the brandy had dulled most of the pain she was feeling. He smiled in spite of himself. She was a little more than tipsy and trying very hard not to show it.

Bandage in place, Lauriette sat back on her heels to view her handiwork.

"You are well on your way to recovery, sir," she smiled, then placed her hand quickly over her mouth to hold in a hiccup.

Devlin lightly caressed her cheek. "You are very lovely," he barely whispered.

Lauriette's heart was pounding madly. She looked at him through hazy eyes swimming in tears. Hastily, she jumped to her feet, dizziness causing her to grab at the bedpost. "You musn't say things like that!"

Devlin chuckled softly, his eyes resting on the opened nightshirt, revealing the deep cleft of her breast. "I merely stated an obvious fact," he mused.

Lauriette rested her forehead against the coolness of the bedpost and stared into the leaping flames of the fire. "Of course I'm lovely. I am just the kind of woman who is flattered and put high on a pedestal untouched, uncared for, unloved, to be looked upon as an object to be owned and gullible enough to believe that it is the proper way of life. But no more! Lies! All lies! Please, I don't wish to hear any more!" With a strangled sob, Lauriette covered her face with her hands and wept.

Devlin folded the girl into his arms, a warmth flooding over him. Someone, somewhere was responsible for her grief and his brows drew downward at the thought.

"I . . . I cannot stay here," she whispered shakily, withdrawing from his embrace. She was experiencing a multitude of emotions created by his touch, bringing about even more turmoil inside.

"What will you do if you don't stay?" he questioned. "Where will you go?"

She glared at him, anger and frustration causing more tears. "I don't know! I don't know!" her voice pitched higher. "All I know is I cannot stay here!"

"Why?"

"I don't know!"

"Why, cherub?" this time his voice demanded.

"I should never have come with you!" Nervously she paced back and forth. "I should have listened to Jamie and never come to London in the first place! He was right all along! Don't you see that? Don't you understand?"

Devlin's hands took her shoulders, forcing her to look up at him. "No, I do not understand any of your rantings!" he replied angrily. "Why? Why do you have to leave . . . to run? Answer me!"

"Because!" she blurted out. "Because you frighten me! You . . . you confuse, bewilder me! Everytime you are near I cannot think clearly. You mix me up inside! You pop in and out of my life like a dark angel—as if you were Lucifer himself come to vex me!"

His face was so close, Lauriette could see her reflection in his misty brown eyes. She held her breath. He was going to kiss her. She knew it but was powerless to prevent it. His lips ever so lightly brushed hers, causing tiny shivers to run rampant up her spine.

Devlin looked at Lauriette through half closed eyes. The urge to possess her was overwhelming, filling his loins with fire and his mind with a need to consume. Who was this enchantress with the cherub face?

He embraced her, his lips finding hers once again. It was a gentle, yet urgent kiss. He did not demand of her as Evan had. This man was doing something to her senses, her control gradually ebbing away. I am afraid—yet not afraid! What is this? What is happening?

"Your name, cherub," he whispered huskily. "Tell me your name."

She was breathless, her lips soft and moist from his kiss. Gone were all her fears.

"Lauriette," she whispered back. "I am . . . Lauriette."

Ten

Devlin grinned crookedly, much the same way he did the first time he kissed her.

"Lauriette," he drawled. It sounded so pleasant to the ears, to finally have a name for this enchantress who plagued his dreams. "A beautiful name, little cherub, and well suited to you."

Lauriette nervously lowered her head but Devlin would have none of it. Tenderly, he lifted her chin with his hand. "That is not, I repeat, *not* flattery," he commented lightly. "I very seldom compliment—I never flatter."

She was drawn to this dark angel. He seemed to give her his strength, his courage, merely by gazing into her eyes. She was not afraid of him, not repulsed by his touch.

He stroked her cheek as if memorizing every line, every plane that seemed to make her face unique. She dared not breathe for fear of breaking the spell he weaved. He kissed her, a fiery kiss which sent Lauriette's senses reeling, his tongue softly discovering the sweetness of her mouth. Holding her tightly he buried his face against her neck, inhaling the fragrance of honeysuckle.

It was useless to deny it—he desired her so much he ached. It was as if they had been foredestined from that first moment on the docks.

Devlin's mouth gently plundered hers, his hands gradually removing the nightshirt from her slender shoulders. Tenderly he cupped one breast, teasing the nipple until it grew taut. The nightshirt fell about her ankles and without further hesitation, he carried her to the bed.

Lauriette was astonished by her own willingness at the hands of this man she called Lucifer. It was almost too dreamlike to be happening, but in all her pain, all her sorrow, she desperately needed to feel love and strength, to be desired, to be wanted, if only for this one night. This dark stranger awakened a passionate side she never realized existed.

In the firelight, Devlin's muscular frame was silhouetted against the far wall as he climbed into bed beside her. His mouth tasted the virginal swell of her breasts, his hand lightly caressing the outside of her thigh.

His lips moved sensuously to the cleft of one breast then slowly began its journey downward, his tongue leaving behind a glistening path. Lauriette moaned deliciously.

A gasp escaped her lips as her fingers threaded their way through his dark wavy hair. She was on fire with need, her mind and body drifting away from the pain she had experienced, the brandy heightening her bravery.

Flashes of memory pierced her foggy mind and suddenly her body stiffened. "Please . . . I beg of you . . . don't . . . hurt . . . me, please!"

Devlin stopped abruptly, seeing the terror in her face. Gently, he touched her cheek, brushing away a tear. He smiled, then gradually his smile dimmed, his face taking on a serious, passionate look, his eyes like burning coals.

He showered her face and neck with kisses, his hands massaging the inner part of her thighs in a sensually relaxing manner. The bitter thoughts fleeing her mind, her arms encircled his neck, and instinctively pulled him down to her.

Devlin's lean hands expertly moved over her raised nipples, over the flatness of her belly, roughly cupping her well-rounded buttocks.

"The wonder," he breathed against her ear. "The wonder of you, my little cherub!"

Lauriette was dizzy with want of him, of his strength, his all-encompassing desire for her. Her breath came in short pants, her body arching upward, aching to discover the mystery of this thing poets write of.

Her eyes grew wide as Devlin entered her and she cried out in fear. He grew still, his lips kissing her neck where a pulse throbbed, waiting until she began to respond once again.

Lauriette gasped as he began to move slowly, his mouth softly ravishing her right breast. The first shock of his entry was now replaced by an unfathomable warm sensation that began in the pit of her stomach, spreading throughout her entire being. She moved with him, her body in compatible rhythm with his.

She was carried away by the tide of emotions, her mind whirling, sensation upon sensation mounting until she was consumed in delicious passion.

Devlin came to an almost violent climax, his response to this mysterious girl so overwhelming it frightened him a bit. He rolled away from Lauriette completely drained, a sweet contentment washing over him. What was it about her that touched him deeper than any other woman?

"Cherub?" he whispered. "Lauriette?"

Silence. She was sound asleep, her serene face turned towards him. Smiling crookedly, he brushed a stray curl away from her shoulder and covered her with the quilt. He settled himself beside her and sighed, his hand resting on her hip.

In the sitting room downstairs the clock chimed one, two, three, four times. Four o'clock in the morning and Devlin was wide awake.

Quietly, he stole out of the fourposter, pulling the heavy drapery together to ward off the winter chill. He stood, legs apart, naked before the dying fire, guilt smothering him. He should have been stronger, he told himself, should have never kissed the little tart in the first place!

If the truth were known, she was the first virgin he had ever seduced. Devlin gave a start. That's it! She was an inexperienced innocent who needed comforting. He laughed silently. This little chit was merely something new and different to him—a diversion, nothing more. *I only pray she doesn't become hysterical in the morn and demand I make an honest woman of her!*

Faint moans from the bed caught his attention and he hastily tiptoed towards Lauriette.

"P-please . . . p-please don't hurt him . . ." she cried faintly. "I'll do . . . anything. Don't . . . hurt . . ."

Devlin crawled under the quilt, his gaze settling on the outline of Lauriette's tortured face.

"No! No!" she screamed outright, her arms lashing out at unseen villans. "Peter! Peter!"

"Lauriette!"

Devlin shook her roughly, his hands holding her firmly. She was trembling violently, perspiration beading on her forehead.

"It's all right, little one," he soothed, drawing her into his arms. "You were dreaming, that's all."

"The . . . same dream," she barely whispered, her voice catching in her throat.

"Same dream?"

"Please don't make me remember!" she pleaded. "Hold me tight . . . please, as tight as you can!"

Devlin kissed her trembling mouth. "You're safe here," he murmured. "I won't let anything harm you."

"Make me forget, dark Lucifer," her voice shook. "Make me forget my memory, my thoughts, my fears."

He placed his hand between her parted thighs and found her desperately willing. With a groan, his mouth bruised hers and once more swept her away, far away into loving forgetfulness.

Eleven

The cold winter light of morning filtered through the part in the heavy velvet drapery, a cool draft waking Lauriette. The chill in the air nipped at her nose and she snuggled deeper into the warm quilt.

Her eyes flew open as a flood of the night's events paraded before her. The recollection of the act of love-making hit her with such an impact, she burned with guilt and humiliation. *What have I done?* She swallowed nervously. *Oh, Lauriette! Did you have to prove yourself a wanton? A slut? Did you have to encourage the man? Oh fool—fool!*

Inching her way, she eased herself from underneath the quilts and through the opening in the drapery. With quick haste, Lauriette dressed in her chemise and ruined ballgown, closely watching the sleeping man. His breathing seemed very slow and deep, the furry mat of dark hair on his chest calmly rising and falling.

She stood for a fleeting moment just to gaze at him. *How peacefully he sleeps,* she mused and had to stifle an impulse to touch his cheek.

Looking down at her gown, another pang of guilt

stabbed her. Henry! *He'll be full of questions of where I've been and why! Oh, Laurie, Laurie, what have you done?*

She made not a sound as she tiptoed from the room, closing the door behind her. Scanning the empty staircase and anteroom below, she breathed a sigh of relief. *I have to go!* she thought frantically.

She had no cloak! The man's greatcoat was still draped across the chair from the night before. She decided to borrow it, vowing to have Dolly return it.

Pulling the coat tightly about her, she ran out into the cool, crisp air. She hailed a hansom at the corner, then quickly glanced over her shoulder at the house—and thinking of the nameless man who had comforted her through the night.

The hansom came to a stop in front of the Branscombe House; Lauriette bounded out before the coachman reached the door and hurriedly asked the man to wait a moment for his fee.

"Lolly!"

Jean reached her before she knocked on the door and whirled her about. He stared at her dumbfounded, taking in disheveled state and tangled mass of curls.

"Jean, how long have you been here?" she asked breathlessly.

"We have been looking all over for you, *ma petite.*"

"Please, let's get in out of this cold and we'll talk," she turned and rapped on the door.

"Lolly, there is something—"

Jonas slowly opened the door, his face lined with sadness. His dark eyes brightened at the sight of his favorite.

"Missie!" he cried, pulling her inside.

"Would you pay the driver outside?" she asked quickly. Something was wrong, the house was too quiet. "Are they very angry at me, Jonas?"

The servant bowed his head, not about to meet her

questioning eyes. "Missie," he whispered, his eyes filling with tears. "Missie, Master Henry—he—"

A cold foreboding gripped her. "What has happened? Jonas?" Her voice trembled. "Where is Henry? Tell me!"

"He . . . he . . ." Jonas's voice trailed off.

"Lolly," Jean's hand rested on her shoulder. "Henry is . . . severely wounded."

Her eyes widened with surprise and concern. "No!"

"Come into the sitting room, Lolly," Jean said softly.

They moved into the sitting room and an agitated Lauriette restlessly paced back and forth across the room.

"Henry challenged Brimley."

She drew in her breath and turned to face Jean, her face cold and hard. "Evan," she breathed just above a whisper.

"Henry entered the library only moments after you ran out and it did not take him long to understand the situation," Jean explained. "But, Lolly, the duel was fought fairly."

"Fairly!" she mocked, tears glistening on her cheeks. Her thoughts turned to her sister. "Marie-Claire! She must be devastated! I should go to her!"

"There is no need for your comfort, dear sister," came Marie-Claire's calm voice. "I am just fine."

Lauriette whirled about coming face to face with Marie-Claire. She was no longer wearing her silver ballgown but was clothed in her usual flair. Her lovely face bore no trace of worry or regret.

She could not believe her sister's cool composure. Her husband was critically wounded and she showed not one shred of remorse or guilt. "How can you stand there with that satisfied look on your face when Henry could be dying?"

"Lolly!"

Lauriette jerked away from Jean's restraining hand. Her eyes were flashing with hurt.

"It is all your fault!" she accused. "You supplied the motive and Evan, your lover, carried it through. Why, Marie? You've nearly destroyed two lives, mine and poor Henry's. For what purpose? Well, there is no one in your path now—you and Evan deserve each other!"

Turning on a stunned Marie-Claire, Lauriette fled the room with Jean following closely behind.

Devlin woke feeling rested and in good spirits. Rolling over he reached for the girl's velvety softness and instead found cold linen under his touch, his eyes flew open. With one violent sweep of his arm, the drapery flew back. He scanned the quiet room and found nothing out of place.

Perhaps he had dreamed the young woman up, imagined the yielding supple body against his. Gingerly, he touched the indentation on the pillow next to his and smiled as he found a small yellow tea rose. No, she had not been a figment of his imagination. Absently, he twirled the flower in his fingertips, remembering vividly the tender night.

He swung his legs over the side of the bed, pulling on his robe. "Judd?" he bellowed. "Are you up yet?

He picked up the discarded nightshirt beside the bed and with a growl, crumpled it in his hands. The little minx slipped out on him and all he knew was her first name!

Judd appeared in the doorway. "It's about time you got up." He grinned knowingly. "It seems strange that we have two beds made up that haven't been slept in. Care to venture why?"

Devlin gave him a sidelong glance. "Did you see our little guest leave?"

Judd's twinkling eyes were fixed on the disarrayed bed. "No, but I did find your greatcoat missing a few minutes ago."

He nodded absently, picking up the nightshirt again. "Did Bourget arrive last night?"

Judd shook his head. "The bed wasn't slept in."

"I need a good bath," he sighed.

"I'll send Marshall in to you and have cook make you breakfast." Judd turned to leave then turned to look at Devlin from the doorway. "Care to discuss the events of last night?"

With a wild oath, Devlin sent the nightshirt hurling towards a laughing Judd. His footsteps echoed in the hall as he disappeared.

"Well," he said aloud, opening the bureau drawer, "at least she didn't demand my name." Hesitantly, he laid the tea rose on top of the sketches.

His bath ready, he relaxed in the hot water, his thoughts drifting back. A choice piece, that little lady fate had placed in his lap. It was still difficult for him to understand what had passed between them. He had never felt desire so strong before. It was only the circumstances, he repeated to himself, the right moment, the right atmosphere, a different breed of woman . . . it just naturally had to happen.

"You told me to remind you," Judd cut into his thoughts, "Lord David is expecting you at noon."

A frown crossed Devlin's face. "Must you spoil a perfectly delightful daydream?"

Judd laughed. "Some of us have to keep our heads on our shoulders. By the way, how is your arm? I thought to help you dress it last night, but your bed was empty."

Devlin looked down at the arm that was neatly bandaged. "The touch I felt last night was much more soothing than yours! It seems to be healing already."

"Must be," he returned, an amused look on his face. "It didn't seem to bother you any last night." And before Devlin could retort, he bowed out of the room.

In spite of himself, Devlin laughed. Judd was his third cousin and his almost constant companion for the last ten years. Being distantly related only secured the bond between them and they became as close as brothers.

He stood before a blazing fire, drying himself, thoughtfully chewing on the end of a cheroot. Another summons from the dynamic Lord David Essex, Marquess of Sutherford. He managed to avoid seeing his father several times, but now? He could not ignore a demand for his presence.

Grimly, he bit down harder on the cigar. His visits always ended in argument, it had always been this way. But his father was not getting any younger and he did have an obligation to him, did he not? The best way was to face the old man and get it over with!

Twelve

The threat of rain was evident as Devlin emerged from his coach, tastefully dressed in dark blue. He entered Ellsworth Inn, inquiring as to the rooms of Lord David Essex.

The innkeeper smiled broadly. "Most certainly," he ventured, "he has been expecting you, your lordship."

It took some time for Devlin's eyes to adjust to the darkened room. The heavy velvet drapery was pulled against the draft and the only source of light came from the cavernous fireplace.

"Well, scamp, once again you've made it back from those damn savage colonies," the scratchy voice came from behind him.

He turned, taking in the slight form that had once been as impressive as his own. Lord David Essex walked carefully with the aid of a cane, his hand haplessly trembling. The man's hair was a snowy white, tied at the nape of his neck by a black velvet ribbon. But it was Lord David's eyes that matched Devlin's, the misty brown that could blend into black in the wink of an eye.

Devlin smiled affectionately, extending his hand. "We're not colonies any longer, father, we're Americans."

"Of course, of course," he returned roughly, taking his son's hand, "I had forgotten. You're an American now. You gave up your heritage to become one of those savages."

Devlin clutched his fists. His father was deliberately trying to goad him into a confrontation. *Not this time, old man,* he thought warily, *not this time!*

He merely smiled lazily, leaning back against the desk. Slowly, he folded his arms across his chest and for a long moment, contemplated his father.

"As you say, father, we are called savages," he drawled. "But then, we have been called much worse."

"I imagine so," Lord David agreed. "I understand it is quite a hardship waiting for Neville to return, your loathing of the society which gave you succor and treated you with such respect."

Devlin's eyes narrowed, his temper taking a gradual rise. Lord David would never forgive him for his passionate support of the American Revolution. Why could he not understand it takes more than a title and wealth to make a man? He needed the freedom, the need to carve out a life for himself—if ever he was to become a real man!

"You invited me to dine," he said in a low voice. "Unless you intend to go on with this sordid conversation and pitch me out as you did ten years ago!"

Lord David's eyes changed to coal black. "You keep a civil tongue in your head, boy, or I'll—" A wracking cough seized him and he sat down heavily. The man could hardly breathe, tears streaming from his eyes. Devlin watched in horror as his father fought for control. He hastened to the dining table, quickly pouring a glass of brandy.

With trembling hands, Lord David sipped the strong liquid. His breath was beginning to return to normal.

Davlin felt love, as well as pity, swell from deep within his chest. Suddenly, his father looked very old to him. This man was as a stranger, an aloof, cold man.

Lord David gazed up at his son's concerned face. "Devlin," he whispered weakly, "I am dying."

"Father—"

Lord David waved his words away. " 'Tis time to face the inevitable," he stated quietly. "I am slowly dying and nothing on earth can change that."

Devlin bowed his head, not wanting to accept his father's words.

"I have no idea how much time I have left. The doctors tell me it could be two months to a year." Lord David stood and made his way to the closed drapery. The silence was deafening, Devlin stunned and confused.

With an enraged cry, Lord David hurled his cane across the room. "I'll be damned to hell and back if I'm going to die all alone with one son in India and the other rake in the colonies!" he roared. "I want my flesh and blood with me when I die—not those two vultures of my brother's!"

Devlin picked up his father's cane and stood looking at him, his eyes truly seeing him as a man and not a god.

Lord David faced him, a determined set to his jaw. "I want at least one legitimate grandchild to hold on my lap before I die!"

Devlin was completely speechless for an unending moment. Slowly his father's words sunk in and he backed away from Lord David.

"B-but . . . but, fa—"

"I want a grandchild before I die, scamp!" he bellowed. "So, get to it and wed! Do you hear? I want a grandson!''

''A grandchild! Do you hear me, scamp? A grandson!''

Two days had passed and still Devlin's father's words echoed in his ears. Even now it was still difficult for him to grasp what was happening. Within forty-eight hours, his entire life was out of control and for the first time he was not sure what to do.

He had taken Nomad, his prize stallion, out for exercise in the crisp December air. What to do, how to find the answer . . .

The countryside was completely deserted, the cold air no doubt keeping people in. His eyes scanned the barren grounds and for a reason he could not understand, Devlin felt disappointment in not running into the little artist with the cherub face—Lauriette.

''Come on, Nomad,'' he said aloud, patting the stallion's mane, ''time to get you home.''

Where had the little imp vanished to? It was as if she had been only a dream . . . but she was real! Inwardly, it irked him that she could elude him so successfully, without so much as one solid clue to her identity. She fascinated him. Even her name—Lauriette—sounded intriguing.

It began to rain, the cold icy drops sneaking down the neck of his greatcoat. Devlin's mind returned to family, as he rounded the street corner. The Essexes were not an openly affectionate family. For years there had been only the three of them: Neville, Devlin, and Lord David. A house of men soon forget the soft touch of a woman.

Devlin dismounted, leading Nomad into the dry comfort of the stable. Handing the reins to Timothy, one of his livery, he stood leaning against the door frame and stared out at the torrential downpour.

He barely remembered his mother; only the portrait

which hung in the library at Essex Hall kept her memory alive. Lady Marianne had died in a fall from a horse when he and Neville were but eight years old. Over the years the two things he did recall time and again were his mother's gentle laugh and her slender, delicate hands. Odd things for a small lad to remember. . . .

Devlin stared into an ever-widening puddle at his feet, his brows drawn downward in a frown. He had been no more than fourteen when his uncle's children came to live with them. After they had moved in with them, their peaceful existence was turned topsy-turvey.

He returned to his house, waspishly slamming the door after him. Remembering the past only succeeded in making his mood blacker.

Well, no matter what, his father had another think coming! He was not ready to tie himself down and he honestly doubted he ever would. Neville would return in April, let *him* be the one to take the agonizing plunge.

Love! he thought disgustedly. *Bah! There is no such thing! A bewildered losing of one's senses. An imaginary emotion poets write of.*

He had sailed the oceans and pioneered land. He had known enough women to realize what a hoax it all was. A mutual attraction of two bodies and immediately the fairer sex proclaims it love. *Bah!*

Carelessly tossing the drenched greatcoat on a chair, he completely ignored the track left by his muddy boots. Devlin was in a dark, dangerous mood, the scowl on his face reflecting his thoughts.

"Devlin." The soft voice interrupted his ugly thoughts. Anger quickly forgotten, he grasped the outstretched hand of Jean Bourget.

"It has been a long time, my friend," he half smiled. "At least two years, perhaps longer."

Jean nodded absentmindedly. Devlin felt his friend's preoccupation. This man who normally smiled continually now wore a worried, downhearted expression, his gray eyes swollen and bloodshot.

"What's amiss, Jean?" he asked bluntly. "I expected you two days ago."

Jean sunk to the sofa, head resting in hands. He was beside himself with worry about Lolly. He searched everywhere the night of the ball but to no avail. Then she appeared as suddenly as she vanished, looking as wild and beautiful as the Louisiana wilderness. He was full of questions, but they had to be set aside. He had to be the one to tell her of Henry's duel.

"Dev, are you acquainted with the Branscombes?" he asked slowly.

Listening with only half an ear, Devlin shook his head absently.

"I had to tell a lovely young woman her brother-in-law, whom she is very fond of, was almost killed in a duel," he sadly began. "Sir Henry Branscombe. I just met him that night. I am a close friend to the girl's brother, James Claymoor. He and I have had many a good brawl together."

Jean gratefully accepted the brandy Devlin offered. Thoughtfully, he stared into the potent liquid. "The grief that little one carries! She turned on her sister, Lady Marie-Claire, accusing her of being just as guilty as Sir Evan Brimley. She is so beside herself, I fear for her."

The brandy snifter raised to his lips, Devlin froze. It was the mention of Brimley's name.

"What did you say about Brimley?"

"Brimley fought a duel with Branscombe," he repeated. "It happened the night of the Winter Ball. She could not even bear to see him. I, too, feel responsible for what happened. If you could have but seen the pain in those blue-green eyes of hers. Sweet little Lolly!"

"Did you call her . . . Lolly?"

Jean nodded dumbly.

"Is that her given name?"

Jean grinned, his eyes holding a faraway look. "No, it's but a nickname I gave her. She has a lovely French name, one that is not heard of too often . . . Lauriette."

Devlin paled, his mind in a turmoil. Finally, he had a link between himself and his mysterious little artist. And now he had a last name to go with the first—Lauriette Claymoor!

Instinct told him to see her, he *must* see her, to be sure she was all right.

"I encountered a young lady in the rain three nights ago." he said. "The fact is, she ran in front of my coach."

"What?"

Devlin nodded his head. "I offered her lodgings for the night, as she would not tell me her name or where I could take her. She was gone the next morn—disappeared."

Rising, Jean threw Devlin a questioning look, remembering Lolly's appearance.

"I need to see her!" he said to a much surprised Jean. "I would like to see for myself that she is . . . all right. She was quite distressed that night. Will you take me there?"

A strange, unfamiliar look filled Devlin's misty brown eyes. Jean was compelled to take him to Lauriette, though he could not fathom why.

"I cannot say if we will be welcomed, *mon ami,* but I will take you," Jean stated uncomfortably.

Thirteen

Devlin could not help but grin, imagining the expression Lauriette would wear when they came face to face. The lovely phantom was no longer a memory and within moments he would be seeing for himself if his mind held the proper picture of her.

"Marie-Claire is quite upset with Lolly," Jean stated, his hand absently rubbing his chin. "She was none too happy with my interfering and demanded I leave posthaste."

Half of Devlin listened to Jean's ramblings while the other half was remembering the one night he had spent with Mistress Lauriette Claymoor. She was quite a charming bit of baggage and with that pleasant thought, he grinned crookedly.

The Branscombe townhouse was impressive with an eight-foot iron fence surrounding the grounds. Somehow he could not picture Lauriette in this setting, with a huge fence keeping people out.

Jean glanced over at Devlin as they passed through the gates. "This was Lord Craymoor's wedding gift to his son," he informed him. "Quite something, is it not?"

Jean rapped the brass knocker several times before they heard echoing footsteps inside. The door gradually opened.

"Good afternoon, Jonas," Jean smiled amiably, stepping quickly inside. "I have brought a gentleman to see Mistress Claymoor, Sir Devlin Essex, Viscount of Delbridge."

Jonas was openly awed by Devlin's rank but worried nonetheless. "I'm sorry, Mr. Jean, but I can't let you see missie," he said in a low voice. "My lady's orders. You understand, sir, I have to do what I'm told."

"I thought I made myself clear two days ago, M'sieu Bourget," Marie-Claire's cold voice rang through the foyer.

Devlin arched a brow, his keen eyes following the attractive woman's steps. There was no trace of any resemblance to Lauriette, he noted.

Marie-Claire stood face to face with Jean, her manner very cool and indifferent. "Please be good enough to leave my house."

"You cannot keep me from seeing Lolly, Marie-Claire," Jean replied harshly.

"I can and will," she replied curtly. "Lauriette is in no condition to receive any visitors."

"This is a matter of importance."

"Do you think I will let you influence her any more than you already have?" she questioned. "Because of you she thinks she has broken her betrothal! Now, please be good enough to leave before I have you forcibly removed! Is that clear?"

Jean felt totally helpless, his mouth agape. Marie-Claire turned toward the sitting room.

"My lady," Devlin said softly and smiled inwardly as the woman turned and regarded him for the first time. "I am Sir Devlin Essex, Viscount Delbridge.

Perhaps you know my father, Lord David Essex, the Marquess?''

Marie-Claire smiled cooly. Everyone in England knew of Lord David Essex, a very wealthy and powerful man. Slowly her eyes appraised Devlin's broad frame. Yes . . . and everyone in London knew of Lord David's hellrake son, too!

He put on his most charming smile. ''Surely this once a lovely lady like yourself could make an exception,'' he said. ''I wish to see Mistress Claymoor . . . on a matter of some sketches she did.''

Marie-Claire smiled very sweetly and answered, ''Lauriette is now in my charge, my responsibility. She sees no one at this time. Now leave!''

''Elliott is her legal guardian!'' Jean exploded. ''You have no right—''

''No right!'' she shouted. ''Elliott gave up his guardianship when she came here to marry! Jonas! Assist these good gentlemen to the door. If they do not leave, have Tom and Jonathan throw them out!''

In a whirl of crisp skirts, Marie-Claire stormed toward the sitting room. Devlin took a step towards her then felt Jonas's hand on his arm.

''It will do no good to vex her further,'' Jean whispered angrily. ''Perhaps we better wait.''

Devlin nodded and without any trouble they headed towards the door.

''I'm sorry, Mr. Jean,'' Jonas whispered as he opened the door.

''It's not your fault, Jonas,'' he replied. ''Good day.''

''Devlin, I'll hail a hansom to take me to the docks,'' Jean said, once outside the gates. ''So much has happened. I need to see my ship and become involved with something I can control.''

''Very well, my friend,'' he answered, extending his

hand. "I will see you soon."

Devlin was in a somber frame of mind as he reached the coach. Something was not quite right, he could sense it. *Well, there's nothing to be done about it tonight,* he reasoned.

"Hurry and shut th' door, quickly!" The frantic voice came from the far corner of the coach.

Devlin sat and immediately closed the door. The coach lurched forward and he leaned back, staring for a long moment at the woman. There was something very familiar about her.

"You have business with me?"

"Are ye th' owner of this fine coat?" she asked, placing the neatly folded garment in his hands.

"I am."

"Me mistress asked me to return it and express her thanks," she told him. "I saw ye leave yer place and followed ye back here."

"I remember you," he smiled. "You are Mistress Claymoor's maid."

She blushed shyly. "I'm Dolly, yer lordship. I placed ye, too, th' moment ye walked out yer door."

"I am sorry to hear of Sir Henry's misfortune," he said. "Your mistress, is she faring well?"

Dolly's eyes lowered in a heartbroken fashion. "The missie is not well, sir," she admitted. "She feels so much pain and hurt inside. She feels responsible for what happened." Then she raised her eyes to his unspoken plea. "Ye could not see Mistress Lauriette . . . because she is not there."

"What?"

"She ran from th' house after she found out about Sir Henry," she added. "I was th' only one what talked ta her before she disappeared."

Devlin looked at the maid closely, his brown eyes turning black. "And tell me, Dolly, do you know where she's gone?''

She looked away, avoiding his piercing stare.

''Dolly,'' he drawled slowly, ''do you know where Mistress Claymoor is?''

The maid nodded dumbly.

''Where is she, Dolly?''

''She's . . . she's gone to Claymoor,'' she answered softly. ''Master Elliott's estate in Dorset. Please, sir, ye won't tell a soul, will ye? I worry so fer her safety. . . . Her world's been ripped apart these days. I can't hardly bear the idea of her out there alone. . . .'' She glanced out the window at the pouring rain. ''It's gettin' dark. Would ye have yer man stop here? The walk will do me good.''

''Rest assured, Dolly,'' he smiled comfortingly, ''your secret will be safe with me.''

Fourteen

Lauriette stood on the steps of the Claymoor Estate and gazed upward at the neglected stone house. Yes, it was the same house of which she held many fond memories—but it was so overrun with weeds and dead vines—hardly as she remembered it. All the money Elliott sent for the upkeep year after year—evidently, it had not gone to Claymoor!

With a nervous gulp, she lifted her skirts and mounted the steps. The grounds looked so sad and unwanted. She rapped the knocker soundly and waited for the sound of footsteps. Anxiously, she glanced about. There should have been someone about!

Once again Lauriette rapped the knocker hard against the huge wooden door and waited. Still no sound from within. Holding the door ring, she shoved against the door and it opened smoothly.

"Hello!" Her echo was all that answered back. The house was dark and eerie; where were all the servants?

Lauriette moved to the drawing room and was surprised to find a blazing fire in the cavernous fireplace, everything in order and neatly dusted. This room looked very lived in.

"Who are you? What do you want?"

Lauriette gave out a startled cry at the sound of the harsh voice. An old woman stood in the doorway, her faded gray dress neatly pressed, giving her a matronly look. Her white hair was pushed under a white mob-cap, her blue eyes straining to see the intruder in the poor light.

"Clara?" Lauriette barely uttered the name. "Is it really you, Clara? 'Tis me, Lauriette . . . Lauriette Claymoor."

A disbelieving gasp escaped the woman as she rushed across the floor to embrace the young girl. It had been so many years! So many years!

"Child, child!" Clara cried softly. "What are you doing here?"

She gazed up at the old woman, tears glistening in her eyes. "I . . . I want to stay here," she stammered. "Please, Clara, don't send me away, please!"

"Hush, dear," she soothed. "Such talk! I would never send you away."

Clara Gordon watched from the doorway the diligent figure scrubbing the foyer floor. With a disapproving shake of her head, the housekeeper of Claymoor returned to the warmth of the kitchen.

Seth, her husband of more than five years, sat at the table munching on a cold biscuit. She looked at him with a bewildered expression and he smiled sympathetically.

"Dear me!" she sighed, sitting next to her husband. "What am I to do with the child? She insists on doing tasks that Emma should be a-doing!"

"Now, just calm yerself, Clara," Seth warned, patting her hand. "Ye can't stop her."

"But scrubbing floors, Seth!" she exclaimed. "Why,

Master Jamie would be furious if he knew. He always protected her, spoiled her—"

"Now, Clara."

"It's because of Sir Henry," she went on. "The poor dear blames herself, I know she does!"

"But Sir Henry is Lady Marie-Claire's husband, is he not?"

Clara nodded. " 'Tis a long story," she said confidentially. "Sir Henry and Miss Lauriette had an understanding a long time ago. I'm not sure how but Miss Marie found a way to weasel herself into Sir Henry's father's affection and he requested a betrothal between Sir Henry and Miss Marie. But even before it was announced, Miss Lauriette found the two of them together—*together,* if you know what I mean—"

At the sound of footsteps they became silent as Lauriette entered the kitchen.

"The foyer is finished, Clara."

"And so are you, sweet," she replied sternly. "Now, you sit and have a bite to eat. You never touched your breakfast this morn."

Lauriette heaved a sigh. "I wasn't hungry this morning."

Clara placed a bowl of soup in front of her. "I expect you to eat every bit of it, too!"

Lauriette smiled affectionately at Seth and Clara. They had taken her in that first night and never once did either of them pry. They waited patiently for her to talk with them.

She had made the right decision in coming to Claymoor. She felt safe and secure from the world in this huge house, and here no one could hurt her.

Seth stood up and reached for his coat. "Well, ladies, 'tis time for this gardener to get back to Essex House."

"You button up, old man," Clara called after him.

" 'Tis cold outside!"

Clara turned her attention to Lauriette. "I want you to finish that soup, then upstairs with you."

"Clara . . ."

"I am still spry enough to turn you over my knee, child," she warned. "A nap is what you need and a nap you will get."

Lauriette shook her head, her eyes filling with tears. "I'm glad I came."

"So am I, dear," Clara answered.

It was a glorious day, the sun brilliantly shining. *He* was with her, softly gazing into her eyes. He smiled a somewhat crooked smile and moved towards her.

"I have finally found you," he whispered.

"I have been waiting for you to come," she replied and opened her arms to him.

His embrace was strong and secure. She was safe with him and felt no fear. Dark Lucifer was her courage, her will, her faith and with him to love she could face anything.

Suddenly her eyes widened in horror as Evan held her fast. "Thought you could escape me, didn't you!" he growled, eyes hard and glinting. "I told you; you are mine and no one will ever take you from me!"

She screamed, beating her fists, shoving herself away from him. She was suffocating, her breath coming in short, painful gasps.

"Help me, someone, please . . . please.."

"Lauriette," Clara whispered, shaking her shoulders. "Lauriette, dear, wake up."

She opened her eyes and blankly stared for a long moment at the woman, trying to rid herself of that horrible nightmare.

"Are you all right, child?"

Lauriette rubbed her eyes. "I—I was dreaming,"

she answered sleepily. "What time is it?"

Clara laughed. "Time to get up! You have a visitor in the drawing room."

"Me? Are you certain?" she stammered. "But—but no one knows I'm here. Oh, Clara!"

"Now, now," Clara soothed, patting her shoulder. "The visitor is Sir Devlin Essex. His father owns Essex Hall, the nearest estate to us."

Lauriette slipped out of bed and began to dress hastily. "Why would he wish to see me?" she questioned aloud. "How did he know I was here?"

"Perhaps Seth said something to him," she answered, helping to button the back of Lauriette's dress. "Why are you so suspicious?"

"It's just . . ." Lauriette sighed. "I'm sorry, Clara, it's silly of me to be so jumpy."

"Now turn around and let me have a look." Lauriette wore a simple blue muslin daygown. "You look lovely, child."

Arm in arm they descended the stairs. "I took the liberty of serving Sir Devlin tea," Clara whispered, then smiled impishly. "He's quite a handsome devil, I might add."

"Oh, Clara!" Lauriette scoffed. "Will you ever change?"

"Too old to change now, my dear," she replied. "Now, if you need me, just ring."

Lauriette took several deep breaths before opening the door. The room was illuminated by the fireplace, a friendly sight on such a cold and dreary afternoon.

Sir Devlin Essex stood at the bay window, his back to her, staring out at the unkept grounds. He was dressed in an emerald green coat and cream-colored trousers, his black Hessian boots reflecting the fire. He was quite an impressive man—broad shoulders, narrowing hips . . . black hair curling over his coat collar.

She quietly closed the door behind her and leaned against it, silently appraising the man. Why on earth would he come to see her—and on such a depressing afternoon? Perhaps he knew her family. . . .

"My lord?" she softly broke the silence. "You wished to see me?"

The man turned and gazed at her, causing her to feel a strange trembling, her pulse quickening. She could not make out his features, he was half standing in the shadows.

"Mistress Claymoor," his voice was deep and husky. "I trust you are well?"

His voice! There was a ring to it triggering her memory. Sir Devlin Essex moved to the fire, his cool brown eyes still holding her transfixed.

From her shocked expression he saw that she recognized him and he grinned crookedly. Sir Devlin and her Lucifer were one in the same from the long straight nose to the deep slashed dimples. There was no mistaking it!

"You!" she exclaimed through clenched teeth. "What on earth are you doing here! How did you find me?"

Devlin graced her with a slight mocking bow. She was exactly as he remembered, only lovelier. "I had hoped you'd be a bit more cordial," he drawled, moving closer to her. "Such an elusive lady."

Lauriette blushed deeply and retreated a step. The effect this rogue had upon her was overpowering. He had an uncanny ability to confuse and bewilder her, part of her wanting to run to him—part of her wanting to stay away.

Devlin could not understand the strange attraction this girl had for him. It had taken him days to decide to come to Dorset. There had been been a struggle taking place inside him, which caused him many a sleepless night! Should he mind his own business and stay in London or go to Essex Hall only a few miles from this little enchantress and take his chances? Well, the decision was finally made. . . .

"Does anyone else know I am here?" she asked slowly.

She was too young to be hurt so much. Her eyes were glistening with unshed tears, her bottom lip trembling.

"Dolly returned my coat," he answered. "But as it so happens I learned of your identity from a common friend quite by accident."

"A common friend?"

"Jean Bourget."

"Jean?"

Devlin nodded. "Your maid then confided in me as to your whereabouts."

"And, of course, you took it upon yourself to make certain I hadn't done anything drastic," she said bitterly. "As you can see, I am just fine and I intend to stay that way."

Devlin's eyes narrowed as he stared at her. "As you say, Mistress Claymoor, I do see that you are the same bad-tempered little shrew I encountered weeks ago," came his cool reply. "What you aren't is the warm, enchanting little imp that occupied—"

"That night was a terrible mistake," she cut in. "It should never have happened. If only I hadn't partaken of so much of your brandy!"

"I see."

"You're not to blame, my lord," she hurried on. " 'Twas my fault—all my fault. If I hadn't left the ball, if I hadn't gone with you . . . I'm not a loose woman. And that was the first . . . the first. . ." her voice trailed off.

"The first time you had been made love to," he finished, a devilish gleam in his eye. "I'm not certain whether to be relieved or offended. A man doesn't like to think a woman is repulsed by his caress."

"Sir, you know exactly what I mean!" she responded angrily. "I only wish to forget that entire night!"

He stood only a heartbeat away from her, his eyes softly holding hers. "I see now, cherub," he whispered. "You would like to forget the light touch of my hand caressing your cheek, my arm about your waist, my lips tasting yours . . ."

His mouth covered hers, his arm encircling her waist, gently pulling her to him. Lauriette closed her eyes and with a unconscious relief, melted against him. She was on fire, her heart pounding furiously.

Her logical mind began to fight against her heart and with all her will, she pulled away from his embrace. She was trembling, her mind confused and numb.

"Please—please go," she said breathlessly.

Devlin grasped her arm, pulling her back to him. "Are you sure you want me to go?"

The meaning of his words twisted like a knife in her heart. She slapped Devlin smartly, the shock of her act stunning him.

"How dare you!" she stormed. "How dare you presume I would fall into bed with you! Just because you plied me with drink and seduced me in a very weak moment when I was so vulnerable, do not think for one moment that there will be a repeat! I don't want you or any man! I need no one!"

"Mistress Claymoor, I—" Devlin angrily began.

"Such arrogance!" she cut him off sharply. "I am certain you know how to find your way out!" Her voice caught in her throat and she ran from the room, slamming the door behind her.

Devlin stared intently at the door Lauriette disappeared through, his temper struggling to be loose. He had never encountered a woman with such pride and stubborness before. That hot-tempered little minx! Thoughtfully he rubbed his inflamed cheek and gradually a grin broke into a smile.

She was quite a handful, filled with fire and spirit. Those eyes! Those damnable horizon blue eyes intrigued him so. They said so much more than the little baggage realized.

"Mistress Claymoor," he whispered, staring into the fire, "you've not seen the last of me! Fortunately for you your eyes say differently than your words."

Fifteen

Devlin woke in an unfamiliar bed, the sun filtering through a dirty paned window. One eye opened, then the other, his mind filled with ache. Did he go to the tavern the night before? He did. He groaned, rolling to his back. There had been a wench the night before. The bed now held only him but the other pillow still held an impression. *My god! Must have been a wild night!* he inwardly groaned.

"Y-yer lordship?" a timid voice inquired.

Devlin scowled, peering over the rough comfort. At the foot of the bed was Timothy, one of his livery, nervously fingering his hat.

"Well?" he growled impatiently.

"Yer lordship," he began, "Mr. Judd, he's a-waitin' yer pleasure at Essex Hall."

Angrily, he threw back the covers hurling curses to every part of the scarcely furnished room.

"Well, just don't stand there, damn it," he shouted. "Fetch my horse!"

"Right away, yer lordship, right away!" Timothy stammered, tripping himself in an attempt to get to the door.

Devlin violently shook his head in an effort to clear it. What on earth had possessed him to drink so much? Lauriette! That little imp had an amazing ability to infuriate him.

Being so close to her only caused him to want her that much more. It was ego that made him think she would fall into his bed willingly; after all, the first time there had been extenuating circumstances . . . and brandy!

The biggest mistake he had made was underestimating her. She was certainly not like the women he knew before. In fact, he had never met anyone like her.

Judd was relaxing in front of the fire, his boots and trousers muddy from the long journey. Devlin seated himself in a chair closer to the fire, his head still throbbing.

"Seems you rode in great haste, cousin," he said, stretching his legs out before the fire.

Judd nodded, still staring straight ahead. "You told me to let you know of any activity."

Devlin sat up abruptly and looked at Judd. "Well?"

"Where would you like me to start?" he asked, a mischievous glint in his eyes. " 'Tis a long, involved story."

"Damn it, man, now is not the time for jesting!" Devlin shouted, then calmed himself. "Your sense of humor is not helping my sick head one whit!"

"My apologies," he said lightly. "Mistress Lauriette Claymoor came from Philadelphia to wed none other than Sir Evan Brimley. Dev, you don't seem surprised."

Devlin was thinking of the duel. "I, more or less, suspected as much."

Judd leaned forward, extending hands toward the fire. "The night of the Winter Ball Mistress Claymoor caught Brimley in a very compromising situation with her sister, Lady Marie-Claire."

Devlin grinned. "I've had the pleasure of meeting her ladyship. Her husband, Sir Henry, was severely wounded in a duel that same night—"

"Brimley," Judd cut in. "Branscombe is not a man to be openly cuckolded and challenged him to a duel."

Devlin rubbed his chin, his head beginning to clear. "I imagine that bastard enjoyed every minute of the duel."

"Mistress Claymoor backed out of the betrothal, and according to my sources, she told Brimley in no uncertain terms." He grinned. "I'm told Brimley stands firm that their wedding will take place."

"When were they betrothed?"

"Almost two years ago in Philadelphia," he answered. "Her brother introduced them. Elliott Claymoor is a member of the Assembly—he is a very influential man, very ambitious."

"Ended the betrothal, eh?"

Judd chuckled. "Full of sass and spice," he laughed. "I'm certain Mistress Claymoor had no idea of Brimley's sordid past."

"Of course not," Devlin agreed.

"You realize, Brimley isn't one to bow out gracefully," Judd reminded. "He won't let go."

Devlin's expression became sober. "I know but I don't believe Mistress Claymoor understands this."

"There's something new," Judd said slowly. "The Lady Marie-Claire is on her way to Claymoor."

"What? But how did she find out?"

Judd shrugged his shoulders. "Who knows? Probably a matter of deduction. I should imagine Lady Marie-Claire knows her sister quite well or perhaps there's a spy in the village or even at Claymoor."

Devlin paced the floor in front of the fire. "Is Brimley traveling with her?''

''No, it seems his uncle sent him to Scotland until the scandal cools a bit,'' he replied. ''But he will definitely be back to collect his bride as soon as all this dies down.''

Devlin turned sharply, an inspired glow on his face. ''Brimley will not let Mistress Claymoor go willingly.''

''Of that you can be sure.''

''Then perhaps we will give her some assistance, eh?''

Judd looked concerned. ''What are you up to, Dev?''

He smiled wickedly and clasped his cousin's shoulder. ''You'll see soon enough, Judd.''

Sixteen

Lauriette strolled along the unkept grounds of Claymoor; her spirits were at low ebb. Her mind was filled with memories of the past—good, happy memories of a time when laughter filled the house on a warm summer's day and the grounds bloomed with a rainbow of colored flowers.

The sun came streaming through a parade of fluffy white clouds and Lauriette looked skyward, thoughts of Philadelphia causing waves of homesickness. If only she had refused Evan's offer of marriage perhaps Henry would not have had to suffer and she would still be safe and sound on the farm.

Lauriette entered the barren woods and meandered down the well-trodden path. Son she came to a clearing and stopped, her mouth turning into a saddened smile. A half-frozen pond was partially concealed by underbrush. She could almost envision Henry and herself sitting on a blanket, laughing and enjoying their moments together.

A single tear trickled down her cheek. A sob caught in her throat as she quickly turned away. "Oh Henry,

Henry!" she whispered aloud. "I'm so sorry . . . for everything."

A rustling sound from behind caught her attention and she turned to find Sir Devlin Essex astride his horse, Nomad.

"Good afternoon, Mistress Claymoor," he smiled, slinging his leg over the saddle horn.

"It was until you popped in!" she replied tartly.

"Faith, and I came to make peace between us," he laughed, jumping down. "I came to apologize for my abominable actions of yesterday."

She was taken back by his passive mood. "I suppose it would be good manners to accept your apology," she grudgingly returned.

He looked around the secluded spot and nodded in approval. " 'Tis a pretty spot here."

She smiled demurely. "Yet, it's quite beautiful in the summer."

"Have you visited here often?"

"No," she said slowly. " 'Twas four years ago I was here. We returned home . . . I don't remember exactly when . . . September perhaps."

Devlin looked at her curiously.

"I—I fell ill and had to return to Philadelphia, my home," she explained, though not understanding why she did so. "I—I cannot recall the last days of my visit, I was so ill." She sat down on a large rock and silently began to massage her temples. Talking of that summer always brought on a heaviness in her brain.

Devlin knelt beside her. "I've something very important to discuss with you."

"Important?" she asked. "What?"

"A matter which concerns both you and I," he said softly. "A matter of giving you my name."

Her brows drawn downward in study now shot upward in surprise. "You . . . want to marry me?"

He nodded. "Isn't that just what I asked?"

Panic rose within, Lauriette jumped up and moved away from him. "But—but you know nothing about me," she stammered. "You don't love me."

He stared at her, a subdued scowl upon his face. "I fail to see what love has to do with marriage."

Lauriette was at a loss for words. Never in her wildest dreams did she expect this!

Devlin took advantage of her silence and plunged on. "My father has been pressing me to marry and I'm not one to go into anything blindly. Our marriage would be one of convenience, that is—"

"Yes, yes! I know exactly what that term means!" she cut in impatiently, anger boiling inside. The bloody gall of this man! "And just why, exactly, would this marriage of convenience be advantageous to me?"

"My name will give you protection. I'm wealthy by inheritance and by my own right," he said in a very businesslike tone. "You'll have nothing to worry about for the rest of your life and a very enviable social position will be yours for the asking. Also, I'm not exactly a bad-looking fellow—you could do a lot worse."

Her eyes were blazing with anger, but she kept her tone calm. "And in return what would you expect from me?"

He grinned lazily. "Your loyalty, cherub," he said so softly. Devlin stood now and pulled her to her feet. "And my rights as a husband—only until you conceive. From then on you'll be amply taken care of and I'll keep my little indiscretions very private."

"I see," she replied quietly, then stared straight into his eyes. "And if I too desire a few little *indiscretions* myself?"

Devlin's mouth flew open, shocked that she would even consider such an act.

"You self-centered, arrogant cur!" Lauriette burst

out in rage. "What on earth ever gave you the idea that I would even consider marrying you! Of all the audacity! Just like a man! An affair or two for a man only adds to his character—but a woman? Well, let me tell you, your lordship, I wouldn't have you or any other man for that matter!"

He looked at the young woman patiently. "And what if you are with child?"

She ceased her pacing and glared at him. "What would lead you to believe the child would be yours?"

His temper burst like a clap of thunder. Before Lauriette could move, Devlin's hands were on her shoulders and he shook her soundly. "I should throttle you proper!" he growled. "That remark is beneath you."

A golden brown curl escaped her bonnet. She was close to tears but stubbornly refused to let Devlin see her weaken.

He let the curl slide from his hand, the silky texture softening his anger. It would be so easy, so damnably easy, to throw her to the ground and ravish her!

"I've asked you to accept my name," he repeated gently. "Would I be so hard to live with?"

As he gazed upon her, all the lovely softness in her eyes disappeared and she became cold and remote.

"The Claymoor name has always set well with me," she answered curtly. "I need neither your name nor your protection."

His face hardened, his eyes glistening like onyx. "You would rather suffer the attentions of Brimley?"

Lauriette stiffened at the mention of Evan's name. Her eyes were full of unleashed fury as she faced Devlin, her arms akimbo. "There will be no vows spoken, he understood perfectly—and now you do, too!"

He grasped her hands quickly and held them tightly. "Brimley won't stop just because you wish it," he snapped, making her face him. "At this moment your sister is on her way here."

Lauriette stared at him in disbelief. "You told her!"

Devlin hurriedly shook his head. "I told no one," he said emphatically. "You cannot go on running, you little fool! I'm offering you a way out. Can you not see that? Your sister will be here soon and before you know it, Brimley will be here to collect his bride!"

She twisted free of his hands and shoved him from her. "I don't need your protection, can you not get that through your thick brain? I'm big enough to handle my own problems and I *do not need* you in my affairs!"

He never encountered a woman in his entire life to match her! At that moment he wanted nothing more than to throw her over his knee and give her a thrashing she would long remember!

With a curt nod of her head, Lauriette stormed through the woods leaving Devlin standing silently, his fists clenched tightly.

Well, if she wants to be left alone, that's exactly what she'll get from me! he fumed. *I wouldn't lift a finger to help her if —even if the devil himself was ravishing her!*

Seventeen

Night was quietly descending upon Claymoor; the winter wind eerily howled through small cracks in the wood around the windows. Lauriette sat before the fire staring intently into the flames. She was no longer the blazing, bad-tempered shrew of that afternoon but now a composed, serene young lady, her elbows gently resting on her knees.

She became very docile after her explosive encounter with that man. He was right; she could not keep on running forever. It was time to take a stand and face Marie-Claire once and for all.

The thought of marriage now was the furthest thing from her mind; in fact, she would never be able to trust a man again. Jamie had been right all along and as much as she desired to see him, she hated the thought of that smug, I-told-you-so expression he would wear!

No doubt guilt prompted his proposal, she thought angrily. How she had hated that confident look he wore while stating the conditions of marriage! He was so sure of himself! So positive that she would jump at the chance to marry him. Devlin had been genuinely shocked at her refusal.

Lauriette laughed in spite of the anger she felt. Obviously, many women had set their caps for Devlin Essex and he was very sure of his magnetic charm. He surely was a charming devil too, with that dark hair curling over his collar, his crooked smile . . .

Lauriette sat up stiffly and mentally took hold of herself. She had to stop all this foolish dreaming and try to look at life realistically. Well, she was rather pleased with herself. She had sent Devlin Essex packing, good and proper! To leave herself open to a man like that—or to any man for that matter—would only lead to further hurt.

The double doors to the sitting room flew open, light from the foyer flooding in. Marie-Claire stood poised in the doorway, her hands still neatly tucked into a fur muff. She was richly dressed in a maroon velvet traveling dress, an intricately designed ruby brooch glistening at her throat. Her light blue eyes looked upon Lauriette with disfavor as she stood.

"Are you not going to invite me to share the warmth of your fire, little sister?" her voice sounded more like a demand rather than a request. She tossed the fur muff on a chair and began to remove her kid gloves.

Clara appeared in the room, nervously wiping her hands on her apron. "My lady!" she exclaimed. "We didn't know you were to visit."

"There is no need for you to make an appearance, Clara," Marie-Claire said coldly. "As you can see, my sister and I are not at one another's throat. Please be good enough to return to your kitchen and stay there."

Clara anxiously looked to Lauriette, determined not to leave, but Lauriette nodded and she vanished quietly.

Lauriette turned back to the fire, her anger gradually rising. "How did you find me?"

Marie-Claire gave a short, brittle laugh. "You are not very inventive, dear sister," she said, moving towards the fireplace. "Claymoor was the only place you would feel safe. Actually, the deduction was quite simple."

"And how is Henry?" she asked, almost afraid of the answer.

"He is steadily improving," Marie answered. "The doctors say he will be able to get out of bed within a few weeks. Of course, he was very concerned about your disappearance." She was carefully surveying the dimly lit room until her gaze rested on the filled crystal decanters in the far corner. With a satisfied smile, she walked to them.

"You have given me a great deal of worry, Lauriette," she said evenly. "You created quite a scandal, you know."

"No more so than you, Marie," she returned coldly.

Marie-Claire filled two glasses with sherry then approached her sister. She held the glass out to her, and without a word, Lauriette accepted it.

"A toast," Marie lifted her glass, "to a better understanding between us."

Lauriette lifted the glass to her lips and drank. She made a sour face. The sherry tasted particularly bitter.

"Now," Marie began, "I came on ahead to talk with you about the plans."

"Plans?" Lauriette moved away from the fire; she was feeling increasingly warm.

"Why, your wedding plans of course!"

Her eyes widened as she glared at Marie-Claire. "What on earth are you talking about?"

"My dear, just because of a little indiscretion, you're not going to back out of your marriage to Evan!" she exclaimed.

"Your trip was for nothing, Marie-Claire," Lauriette replied hotly. "Did you hear me? For nothing! I want no part of Evan Brimley now or ever! How dare you even suggest my going through with it after everything that has come about!"

"Now let me tell you, Lauriette!" Marie-Claire snapped. "You are not going to ruin everything I've worked for! You're going to marry Evan and there's nothing you can do about it. You ingrate! My reputation is on the line and I'll be damned if I'll let some stubborn little piece of baggage undermine it. You'll do as I say!"

"Indeed!" Lauriette retorted breathlessly. She was finding it difficult to breath. She grabbed the back of the sofa. "I'm not afraid of you any longer! I'm going to walk out of this room and away from you!"

Lauriette took a step and felt her knees give way. She was losing control of her limbs. What was happening? She looked to Marie, a frightened and bewildered look upon her face.

"Little fool!" she spat. "Did you actually think I would face you without some guarantee?" Marie-Claire held out a small vial, a strange smile played on her lips. "It will only render you unconscious a short time, but before Evan arrives you will agree to this marriage—or you'll die a slow death!"

Lauriette could no longer feel her legs. Her mind was beginning to drown in blackness and as if in slow motion, she felt herself sinking and could faintly hear Clara screaming.

Eighteen

It had rained most of the day and Devlin kept his restless spirit in check by sleeping into the late afternoon. Three days had gone by and not one word from Lauriette.

Damn her! he thought angrily. Never had a woman talked to him the way she had. He had only tried to help her and she had all but spit in his face. She was a stubborn, hard-headed . . . He had honestly been taken by surprise when she turned him down. There were always women wanting him, his name, a place in his bed, and when he finally decided to take a wife—the imp turned him down without a second thought!

Perhaps he had been a bit high-handed and too blunt for her. After all, a woman wants a man to be romantic when proposing but dammit all, he just wasn't a man to use flowery words and poetry!

Devlin shortened the distance between him and the fire in an instant and shook his head, a scowl causing wrinkles to appear on his forehead. Well, what was done could not be undone. She could rot in hell for all he cared. He would not lift a finger to help her—not one finger! Mistress Lauriette Claymoor was now on her own—far be it from him to interfere!

Tomorrow he would return to London and resume his normal life, just as if *she* had never entered it. He had never lacked feminine company before, and he would not suffer now.

A commotion from the foyer caught his attention and as he moved towards the door, it burst open and Clara Gordon ran into the room, quickly followed by Judd and Seth.

"I ran into Mrs. Gordon and Seth on the steps," Judd explained.

"Your lordship!" Clara rushed at Devlin. "You've got to help her! You've just got to!"

"Calm down, Clara," Devlin soothed. "Calm down. Judd, fix Mrs. Gordon a brandy. I think she could use it."

Clara gratefully accepted the brandy and sipped it slowly. Seth stood beside her his eyes full of concern.

"You've got to come, your lordship!" she began again. "You've got to help!"

"Mistress Claymoor has made it perfectly clear that she doesn't want or need my help," he said gravely.

"Clara, what is all this about?" Seth questioned.

"It's Lady Marie-Claire," she told him, then turned back to Devlin. "You don't understand, your lordship. I—I thought I could come to you—because you came to see her the other day. She's in terrible trouble!"

"Mrs. Gordon, I do not see what—"

"Lady Marie-Claire has done something terrible to her!" she cried.

"Now, Clara," Seth said in a disbelieving voice, "ye can't mean that."

"I do!" she staunchly replied. "They won't let me see her, won't let me near her room!"

"Start at the beginning, Mrs. Gordon."

Clara nervously picked at her dress. "They were arguing. Lady Marie-Claire dismissed me from the room. Her ladyship's voice became shrill then quiet all of a sudden. The next thing I saw was Lauriette slump to the floor!"

"What?"

"That's right, that's right," she excitedly went on. "I screamed, but Lady Marie-Claire told me she fainted and to fetch young Jonathan Dell to carry her upstairs to her room."

"Perhaps she did faint."

Clara eyed him critically. "Your lordship," she said slowly, as if speaking to a child, "I've known Miss Lauriette most of her young life and she does not faint in the middle of a heated argument! Anyway, I hurried to her room as soon as I could but Jonathan wouldn't let me in! Orders, he said! From her ladyship, he said! They locked her in her room they did! Her ladyship even ordered cook not to send any food up to her chamber and no fire to be lit! Lady Marie-Claire has kept a close watch on me and I came for help the moment I felt it was safe enough."

Clara brushed away a tear. "Three days that child has been up there with no food, no warmth. Please, your lordship, she could be dead!"

"Judd, have horses saddled and tell young Tim to leave for Claymoor five minutes after we depart. We don't want them to hear us," Devlin ordered quickly then turned to Clara. "Don't worry, Mrs. Gordon, you stay here with Seth and we'lll get her out—in spite of herself!"

Marie-Claire relaxed on the sitting room sofa, a satisfied smile on her face. It was going as well as could be expected, and after another cold night in that room, Lauriette would consent to sign her soul to the Devil himself. She had to admit having Lauriette under her thumb gave her a great deal of pleasure. Sister or no, Lauriette never meant anything more to her than a beauty who always seemed to get in the way. From the time Lauriette was born and she was seven years old, she had hated her. She hated the way her mother had cooed over her and her brothers adored her. No one had ever paid attention to her the way they did Lauriette. As far as she was concerned Lauriette had taken everything away that was rightfully hers.

A maddening crash at the main door brought Marie-Claire to her feet. She ran from the room only to be stopped in her tracks by the charming smile and two cocked pistols of Devlin Essex. Behind him stood another man, younger but the same in height and stature.

"Good evening, your ladyship." he said graciously bowing.

Marie-Claire coldly nodded. Two burly men came running from the corridor and stopped next to her.

"Where is your sister?" he asked politely.

"She has returned to London," came her answer.

"You'll excuse me if I don't believe you." The smile was still there but his eyes were sparkling black.

"Come wi' me, yer lordship." Dolly came rushing from the stairs. "I'll show yer."

Marie-Claire's eyes widened in recognition, anger radiating from them as the plump maid motioned to the stairs.

"Judd, stand guard at my back."

Devlin took the stairs two at a time then impatiently waited at the top for Dolly to catch up. Judd stood near the banister, his pistols leveled at Marie-Claire and her two henchmen.

"Now, gents, let's not try anything foolish," he said, his smile none too pleasant.

Devlin found Jonathan Dell leaning against the wall

near Lauriette's door. He cocked one pistol and at the sound the burly young man stood frozen to the spot. His eyes were full of fear. He had no desire to lose his life because of some rift between her ladyship and this dangerous man.

Devlin motioned the man away from the door and Jonathan eagerly complied.

"The key, man, give me the key!" he demanded.

Jonathan nervously fumbled in his pocket and finally produced it. Devlin quickly grabbed it from him.

"Now, if you'll do me the honor . . ." Devlin nodded to the open bedroom door behind the man.

Without an argument, Jonathan quickly backed into the empty bedroom and Devlin immediately slammed the door shut, locking it securely.

"Go and ready my coach," he ordered Dolly with a half-smile. "Your mistress will need you."

"God bless ye," she whispered and hurried down the corridor to the stairs.

The door unlocked without much struggle and Devlin stood in the doorway a long moment before entering. The neat little room was deathly cold and quiet, not a thing out of place.

He found her on the bed, bundled up in the quilt. She seemed to be asleep, but upon a closer look, she was unconscious, an ugly gash on her forehead. Devlin kneeled before her.

"Lauriette!" he said softly. She was so still and so terribly pale. " 'Tis a fine mess you've gotten yourself into!"

Reaching underneath the quilt, he lifted her into his strong arms. Her eyelids fluttered, then half opened.

"Dev?" Her voice was but a faint whisper.

It was the first time she used his name and he felt pleased that she used his nickname.

"That's right, cherub," he whispered, his voice taking on a choked huskiness. "I've come to take you home. You'll never be hurt again, my promise."

"Home," she murmured, but Philadelphia was so far away! "I—I prayed . . . for you . . . to come . . ." She slipped back into unconsciousness.

Devlin stopped and beheld her thin, pale face. He had to get her back to Essex Hall into a warm bed and pour some hot soup down her. That wound—she needed a doctor.

As Devlin reached the stairs, Judd glanced up at him for a moment. The expression Devlin wore was dark and severe, his black eyes conveying contempt for Marie-Claire. Never had Judd seen such controlled anger in Devlin before. With caution, he moved near the door, leaving the stairs clear for his cousin.

At the foot of the stairs Devlin paused, his hard gaze causing Marie-Claire to step back. The man looked as if he were going to kill her!

Devlin's voice was low and murderous. "If she dies, your ladyship," he spoke calmly, "be prepared to suffer the consequences."

"Sir Evan will be furious at your interference!" she boldly shouted.

Devlin laughed harshly. "Your Sir Evan knows where he can find me."

He turned on his heel and stormed out, leaving Judd to guard his back. At the door, Judd mockingly saluted Lady Marie-Claire, then exited through the open door.

Nineteen

Devlin paced back and forth at the foot of the bed, a slender thread of reasoning holding his anger in check. The doctor had been there to see Lauriette and ordered nourishing broth and plenty of bed rest.

Lauriette had been slipping in and out of consciousness and was hardly aware of what was taking place. She was so tired and hungry—and wished that she were strong enough to tell them all to leave the room and let her sleep.

There came a soft rap on the door and Dolly hurried to answer it.

" 'Tis the Reverend Birnham, yer lordship," she whispered, a questioning look on her face.

Devlin knelt beside the bed, gently taking Lauriette's hand. Slowly, her eyes half opened.

"Lauriette, we're going to do it my way," he said softly but sternly. "Reverend Birnham from the village is here and he's going to marry us right now. You're in no condition to argue with me, and if you do, I'll toss you out on your pretty little behind. Is that understood?"

Lauriette weakly squeezed his hand. "Yes, Dev," she whispered. "You—you win."

"All right, Dolly, let the good reverend in," Devlin said.

The Reverend Birnham was a portly fellow who actually looked like a parson. He was dressed in somber gray from head to toe.

"My lord," said he, "I was asked to come post-haste." He peered over his spectacles at the frail woman in the bed. "What may I do for you?"

Devlin produced a paper from the bureau drawer. "One marriage, parson." He handed the special license to him. "I am certain that the good doctor and Dolly will be only too happy to witness the nuptials."

Reverend Birnham drew his bushy brows together, his eyes remaining on the young viscount. "You, my lord?"

Devlin nodded curtly. "Now."

"But, b-but, my lord," the parson stammered. "This—this is highly irregular. Once it is done, it cannot be—"

"Damn it, man, get to it!" Devlin roared, his patience at an end. "I mean to marry Mistress Claymoor and I mean to marry her tonight!"

Lauriette faintly heard Reverend Birnham's solemn words and rallied her strength long enough to acknowledge her vows. He was actually doing it! He was marrying her and she was too weak to protest. She felt his lips brush her cheek as the parson pronounced them man and wife. It was done and for some unknown reason, she felt relieved.

A loud, piercing scream filled every room in Essex Hall. Devlin, a brandy in hand, dropped the snifter and ran for the upstairs with Judd hounding his heels.

As he entered the room, he found Dolly doing her

best to restrain the hysterical Lauriette.

"Let me go! Let me go, I say!" she demanded. "I have to leave, to get out!"

Devlin pushed Dolly aside and ordered her and Judd out of the room with, "Leave us alone"

Lauriette shoved him away from her, struggling to get to her feet. Devlin grabbed her arms and did his best to hold her.

"Let me go!" she shrieked. "I can't stand any more of this, please! Let me go!"

Having no other choice, Devlin drew back and hit her soundly with the flat of his hand. She grew still, her eyes filled with terror. Where was she? Her head throbbed unmercifully.

Tears welled up and overflowed down her cheeks as she blinked them away. "S-she shut me away," she sobbed. "S-she drugged me a-and s-shut me away."

Devlin drew her into the security of his arms and gently stroked her hair. "It's all right, cherub," he whispered. "You're safe with me. No one will ever hurt you again."

"Clara!" she cried. "I—I remember Clara screaming . . ."

"She's fine," he reassured her. "She and Seth have moved into a cottage on the estate. You're not to worry about anything . . . Viscountess."

She looked up at him with a puzzled expression. Could it be she did not remember the ceremony?

"Don't you remember, cherub?" he asked. "Reverend Birnham was here earlier. It's all very legal."

She stiffened in his arms. "Then I—I wasn't dreaming?" she stammered. "It really—I mean you and I—you are my—"

Devlin laughed in spite of himself. "Yes to every one of your questions." He lightly touched her cheek. "We'll talk more on the morrow when you're feeling better. Now sleep, my lady."

She reluctantly lay back but held onto his hand. "Will you stay with me?" she meekly asked. "Just until I'm asleep?"

"Until you are asleep," he agreed, "even long after if you prefer."

Lauriette drifted off to sleep before Devlin finished his sentence. Her face was calm and peaceful, gone was any trace of the hysterical girl she had been minutes before.

She was too innocent for her own good. He would see that she forgot all of the hellish nightmares as soon as she recovered. He would shower her with attention and gather around her only the kindest people. No one would ever hurt her again! Not even a harsh word or disapproving look!

Devlin's head came up with a start. What in heaven's name was he going on about? He was beginning to sound like a lovestruck swain! It was guilt, that's it, guilt! He felt responsibility toward her ever since that first night near the docks.

Damnation! He wanted no part of tender feelings for anyone—and that included the moppet who now shared his name. In the formulation of his plan, he logically reasoned Lauriette would be as any other woman had been in his life and it unnerved him to feel such a strong, undefinable urge to protect her. He had to get hold of himself!

She was sleeping soundly now; her hand had gradually relaxed and he removed his. Things would work out, he surmised, but he would have to take one day at a time.

Devlin returned to the drawing room where Judd greeted him at the door.

"Is she all right?"

He sunk in the chair in front of the fire. "She had a nightmare," he explained, rubbing a hand across his eyes. "That damn bump on her head."

"She's the one, isn't she," Judd stated.

Devlin looked at him and nodded.

"That bump is a nasty one according to Dr. Quade," Judd said. "Dev, why did you send me to fetch Reverend Birnham if she is going to be all right?"

"I thought you would have guessed," he smiled slowly. "Mistress Claymoor is now Viscountess of Delbridge."

Judd looked at Devlin as if he were insane. "What?"

"Tomorrow I want you to return to London," he said seriously. "By the end of this week I want my marriage to be the talk of the city. We'll see how Sir Evan Brimley likes the news."

"Dev, I never argue with your logic," Judd said softly, "but in this case, aren't you asking for trouble?"

Devlin's face was a mask of stone. "I've been waiting for this moment too long," he declared. "What he believed to be his now belongs to me and I want him to know that it is Devlin Essex he'll be facing and not Neville!"

"But Mistress Claymoor is not Theresa Whitley," Judd reasoned. "And you are not Neville. He called Brimley out—"

"But Brimley was more experienced than Nev," Devlin stormed. "He knew Nev had very little to do with rapiers and he sought to kill him, not just to draw blood!"

"Dev, that was all years ago," Judd argued. "It was seven years to be exact. And what of your bride? Does she know she's been used as a pawn?"

Devlin grabbed Judd by his cravat, startling him. He had gone too far and knew it the moment the fatal words escaped his lips. Devlin was doing his best to curb his black temper.

"Thank the gods you're my flesh and blood!" his voice was hard, his eyes shining as two black coals. He quickly released him, then turned toward the fire.

"I—I did not mean to goad you, cousin," he said apologetically. "It's just—you have said yourself she is an innocent in this plot. But what has transpired, Dev—marriage vows are forever."

Devlin stood before the fireplace, one arm resting on the mantel. "She has come into this marriage with her eyes wide open," he said calmly. "I could not leave her to her sister and the likes of Brimley, surely you can see that! Believe me, it has been a fair bargain for both of us."

Judd straightened his cravat and nervously ran a hand through his hair. "I hope you're right," he frowned, "but everything I've heard indicates you're going to have your hands full. Her ladyship is no ordinary Englishwoman but an independent-thinking Yankee."

"You think so?" Devlin laughed. "Well, we'll just have to wait and see."

Twenty

Lauriette awoke from sleep early, hearing a tree branch banging against the bedroom window. The house was quite still in the morning hour and she sighed dreamily, feeling secure in the house of Lord Essex.

Her head still thumped from the bandaged cut on her forehead but it was not nearly so painful as the night before. So many pieces of the last few days were still jumbled and she pressed her hands to her aching head in hopes she could put the days in sequence.

Marie had actually drugged her and imprisoned her in her own room! That was still so hard for her to believe. Why? Why was it so important for her to marry Evan? And why would it ruin her sister's reputation if she did not? She could make no sense out of Marie's rantings.

Tossing back the quilts, she eased her way out of the enormous bed. She needed to be on her feet, pacing back and forth in order to think clearly. Dizziness encompassed her as she stood and she grabbed for the bedpost.

She refused to weaken and crawl back into the bed. After all, she was no cripple! She would not depend upon anyone.

Feeling her way along the wall, Lauriette made it to the window and leaned her head against the coolness of it. No longer Lauriette Claymoor. It was no dream—Lady Lauriette Essex, Viscountess of Delbridge!

Their arrangement was not uncommon in England, but still it seemed absurd to her. How could she marry a man who was a complete stranger to her? Well, being fair to Devlin Essex, she did admit that Evan had ended up a complete stranger to her, too. She traded one Englishman for another. Was she any better off? A loveless, cold marriage was what she had to look forward to.

Perhaps if she were patient, Devlin would allow her to return to Philadelphia when Jamie came. And Jamie! What would his reaction be when he found out! "My god!" she grimaced. "He'll be beside himself with laughter!"

"You're awake early, my lady."

Devlin's gentle voice startled her as she whirled about. He was leaning against the closed door wearing only his dressing gown. His dark eyes were swollen from sleep, his black hair tousled about.

"It seems I'm not the only early riser," she remarked.

"The wind woke me." He yawned, stretching towards the ceiling. "I was anxious to see about you."

"As you can see, I am much better." Lauriette sighed, wishing her heart would stop pounding so.

"The nightshirt does not do you justice," he drawled, his soft brown eyes openly appraising her. "I'll send Clara Gordon to London to buy you an entire wardrobe."

" 'Tis not necessary," she said quickly, not wanting anything from him. "If you would but send her to Branscombe Manor I've a trunk full of new clothing."

"Your trousseau?"

She nodded silently, her eyes unwilling to meet his.

"No," he said definitely, his face taking on a stubborn, prideful look. "You'll have new gowns to suit your station. The clothing you brought was to please Brimley. I'm wealthy enough to buy you a trousseau a hundred times over."

The man was exasperating! "You are insane," she returned saucily, hands resting on hips. "I did not know Evan well enough to know his likes or dislikes. My gowns were tastefully made to suit me and no other! I feel I dress as well as any grand lady of your acquaintance and if that is not enough, then I shall spend all my time right here in this room . . . wearing this silly nightshirt!"

"Cherub, I don't wish to argue the point with you," he said softly. "I only want to please you." If he could not goad her into doing what he wanted and if a little thing like the clothing she brought from Philadelphia would please her, then he would give in. "You shall have *your* clothes by tomorrow."

Lauriette was grateful to him for giving in. She wanted her trousseau mainly because Jamie had helped her with it and she needed this to remind her of home.

Devlin stoked up the fire and added another log to it. Perhaps it was best to let her have her way on small matters. After all, gowns were gowns.

"Why?" she asked quietly. "Why did you marry me? I did not expect you to actually do it."

He looked at her young face for a long moment, then replaced the poker. "Perhaps it is because you refused me. You aren't after my title, my money . . . There are many reasons yet there are none."

"May I ask to have one stipulation put into our silent agreement?" she questioned, hands gripping the back of the satin chair.

"Within reason," he replied.

"I only want to ask that you never—*never* flaunt one of your . . . your liaisons before me," she strongly stated.

He came to her quietly, his eyes softening at the lost look she wore.

She gazed up at him, her eyes filling with tears. "Whether I would love you or no, I couldn't—couldn't bear to see it with my own eyes," she whispered, choking back a sob.

Devlin lifted her chin and smiled a warm, reassuring smile. "On my oath, madam," he answered.

Her head was aching brutally as her hand lightly touched the bandage. Before she realized what he was about, Devlin swooped her up in his arms and walked to the bed.

"I'm afraid I'll have to deny you the pleasure of my company for a time, cherub," he stated as he laid her on the bed.

"But—but—"

He hushed her protests with his lips. "I have business in Cornwall that needs my immediate attention," he whispered. "You needn't worry, Lauriette, no one would dare harm you here. Believe me when I say you are safe as can be."

"I . . . do not . . . understand."

"Even a lowly viscount has duties, wife." He grinned. "Besides, Dr. Quade has ordered bed rest for you and 'twould be in your best interests if I were not loitering about."

Lauriette blushed prettily, noting his devilish gaze resting on the outline of her hardened nipples against the nightshirt.

Devlin kissed her long and tenderly, then smiled wickedly. "We'll have plenty of time to consummate our marriage after you've completely recovered."

Twenty-One

With Devlin absent from Essex Hall, Lauriette began to take each day as it came. Her recovery came that much quicker with the quiet hours spent reading and a doting staff to look after her. At first Devlin's servants were a bit anxious about the new mistress of Essex Hall, but after the first few days they found Lady Lauriette to be soft-spoken, kind and easy to serve.

Lauriette spent her days sitting comfortably in the drawing room, a lap blanket covering her legs. With the help of several good books borrowed from the library, she whiled away hours in front of the cheerful fire. Devlin's reassuring parting words came to her time and again as she regained her strength, for not once did she feel the cold chill of fear upon her shoulders.

The day began with the winter sun streaming in the windows and she smiled brightly, feeling not the slightest trace of a headache. Against Dolly's better judgment, she dressed in a blue velvet daygown and insisted stubbornly that this very day she was a well woman.

Lauriette descended the stairs slowly, tightening her hold on the banister. It felt wonderful to finally feel completely well.

"Good morning, Lady Essex."

Lauriette stopped abruptly on the stair, her eyes taking in the broad form of a neatly dressed man with light brown hair and deep gray eyes. He casually stood at the bottom of the stairs awaiting her company.

"You needn't fear me, my lady," he said quickly. "Did Dev not mention me to you?"

"I am sorry," she apologized, still wary of him. "Your voice sounds familiar—"

"Allow me to introduce myself," he interrupted, bowing gracefully. "I am Judson Clarke Oakes, Esquire, untitled cousin and close friend—at your service."

Lauriette smiled graciously and continued down the stairs, accepting Judd's outstretched hand as he escorted her into the drawing room.

"I can see for myself that you have recovered, Lady Essex." he smiled. "I must say you are lovelier without the bandages."

Lauriette laughed at Judd's flattery. "You are too kind, sir," she replied.

"Indeed not, Lady Essex," he protested. " 'Twas like an answer to prayer when Dev sent word for me to come to Essex Hall. He wished me to ease any fears you may have or problems that could arise until he could return."

"You . . . you mean Devlin sent you here to watch over me?"

"Please, my lady," he said quickly, "do not misinterpret. 'Twas his concern for your well-being—not that you cannot take care of yourself."

"I understand, sir," she said gently. "I'm very grateful to his lordship that he is concerned—and very pleased that I have your company."

Judd's boyish smile brightened. " 'Twill be a joy to serve you, your ladyship."

"If we are related, would it not be proper for you to call me Lauriette?" she asked. "I prefer that to 'your ladyship' or 'Lady Essex.' "

" 'Tis done then, Lauriette," he proudly agreed.

Barton entered the room and stood, mouth agape at the sight of his mistress dressed and looking ready for a full day.

"Your ladyship!" he exclaimed. "Your ladyship, you should not be out of bed."

"Barton, thank you for your concern but I feel just fine," she said softly. "I think Mr. Oakes would like breakfast and I would like a steaming cup of Kerry's delicious hot chocolate. We'll have it served here."

Barton opened his mouth to protest, then shut it quickly. Since his lordship brought the mistress to the Hall, he came to realize it was useless to argue. He bowed curtly and scurried from the room.

"You were in London?"

"At the Essex Townhouse," he answered. "Dev and I take spells. At times we are closer than brothers and other times we need to be apart. He is a very complex man."

"Yes, he is," she absently replied.

"Has he mentioned any of the family?" Judd asked, but by Lauriette's confused expression he grimaced. "No, of course he didn't. That's Devlin's way and in time you'll come to understand it. He is his own man."

Lauriette sat back contemplating. Judd Clarke Oakes reminded her so much of Jamie she wanted to cry. "Tell me, Judd," she insisted excitedly. "Tell me about his family. I want to know."

Judd relaxed in the satin chair, propping his feet up on an ottoman. "Well, I suppose we should begin with

The Dragon. That is Lord David Essex, Marquess of Sutherford, Devlin's father, my esteemed uncle," he began. "He is a stern old man with little tolerance for flattery or people who put on airs. He and Dev have been at odds ever since I can remember. Uncle is from the old school and expects to be obeyed regardless of what one feels. He is no easy man to live with.

"Next is Devlin's brother Neville. At the moment he is in India but should be returning soon. You will find him quiet—a bit unusual and moody at times, but he is really not a bad sort."

"Are there any more?"

Judd's face grew sober. "Lord David also has a niece and nephew from his side of the family but they can be discussed at a later time."

"Then you are from Devlin's mother's side?"

"Yes, Aunt Marianne was my father's younger sister," he replied.

Lauriette was going to question Judd further when Barton appeared carrying a large tray filled with hot muffins, eggs, ham, and steaming hot chocolate.

"Barton!" she protested. "This is quite a feast. I only asked for chocolate."

Barton smiled awkwardly, as if not used to doing such a silly thing. "My apologies, your ladyship," he said, "but you understand how Ketty takes on when a nourishing breakfast is not eaten."

Judd watched with growing amusement as Barton quickly departed, then laughed. "I believe you've melted old Barton's heart," he informed her. "I've never seen him fuss so over breakfast."

Over the weeks that quickly flew by, Lauriette came to know Devlin's young cousin and welcomed their lengthy chats and long walks. It was clear to her that Judd held Devlin with great respect and admiration.

He was totally committed to the man that she barely knew.

The house was extremely quiet that afternoon. Lauriette finally took an early nap after Dolly's prompting and when she awoke, found Judd had gone horseback riding across the estate.

Lauriette decided the time had come for her to acquaint herself with the great Essex Hall, to acquire as warm a feel for it as she had for Claymoor. Each room she found as lovely as the one before, the windows tastefully draped with velvets, the expensive Oriental carpets gracing each and every bedroom, fascinating her and urging her onto the next room.

Essex Hall was so rich, so splendid, it saddened Lauriette to think of the impoverished Claymoor with its bare floors and tattered draperies. Once upon a time, long, long ago Claymoor had been as grand as Essex Hall.

She stool transfixed in the doorway of a room in the tower, her eyes taking in the neatly placed trunks and baskets. Quietly, she entered the small room, a wistful smile playing on her lips. Everywhere her eyes roamed she found traces of childhood. Brightly colored toy soldiers, several wooden swords, in one corner a small drum. It was as if she stepped into the past—Devlin's past. It was strange yet comforting—the room seemed so out of place in this ancient house.

Lauriette's eyes lingered on a yellow object near the window. Curious, she moved toward it. It was a child's rocking horse painted a bright yellow and next to it a small cradle. Lovingly her fingers touched the head of the wooden horse and rocked it back and forth easily. It was a room filled with wonder and surprise.

"Devlin must have grown up here at Essex Hall," she mused. It was difficult for her to imagine the enigmatic man as a child, he was always so arrogant and headstrong. Had he ever laughed and played upon this horse? Her hand rocked the wooden steed. Was this, his first Nomad? What kind of a child had he been?

"He's here! His lordship's back!" she heard Flora, one of the maids, exclaim excitedly.

Lauriette jumped to her feet, glancing out at the withering sun in the process. It had been early afternoon when she entered this strange little room. Could she have been here for hours?

In haste, she hurried down the spiral staircase, down the long corridor, and by the time she reached the head of the stairs, she was breathless, her cheeks flushed.

The great door flew open, Devlin and Judd laughing heartily as they entered. Lauriette started down the stairs and as her eyes met Devlin's, his laughing ceased but the smile remained.

Devlin took her hand, assisting her down the last few steps. "My lady," his voice was caressingly soft, "I'm happy to see you've regained your color."

Lauriette could not help but return his smile. "I'm afraid I've been spoiled by your staff." she replied.

His hand still holding hers, Devlin slowly pulled her toward him until they were only a breath apart. "Why, my lady?" he said, his dark eyes dancing. "No welcome kiss for your husband?"

"My lord!" she protested weakly, her heart violently pounding. "Your cousin! The servants!"

Devlin eyed Judd, then laughed. "The servants see nothing and I'm sure cousin Judd will look the other way for me to properly greet my wife."

"By all means," Judd agreed "I would never interfere. Allow me to fix drinks in the sitting room." And with his last words, he disappeared into the next room.

Devlin drew her into his arms and the moment his lips met hers, gone was all thought of Judd or anything else. She felt so relieved that he had returned and seemed happy to see her.

"Your mouth is still as sweet as I remembered," he whispered for her ears only. " 'Tis good to be home."

The huge table in the dining room had been set as exquisitely as only Barton could set it, the candles glowed in the middle of the flowered centerpiece. Lauriette sat at one end of the long table, while Devlin was seated at the head and Judd somewhere in the middle.

Lauriette sat quietly, picking over the delicious meal Ketty had carefully prepared. She had not entered the conversation between Judd and Devlin, her own thoughts trying to deal with her explosive emotions at her husband's homecoming. He had kissed her so tenderly, so passionately and she had responded—even after vowing she wouldn't.

Several times during the meal, and afterward in the sitting room, Lauriette felt unsettled and looked up to find Devlin's dark stare resting on her, a mysterious smile tugging at the corners of his sensuous mouth.

Finally out of sheer nervousness she excused herself and hastily climbed the stairs to the security of her room.

Dolly was readying Lauriette for bed, a lovely blue silk nightgown and matching wrapper laid out across the bed. Curious, Lauriette picked up the seductive gown and threw the maid a questioning look.

"A gift from 'is lordship," she said happily. "He asked ye ta wear it tonight."

Lauriette shut her eyes tightly. No wonder he had eyed her so mysteriously. He was going to claim his husband's rights and she could not refuse him. She bit down on her lip. Could she go through with it?

Dolly helped her into the beautiful blue gown, then turned her to the mirror. Her reflection brought a scarlet blush to her cheeks. To be sure, it was something *he* would select! The silk clinging to her shapely form, the neckline cut to the waist exposing most of her firm breasts. Ah, yes, a very seductive gown indeed!

"You can go, Dolly," she said quietly. "I can do my hair tonight."

"As ye say, my lady," Dolly curtsied and hurried out of the room.

The candle on the dressing table flickered several times as the hot wax slithered down the side of it.

"Ninety-seven, ninety-eight, ninety-nine, one hundred," Lauriette counted the strokes aloud. Her golden brown hair shimmered in the candlelight.

It was difficult for her mind not to dwell on what was to come. She was not even sure she could go through with it; the vivid memory of Marie and Evan kept popping up before her eyes. *Did we look like that, that night?* she silently questioned. *They were like two animals in heat, thrashing and grunting—*

She moved from the dressing table to stand at the window, staring out at the darkness. Love between a man and a woman was not supposed to be like that, she was certain of it! Love was to be a warm, wondrous merging of two bodies; a kind of rapturous blending of two souls, not rutting and grunting like beasts in a field! There had to be more to it than that, there just had to be!

"You look absolutely breathtaking," a soft voice whispered.

Lauriette gave out a startled gasp as she jumped. Devlin stood by the bed, his dressing robe open to the waist, dark curly hair covering his muscular chest. His intense gaze lingered on the rise and fall of her breasts, then upward to the fullness of her lips, then on her horizon blue eyes.

She blushed deeply. "It's quite . . . quite lovely."

Devlin took her by the hand and guided her nearer the fire. He was pleased with himself in his selection of the garments. Taking her by the hand he led her to the bed and then sat down beside her.

"I have something for you," he whispered. He grasped her left hand and with slightly trembling fingers, eased an exquisite gold band onto her finger. The ring was detailed with engraved orange blossoms and a small diamond in the middle of each flower.

Lauriette was enchanted by the dainty ring, a perfect fit. "It is so lovely," she breathed. "It is the most beautiful ring I have ever seen."

Devlin was somewhat surprised by her reaction. "It belonged to my mother," he said in a tender voice. "Her hands were like yours, small and delicate. I'm happy it fits so well."

She was overcome with wonder at the sentiment this man could show. "I am honored," she murmured, "that you wish me to wear it. Thank you."

"Dunstan in Cornwall belonged to my mother," he explained, his fingers running over the tiny ring on her finger. "I had a need to see the old place once again—and I wanted to get this ring."

Impulsively, she leaned over and kissed him lightly on his surprised lips. She went to draw away when his hands cupped her elbow and pulled her into his arms. His lips touched hers, spreading a fiery warmth throughout her body. His tongue gently forced its way through her teeth and came into contact with hers, causing a quivering sensation in the pit of her stomach.

His hand lightly stroked her neck, feeling the pulse quicken, then slowly moved to her shoulder, gently squeezing it.

"I've waited so long for this night," he breathed, running his tongue down the length of her throat.

"I—I don't—know," she stammered, her will to resist quickly dwindling away.

He chuckled deeply, his eyes merrily dancing. "This is not the time for words, cherub," he grinned crookedly. "Close those damn captivating eyes and let your senses take over."

"B-but—but, I—"

"Quiet!" he shushed, his hands quickly divesting her of the wrapper. " 'Tis the bewitching hour and Lucifer is here to teach you the delights of passion." And with his last words, Devlin snuffed the candle.

He laid her back against the downy pillows, his hands stroking her slender arms. He tenderly claimed her mouth, his hands cupping her face. She was so different from any other woman he had been intimate with. She was a novice. It was up to him to teach her the ways of love, to learn how to give pleasure as well as receive it. He wanted to show her, to make her revel in their lovemaking.

"Laurie," he whispered breathlessly. "Laurie, love, put your arms around me."

In silence, her arms encircled his neck and in the darkness he smiled. His hands moved to the front of her gown and gently touched her breast, feeling it grow taut in his hand. It was so perfectly formed, the right size for his hand to cover.

Lauriette gasped as his teeth tenderly teased the nipple, the shock of it causing ripples of excitement to flood over her. His hands moved over her body like a master craftsman, shaping and molding her into an object of passion.

Her mind floating elsewhere, Lauriette sighed deeply and Devlin chuckled deep within his throat. She was responding to his foreplay and he was on fire for her. He held himself in check; he must move slowly. He wanted her to enjoy every moment of their intimate night.

He was lying beside her, his mouth passionately attacking hers, causing her to tremble with a mixture of fear and anticipation. Her body began to relax, molding itself against his in final surrender. She needed him desperately, wanting him to take her soul and merge it with his. It was all so dreamlike, as if they were both living a fairy tale and it startled Lauriette to find she did not want this incredible ecstasy to end.

Lauriette felt his hardness against her thigh and she gasped. Devlin kissed the lobe of her ear, sending shivers up her spine.

"Should I continue, cherub?" he whispered hungrily. "Tell me you want me, love. I want to hear it from your sweet lips."

She touched his face, her fingers tracing the outline of his lips. His hands sensuously moved to her thighs, then to the silkened mound that waited for him to explore what belonged only to him.

She was lost to wild desire as his hand found her hidden treasure. "Yes!" she cried out. "I want you, Dev! I want you now!"

Her passionate words spurred him on and suddenly he was on top of her, his mouth covering hers, his tongue in pursuit of hers. He could wait no longer for the paradise he sought and plunged into her.

She cried out, gripping his shoulders. The sudden entry caused her emotions to soar. His manhood was like solid iron, strongly moving in and out, taking her with him. He wanted her to feel everything, to know the sweetness of it, to never fear it is wrong to enjoy.

Lauriette began to move with him, her arms willingly stroking his back, kneading his buttocks as he moved slowly, deliberately holding back. He had taken her virginity weeks before and smiled contentedly as his bulging manhood enjoyed the tightness of her treasure. He was caught up in the rightness of it all, the joy he felt as she moaned with pleasure. Never before had he the uninhibited desire to please a woman as he did now. Devlin was filled with want of her, blocking out memories of any other woman before her.

Lauriette felt a strange, tingling sensation as she moved with him and she began to undulate faster, a hunger to know more about the exotic feeling pushing her onward. It exploded and began to spread throughout her loins until it consumed her and she clung to Devlin, moving rhythmically against him until she could no longer stand the sweet pain.

Lauriette's seductive movements surprised Devlin and as she climaxed, he plunged deeply into her and moaned contentedly as she drained him of passion in a fulfilling way he had never before experienced.

She lay in the strength of his arms, tears wetting his chest. Never had she known anything that was so rapturous and wonderful before. She was totally drained, her eyes heavy with sleep.

"You're a passionate imp, Laurie," he whispered huskily, placing a kiss on her temple. "Are you content?"

"More than content," she answered shyly. "Is . . . is lovemaking always so . . . so ardent, so explosive?"

Devlin kissed her swollen lips softly. "For the most part, love," he replied. "Then you aren't disappointed?"

She laughed gently. "How could I be? Did I not have dark Lucifer as my teacher and was it not the bewitching hour?"

Like the tinkling of chimes, her laughter filled his ears and he was pleased, though it affected him more than he cared to admit.

"You are an apt pupil, cherub," he complimented, his voice still thickly laced with desire. He brought her hand to his lips, kissing each finger slowly. "There is so much to show you—but we have time for that. Years and years."

"I look forward to it," she murmured sleepily against his chest.

Devlin held her tightly against him until Lauriette sighed, rolling over to her side.

Devlin was abruptly awakened by the sound of sobbing. He raised himself on one arm and gazed down at Lauriette. Her sleeping face held a tense look, she was silently sobbing, tears streaming down her cheeks.

"N-no," she whispered fitfully, her head thrashing from side to side. "P-please, no!"

"Laurie," he whispered, touching her shoulder.

"No!" she shrieked, bolting upright. "Don't touch me!"

Devlin grabbed her shoulders, shaking her soundly.

"Wake up!" he said sternly. "Laurie, wake up!"

She sucked in her breath, her blue eyes wide and frightened. "Dev?"

"It's all right, love," he reassured, taking her into his arms.

She snuggled closer to him, feeling the warmth from his body caress hers. "It was horrible," her voice trembled. "There . . . there was blood everywhere . . . on the horse."

"Blood?"

"Hold me tighter," she begged. "I'm still afraid."

Devlin tightened his hold on her. "There's nothing to be afraid of," he replied sleepily. "No one can hurt you while in my arms."

"Then you must hold me forever," she murmured against his neck, "for I fear many things."

Twenty-Two

Devlin woke slowly, savoring the smell of bacon in the air. He knew it was a glorious morning before he opened his eyes. It had to be glorious, for what else could it be after such a satisfying night!

He lay there quietly, reliving each moment of the night before. It had been a delight to learn he was wedded to such a passionate little minx. It was going to be a pleasure teaching her, molding her into an instrument of love. These feelings were strange to him, so strong was his attraction for Lauriette. *Well, enjoy it, man,* he thought to himself, *for as long as it will last.*

His eyes opened only to find himself alone in the huge bed. "Lauriette?" The room was silent.

"Damnation!" he cursed aloud, recalling the last time they slept together.

Devlin jumped out of bed, hastily donning his robe. Surely she hadn't run from him! Not now, she was his wife! She belonged to him and as he quickly dressed, for the first time he actually thought of her possessively. *His* wife, *his* lover, *his* Lauriette!

* * *

Lauriette shivered despite the warm cloak which covered her. She woke feeling rested and happily content, her leg touching Devlin's. As quietly as possible, she turned on her side and gazed at him for the longest time. He slept deeply, the lines in his face smoothed, making him more like a little boy. How utterly perfect he was made! He was a superbly built man whose muscles bulged even while sleeping.

Gingerly, she barely touched his full lips and noted how long his dark eyelashes were. She then traced one of his dimples down the full length of his lean jaw.

Standing in the circle of sunlight, Lauriette closed her eyes and once again saw Devlin's sleeping form. She could not suppress the smile that emerged, knowing he had shared the same bed with her throughout the night.

She wondered if all men were as Devlin, such tender lovers. The night before taught her that lovemaking was not coupling as Evan and Marie-Claire. She was overjoyed that Devlin had banished those terrible doubts.

Lauriette, the woman; Lauriette, the wife; Lauriette, the lover! *Lady Essex*—she mentally tested the way it sounded—*Lauriette Essex*. It had a nice sound to it.

Emotions flowed like a waterfall as she strolled along the grounds. To feel so happy, so safe—it overwhelmed and frightened her. Was it right to feel like this? She had not felt such joy ever, even in Philadelphia with her family.

She thought of Jamie and would he not be shocked! She imagined he would carefully appraise Devlin, then he would no doubt approve of him. After a time he would grow to love him as she did. . . .

She froze, hand to her mouth. Faith! What was she thinking! Love? That was ridiculous! Attracted to him, yes. Grateful to him, yes. But love? She had to remind herself of the circumstances surrounding their marriage. No words of love were ever spoken and in the end she had agreed to his conditions, adding one herself.

Of course he made love to her. He had been very gentle, very tender, but he was no doubt that way with every woman he bedded. He was attracted to her, he bluntly told her so, and she was not ignorant of the way he made her feel.

Absently she sighed. No, she had no right to expect love from a virile man like Devlin. He had tasted the delights of scores of women, and before his lifetime ended he would undoubtedly sample many more.

An agreement was an agreement and she vowed then and there never to cling to him, never to leave herself open to hurt, never to expect more than he was willing to give. It would have to be this way, she could not afford to be hurt again.

"Do you always disappear like a phantom?" Devlin's serious voice cut into her thoughts.

He stood only a few feet from her, hands clasped behind his back, his legs slightly parted. He had dressed hastily, his shirt haphazardly stuffed into his tight breeches, his hair a mass of tangles.

The smile she wore vanished as his scowl deepened. "Are you always so cross in the mornings?" she countered.

Devlin felt an overwhelming sense of relief upon seeing her quietly strolling the grounds. She looked so lovely, so totally innocent.

His frown was replaced by a charming smile. "Only when I wake and find my bride gone from my bed."

Lauriette blushed deeply and turned to eye the blooming tree. "Spring has finally arrived, I think," she said. " 'Twill be nice to feel a warm gentle breeze against my face once again."

"So here you are," Judd's voice boomed from the

door. "Come! Breakfast is ready and I have news of London."

"You go on," she told Devlin, "I'll be but a moment."

Devlin nodded and strode toward the house. She watched as he met Judd on the steps and they walked into the house together.

Turning, she moved along the edge of the grounds nearer the woods. Yes, April was going to be a beautiful month when everything that nature offers comes alive. In fact it was in April, four years before, that the American Claymoors had come to visit.

Lauriette stopped abruptly, creases wrinkling her forehead. Why had that thought entered her mind? Her holiday four years before had nothing to do with her living here now. But then, those hideous, undefinable nightmares kept recurring. Why? What was there in the past that would cause such unease and terrifying dreams?

"Lauriette!"

Judd met her at the door, his mouth split in a wide grin.

"Well, it is time."

"Time?" she repeated.

"Time for you to meet the old dragon."

"Devlin's father? Here?"

"He arrived only moments ago," he said, taking her arm.

Lauriette had no time to think about the man she was hurrying to meet. In all the weeks she had known Judd, he only spoke of Lord David just that once. He opened the library door and ushered her into the room.

A pair of soft brown eyes, much like Devlin's, slowly looked her over from her golden brown tresses neatly tied back with a ribbon to the tip of her satin slippers wet with dew. The old gentleman sat like a reigning monarch in the overstuffed chair, his elegant black cane resting across his knees. His face was lined with age, his hair white as snow. But his square chin was as firm as any young man's, as was the lively sparkle in his eyes.

Devlin stood with his back to his father, gazing out the window, a deep frown covering his face.

"So, this is the Viscountess of Delbridge," he drawled, his voice barely above a whisper. "At least she does not look like a tavern wench or a little adventuress as the gossips in London are spreading. Stand nearer the fire, girl, so I may get a closer look at you."

She moved closer, feeling much irritation at Lord David's manner.

"You can tell she comes from good stock," he said bluntly to Devlin. "What family did you steal her from, scamp? She Lord Farley's child? Perhaps Lord Anderson's?"

"While I'm standing here thusly, would you care to inspect my teeth?" she asked tartly. "Or perhaps you would like to know how many children my mother had so you may be sure I'll breed!"

Devlin's eyes grew wide and he turned and stared at Lauriette.

"I am no Englishman's daughter," she informed him. "I am neither tavern wench nor adventuress. My parents were hardworking, honest Americans from Philadelphia! And let me tell you, my name is Lauriette and I am neither dumb nor ignorant and I wish that you would not talk around me as if I weren't here!"

Lord Essex looked up at the young unafraid girl and gradually his lips broke into a smile. This child-bride of Devlin's possessed a spirit that reminded him of his beloved Marianne.

"And you needn't worry about your son, either!" she went on with her tirade. "I did not marry him for money or title. I've money enough of my own to suit me and there is a handsome dowry awaiting your son in London. And as for the title, we patriots do not have much use for them."

"You are quite outspoken, Laurie," he said, his voice softening a bit. "I imagine most women are that way—over there."

"There is no written law which states a woman cannot be honest and forthright," she replied, then walked to the door. "If you are through with your inspection of me, your lordship, I shall see to breakfast . . . and my name is Lauriette!" She disappeared from the room, her skirts rustling behind her.

He looked at Devlin. "She's got spirit," he said grudgingly. "I like that, scamp."

Devlin returned his father's stare but said nothing. He was pleased and impressed by the way Lauriette had handled his father. Slowly but surely, he was finding out that there was more to his bride than a pretty face and a comely figure.

"Well? Have you nothing to say to me?" the old man rasped.

"What would you have me say?" Devlin countered.

" 'Tis such a damn shame I had to find out from the gossipmongers in London," he snapped. "To be sure, though, you're running true to form."

Devlin stiffened at his father's remark. "We did not have the time to send out formal invitations, Father."

"I trust there was no problem," Lord David stated evenly.

Devlin shot his father a black look. "As my wife stated, Father, she is wealthy in her own right."

"I was thinking of the girl, scamp," he retorted. "I understand she was betrothed to Brimley."

"I can take care of any misfortune which may come." He grinned. "She is much better off with me than Brimley, you have to admit that."

Lord David looked questioningly at his son. "You do have some feelings for the girl, don't you?" he asked gently. "What I mean is, you did not marry her . . . for revenge?"

Devlin laughed harshly. "Lauriette is not without certain . . . er . . . *charms* that fascinate me. Does that answer your question? There is no one here to oppose me; where does revenge come in? I would think you'd be pleased. I did as you demanded—I married!"

Lord David eyed his son closely. "I am pleased," he said roughly. "She will most certainly be a match for you!"

Twenty-Three

Lauriette stood near the edge of the woods, a thoughtful frown darkening her face. For weeks she indulged herself in these long walks and always it seemed she found herself abruptly stopping where the woods began. It was as if some inner voice warned her against entering the forest and for some unknown reason, she listened.

Dejectedly, she hung her head. The preceding weeks with Devlin were almost dreamlike. The days were filled with the running of Essex Hall—the nights filled with passion in Devlin's arms. He truly taught her the meaning of ecstasy and she looked forward to the tender nights with eager anticipation.

But no matter how happy, how content, each night's sleep was disturbed by those terrifying nightmares. Many a night passed that Devlin woke her, saved her, from the dream but many more went by that she woke herself, a cold sweat beading on her forehead, her heart pounding out of control. What was causing those dreams to come so frequently?

''Well, Laurie, out for your morning constitutional I

see.''

She turned to find Lord David slowly walking towards her.

''I was just appreciating the sweet spring air,'' she replied distantly. ''The forest is in bloom.''

''Are you still angry with me?'' he asked rather bluntly.

Lauriette laughed lightly. ''Not angry,'' she smiled, ''merely perturbed that you cannot see America as I do.''

Lord David cleared his throat, then scowled at his daughter-in-law. ''I do not believe we should discuss politics on such a sunny day,'' he grunted, then changed the subject. ''Have you eaten?''

''I—I had some hot chocolate.''

Together they walked towards the Hall in companionable silence, each content to be in the other's company. Since he had established himself at Essex Hall, Lauriette found she liked Lord David more with each passing day.

''You speak of the American Revolution with such emotion, child,'' Lord David commented slowly. ''Yet you were just a child when it came about.''

''My father was killed at Yorktown right before Cornwallis surrendered.''

''I'm sorry,'' he sincerely replied, ''and your mother?''

''She died right after my seventh birthday,'' she told him. She looked up and smiled. ''But life has been very good to me.''

''Most ladies would whine incessantly to be imprisoned out here in the country, away from the glittering balls and the companionship of other ladies. Do you like this quiet a life?''

''There has to be more to life than glittering balls and the constant round of teas,'' she explained. ''What a way to waste one's life.''

They entered the sitting room and Lord David seated himself, exhausted from the walk. ''And where is my son?''

Lauriette removed her cloak, draping it over the chair. ''He went to see Judd off to London,'' she said. ''Dev also had to see the constable about Jacob Enders.''

''I cannot understand it,'' he reflected. ''Devlin never was interested in the estates before. He would have sooner seen it go to ruin.''

She looked at Lord David critically. ''I think you underestimate your son, milord.''

Immediately a brow shot up. ''I think not, milady,'' he returned roughly. ''My son has never lived up to my expectations and I do not believe this little respite will last.''

''You're being unfair,'' she accused. ''No man can live by another's expectations of him and Devlin is no different. He is his own man and you should be proud that he is!''

Lord David's mouth gradually broke into a grin. ''You are fiercely loyal to him.''

''Would you have me otherwise?'' she asked, some of her anger diminishing.

''I would not have my daughter-in-law any other way,'' he answered, a twinkle in his brown eyes.

''What is going on?'' Devlin's voice came from the doorway. ''A conspiracy?''

Devlin entered the drawing room, placing a brief kiss on Lauriette's forehead. From behind his back he produced a sketch pad.

''Devlin—thank you,'' she stammered, quite taken back by his thoughtfulness.

''I have missed your sketchings, madam,'' he smiled, then turned to Lord David. ''What were you two arguing about this time?"

"Laurie has been defending your honor."

Devlin looked at her curiously, but she refused to be baited. Instead, she grabbed up her cloak and marched out of the room without even as much as a by-your-leave. Devlin watched the closing of the door then looked quizzically at Lord David.

"She is quite remarkable," Lord David sighed. "Put me in my place, pretty as you please—just like Marianne could."

Lauriette sat down on the bed, sketch pad in hand, her head beginning to throb. What had come over her to talk to Lord David in such a manner? Surely he knew his son a lot better than she! But there was something inside her that would not let her stand by and listen to anyone criticize Devlin—not even his father!

The sound of approaching horses brought her out of her thoughts as she rushed to the window. An elegant coach-and-four was rounding the bend, the horses beautifully matched grays. They were receiving company and this would be the first time she would entertain as Lady Essex.

Lauriette hurried from their room only to freeze at the top of the stairs, her eyes drawn to the scene. A stunning woman with raven black hair, very fashionably dressed, was kissing Devlin squarely on the mouth.

Devlin's hands tightened on the woman's wrists as he disengaged himself from her, his eyes cold with age-old indifference.

"Oh, Devlin!" she squealed. "I came as soon as word of your return reached me in Durham. Harry was good enough to visit, he came with me, you know."

Devlin's eyes found Lauriette's and a smile broke showing his deep slashed dimples. "We have guests, my love,'' he said, relief written over his face. ''Come and meet them.''

Lauriette slowly descended the stairs, fully aware of the woman's eyes upon her. Devlin tightly grasped her hand and pulled her against his side, his hand resting snugly on her waist.

''Lauriette, may I introduce Lady Muriel Horton, my cousin,'' he said. ''Muriel, my wife, Lady Lauriette Essex.''

The amazement was clearly registered on Muriel Horton's face, her green eyes widening in disbelief.

''The gawdawful trip has left me crippled for life!'' a voice drawled from the door.

Muriel made an effort to regain her badly shattered composure. ''Harry, come meet Lauriette,'' she exclaimed.

Lauriette stiffened as Harry casually strolled from the open doorway. It was the same distasteful man she met the night of the Winter Ball.

''Oh, yes, the lovely Lauriette Claymoor,'' he said, his eyes noting the flush of her cheeks. ''I heard of your marriage to Devlin in London. The greatest happiness to you both.''

''Thank you, Harry,'' Devlin returned.

''What in damnation is going on!'' Lord David demanded.

''Why, we came for a visit, Uncle,'' Muriel said sweetly. She went to embrace the old man but he waved her away.

''You're looking well, Uncle,'' Harry complimented.

''You know damn well I look nothing of the sort!'' he growled. ''Let's not try flattery. It will get you nowhere!''

Lauriette was truly shocked by Lord David's cold, bitter attitude toward his niece and nephew. Immediately, a wracking cough seized him and Lauriette hurried over to him.

"Dev, get his medicine. Hurry!" she called over her shoulder.

She managed to get him to the nearest chair in the sitting room. Devlin handed her the medication and she mixed with water as Muriel and Harry looked on.

She held the glass to his lips. "Drink all of it, Father," she whispered, a worried expression on her face. "Now lean back and let the medication work for you."

Silently Muriel cast an angry glance at her brother. He knew of Devlin's marriage yet had neglected to tell her. She watched with glowing ire the touching scene between the old man and Devlin's bride. It was plain as day that she was not their equal in any respect. Why, no woman of breeding would be down on her knees nursing Lord David! Not when there were servants handy!

"I'm all right now, Laurie," Lord David choked brokenly. "Don't fuss! It is not my first attack and 'twill not be my last!"

Lauriette looked up worriedly at Devlin's sober face. She took the glass and returned the medicine to the shelf. His attacks were becoming more and more frequent.

"Is—is he all right now?" Muriel asked.

"He'll be just fine," Lauriette answered. "Please, let me show you to your rooms."

Muriel tittered on and on during supper of her year in mourning and her time spent in the country. Lauriette did her best to be gracious and listen with interest, but Lauriette hadn't the foggiest notion who most of the people she spoke of were.

"Then last month Lord Avery Barrows spent a fortnight at Dayton House as my guest," Muriel announced smugly.

"Lord Barrows?"

Muriel looked at Lauriette as if shocked. "You do not know of Lord Avery Barrows?"

Lauriette shook her head.

"Devlin, where have you kept this sweet innocent?" she asked. She then turned back to Lauriette. "My dear, everyone who is anyone knows of Lord Avery Barrows. Why, he is the richest, most sought after widower in London! I am quite taken that you did not know this—being married to such an influential man as Devlin."

"I haven't been in England very long," she replied quietly, feeling the sting of Muriel's sarcasm.

"You must forgive my sister, Lady Lauriette," Harry apologized. "She has been hidden in Durham so long, she thinks everyone has the same tastes in men."

"I believe we've heard enough chattering for now, Muriel," Devlin cut in sharply. He did not like where the conversation was leading.

"You needn't apologize for me, brother," Muriel pouted.

Harry smiled wickedly. "Of course I do, Muriel," returned. He looked once again on Lauriette, his green eyes boldly assessing her. "You are much lovelier than I remembered, if your ladyship will permit the compliment."

A brow shot upward as Devlin glanced from Harry's face to Lauriette's blazing crimson cheeks. "You have met before?"

"We met briefly at the Winter Ball," she meekly answered. How dare that man bring up that horrid night!

"What a night to remember!" he mused, enjoying Lauriette's discomfort. "Poor Henry caught in a duel. . . . I understand he is recovering quite nicely from that nasty wound. . . ."

"His arm," Lauriette anxiously cut in, "has he regained the use of his arm?" Her nerves were tight as a bowstring, waiting his answer.

"Yes," he replied and watched as the look of relief flooded across her face.

Muriel eyed Lauriette closely, noting the changes in the young woman's expression. "You seem very close to your sister's husband," she commented slyly.

Lauriette's head jerked up at Muriel's curt remark and she saw the knowing, arrogant look she wore. "If you will excuse me," she said cooly, "I will see if Lord David requires anything."

As Lauriette left the dining room, Muriel gazed innocently at Devlin's face. "She is quite sensitive, is she not?"

"Lauriette does not know the workings of nobility politics," he stressed. "As you could undoubtedly tell by her accent she is not English. She has no reason to know all the elite of London, no reason at all to even be interested in them. If you try to belittle her again, I'll order you out of this house!"

"Devlin, what a horrible thing to say!" she whined. "I was only trying to enlighten her, that is all. You've cut me to the quick, you awful cad!"

"He is right, Muriel," Harry interrupted, leaning back in his chair. "You are not superior to everyone—and Mistress Claymoor is a living, breathing example."

Devlin turned his hardened stare on Harry. "A very commendable speech," he remarked with a low, even tone. "But she is no longer Mistress Claymoor but Lady Essex—and I suggest you not forget that little item, Harry."

"Devlin, you do me an injustice," Harry's voice sounded crushed.

"Never an injustice," Devlin drawled. "I know you too well."

Lauriette looked in on Lord David and found him sleeping soundly, his supper tray sitting on the floor. He had not touched his food. She stood at the foot of his bed affectionately gazing down at his white head. She was growing so very fond of him! Lord David was slowly replacing the father she barely knew.

Quietly, she picked up the untouched tray and snuffed out the candle by his bedside. She tiptoed out and took the servants' stairs down to the kitchen, surprising Ketty in the process.

"Yer ladyship shouldna' tote that!" she scolded gently. "That's wha' servants o' fer!"

Lauriette looked at the cook worriedly. "I don't believe Lord David touched his food at all."

Ketty sat down heavily at the table. "There's nothin' ye kin do, milady," she said sadly. " 'is lordship's been a-slippin' away a long time."

"And it is hopeless?"

Lauriette said no more. She quietly padded down the long corridor into the foyer, picking up her shawl folded neatly on the side table. Solemnly, she lifted the latch, letting herself out into the warm night air filled with the scent of lilacs.

She greedily inhaled the fragrant breeze; a starlit sky graced the heavens and a mellow moon lighted the garden she strolled in. The gentle glow of it caught the sparkle of a crystal blue tear that found its way to her pert little chin.

Lauriette knew not why she cried. Perhaps it was because her feelings had been tramped upon during supper; perhaps it was because of her feelings for Lord David. She feared for her little world here. She never realized before just how different she and Devlin were. In

Philadelphia she was known and liked for what she was, not who she was or the important company she kept! There had been no special little clique which had the power to accept or discard a person.

Muriel was so beautiful. She knew just the right thing to say and do. Her clothing was the very latest fashion, making Lauriette's trousseau look outdated. Why did the woman intimidate her so?

Then strange Harry. From the first time she encountered him, there was something about him she did not trust. She did not understand why he repulsed her; it could have been his overbearing attitude or perhaps the way he would look at her, as if mesmerized by her features. There was a certain cruelty in him, she sensed, as if hurting gave him pleasure.

Lauriette was concerned about fitting in. Being a witty conversationalist was never her strong point. She always loathed the dinners in Philadelphia that the women were so fond of. They would retire to the sitting room to gossip while the men smoked their cigars and sipped brandy. How she had longed, many a time, to be in there with them. Their talks were so full of politics, hunting, the state of the country—everything that would give one food for thought. Now, she was married to a titled gentleman and had to make distasteful small talk to a woman with whom she had nothing in common.

"Looks as if you need this." A hand held out a lacy handkerchief. Lauriette looked up to see Devlin smiling down at her. "What is the matter?"

"Where are our guests?"

"Muriel has already retired," he said indifferently, "and I left Harry refilling his brandy snifter. I asked you what is the matter?"

"Nothing—everything!" she sniffed.

"You've a very logical way of putting things," he

laughed softly.

"I know of no other way to tell you," she defended.

"Did you look in on my father?"

Lauriette nodded. "You've known for some time that he's going to die, haven't you." The smile vanished from Devlin's face. "Is there nothing we can do?" Tears blurred her vision.

"Only to keep him as comfortable as possible," he whispered. "You are a bright spot in his life. He cares for you, Laurie."

"He is a very special man," she confided sadly. "I love him."

Devlin looked at her quite startled. "I almost believe you mean that."

Lauriette turned on him, her eyes snapping with anger. "*Almost* believe!" she repeated harshly. "Have you known so many insincere women in your lifetime you have to question a simple, honest declaration?"

"What I meant—"

"You needn't explain further!" she stormed. "If you'll excuse me, I'll retire now!"

Devlin stood there in the darkness looking after the slight form running towards the house. Women! She was being honest in her feelings for his father and he mocked her. Devlin was so used to women saying things to please him, never meaning what they say, barely remembering their words at all. It was difficult for him to believe a woman could be totally honest.

The hour had advanced far into morning by the time Devlin climbed the stairs to bed. The evening had drifted by slowly after his little scene with Lauriette. But after a victorious game of chess with Harry and a few brandies to mellow his mood, he was ready to play the apologetic husband.

The room was completely dark as he entered, and

leaving the candle unlit, he quickly disrobed. He slid underneath the coverlet and felt Lauriette move on her back. Devlin leaned over her, placing a light kiss at her temple.

"It is only me, my dear," he whispered quite low.

Lauriette opened her eyes, a scream frozen in her throat. Awakening gradually from sleep, all she heard was the low rumbled voice and a shadowed man leaning over her. Where was Devlin? How did Evan manage to sneak into the house?

"No!" she shrieked as one of her hands lashed at the man's face.

Her mood had caught Devlin off guard and he felt her sharp nails graze his cheek. She managed to unbalance him and jumped from the bed. Devlin lunged for her and brought her down hard to the floor, knocking the breath from her. Lauriette kicked and fought like a she-cat, hurling vile oaths at his head.

"He'll kill you for what you're doing!" she raged, straining against the strong arms that held her in their steel grip.

"It's me!" Devlin shouted back. "My god, Laurie, it's Dev!"

Pinning her down with his legs, he managed to light the candle, sending a bright glow across the room. The look on Lauriette's face was that of sheer terror. She had actually thought he was Evan!

"Who did you think I was?" he finally asked.

Tears stung the back of her eyes. "I—I thought—you were—Evan!" she stammered.

"What?" he cried. "How in the devil could you have mistook me for him?"

She wiped a stray tear with the back of her hand. "Your voice," she answered. "You—you called me 'my dear' ."

"So I did."

"It was the only—only thing he ever called me."

She reached up gently and touched one of the bloody creases.

"Forgive me—please."

"There's nothing to forgive," he said sullenly.

"But—but I hurt you," she returned very gently. "I would never—never have consciously hurt you."

"Oh, Laurie, Laurie," Dev sighed, gathering her into his arms. "Haven't you realized yet that he cannot hurt you ever again? You're safe here with me. I'll never let anyone cause you pain again."

Her bruised arm silently slipped around his neck as she raised her head, offering for the first time her full lips to his own. His mouth claimed hers and she felt a tremor of anticipation sweep through her. It was *she* who desired him more than anything and *she* felt driven to make the advances. She wanted to be the conqueror tonight.

Lauriette turned toward Devlin, deepening the kiss, entwining her tongue with his. Her arms traveled down the length of his arm, enjoying the feel of his warm flesh against her palm. She pulled him ever closer, drinking in the heated nearness of him.

Devlin's expression was unfathomable, deep with passion. In that moment he smiled affectionately, knowing now his nights with her had not been in vain.

Letting her emotions control the night, Lauriette buried her face in his neck, kissing, teasing him. She was enjoying the part of a wanton and desire grew inside to explore further.

She moved down further to his chest, placing tiny kisses across it. He was so exquisitely handsome, she wanted to devour him.

"Oh, cherub!" he moaned, deep within his throat. "My darling cherub."

Lauriette caressed his broad shoulders, massaging

his muscular chest and flat abdomen. As she reached his thigh, her hand faltered and stopped. It was the first time they had made love in the dimmed candlelight, the first time she had taken the initiative, the first time she had actually seen his manhood and she gasped. It was the most fascinating, most unusual thing she ever seen in her life and nothing like she imagined it would be.

"Don't be afraid of him, Laurie," Devlin whispered, his dark eyes drunk with passion. "Touch him. You'll find he is a very warm and accommodating fellow."

Taking her hand, he slowly guided it to his swollen member. Lauriette tightly closed her eyes but opened them quickly as she felt her hand enclosing his bulging manhood. It was warm and truly beating with a life of its own. She gazed up at him with eyes of amazement and he grinned crookedly.

Devlin pressed her against the Turkish carpet, his hand quickly unbuttoning her shift exposing her firm, solid breasts. His hand cupped them, his mouth feasting on one then the other. Lauriette was on fire with want of him. She willingly parted her thighs, pulling him to her, needing to feel his hardness inside her, quenching the aching thirst that had built up.

Devlin's own emotions were confused as he moved atop her. He had an unexplainable need for this woman, from the first time he laid eyes upon her. He could not get enough of her, could not tire of her. Lauriette Claymoor Essex had set his soul aflame.

Lauriette raised her hips to meet his thrusts, her movements natural and passionate. She could feel his hands moving against her skin, encouraging, teasing, praising. She was only alive when Devlin touched her, possessed her.

His lips moved to her ear, his teeth gently teasing the lobe, and she began to tremble with the mounting of her own desire. A cry of pleasure escaped her lips as her arms and legs clung to him, tears spilling over her cheeks. He was consuming her, devouring her and she soared with joy.

Devlin's manhood peaked with desire as he moaned in her ear, his body shuddering time and again with shock waves of ecstasy.

They lay a long while, arms and legs entwined. A strong bond surged between them like a lightning bolt, their emotions still running rampant.

Devlin begrudgingly moved away a bit, leaning on his elbow. He smiled that boyish, crooked smile of his and Lauriette beamed when the softness in his eyes caressed her face.

"Come, my love, I think it is time for sleep," he whispered, picking her up in his arms.

Once in their huge bed, Devlin covered them both then gathered her into his arms. Without words, Lauriette completely surrendered herself into his hands, now stroking her hair. She was becoming more and more dependent on this strange, fascinating man, and this worried her, for she knew not where it would lead.

She would think on it later, she reasoned sleepily. But for tonight she would sleep securely in her husband's arms.

Twenty-Four

"As I said before, Devlin, it really is wonderful to have you home where you belong," Muriel smiled sweetly. "It has been quite lonesome since Frederick passed on. He was very amusing in his own little way and we did have so many delightful times together. I know what you are thinking, my dear. Frederick was much older than I, but he possessed a young mind . . . and liberal views of our lives together."

Devlin never heard a word as Muriel continued on and on. He stood at the French doors with hands clasped behind him, legs apart slightly. His eyes rested on Lauriette in the garden. On her arm hung a woven basket filled with multicolored flowers. He could hear the tinkling sound of her laughter even behind the closed doors as she conversed with Seth Gordon, the gardener. In the sunlight Lauriette's hair shone with brilliance, her rather large straw hat neglected on the ground. He could not take his eyes from her.

"Devlin, you've not heard a word I've said," Muriel scolded.

"What? I am sorry, Muriel, I've been preoccupied

this morn,'' he answered absently. ''Have you seen my father yet?''

''You mean 'his lordship','' she said sarcastically. ''I truly think he would prefer me not to call him anything at all!''

Devlin looked at her for a long moment, then smiled. ''Come, Muriel, do you really expect me to believe you would have it otherwise? We both know how much you dislike my father—and you always have.''

Muriel locked her arm in his, pressing herself against him. ''I should have known better than to put up a pretense with you, my dear,'' she whispered, but again Devlin was not listening to her. He was staring out the window.

Lauriette was seated on the ground while one of the servants knelt beside her, a wooden crate in hand. She laughed with delight as she picked up a young black pup and held it to her cheek. The servant turned the crate on its side and out came four more.

''How utterly beneath her station!'' The words came tumbling out before Muriel could stop them.

Devlin looked at her sharply. ''I see nothing wrong.''

''Why—why a lady should not be out there on the ground romping with a litter of pups like a peasant wench,'' she sniffed.

''My wife is very much the lady and handles herself very well—even when playing with a litter of pups,'' he snapped. '' 'Tis a pity Englishwomen could not follow the examples of American women. You would no doubt find yourself less a snob!''

Devlin pulled away from Muriel and left the room without another word. She angrily stamped her foot at the closing of the door. Why, he was actually taken with that little twit! How could he have married her, how? Without giving her so much as a chance to compete for his affections. Well, it was not over yet! In fact, her holiday at Essex Hall had just begun!

Lauriette spied Devlin near the grounds and waved. "Dev!" she shouted merrily. "Come see what Pauley found in the stables!"

Devlin stood over her smiling, then knelt down beside her and picked up a brown-and-white speckled pup.

"Aren't they beautiful?"

"Beautiful? I think not, my lady," he laughed. "A pup is a pup to me."

"No, Dev, you're wrong," she stated, gathering three of them into her full skirt. "They each have personalities of their own. Just look at them!"

He took a long look at the pup he held, then smiled. "I dare say you're right, cherub."

She returned the pups, one by one, to the crate. "I imagine Pauley should return these little heartbreakers to the barn," she sighed. "Are you going to ride today?"

"I promised old Whit Myer to check on an old abandoned cottage on our land. He needs a place now that he is too old to work and I think he'd rather stay on Essex property."

"May I ride with you?"

Devlin grinned crookedly. "Can you ride?"

"Why not see for yourself?" she replied saucily.

"How long will it take you to change?"

"As long as it takes you to have the horses saddled," she said over her shoulder and hurried toward the house.

The spring day was perfect for a horseback ride and Lauriette looked lovely in her green velvet riding habit. Devlin smiled his approval as she came tripping down the steps.

Beside Nomad stood a beautiful white Arabian Stallion. Lauriette's eyes widened with pleasure at the sight of the noble beast.

"His name is Caesar," Devlin said.

"Is he as spirited as Nomad?"

"There is only one way to find out," he replied.

Taking her by the waist, he easily lifted her onto the sidesaddle and before Devlin could mount, she was off. Devlin's laughter echoed through the wind as he kneed Nomad and was on the chase.

They raced over the open countryside, Devlin holding back Nomad to give Lauriette the lead. She was exhilarated, feeling the fresh country air whip at her clothes.

She finally halted the horse at the top of a grassy knoll and waited for Devlin to catch up. "Well?"

"Well, he is most spirited indeed," she laughed breathlessly. "He is magnificent!"

"Then he is yours."

Lauriette stared at him. "I—I can't accept such a generous gift."

Devlin could not believe the simplicity of the woman. "Why can you not just gracefully accept the horse and say thank you?" he countered hotly.

"Thank you, Dev," she replied meekly.

"The cottage is just over the rise," he said. "We'll rest there for a while before turning back."

She waited as Devlin took the lead, then fell in behind him. She had mixed emotions over accepting this generous gift from him, for though she already loved the giant beast, Lauriette did not dare become too engrossed with Devlin. She had no intention of becoming obligated to him any more than she already had. Being indebted to a man—any man—could prove dangerous.

The cottage lay straight ahead, hidden by trees. Closer and closer they came. Lauriette felt a cold chill envelop her as Devlin halted and lifted her from her horse.

Devlin noted the look of dismay upon her face, even the pretty flush to her cheeks had paled somewhat. As he placed her on her feet, he found her to be trembling.

"What is wrong, cherub?"

"I—I don't know," she barely whispered, her eyes darting about. "It—it is this place. It seems very familiar to me yet I know I've never been here before."

"It is possible you were," he said lightly, tethering both animals. "This vast forest connects Essex Hall to Claymoor and you told me yourself of your visit to Claymoor four years ago."

Lauriette slowly, cautiously moved about, the uneasy feeling growing at an alarming rate. They entered the disheveled, broken down cottage and as Devlin checked the damages to the place, Lauriette stood near the door, her heart pounding murderously.

"How . . . how long has it been empty?" she asked quietly.

Devlin stopped his inspection and looked at Lauriette closely. "A long time, Laurie," came his reply. "As long as I can remember."

Lauriette bent to straighten an overturned chair. "This cottage has known great sorrow," she whispered strangely. "It is evil, Dev, I can feel it."

Devlin held her at arms length and looked into her frightened eyes. "Lauriette, what in the devil's wrong?" he demanded. "This cottage has been deserted as far back as I can remember."

"Not always deserted, Dev."

"What in hell are you going on about?" he asked crossly. "You say you've never been here, yet you mumble on about sorrow and evil."

Lauriette felt panic rising within her, as if this small cottage would devour her whole. "Please, Dev, believe me!'' she cried, her voice trembling. ''I don't know how I know, only that I do. I'm frightened! Please, please take me away from here!''

Without further prompting, Devlin escorted Lauriette out and away from the cottage. Untying the horses, they walked with them to the top of the hill.

''Laurie,'' he said finally, ''are you all right?''

''Yes . . . no . . . I don't know,'' she answered. ''I had this . . . this overwhelming fear of that place. It's real, Dev, my fear of it is real!''

He placed an arm around her and drew her close to him. Devlin was becoming more and more concerned with each passing moment.

''Laurie, are you absolutely certain you've never seen that cottage before?'' he asked.

''Yes, I am certain,'' she returned sharply. ''When I was here four years ago, I never, *never* set foot on Essex land. Please, take me home.''

The ride back to Essex Hall was nothing like their leaving. Lauriette was silent, brooding about what had taken place. Devlin was much concerned over Lauriette's unusual behavior. She had been so terrified.

The morning had started out so promising, so full of warmth and laughter. And now? She had ruined it all with that crazy premonition of hers!

Returning to the stables, she slid off Caesar with ease. Without waiting for Devlin, she walked toward the house, her heart very heavy. What was happening to her? She felt herself slipping away bit by bit and knew not the reason shy.

''Laurie! Laurie!'' Devlin called, but she hurried on.

In three long strides he caught up to her. Grasping her arm, he gently turned her around. Tears wet her cheeks; tenderly Devlin wiped them away with the palm of his hand.

''Laurie, love, everything will be all right,'' he whispered encouragingly.

Tears filled her eyes once more. "Oh, Dev, Dev!" she sobbed and threw her arms around his neck. "I'm so sorry! I've done nothing but cause you problems."

"Sh-h, cherub," he soothed, brushing away a strand of hair from her face. "That's not true. Other people caused your problems. Now, dry those lovely tears of yours. After all, we can't have Father thinking I've done you a wrong."

Devlin watched as Lauriette mounted the stairs, then thoughtfully sought out the sitting room and the nearest decanter of brandy. He was very disturbed at what had taken place at the cottage and wondered if her terror of that place was linked in some way to the recurring dreams she had. She was so terrified there and he had to swallow the overwhelming impulse to protect her. Never before had he felt the need to fiercely protect a woman and the thought of it only made him more uncomfortable.

"Whatever put such a scowl on your ugly face!"

Devlin looked up to see Judd's smiling face. "Judd!" he beamed, jumping to his feet. They hugged each other affectionately.

"Well, how is the husband doing?"

Devlin laughed, slapping him on the back. "Making progress, cousin," he replied.

"How is Lauriette?"

"She is fine," he said quietly. "She'll be pleased to see you. Now, what brings you back to Essex Hall so soon? Have we news of Brimley?"

"No, Dev," Judd answered. "He is still in Scotland. Actually I've an important letter for his lordship. I was asked to hand deliver it. From Lord Bottomsley."

"Bottomsley, you say?"

"None other," Judd replied. "Evidently, it is quite

important. His lordship dismissed me on the spot."

"Can't say as I'm disappointed you're here," Devlin smiled. "How is London?"

"Very boring, cousin," he sighed, sliding into an overstuffed chair. "Everyone is heading for the country, leaving only the dregs."

"Well, perhaps we'll have a peaceful summer then."

"Hardly," Judd scoffed. "Considering Harry and Muriel are residing here. How is the family getting along?"

Devlin produced a cheroot from his pocket, lighting it. "Well, Father was fit to be tied when they came," he drawled, blowing tiny smoke rings. "Muriel and Laurie seem to have an uneasy truce. Naturally, Laurie is trying to be as gracious as possible—but no one can please Muriel."

"And Harry?"

Devlin's face darkened. "As long as I do not find out about him taking his *pleasures* on any of the people in my area, I cannot in good conscience, send him packing. I'll keep a close watch on him," came his cool reply. "Now, what of our friends in London?"

"Lady Marie-Claire is traveling with friends to Vienna for the summer," he informed Devlin. "I understand, though, that Sir Henry is taking up residence—at Claymoor."

"I see," Devlin said slowly. "Strange he should wish to live in that drafty, decaying old place."

"Well, the scandal of his duel with Brimley left him without much pride, so I understand," Judd enlightened. "I imagine he would like to become a recluse for a while. At least until the scandal becomes old news."

"Or he feels the need to be near Lauriette."

"Dev, do you realize what you're saying?" Judd questioned. "If I didn't know better, I'd swear you wear the look of a jealous man.''

''No, cousin, not jealous,'' he returned. ''Just cautious. I do not take kindly to anyone meddling with what belongs to me.''

''Scamp!'' came Lord David's raspy voice. ''Scamp! I need you.''

''Well,'' Devlin sighed, setting down his brandy snifter, ''the time for pleasure is at an end. The dragon is bellowing.''

Twenty-Five

Lord David sat at the desk in the library, shoulders hunched, pondering over the letter in his trembling hands. His face wore a most serious expression, his eyes black with anger and concern.

"Judd brought me a letter from Bottomsley," he began slowly, not bothering to look up.

Devlin quietly moved away from the desk and seated himself in a chair overlooking the grounds. The one thing he did not want to hear from his father was a long, boring account of the affairs of Lord Craigmore Bottomsley.

"I need you to make a run across the channel," Lord David said evenly.

Devlin turned and looked at his father. "Another émigré, Father?" he drawled.

Lord David threw him a bleak look, silencing him immediately. "There is a passenger to be brought aboard your ship after nightfall in mid-channel. You still have your ship, do you not?"

"Of course I have my ship!" he returned rather gruffly. "She's docked in Cornwall."

"Good," Lord David went on. "In mid-channel you will intercept a small fishing boat. The boat will signal you with one light, then two, then one again. You will return the signal, then take on a single passenger."

Devlin arched a brow. "Just who is being smuggled into England this time?" he questioned sarcastically. "Another old chum who ran with you about the country?"

Lord David's white head came up with a jerk, his eyes narrowing. "Your passanger will be Lady Raine Whitley."

Devlin paled a bit. "Theresa's mother!" he whispered. "What the devil's she doing in France?"

"Her other daughter, Irene, married a French nobleman," he replied. "Raine traveled to Montbard to be with her during the birth of her first child. I am sorry to say Irene died in childbirth. The babe, a boy, died some hours later. Now, with all the peasant uprising over there, she cannot leave as a woman of station. At the moment she is in Douarnenez awaiting to be returned to England."

"When do I leave for Cornwall?"

"Daybreak," came the answer. "And, scamp, I think it best to keep this to yourself. Lady Raine's life could depend upon your discretion. Have you any questions?"

"None."

"You will escort her to London," he instructed. "Once Raine is safe inside the walls of Whitley House, your task will be complete." Lord David slowly stood up, taking cane in hand. "I am thoroughly exhausted, scamp. Have cook send my meal to my room. I cannot abide the presence of those two at my table tonight. Just make my usual excuses."

Devlin stood alone in the silence of the room as the door quietly closed behind Lord David. After so short a time, another separation from Lauriette. Eyes closed, he shook his head. Logically, it was best for him to be away from her for a while. Their lives were following too regular a pattern and this disturbed him a great deal. He had no use to be bound so tightly to a woman. After all, he had married the pretty Mistress Claymoor and that alone bound him more than he anticipated. No, he needed this time away from her to get this little enchantress out of his mind and put her into proper perspective. It had been a long time since he had been to London.

Supper had been a quiet affair. Lauriette decided to have her meal with Lord David in his room. Muriel felt very much the adored lady with three gentlemen dancing attendance but was sorely disappointed when Devlin and Judd seemed to be preoccupied. Brother Harry was openly amused at his sister's attempts at witty conversation that failed.

She had been so confident, so cheered by the news that Lauriette would not dine with them. She had taken much longer to dress than usual, taking great pains with her hair and makeup. Dejectedly, she slumped back in her chair and sulked. She could have been dressed in a sackcloth and ashes for the attention Devlin paid her! It was the final blow to her ego and without waiting for the meal to be finished, she rudely excused herself and sought the darkness of her bedroom and a decanter of wine.

Harry pushed his half-eaten plate away from him and sat back, dabbing his mouth with a napkin. "Dinner was a bit boring," he sighed. "It would have been much more interesting if her ladyship would have been present."

Judd's eyes darted from Harry to Devlin, knowing how Harry's goading humor irritated his cousin.

"And supper would have been even more interesting if Percey Edgewood had graced the table," Judd carelessly threw out, watching as the comment hit its mark.

Devlin smiled lazily, knowing his cousin Harry's appetite for the unusual. "There are times when my wife prefers a more dynamic dinner partner than one who spends his time doing things she has no idea even exist."

Harry stiffened in his chair, his eyes staring straight into Devlin's. His face was a stoney mask of rising anger at the insult. Judd grinned triumphantly as Devlin's biting remark stung Harry.

"At least I do not play the loving swain," Harry announced boldly. "My jaded appetite is my own business."

Harry left the room in a huff and Judd burst out laughing.

"I tell you, that *man*"—and Judd stressed the word—"has guts. I wonder why he has stayed so long. Essex Hall does not cater the kind of companionship he desires."

"I imagine he is running again from his debts," Devlin surmised. "That is usually the only time he ends up here." His smiled disappeared and he became serious. "Judd, I'm leaving tomorrow for Cornwall and the ship."

Judd's gray eyes twinkled merrily, a broad smile flashing across his face. "I've been itching to get back to sea—"

"You can't go this trip," Devlin hurriedly cut in. "I'm sorry, but I need you here." In a hushed tone, he explained in detail the nature of his journey. Judd listened closely, his face revealing the seriousness of the situation. "So you see, I would feel much better about everything if I knew you were here to oversee things. I trust no one else."

"There is no doubt I'll stay," Judd said firmly. "I would be more help here. Have you told Lauriette yet?"

Devlin shook his head. "No," he answered, "I plan to tell her tonight."

"Are you going to tell her everything?"

"Just that I have some business that has to be taken care of," he explained. "She doesn't need to know any more than that."

"But, Dev," Judd argued, "she's your wife. She has a right to know—"

"She only need know what I wish to tell her!" he snapped. "It is none of Lauriette's business what I do! I live my life the way I see fit. As long as Lauriette is provided for, she should have no complaints—and neither should you!"

Judd stood up from the table, his fear of Devlin's wrath overpowering his own anger. "You have no complaints from me, cousin, at least not yet," he replied coldly. "I'll stay here. Now, I bid you good night." Turning on his heel, he left the room.

With an enraged growl, Devlin sent china flying against the far wall. His black mood was almost unmanageable. He could not understand himself at all! Judd innocently commented on Lauriette, more or less protecting her rights, and immediately he flew into a boiling rage. Why was it that he did not want anyone to be concerned over her? What did it matter? He should be grateful that Judd cared about her. After all, he would not be there forever and she should have people around her who care.

Devlin attributed his irritability to his upcoming journey. He was spending too much time at Essex Hall with Lauriette. The next few weeks away from her would clear his head.

* * *

Lauriette sat curled up in the window seat of their bedroom, the darkness of night comforting her. Her knees drawn up to her chin, she peered out the window at the eerie view of fog rising over the forest.

It had been a most unnerving day and even after the quiet evening meal and a game of chess with Lord David, her nerves were still shattered. Tiredly, she pressed her forehead against the cool glass. Her thoughts repeatedly turned to the afternoon at Myer's cottage. It was so silly to be frightened of a deserted, rundown mass of stone that she had never seen before! How utterly ridiculous she felt, panicking like some spineless little child afraid of her own shadow! Surely Devlin thought her insane!

Lauriette's thoughts turned to Lord David and she frowned. He was becoming weaker, and the medicine Dr. Quade had given him was now having no soothing effect whatsoever. *Please,* she silently prayed, *please give him a little more time here with us, please* . . .

The door slammed shut bringing Lauriette out of her sober thoughts. She could hear Devlin cursing under his breath as he fumbled for the candles. The room gradually was illuminated with faint light.

Devlin grinned crookedly as his eyes found Lauriette curled up on the window seat already dressed for bed, her hair brushed to a golden brown, her satin wrapper tied neatly at the waist, revealing the fullness of her breasts and the rounded softness of her hips.

She felt his eyes rake over her and blushed in spite of herself. Would she ever grow accustomed to Devlin's bold stare?

"It has been an unusual night, my lady," he commented drily, removing his cravat and shirt. "You were missed at supper. Harry inquired after you."

Lauriette looked at him sharply. "With all due respect to your cousin, I enjoyed my meal with your father,'' she answered defensively. ''It is not good for him to eat alone so often.''

''I have business to attend to,'' he announced suddenly, causing Lauriette to stare at him. ''I'm not certain how long I'll be gone.''

''I see,'' she said quietly, her gaze lowered to her hands.

Devlin turned and regarded her closely. ''Are you not going to ask where I'm going or to come with me?'''

He was baiting her, goading her, she could sense it. She calmly raised her eyes to meet his. ''If you had wanted me to know your destination, you would have told me,'' she answered simply. ''If you had a desire for my company, you would ask me to come along.''

Devlin was at a loss for words. Her answer had been straightforward and honest and once again he had underestimated her. Gradually, a grin broke out on his lips. No matter how angry and disturbed he became, everything seemed to vanish when he was with her.

Devlin reached for her, pulling her to her feet. ''I've some matters to take care of for father,'' he told her. ''I'll be gone no longer than need be.'' Devlin took her into his arms. ''Now tell me, wife, what little trinket would you like me to bring back from my journey to please you?''

Lauriette gazed up at him, her horizon blue eyes shining. ''I ask only your safe return, husband,'' she replied softly.

Devlin stared down at her for a long, long moment. Would this strange woman ever ask anything of him? Never question or beg anything of him? He was amazed, baffled and puzzled by her. He had never met anyone like her before and he was unsure of everything that concerned her.

''It's time for bed, cherub,'' he whispered with a

wicked smile. "Give me something tonight that will keep me warm till I return."

To touch, to feel, to know. Devlin gazed down at the sleeping Lauriette beside him, his eyes taking in her slender frame. What was there about her that intoxicated him? It was true she was lovely in her own quiet way; but he had made love to many beautiful women, some much lovelier than Lauriette. But there was something—something unique which set her apart from every other woman he had known.

Her eyes flickered, then opened and he gently smiled at her. She hesitated but a moment, then reached up and lightly touched his cheek.

"What time is it?" she asked sleepily.

"Shortly before dawn, my lady," he whispered, pressing a kiss into the palm of her hand.

"You should be sleeping," she lightly scolded.

" 'Tis hard to sleep when we have so little time left," his voice became deep and husky.

In an impulsive moment, Lauriette threw her arms around his neck pulling him closer to her. "I shall miss you so much, Dev."

Lauriette's gesture melted any resolve Devlin could have had as he kissed her with great longing, her lips sweet and giving. She was such a wonder to him, such a puzzling wonder.

Devlin's fingers softly touched her forehead, then gingerly moved to her left cheek causing shivers of anticipation to wiggle up her spine. He was teasing her in a most loving fashion, his fingers tracing the outline of her mouth, her chin, now making their way to her ear.

Lauriette gasped as his tongue replaced his fingers. "Dev!" she cried breathlessly. "I am too filled with fire for this teasing!"

He chuckled deeply. "Filled with fire, you say?" he

murmured against her ear. "Then let us see if we cannot quench that fire!"

With one gentle thrust, he had pulled her atop of him and Lauriette squealed with delight. "I am yours, my cherub," he grinned wickedly. "Show me the wonders you have learned. Give me a sinfully delightful memory to fill my coming nights!"

She started to laugh but the laugh died in her throat as she gazed into his smoky brown eyes. There was something there, something more than the unspent passion of the moment. Could it be—no! It was only her mind playing tricks on her. Love, real honest-to-goodness love for them was out of the question.

Devlin gazed into pools of blue in her eyes and a sigh caught in his throat. Those damnable eyes he could read so easily were now filled with an expression he did not understand.

Outside their window the first few traces of daylight were beginning to appear, giving the earth a sense of magic. Her lips touched his, so soft, so warm, so moist, so gently at first. But as her tongue sought his, her mouth became like a finely edged sword, sharp, searing, thrusting to plunder the inner part of his.

Devlin's silken chest was crushed against her breasts, his hands tenderly stroking her back. Urged on by his ragged breathing and her own mounting excitement, Lauriette began kissing, nibbling underneath his hard chin and began a gradual descent. Down to his chest, kissing every inch, leaving no part unaffected by her hot breath and scorching tongue; down to his taut flat stomach, her mouth spending a few moments longer over his navel.

She was being swept away on a torrent of unleashed passion, wanting to go on, to discover all there was to know about this man, this beautiful body that had taught her so much.

Devlin moaned aloud as Lauriette's lips found his most vulnerable spot and his hands entwined themselves in her velvety brown hair. She was no longer afraid of the unknown, no longer uncertain of herself. She was an instrument of pleasure, a whole woman wanting to give this man all she had to give and to receive from him, to drain from him until he was weak with spent passion.

His hands on her shoulders, Devlin could stand no longer to hold back his desire for her. To feel her body merge with his became an almost uncontrollable urge as he pulled her up to him, kissing her fiercely.

With growing confidence she straddled him, feeling his hands hot and trembling on her waist guiding and directing her. The time for fulfillment arrived. She could wait no longer to be made whole once more. Her body shuddered as he savagely arched upward, hands hurtfully gripping her hips.

Lauriette rocked backward as his manhood filled her, consumed her. Only his hands, his gentle yet demanding hands kept her from falling. She was moving in perfect rhythm with him, her passion climbing ever higher and higher.

Finally, she could hold back no longer. She was beyond logical thinking, beyond anything that had to do with her future. Gone were the resolutions she had so fervently made, gone were all the barriers she had so foolishly put up. She was a woman. A woman made for the love of one man—*this* man!

Her fingers dug into his chest as she cried out to Devlin, begging, pleading with him to quench the burning that was consuming her.

Feverishly, Devlin moved, his thrusts becoming quick and fast. Lauriette stiffened as the first wave of fulfillment hit her with such force she thought she would faint. Devlin groaned, his hands digging into her hips as he, too, rocked with ecstasy. They were one. There were no more secrets, nothing held back. They both had reached for the stars and found a magnificent pool of exquisite torment and unfathomable joy beyond their wildest dreams.

"Oh, Dev, Dev," she moaned, collapsing on top of him. "My love . . . my dearest love . . ."

Rays from the sun gradually filtered through the bedroom curtains, a warm breeze gently rustled the trees outside the window. Devlin dressed quietly, his brown eyes resting on the sleeping face of Lauriette.

He stopped midway in pulling on his boots and smiled as she turned on her side, nestling further into the covers. Her hair was a tangled mass of curls falling over one bare shoulder, her hand that was adorned by his mother's ring resting against the pillow by her cheek. She smiled in her sleep and automatically he smiled back.

Enough of this nonsense! he told himself and finished pulling on his boots. What was he coming to, to sit all moon-eyed watching her sleep like some soppy schoolboy!

His emotions were becoming too complicated for comfort and immediately he turned away from the bed to finish dressing. It would be a long ride to Cornwall and he welcomed the thought of riding Nomad rather than taking a coach. He would travel much faster that way and perhaps the journey in open air would clear his head considerably.

He was ready to go. Turning back, Devlin threw a kiss toward the bed. He stood for a long moment staring at her as if trying to burn into his memory every inch of her. Much to his surprise and dismay, a hot stab of regret bolted through him. *It would be so easy to crawl back into bed with her and stay.*

Devlin gave his head a vigorous shake as if to clear it of all foolish notions. After all, he would have her in bed when he returned.

The servants were already up and bustling about as Devlin descended the stairs. Flora, the downstairs maid, dropped a brief curtsey then hurried to the kitchen.

"It certainly took you long enough to dress," Judd complained. He was comfortably leaning against the drawing room door frame, one leg cocked over the other, arms folded across his chest.

"Up to see me off, eh?" Devlin commented. "Quite a feat, seeing that everyone else in the house is still sound asleep."

"I only wanted to wish you luck and God speed," he said, extending his hand in an unspoken apology.

Devlin heartily gripped his cousin's hand with much affection. "I explained to Laurie I had to tend to father's business," he informed Judd.

"Did she ask you?"

Devlin slowly shook his head. "She has a way about her—" His voice trailed off. "Before I leave, I want you to make certain dear Harry leaves as soon as possible. Give him money—whatever it takes, but I want him gone by tomorrow morn."

"But what if he'll not take money?"

Devlin's expression was grim. "He will. His kind always does."

"I will see to it," Judd replied.

"Well, cousin, it is time."

"Have no worry about Essex Hall," he reassured. "All will be well when you return."

Devlin slapped Judd on the back. "With you here, how could it be otherwise," he smiled. "Guard my possessions jealously, Judd."

"On that you can depend," came Judd's confident reply.

Twenty-Six

Lauriette sat in a comfortable rocking chair, her blue eyes staring at the page of the book but not reading. The household had long since gone to bed, but here she sat in her bedroom, the candles on the night table allowing her the pleasure of reading.

Wearily, she rubbed her eyes. In the sitting room downstairs, the clock struck two. Five days had gone by since she woke and found Devlin already on the road to Cornwall. Five very long and lonely nights had passed without the warmth of him against her.

Rain splattered against the windows, the house creaked and Lauriette jumped. Her eyes darted about the room as if expecting to find someone lurking in the shadows.

"Faith!" she exclaimed aloud to herself. "And you're a grown woman!"

She *must* get her nerves under control! What was happening to her? With Devlin away, she became afraid even though she rationalized there was nothing to fear at Essex Hall. Lord David's room was only several doors away and Judd was closer than that. But she could not shake the feeling of apprehension.

Her mind drifting back to Devlin, Lauriette closed her eyes, a lazy smile crossing her face. She never once realized how terribly lonely it would be without him. It was difficult not to look for his dignified, sober face in the drawing room or listen for his footsteps in the foyer after his daily rides. Lauriette signed deeply. She was becoming too obsessed with Lord Delbridge for her own good! But she could not stop herself from thinking about him over . . . and over . . . and over . . .

Outside the snarling storm whipped and slashed at the trees; inside Lauriette slept in the chair, the book of sonnets slipping from her lap. Her face was calm and serene, her head resting against the wing of the rocking chair.

From her deep sleep, she heard the vague sound of a light-hearted voice calling to her. Moaning lightly, she shifted in the chair.

"Lauriette!" the voice called, so light and filled with warm amusement. "Lauriette, my puppet! Come here!"

Lauriette tried to open her eyes. Was she awake or sleeping?

"Lauriette, my puppet."

The voice was so full of warmth, so familiar. Valiantly, she struggled to wake.

"Lauriette, I'm here . . . here . . . here . . ."

Her eyes fluttered open and widened as she gazed about the room.

"Lauriette . . ."

The voice again! Downstairs! She had to go downstairs! Lauriette flew to the door, her body trembling. She was on the verge of something, something from her past, something of the times she could not remember, and she was afraid.

"Lauriette, my puppet . . ."

She froze at the top of the stairs at the sound of the voice again, now sounding so far away. Her heart pounded rapidly. Where was it coming from?

Descending the stairs seemed to take an eternity to her, taking them slowly, one at a time. Her anxious blue eyes stared at the drawing room door standing ajar. Whoever had called her name was in there, she was certain of it. Stealthily, she crossed the foyer towards the door.

Lauriette silently pushed it back. The room was dimly lit by a single candle and in the far corner she could make out a pair of legs and muddy boots relaxing on an ottoman and draped over a chair was a rain-soaked greatcoat.

He's here! her heart cried out. *He hurried back!*

"Devlin!" she said, her voice trembling with emotion.

The muddied boots quickly hit the floor as the man stood. Lauriette squinted as he stood covered by the shadows of the room. She could hear his ragged breathing, then the sharp intake of breath as his eyes found her just inside the door.

Her eyes misted as she rushed forward. "Why did you call for me?" she asked softly. "Why did you not—"

The man stepped out of the shadows toward her. Lauriette halted suddenly, her eyes taking in the man who stood by the chair. His stature, his hair, his mouth was that of Devlin but he had only one arm! Her mind raced with horror and she felt herself being dragged down into a black pit as she cried out Devlin's name.

The man ran forward as Lauriette sunk to the floor, his own heart racing. He had been stunned by the sound of a soft, feminine voice and thought he was dreaming when he stood and gazed at the young woman. For a fleeting moment he thought it was Terri, his beloved Terri! Who was she and what was she doing at Essex Hall?

He knelt beside her, his right arm sliding underneath her head. She had fainted at the sight of him. Grimly, he set his jaw. He could not blame anyone at being repulsed by his stub of an arm!

No, up close he could see she was not Terri. Terri had been dead for ten years and no amount of wishing or praying could ever bring her back. But this young lady was a pretty one, he thought.

''Neville!'' Judd's surprised voice brought his head around. ''My lord, Lauriette!''

He ran to where Neville knelt and with tender hands picked up the unconscious girl and laid her on the sofa.

''Get me a brandy,'' Judd gold him.

He held the brandy to Lauriette's lips as Neville anxiously looked on. Lauriette began to come around, coughing and sputtering as the bitter liquid passed her lips.

''No!'' she cried out, pushing Judd's hand away. ''Please! Do something! It's Dev, Dev!''

Judd looked from Lauriette to Neville then back again to Lauriette, realization dawning on him.

''This is not Dev, Lauriette,'' he said, taking her by the shoulders. ''This is Neville, Devlin's twin brother.''

Judd's words sunk through her growing hysteria and Lauriette looked at Neville, then began to cry from relief.

''Is she going to be all right?'' Neville asked.

Judd nodded. ''Quite a homecoming, eh?''

''I rode all this way in the rain,'' Neville replied. ''I wanted to surprise everyone—but this exceeded my imagination. Who is she?''

Judd smiled. ''Lady Lauriette Essex, Viscountess Delbridge—Dev's wife.''

"Wife!" Neville exclaimed. "Devlin?"

He could not help but laugh at Neville's expression. "They married in December," he said, then turned to the subdued Lauriette, who was watching them both closely. "Are you all right?"

She nodded slowly. "My—my apologies, sir," she murmured. "It is only—you look—I thought—"

"Say no more, my lady," Neville smiled softly. "At times it is very frustrating to look almost like Devlin. Please forgive me. I did not mean to frighten you so."

Lauriette managed to sit up and returned Neville's smile. "But how did you know my name?"

"My lady?"

She looked at Neville with growing alarm. "Did . . . you not call for me? Telling me to come?"

Neville glanced curiously at Judd then back to Lauriette. "No."

Lauriette fiercely gripped Judd's hand, her face void of color. "Someone woke me from sound sleep," she whispered. "Someone calling my name."

"Lauriette, you're tired and distraught," Judd soothed. "You were probably dreaming, that's all."

"No!" she cried frantically. "I was wide awake, there at the top of the stairs!"

Judd's brow drew together. With the thunderstorm outside it was impossible to hear anything out there.

"You believe me, don't you?"

Judd looked at Neville, then at Lauriette. "Of course I do," he said. "Come. Let's get you back to bed."

"You're right," she quietly agreed. "I am tired." She turned to Neville. "I am sorry about the fright I gave you."

"Rest well, my lady," he replied softly.

The late morning found Neville at the dining table absently toying with his food, a frown clouding his handsome face. First, he had paid his respects to Lord David and was shocked to find him so ill. It was still hard for him to believe that the man who occupied the south wing of Essex Hall was his father. When he left for India, Lord David had still been robust and impressive. Now he was only a deteriorated shell of what he had been. His father had been pleased to see him, a bit of his old self showing through his eyes.

"Good heavens, Neville, you startled me!"

He looked up from his breakfast to see Muriel standing in the doorway, her hair piled fashionably high, her blue morning dress the latest style. She was still as lovely as he remembered—and still as scheming.

"Hello, Muriel," he said easily.

"It has been so long, my dear," she cooed, seating herself beside him. "At least four years, has it not?"

"I believe it has," he replied. "My condolences."

"Yes. Frederick," she pouted. "It was a great blow to me but I am now learning to live with it."

"I can see you are," he commented drily. "Tell me, have you been at the Hall long?"

"A month or so," she answered. "Did you know Devlin married?"

"Indeed."

"Oh, yes, it came as a great shock to all of us," she went on. "A little provincial miss from America. Have you ever heard anything so scandalous? She is a strange one, too. She does not care to mix with people of taste and quality either. I have no idea where Devlin's mind was, it certainly was not on his well-bred heritage."

"I am sure my brother knew what he was doing."

"You think so?" she countered, then leaned closer to him. "Mistress Claymoor had been the betrothed of the Honorable Evan Brimley."

Neville's fork dropped with quite a clatter as his expression turned to stone.

"Oh, Neville, I am so sorry!" she flustered. "I should have never mentioned his name!"

Neville stood, his eyes hard upon her.

"Where are you going?" she asked as he trudged by her chair. "Neville! I said I was sorry!"

Inside his head tiny fireworks were exploding; his shoulder began to throb. He needed a drink in the worst possible way and he headed for the drawing room.

His hand trembled as he lifted the whiskey to his lips. After ten years, Evan Brimley's name still caused deep hatred to surge through him. Would he ever be able to forget? Neville stared down at the empty sleeve pinned back. No, he would never forget that he was only half a man and that Brimley was responsible!

God, his arm ached! Again he filled the glass. He downed the whiskey in one burning gulp. Theresa, sweet Terri!

Lauriette gazed up the stairs, her thoughts sad and confused. She had spent the better part of her morning playing piquet with Lord David in his room. He was growing weaker with each passing day and it was tearing her apart.

Closing the drawing room door behind her, she moved swiftly across the room and stood staring out the French doors at the rain-drenched garden.

She wondered what Devlin was doing at the moment. She wondered if he ever thought of her.

"Good morning."

Lauriette jumped at Neville's voice. "Good morning," she returned hastily. "I didn't know you were in here."

He smiled lazily, a smile so much like Devlin's her heart gave a lurch. She noticed the half empty glass of whiskey in his hand as he came towards her.

"I trust you slept well," she said as he placed the

now empty glass on the table.

"I have had better nights," he drawled. "and you?"

"I have had better nights, too."

He was watching her intensely, a fact which brought a blush to her cheeks. "I can understand."

Lauriette looked at him questioningly.

"I can understand why my brother wanted you."

He stood close to her now. So close, Lauriette held her breath.

"I must see about Lord David," said she and started to leave when he grabbed her arm, gently pulling her back.

"It is truly a prize to take something away from Brimley," he whispered fiercely.

"W-what?"

His hand tightened on her arm. "My brother was wise to keep you from him," he said. "You are very pretty, my lady." His hand gently stroked her cheek. "My Terri was pretty, too. Very much like you. If only . . . if only . . ."

"P-please," she murmured. "Please don't."

"One kiss," he whispered, his face closer. "What harm is there in one kiss?"

Lauriette was rigid, her loyalty overriding her fear. "Because I am Devlin's wife," she said plainly and stepped back.

Neville glared at her for one long moment, then nodded. "I fear I've had too much to drink," he apologized. "I tend to do so when my arm pains me."

"Did—did Evan do this to you?" she asked. "Is that why you hate him?"

Neville backed away from Lauriette, then fled the room. She stared at the open door, holding her breath. That poor man! Her heart went out to him.

Lauriette sought out Judd and found him in the stables. He had ridden the grounds and was very weary as he emerged from the open doors.

"Judd, I need to talk with you."

He smiled. "I am at your disposal, my lady." The look on Lauriette's face caused his smile to vanish. "What is wrong?"

"Tell me about Neville," she pleaded. "I need to know about Evan and what he has to do with this family."

"Let's walk," he told her, taking her arm.

"How did he lose his arm?"

"I will have to go back a way in order for you to understand—about ten years ago," he began. "Devlin and Neville were eighteen. There was a young girl, Lady Theresa Whitley, as lovely and innocent as a fresh summer's day. The first time they met her, both were struck by her but Neville in particular. He fell madly in love with her and even though he was very young, he offered for her."

"And did she love him?"

"Theresa and her mother were both impressed by Neville's offer," he said. "Oh, I suppose she did care for Nev, perhaps even love him, but she was so young and it was her first season—and her eyes did roam to Devlin as well as some other fashionable rakes."

"Surely she didn't play one brother against the other?"

"She was intrigued by Devlin," he replied. "Even though they look alike, they're totally different men. Dev has always been the quiet, sober one never revealing anything of his feelings. On the other hand, Neville has always worn his heart on his sleeve. Devlin interested her I imagine because his interest was elsewhere—with the growing unrest in the colonies."

"Where does Evan fit into all this?"

Judd seated her on a stone bench in the garden. "Devlin and Brimley had words over a—a—er—lady that they were both seen in the company of,'' he recalled. ''Evidently, the lady preferred Devlin's company to Brimley's. Brimley challenged Dev and Dev laughed in his face.''

''Laughed!'' Lauriette gasped.

''He told Brimley that he was not worth getting out of bed to shoot and left him there very much humiliated,'' he said. ''I suppose Brimley caught sight of Theresa with Devlin and it was then and there his little plan was formed.'' Judd's face looked grim. ''He abducted Lady Theresa a few nights after that.''

''Oh, Judd!''

''There is no way to put this delicately, Lauriette,'' he stated. ''Brimley ravished her and then deposited her on Devlin's doorstep in the middle of the night. Dev was not there . . . but Neville was. Amid her hysterics, Lady Theresa managed to tell him and he set out for Brimley's.''

''Neville challenged him?''

Judd nodded. ''Neville was never very good with a rapier. Brimley wounded him seriously. The blade was dirty and infection set in. His arm, from the elbow down, had to be removed.''

Lauriette looked at Judd with sympathetic eyes. ''And what became of Theresa?''

Judd bowed his head. ''She killed herself.''

A cry escaped Lauriette's lips, her eyes filling with tears. ''I—I never realized,'' she whispered brokenly, ''never dreamed—''

''Dev holds himself responsible for everything,'' he said, ''and for a long time Neville blamed him, too. But no more.''

''His hate is so strong,'' she said softly. ''He knew I was betrothed to Evan.''

''He was bound to find out sooner or later,'' Judd shrugged. ''But Neville could not possibly hold you re-

sponsible for anything that happened in the past.''
''Thank you for explaining everything,'' she smiled, placing her hand on his arm. ''It will be far easier to understand him now.''

Twenty-Seven

"Lauriette . . . Lauriette, my puppet . . ." the voice called. "Come! Take a ride with me . . ."

Lauriette lay in her bed frozen, unable to move. It was that voice again, the same warm affectionate voice!

"Lauriette . . . " it called playfully. "Come ride."

It was like an echo. Slowly she eased her way out of bed and quietly walked to the window. A half-moon shed an eerie light on the courtyard below. Lauriette stared into the semi-darkness.

"Lauriette . . ."

She held her breath, becoming increasingly alarmed. Who was he? What did he want of her?

"I'm coming . . ." the voice echoed.

"The door!" she cried and ran from the room. She had to get to the main door, had to make certain the door was bolted. She was frightened, terrified of the unknown man who called to her. He meant to bring something terrible out of the past and cause her world to crumble. She could not let that happen!

Crying and out of breath, Lauriette reached the door, her fingers frantically searching for the bolt.

"What is going on?" Neville's gruff voice called out from the drawing room.

"Please!" she cried out to him. "Help me!"

"Lauriette!" he barely whispered as he reached the door.

"The bolt!" she screamed. "I can't find the bolt!"

Neville's hand enclosed over hers as he brought her hand down on the bolt—the door was securely locked.

"Thank God—thank God!" she half sobbed.

Neville secured his arm around her, leading her into the dimly lit drawing room.

"You are trembling," he said in a very concerned voice.

"Did you not hear him?" she asked anxiously. "He called my name. Please, Neville, you did hear the voice, didn't you?"

He looked at her closely, her face pale with fright.

Gripping his shirt with both shaking hands she shouted, "You had to hear him, you just had to!"

She began to cry and gradually, Neville drew her against him. He gently stroked her hair, murmuring soothing sounds into her ear.

Judd bursting into the room quickly brought Neville out of his entranced state. "What in the hell is going on here?" he angrily demanded upon seeing Lauriette in her thin summer nightgown.

She turned, her face red and swollen from tears. "Someone is out there," she cried. "They were calling me! Oh, Judd, what am I to do?"

He looked at Neville's calm face. "I found her groping for the bolt on the door," he explained almost grudgingly.

"He was . . . coming for me," she said in a whisper. "I . . . I heard him."

"Who?"

"I don't know!" she exclaimed. "But he is out there

in the woods."

"I'll go have a look," Judd said.

"No!" she cried feverishly, hanging onto his arm. "Something will happen to you. I know it! Please, Judd!"

She was on the verge of hysteria, Judd sensed, and placed a reassuring arm around her shoulders.

"Very well, Lauriette," he said gently. "But tomorrow I'll have the entire grounds covered. We'll find him, whoever he is."

"Oh, Judd," she groaned, "what does he want of me?"

"We'll find out, I promise," he reassured. "You're shivering. Let me see you to your room. It is all right, Lauriette, no one will harm you here."

In a few moments Judd was back looking at Neville critically. Neville glared back at him, then turned to the window.

"Did you hear anything, Nev?"

Neville shook his head. "Only Lauriette scrambling at the door," he answered. "Do you believe there is someone out there?"

"Lauriette's life has not been an easy one," he answered evasively.

"Father told me Dev is in Cornwall."

Judd nodded.

"I am surprised he would even leave her," he scoffed.

"Lauriette understands he has business to attend to," Judd snapped. "Dev will be returning soon."

"Think you he will?" he asked crossly. "He would be wise to."

"What is that supposed to mean?"

Neville shrugged. " 'Tis not important."

"Nev, for the love of heaven, do not drag up the past," he warned. "You have not seen Dev for six years. A reunion should be a happy one."

"And so shall this one be, cousin," he returned.

Judd, tiring of the conversation, walked to the door then turned. "Lauriette is an innocent, Neville," he said plainly, "and she is Devlin's wife."

"That, my dear cousin, is a fact I could never forget."

Twenty-Eight

Devlin stood on the deck of the *Horizon Queen* and gazed up at the twinkling sky. There was a fair wind filling the sails and he smiled at the feel of the ship beneath his feet.

He arrived in Plymouth several days after leaving Essex Hall and at first glimpse of his ship, his heart quickened at the prospect of sailing her once again. His faithful crew rounded up, they sailed out on the morning tide.

That night the vessel was sighted and the *Horizon Queen* greeted its noble passenger. Now the ship was heading for London and its captain breathed a sigh of relief that half his mission was over.

Devlin leaned against the rail, his thoughts leading homeward. Before the journey he would not let any thoughts but that of his mission enter his mind. Now the dangerous part of the trip was over, he breathed much easier.

"The sea is beautiful at night, is it not?" a deep, husky voice asked.

Devlin turned, smiling at Lady Raine Whitley. Nine

years had drifted by since he last laid eyes upon her and now even the years had not faded her beauty.

"You should be resting, my lady," he said softly, kindly.

"I am too apprehensive to rest, Devlin," she returned. "It has been so long since I was home. I cannot believe I am going there."

"Rest assured, madam," he said. "I shall personally escort you to your door."

"How is your father?"

"Not well," he said slowly.

"I imagine he is pleased you are back."

"My father has never been one to show emotion, as you well know, madam," he replied.

"And knowing you, my young gentleman, your emotions are kept just as well in secret." She smiled. "And your brother, Neville, is he well?"

Devlin's face sobered. "I believe he's well, madam," he answered. "He has been in India this past year but he's supposed to be returning sometime this month."

"Does he still blame you?" she asked. "For everything that happened?"

Devlin looked down at the rolling waves. "I pray he doesn't, my lady."

"I always hoped to see you married someday," she sighed.

Devlin laughed. "Then I haven't disappointed you, madam," he informed her. "I have been wed these past four months."

"Devlin, you rogue!" she joined in, hugging him affectionately. "Her name?"

"Lauriette," he said softly. "She is an American."

"A lovely name"—Lady Whitley smiled—"and I imagine she is very beautiful."

Devlin gazed out at the boundless sea. "Not beautiful in the sense of London society,'' he said in a deep tone. ''She has a quiet loveliness about her. She stands no taller than my chin, her hair a brilliant golden brown and eyes horizon blue, the color of the sea and the sky combined.''

Lady Raine's hand took his. ''I am very pleased, Devlin,'' she said brightly, ''and from the way you describe her, you love her very much.'' She patted his hand a moment longer. ''Well, I shall retire now, Devlin, good night.''

Devlin did not hear Lady Raine depart. The only thing he heard was the echoing of her words, *you love her very much.* Angrily, he gritted his teeth.

Damnation! Just because he boasted of her virtues does not make him lovesick! He was intrigued by her, amused by her, attracted to her but that did not include love. There was no such thing!

Devlin woke just before dawn, his body drenched in sweat. Damn dreams! he cursed. *She* was there with him, kissing and caressing him, making love to him. Since his talk with Lady Raine, he could not get his mind off Lauriette.

In the dark he could envision her standing there, her golden brown hair curling down her back, that bright smile giving life to her unusual blue-green eyes, her cherub face lifting to look up at him.

''Damn!'' he muttered, slamming his fist into the pillow. He would get her out of his system, by god, somehow, some way! She was just another women who satisfied his desires—nothing more! He would show her—he would show himself!

Twenty-Nine

Lauriette sat quietly, chin resting on hand, concentrating on the chess board. Across from her sat Neville, grinning like a court jester.

"Admit defeat, little one," he cajoled. "Within two moves I shall have your king."

Lauriette gazed at him with warm blue eyes. "You think you have me, sir?" she mocked lightly. She moved her rook into place. "It would seem I have captured your queen, my lord."

"As well as my heart, my lady," he said softly.

Lauriette blushed deeply. "Your move."

Neville stood up and headed toward the liquor. "I concede the game to you," he said, pouring himself a generous glass of whiskey.

"Is your arm hurting?" she asked.

He tenderly massaged his shoulder. "It usually does after a rain." He gulped down the bitter liquid. "Where is Judd this evening?"

She glanced at the clock on the mantel. It was nearly seven o'clock. "He went into the village," she told him. Secretly, she prayed he would bring some word of

Devlin. She looked to Neville who was standing at the French doors, his back to her. He stood so straight and proud, his dark hair curling over his collar, his shoulders so broad. Shamefully, she looked away. She was looking at Neville as if he were Devlin.

"You did not sleep well last night," he commented.

She looked up at him in surprise. "How did you know?"

"I heard you," he answered, "pacing back and forth for hours."

Lauriette looked down at the chess board. Neville came and stood beside her. "It is nothing to be ashamed of, little one," he said sympathetically. "Many sleepless nights drift by me. Did you hear that voice again?"

Lauriette nodded numbly. "I am more afraid to go to sleep," she whispered. "Neville, I don't know what is happening to me . . . or why! Perhaps I'm going crazy. I don't know."

Neville knelt beside her and gently placed his hand on hers. "Judd told me you have gone through some rough times," he said softly, and she nodded. "Tell me."

She looked at him through tear-filled eyes and before she could stop herself, everything came pouring out. She told him of her betrothal to Evan and felt the heavy pressure of his hand on hers.

"And how did you meet my brother?"

Lauriette dried her eyes with the back of one hand. "He was kind enough to—help me when I was so—so desperate," she sighed, careful to omit their bittersweet interlude. "He was kind and gentle, concerned about my welfare, but I was too stubborn, too filled with pride to listen to him."

"He asked you to marry him?"

She nodded. "He wanted to give me his protection

and I refused it," she went on.

"Damnation!" he laughed. "The great Devlin Essex was actually refused? His famous charm did not work on you?"

Lauriette's eyes turned green with anger. "I will not sit here and listen to you berate Devlin!" she snapped.

"My apologies, little one," he retreated quickly. "Please go on. I wish to hear more."

Lauriette came to the most tragic part of her story. With great difficulty, her last days at Claymoor unfolded before Neville. As she told of her rescue, she broke down and could not go any further.

"I am sorry," he soothed, touching her hand to his lips. "I should not have asked you to go through it."

"I'll be all right, really," she gradually pulled her hands from his. "The past is slowly fading. I'm very happy now."

Neville stood, regarding her closely. "Is Devlin good to you?"

"Good?" she repeated, then smiled dreamily. "Yes, he is good to me and kind, generous—"

"So I see," he interrupted. "Good, kind, generous Devlin."

"My, my, such a serious conversation," Muriel's flighty voice brought silence to both of them. She glanced slyly at them, forming her own conclusions. "Lauriette, I spied cousin Judd riding towards the stables."

"Excuse me," she said and quickly departed out the French doors.

Neville watched as she picked up her skirts and ran across the lawn toward the stables. Muriel stood behind him looking directly over his shoulder, anger and jealousy rising within her.

The impatient tinkling of Lord David's bell brought Neville out of his daydreams.

"Never mind," Muriel said with a wave of her hand. "I will see what he wants."

Judd smiled as Lauriette entered the stables, breathless from running.

"Judd—"

"I'm sorry, Lauriette, but there was no news of Dev," he said hastily. "He should have been on his way back by now."

Lauriette looked at him critically. "There is more to this business than he said," she commented, able to clearly read Judd's face. "You need not say anything, my friend. I would not have you betray a trust."

"Lauriette—"

"I'm not asking you, Judd," she sharply cut in. "I have no rights where Devlin is concerned."

"I'm sorry."

"Come!" She smiled sadly, taking his arm. "You look exhausted."

They walked slowly, arm in arm, through the garden towards the house. Lauriette could not dismiss the painful wrenching of her heart. No word from Devlin. He had been gone a fortnight and having Neville at the house was a constant reminder of how much she missed him.

"I ran into Mrs. Gordon in the village," he said, breaking the silence. "She asked me to give you her love."

Lauriette smiled. "I haven't seen Clara since December,'" she whispered. "She must enjoy the gardener's cottage."

Judd laughed. "To be sure. I understand when Seth is finished here, Mrs. Gordon keeps him very busy at home."

As they entered the drawing room from the French doors, they were both startled by Lord David's angry voice then followed by a painful scream for help. Lauriette ran for the other door with Judd on her heels.

"Father!" Her cry was one of shock and horror. Muriel stood frozen, backed against the banister, her mouth wide open in a soundless scream. Lord David was near the head of the stairs, coughing seizing him. He could not catch his breath this time, his face an ugly shade of blue. Falling to his knees, he clutched at his chest.

Lauriette flew up the stairs, screaming for Judd, Neville, the servants to come to Lord David's side.

"The doctor!" she cried. "Fetch Dr. Quade quickly!"

With the assistance of several servants, they managed to get him into his room and back into his bed. Some of the blue had gone out of his face but he could only barely catch his breath.

"L-Laurie!" he rasped, his hand wildly grabbing for hers.

She caught his flailing hand, holding it tightly. "Please, calm yourself, Father," she soothed. "You'll be all right if you'll just calm yourself."

"N-not t-true," he choked. "T-tell me n-not true!"

"No more talk," she whispered, "not until Dr. Quade arrives." He clutched at her hands. "I'll stay here with you. I won't leave."

His tired brown eyes held hers and holding her hand tightly in his, he closed his eyes.

"Am . . . am dying," he moaned.

"No!" she flung at him, determination filling her. "I won't let you die, sir! I will not let you leave us!"

An eternity seemed to pass before she felt the pressure of Neville's hand on her shoulder. "Dr. Quade is here, little one."

Lauriette looked up to see Dr. Quade on the other side of the bed. She smiled down at Lord David's closed eyes. "I will wait outside with Neville," she said quietly, certain that he could hear her. "I will return just as soon as Dr. Quade will allow me."

Downstairs they all waited to hear Dr. Quade's opinion. Muriel sat playing with her fan, her pale face revealing nothing of the argument she'd had with the old man. Judd sat opposite her, quietly staring down at the floor. Neville had just finished a drink and was pouring himself another.

Lauriette stood near the open French doors watching the darkness envelop the grounds. Silently, she brushed away a tear. Why was it taking so long for Dr. Quade to examine him? It seemed as if he had been up there with Lord David forever!

Judd came up and stood beside her, his own thoughts much the same. "Why was he out of bed?" she asked. "He knew the walk would be too much for him. Why did he get up?"

"I have no answers," he said.

"I do not see why all the fuss," Muriel declared haughtily. "After all, he has had these attacks before."

Lauriette's eyes narrowed as she glared at Muriel. "You know as well as I his attacks have never been this severe."

Barton appeared in the drawing room, his face quite drawn. "Dr. Quade has finished, your ladyship."

Lauriette ran from the room with Neville and Judd right behind her. She met Dr. Quade on the stairs, his grave face expressing what Lauriette feared most.

"He is dying," her voice trembled.

Dr. Quade gently held her hands. "I am sorry, your ladyship, but there is nothing more to do but wait." His gray eyes were filled with tears.

"There's nothing I can do?" she asked with a bit of hope in her voice.

Dr. Quade sadly shook his head. "His lordship has been dying for some time, my lady," he whispered.

"I must be with him," she replied.

Neville placed a restraining hand on her arm. "You have been through a lot, little one, perhaps—"

"No!" she cut him off sharply. "He needs me! I will not desert him—ever!"

Two days dragged by slowly. Lauriette kept a constant vigil by Lord David's bedside, dozing now and then in the chair. His breathing was hard and labored, his face a deathly white.

"Laurie," he gasped. "Laurie."

She kneeled by his bed, taking his trembling hand in hers. "Please don't talk, father," she pleaded. "I'm right here with you—I won't leave."

He vaguely smiled at her, his brown eyes holding her so lovingly. "So much . . . like . . . Marianne," he rasped. "So . . . much . . ."

"Please don't tax yourself," she protested. "You must save your strength."

"No . . . time . . ." he murmured. "Devlin . . . where Devlin . . ."

"He's coming, Father," she said quickly. "He's on his way."

"Devlin . . ." he choked. "Dev . . ." His eyes closed as he drifted off once more.

Devlin! If only he were here! she thought desperately. *He should be here!*

"Barton!" Lauriette called as she hurried down the stairs. "Barton, I need you!"

Barton hurried from the kitchen and Neville and Judd came from the drawing room.

"Your ladyship?"

"Send Pauley to Cornwall," she requested, "to

bring back his lordship.''
''What?'' Judd exclaimed.
''Lord David is asking for Devlin,'' she said anxiously, ''and I am determined to have Devlin here!''
''I will send Pauley immediately.''
''Wait!'' Judd called to Barton. ''Lauriette, Dev is not in Cornwall now—he is in London''
Lauriette felt stunned. ''L—London?''
Judd turned to Barton. ''My lord is staying at Whitley House. It is imperative that he return immediately.''
''It shall be done, sir,'' Barton replied and disappeared into the kitchen.
Judd turned to Lauriette, feeling somewhat embarrassed. ''Lady Raine Whitley was in France. Lord David requested Devlin to escort her to London. She was Theresa's mother.''
''You owed me no explanations, Judd,'' she answered quietly.
Neville looked severely at Judd. ''But he did, little one,'' he said harshly. ''It is not easy to take when you are deceived.''
''Now just a min—''
''Please!'' she exclaimed, filled with frustration and weariness. ''Nothing matters except that Devlin return!''
''Little one,'' Neville said softly, ''you have been at Father's side for three days. You should rest, just for a while.''
Lauriette gazed up at the top of the stairs. ''Not yet, Neville,'' she declined. ''I don't want to leave him.''
''But you have to take care of yourself, Lauriette,'' Judd urged.
''I'm fine, Judd, really I am,'' she replied. ''I just can't . . . can't leave him alone.'' She turned and hur-

ried up the stairs.

Judd and Neville looked at each other for a long moment, then went their separate ways.

Thirty

Salene gazed down at Devlin waiting for her in the foyer, a satisfied smile on her face. She had waited several months for him to return to London and she knew eventually he would. Devlin was just not the domesticated type. He thrived on variety and excitement, just as she did.

She slowly descended the stairs, noting the gleam of appreciation in Devlin's dark gaze. Her dress was an empire style, the latest Parisian fashion, its neckline plunged dangerously low exposing most of her full breasts.

Devlin smiled sardonically, lifting her fingertips to his lips. "I received your note," he told her. "How did you know I was in London?"

She motioned toward the drawing room. "There is nothing that goes on in London I do not know about," she replied proudly. Salene turned and looked deeply into his eyes. "I have been waiting a long time for you to return, Devlin,"

"You were that certain of me?"

Salene threw her arms around him. "We are too

much alike, darling,'' she purred. ''You thrive on excitement, just like I do.''

Devlin was becoming aroused by her nearness. He inhaled the exotic perfume she wore; his head clouded.

''I have been so lonely without you,'' she murmured, ''so very lonely.''

Roughly, he crushed her to him, his mouth bruising hers. Salene reacted instantly, her hands hurriedly trying to rid him of his coat.

''Upstairs,'' she whispered urgently, ''take me upstairs!''

Sweeping her up in his arms, he mounted the stairs two at a time.

Within moments they both were divested of their clothing, Salene on the bed anxiously waiting for Devlin to join her. He stood over her for a long moment, taking in her knowing smile and parted lips.

''Please, Devlin,'' she whined. ''I've waited so long.''

His manhood stood out proud and erect, throbbing for release. Playfully, Salene ran her finger from his matted hair to the very tip of it.

''Take me, darling,'' she cried breathlessly. ''Take me!''

Devlin fell upon her, his hands roughly caressing her full breasts. She squirmed underneath him, her nails sadistically raking his back.

''Harder, darling, harder!'' she commanded, as she dug her heels into his buttocks.

He drove into her with such violence, but she begged him for more, cried for him to hurt her. Devlin had to have this release, had to get rid of the anger which had built up inside him. But now all he could see were blue-green eyes smiling at him, trusting him. All he could hear was Lauriette's gentle voice full of passion whispering, *My love, my dearest love!*

He moaned deep in his throat as his release came. "Laurie," he whispered. "Laurie."

Salene's climax was shortlived as Devlin breathed Lauriette's name in her ear. Her body turned to stone even as his hands still brutally caressed her. She struck out at him with all her might as he rolled away from her. Devlin looked confused.

"I should have known," she said in a small, hard voice. He looked up at her, his own anger rising. "It finally happened to you."

Devlin was hastily dressing. "I don't know what the devil you're talking about!" he growled.

"Of course you do!" she retorted. "*She* sent you away from the nuptial bed and you came here looking for comfort!"

"You are insane!" he argued.

She sat in the middle of the bed on her knees, her breasts heaving in anger. "You could have had me any time," she snarled. "We could have been so happy together but you could not bring yourself to marry me! Instead you wedded a girl who has bewitched you into thinking she is so innocent!"

"Lauriette is her name, right?" she went on, ignoring the black storm brewing above her head. "How foolish you were, my dear! I've heard a great deal about your *innocent* bride! You fool! Do you think *she* waits patiently for your return? Hah! Did you even bother to check into her background? Your Miss Innocent was once involved with Sir Henry Branscombe, her sister's husband. Did you not know that? Strange, it is common knowledge in London! What a time she must be having with your loyal cousin to warm her backside while you are here with me! Your Lauriette is nothing but a little American whore acting the part of a grand lady!"

Salene had gone too far and his temper exploded as

nothing she could have imagined. With a deadly growl, he grabbed her up by her shoulders, shaking her murderously.

"You bitch!" he shouted, his eyes black with fury. "You're not even worthy to whisper her name! The only thing that infuriates you is that you could never measure up! Think you she's cold? Hah!" he laughed cruelly. "The lovely lady has more passion than you could act up in months. And that passion belongs to me and me alone!"

Angrily, he flung her from him and grabbed up his coat.

"Where are you going?" she demanded.

Devlin stopped in the doorway and looked back at her, his eyes glistening black. "Away from you, madam," he said lowly. "Away from the stench of this whorehouse."

He left her and hurried down the stairs, hearing Salene's enraged cries and the breaking of glass. Picking up his greatcoat and hat, he opened the door and ran into Pauley, one of his livery.

"Pauley! My god, man, what—"

"Please, your lordship," he blurted out breathlessly, "yer needed at Essex Hall!"

Thirty-One

Lauriette paced back and forth across the drawing room, her nerves wound up tight like a spring. Four more days had gone by since Pauley left for London, four long bitter days and nights sitting by Lord David's bedside, watching him die inch by inch.

Dr. Quade was with him and requested she wait there. It was almost unbearable for her to be so far from him.

"Lauriette," Neville said softly, "Barton has brought you some food." He motioned to the tray on the table.

"Thank you . . . no."

She turned her head, unable to even look at the food. It was hard to even think of eating with Lord David just upstairs, barely hanging onto life.

Neville looked at her with growing concern. Her vigil was beginning to wear her down, her pale face and sunken eyes gave way her lack of sleep and not eating. She was totally exhausted but refused help from him or Judd.

"Little one, please go rest," Neville gently urged.

"I'll stay with Father for awhile."

"I couldn't, Neville," she weakly protested, her eyes filling up again. "He has been the only father I've known. I can't rest. I'll see it through with him."

Muriel came in from the garden dressed in one of her cheeriest dresses. "Good heavens, Lauriette," she said in a surprised voice, "you look absolutely terrible!"

"Shut up, Muriel!" Neville snarled.

She batted her eyes innocently. "My dear Neville, I am only saying this for her own good," she stressed. "After all, she cannot greet Devlin looking this way—not after he has seen so many beauties in London. Do you think he will smile at her if she greets him thus?"

Lauriette felt her anger rising. "I've not the time or patience to primp before a mirror!" she drawled.

Muriel stood before Lauriette, a hard cold look in her eye. "It does you no good to cater to his lordship, you know," she said smartly. "His will was made out long ago. There is nothing you can gain from him now. I cannot believe he has hung on this long! If he is going to die, I wish he would hurry and do it!"

The taut thread that held Lauriette's finely strung nerves was severed by Muriel's cutting words, and with an enraged cry, Lauriette hit the woman with all her might. Muriel cried out as she staggered back, her eyes wide with disbelief.

"How dare you!" Lauriette hissed.

Neville stood still, his mind still rejecting what he had just witnessed.

"Get out of here!" Lauriette screamed almost hysterically. "Get out of my sight!"

Muriel turned and fled out to the gardens leaving Lauriette trembling with anger. At that moment Judd burst into the room, hauling Pauley in with him.

Judd's face was beaming. "He's coming, Lauriette!" he said excitedly. "Dev will be here within the hour!''

''Thank God!'' Lauriette cried, throwing her arms around Judd. ''Thank God! I'll tell Lord David.'' She started up the stairs.

''You found his lordship in London, Pauley?'' Neville asked loudly.

''Aye, milord,'' the young man smiled.

''Was he at Whitely House?''

Pauley's pleased face had fallen and he lowered his head. Lauriette stood silent half way up the stairs.

''Neville!'' Judd began to protest.

Neville angrily held up his hand. ''Pauley, where did you find my brother?'' he demanded sternly.

The young man hesitated.

''Pauley!''

''I . . . I found his lordship . . . at the 'ouse . . . of Lady Salene Thompson.''

Neville gazed up at Lauriette's drawn face, satisfied with Pauley's answer. His brother was not perfect and he desperately wanted her to know.

Dr. Quade met a subdued Lauriette at the door. He spoke not a word, only sadly shaking his head. There was no glimmer of hope.

Lord David was asleep, and quietly Lauriette took her seat by the bedside. She was stunned by Pauley's words. She sighed. It was their agreement. She had agreed to his little indiscretions, as he so delicately put it. She had no right to feel so hurt by the news. After all, he was a virile man.

Lady Salene Thompson. The name sounded familiar. She had seen her once at Madam Charbeau's. The recognition of the woman brought out a hurtful kind of anger and jealousy that surprised Lauriette. Devlin was a man of the world, she could not ask for any more than he was willing to give! She would not think anymore of him . . . his hands, his lips—she must not!

"Laurie!" Her name sounded more like a sweet caress. She looked up; her head swam at the mere sight of his broad frame filling the doorway.

He looked so tired, so worn, she thought. His riding clothes were covered with dust from the hurried journey. Devlin quietly closed the door.

"Scamp," his father rasped weakly.

Devlin seated himself on the bed, his face very grave. "I came as soon as I could, Father."

"L-Lady Whitley?" he managed to get out.

"She is safe," he whispered, his brown eyes misting over. "All went very well."

"L-Laurie."

Devlin motioned for her and quietly Lauriette knelt by his bedside. "She is right here, father."

He smiled weakly. "S-so much . . . like . . . Marianne."

Devlin felt a lump form in this throat. "Aye . . . father."

"I want . . . no . . . no . . . mourning for me. This household . . . is to go . . . go on as it . . . always has . . ."

"Father, we'll talk about this later," Devlin rushed in.

"Love Laurie . . . for always . . . my son." He began to cough.

"I will, I will," Devlin barely murmured.

"I . . . was hard . . . on you"—he could barely form the words now—"because . . . I loved . . . you best . . ."

Devlin rose from the bed, hot tears blurring his vision. Quietly, he found the door and with a sob, let himself out.

"Laurie!" Lord David cried out, grasping for her hands. "Laurie, I . . . cannot . . . find you!"

Lauriette held both his hands tightly. "I'm here, Father, I'm right here,'' she whispered, tears streaming down her face.

''Marianne.'' His face seemed to take on a glow as he said his beloved's name. ''Mari—'' A strange hissing sound came from his throat, his hands relaxed in Lauriette's. It was over. He had finally been reunited with his Marianne.

Lauriette was numb, her grief deeper than anyone could imagine. She sat silently, hands still holding onto his, staring down at his face now calm and serene in death. She had truly loved the old gentleman as she never had her own father. Now he was gone, leaving a cold void deep within her.

''Come, Lauriette.'' She barely heard Judd's soft voice trembling with emotion. ''You can do no more for him.''

He gently took her arm, helping her up. ''He is . . . happy now,'' she murmured in a small, childlike voice. ''He is . . . with his Marianne now.''

''You have to look to yourself now,'' he quietly urged.

Outside, Judd closed the door and turned his full attention to Lauriette. It was plain to see she was in shock. She needed her husband at this time, not him. She needed Devlin!

Thirty-Two

Devlin stood in the shadow of a huge oak tree, silently watching Lauriette sitting quietly on the cold stone bench not more than a few feet from him. She had changed so much in the weeks he had been gone, he hardly recognized her. That she had lost some weight was plainly evident from her sunken cheeks and ill-fitting clothes. Her eyes, red and swollen from crying, wrenched his heart. Judd told him she had stayed with Lord David from the beginning of the last attack. Could she have loved him that much, to sacrifice her own health? Was there truly such a powerful love as that?

He heard her sigh and he smiled sadly. Even in her present disheveled state, she was lovely. Her unselfish attitude toward his father made her even more special to him. He was moved by her, touched by her. He did not like the feelings erupting inside, but yet he could not ignore them. He would have to deal with them realistically, but not now, not when she needed him.

"Laurie."

Devlin stood before her as a towering giant, his

broad shoulders blotting out the lights from the Hall. Her eyes met his and held for the eternity of a moment. Her pain and misery were reflected in his own and at that blunt realization, the feeling of lethargy vanished as a wracking sob tore at her throat.

Kneeling beside her, Devlin tenderly pulled her into his arms. She wept bitterly as he held her to him, his hand stroking her soft mane of brown hair. Lauriette hid her face in his coat and cried till all that came were dry sobs.

"I am home, cherub," he whispered softly. "Everything will be all right now."

In an instant Devlin had her securely in his arms and walked back to the Hall. Lauriette snuggled against his neck, a feeling of warmth flooding over her. Taking a shortcut through the drawing room, Devlin completely ignored the startled expressions of Neville and Judd.

Up the stairs with a sureness the surprised even him, Devlin did not stop until he had Lauriette safely within their bedroom.

In total darkness, he tenderly set her feet on the floor. His hands remained on her waist, and gradually he pulled her to him. It was a dream, she told herself, as he drew her even closer. She had waited so patiently for his return for this moment. . . .

His lips found hers with a sudden brutality which caused her to gasp. He pulled back a moment then kissed her again, crushing her to him. Molding her trembling body against his he breathed in the scent of her.

"Cherub, cherub," he moaned, burying his face in her neck.

Knowing full well the grief he was experiencing, Lauriette held him to her, entwining her fingers in his dark curly hair.

His thumbs, hooked in the shoulders of her gown,

swiftly eased the sleeves down her arms. His lips burned a trail from her neck to her shoulder.

Lauriette was suddenly aware of his seductive moves. Her mind was full of the nearness of him, the clean, manly scent of him, his warm breath against her neck.

Holding her tightly against him, Devlin managed to undo the tiny buttons that traveled down the back of her dress. The dress fell around her ankles. Her now aroused breasts pushed fiercely against the sheer chemise, demanding to be set free.

Devlin's lips, moist and warm, plundered her mouth once again causing her mind to reel. She felt herself being lifted off the floor and tenderly placed on the bed only a few feet away. She lay quietly, her breath panting, waiting . . . waiting.

The huge bed sagged beneath his weight and suddenly Lauriette felt his hands upon her, caressing, loving. Tears stung her eyes as the hurt of a few hours before drifted into her mind. Impulsively, she touched Devlin's face and was seized with the desire to comfort when she found his cheek wet with tears.

"Oh, Dev, Dev," she whispered, a sob choking her. "Please, make this . . . this hurt go . . . away. . . ."

His lips moved possessively over her tearstained face, his hands so gently caressing. He then brushed the hair away from her face, his eyes searching the darkness. Salene's slanderous words came to him and he shoved them away. Lauriette was *his* wife, *his* possession!

His knee parted her thighs and Lauriette urgently pulled him against her. It had been so long . . . so very long! Her arms encircled his neck and she rapidly placed kisses along his neck and ear.

Devlin took her with tenderness and brutality combined, his need for her driving him wild with desire. He bent his head, his mouth finding the taut nipple of her left breast. Lauriette moaned again and again as he came and withdrew slow and easy, prolonging his passionate torture of her.

Her hands traveled over the tense muscle of his back, her heart reveling in his power, his strength. Her entire being was aflame, so white hot that she cried out, "Now! Now!"

Devlin's body shuddered as Lauriette reached that passionate plateau with such abandon, he drove into her again and again, unable to get enough of her.

She lay in the protective circle of his arms, her cheek resting contentedly on the silken hair of his chest. Nothing mattered now except he was home and here in bed with her. It did not seem to matter now how many women he had been with in London or Cornwall or wherever he was. The point was he returned to her—he had not tired of her!

Devlin looked down at Lauriette, her even breathing indicating she was sound asleep. Stroking her tangled brown curls, he felt a pang of guilt. If he had Salene there at that moment, he would have killed her! There was not a shred of truth to anything she'd said. He knew that now. Lauriette was *his*! She carried his name as someday she would his children. She belonged to him and he would never let her go.

Easing himself out of bed, he shrugged on his robe and padded to the window. Love? The word forced its way into his mind and immediately he rejected it. No, there was no such thing as love! It was true he felt affection and obligation towards her, but that was all, nothing more.

Startled, he recalled his father's words. *Love Laurie for always, my son.* And he had answered: *I will.*

Anger shot through him, anger directed at himself.

How could he have promised such a thing when he did not even believe in love! Being away from Lauriette had done no good, it was plain he was obsessed with her.

Lauriette moaned, her head moving from side to side.

"Laurie! Where are you!" the voice called anxiously.

Again, she moaned.

"Laurie, answer me!"

It was the same masculine voice which woke her night after night. Frantically, she tried to open her eyes.

"Laurie, my puppet, I need you! Where are you! Answer me!" the voice was becoming insistent and gruff.

"N—no," she moaned.

"Hurry, Laurie, hurry!"

Her eyes flew open wide as she lay there as in a frozen state, her mind whirling.

"Laurie . . . Laurie . . . Laurie . . ." It sounded so far away.

"Go away!" she cried, sitting up and putting her hands over her ears. "Please go away!"

Devlin was at the bed in two easy strides. "What is wrong?" he asked anxiously.

"Didn't . . . didn't you hear him?" her voice trembled.

Devlin arched a brow. "Who?"

"I . . . I don't know," she barely whispered.

Under his careful gaze she hurried out of the bed, quickly putting on her wrapper. Lauriette walked to the window and stood there for the longest time just staring out.

The moon appeared from behind a cloud, casting its light on Lauriette's troubled face. Devlin gazed at her with a mixture of admiration and awe. Crystal tears trickled from the blue-green eyes.

Devlin moved to her with pantherlike grace. He casually leaned against the wall never taking his eyes from her.

"There is someone out there," she said fearfully. "I don't know who . . . but there is someone, I know it."

"Laurie—"

"You didn't hear the voice, did you?" she said evenly. "The truth."

Devlin bowed his head. "No."

With shaking fingers, she brushed away the tears. "Perhaps I am slowly going crazy. The dreams, the vague recollections, the mysterious voice—"

"*Laurie! Laurie!*"

Lauriette stiffened, her eyes scanning the night. "He's calling me again!" she gasped, backing away from the window. "You had to hear him that time!"

Devlin grabbed her by the shoulders, pressing his face close to hers. "Cherub, look at me," he demanded. She looked up. "Let me help you."

"*Laurie! Laurie!*"

"You don't believe me!" she accused, her hands tightening on his robe. "He's there!"

His hands shook her. "Listen to me!" he urged. "It's only your grief!"

"No, no!" Lauriette cried. "It's real! It happened before . . . when you left . . ."

He kissed her frightened, protesting lips, determined to blot out whatever torment she had. There was such a need, such a damning need to protect her!

Thirty-Three

Lauriette restlessly paced back and forth, her mind in constant turmoil. No matter how she tried, she could not escape her depression. She attributed it to Lord David's death but it was more, much more.

Muriel, dressed in a stunning riding habit, strode in with an air of snobbish arrogance. Her lovely face smiled, but that smile did not extend to her cool brown eyes.

"I have a surprise for you," she said brightly. "You have a visitor, my dear. I ran into him on my way back."

"A—a visitor?" Lauriette looked toward the drawing room doors, a happy cry escaping her lips. "Henry!"

Henry looked at her a long moment, his boyish smile lighting his entire face. Lauriette rushed at him, arms outstretched. They hugged each other tenderly. Henry then stood back, holding her at arm's length.

His brows drew downwards. "You look so pale and thin."

She laughed happily. "Somehow I knew you were

going to say that."

"Well, if you two will excuse me," Muriel said graciously, "I will go and change," and she quickly left the room.

"Please, come in and rest yourself," she urged him. "I'll have Barton fix us some refreshments."

"No, no," he protested. "I can only stay a moment. I would have come sooner but I thought it best to wait at least a fortnight after Lord Essex's death."

Lauriette lowered her eyes.

"So much has happened since the night of the Winter Ball," he continued. "I was frantic with worry when Jonas told me you were missing!"

"Please forgive me for being so thoughtless," she said quietly. "It—it was such a difficult time for me—for both of us."

"And then when Marie told me of your marriage to Essex . . ." Henry faltered.

"You were shocked," she finished for him.

"But why, Lauriette?" he asked harshly, placing a hand on her arm. "Why the devil himself? Did you not know of his dealings, his privateering, his tainted reputation with the ladies?"

Lauriette's eyes narrowed, flashing green. "And did you not know of Evan's exploits and yet fail to warm me?" she countered. "And as for Devlin, I know of no devil! When you are speaking of my husband, sir, you will talk of him with the respect due a Marquess!"

Henry's cheeks flushed red. "I was beside myself with worry!" he exclaimed. "Marquess or no, the man's reputation is sordid!"

Lauriette jumped to her feet, anger boiling inside her. "How dare you!" she stormed.

Henry stood up quickly. "I dare because I care about you!"

The anger died in her eyes as she turned away from

him. Suddenly, his hands were upon her shoulders.

"I have always cared about you," he whispered tenderly. "The duel I fought with Brimley was not because of Marie-Claire. It was because of you—the way he hurt you!"

"Henry, please—"

"I went crazy when I heard you were missing," he railed, turning her around to face him. "Then to find out you refused Marie's help to get away from Brimley and turned and married this—this notorious rake!"

Lauriette went pale. "Marie-Claire was going to—to help me get away?" A surge of hysteria passed through her. "Please leave, Henry."

"But—but, Lauriette!"

"Lord Branscombe, my wife asked you to leave," Devlin's presence filled the doorway.

His face angry and sullen, Henry stiffly bowed to Lauriette then nodded curtly to Devlin. He picked up his hat and gloves, and without further prompting, left.

"That was quite a touching little scene, my lady," Devlin's voice was low and very calm.

He was behind her, roughly turning her to face him. Lauriette was surprised and somewhat frightened by his mask of fury, his eyes like sharp onyxs boring into her.

"Why did you not tell me of your relationship with Branscombe!" he growled.

"Relationship? He's my sister's husband!" she answered hotly.

"I see," he replied in a low tone. "And before he belonged to your sister?"

"I . . . was fond of him," she said defiantly.

"Why did you not tell me this?"

Her face was red with anger. Never had she seen Devlin like this. "I did not think it important!" she replied tartly. "What's past is past! Why have you told me of all the women in your life?''

Devlin stared at Lauriette in exasperation. ''What I do, madam, is none of your business!'' he flung at her, eyes like shining coals.

''If that is your attitude, my lord,'' she replied hotly, ''then you've no right to question me!''

''Right!'' he exploded, grabbing her by the shoulders. ''Madam, you are forgetting one important fact—you are my wife!''

''As you are my husband!'' she cut in. ''But that fact does not stop you from taking your pleasure wherever you are!''

Her taunting words only pushed him further. ''You belong to me, Laurie, to do with as I will,'' he drawled, his face so close she could feel his hot breath. ''No man will ever know you as I do—no man will dare lay a hand on you or I'll kill him!''

She wrenched herself free of his grasp and ran to the door.

''I am no man's chattel!'' she shouted fiercely, her eyes glistening with tears. ''I am your wife but not your possession! You are stronger than I and can rule my body, but not my mind or my heart, sir! Just because you are used to dealing with fine ladies who prostitute themselves, do not put me in the same category!''

With a tearing sob, she fled the room. Devlin hotly pummeled the back of the divan with his fists, his temper out of control. When Muriel had found him in the library and smugly told him of Lauriette's visitor, he could hardly withhold the angered look until she left him. Seeing Branscombe there with her, his hands on her shoulders, his voice telling her how much he cared—he could barely restrain himself.

Lauriette had spoken no words of endearment to him, telling him in fact to leave. But the anger that rose up inside him could not be dealt with and it had to erupt.

Slowly he sat down, head between his hands. He was becoming like a madman and he did not know how to stop these strange emotions bubbling inside him.

Lauriette ran from the house towards the protection of the woods, tears of anger blurring her vision. "Damn him!" she cursed under her breath. "Damn him!"

Out of breath, Lauriette sunk to her knees. She was in a heavily wooded area, and relaxing, she leaned against a huge oak. It was childish of her to run off like that, but after Devlin's outburst she could stand that house not one moment longer!

How could he have spoken to her like that? She did nothing wrong, nothing to deserve the tongue-lashing he had just given her! That man! She had never seen him so angry.

It was almost as if he were—no, it was not jealousy. Couldn't be! Sighing, she closed her eyes. No, he was only angered because he thought someone might want to play with his pleasure-toy!

The sound of breaking twigs caught Lauriette's ear. "Who is there?" she called out.

No answer came.

She stood slowly, cautiously. A feeling of dread came over her, the same kind of feeling she experienced at the cottage. She began to walk slowly at first, then as she heard the heavy footsteps behind her, she broke into a run.

"Laurie, my puppet," the familiar voice called to her. "Laurie . . . Laurie."

Her flight stopped abruptly in a sudden need to know this part of her forgotten past once and for all.

"Laurie . . ." The voice was barely above a whisper; he was standing but a few feet from her.

As in a dream, she turned in slow motion. Lauriette opened her mouth to scream, but terror paralyzed her vocal cords. The human standing before her was but half a man, his face cut and burned beyond recognition, glistening blood covering the white shirt and tan breeches. One arm hung limply by his side, the other pressed against a wound at his throat, blood oozing between his fingers.

"Laurie . . ." The monster reached out a bloody hand to her. "Laurie . . ."

"No . . . no!" a loud strangled scream tore from her throat. "*No!*"

The thing limped toward her and with a cry of horror, Lauriette sunk to the ground, darkness encompassing her.

Thirty-Four

Devlin had just returned from a hard ride on Nomad and was leaving the stable when Neville intercepted him, on his face an expression of concern.

"Have you seen Lauriette?"

Devlin looked at him a long moment, his brows drawn downward. "I do not constantly keep watch on my wife, Nev." he retorted.

Neville's head jerked up in surprise at his brother's tone. "Oh? From the raised voices coming from the drawing room an hour ago, I would dispute that statement."

"What goes on between Lauriette and myself is none of your business!" he said crossly.

"Oh, forgive me, my lord," he replied mockingly, bowing from the waist. "I did not know I was treading upon such dangerous ground."

"Damn you, Nev," he murmured through clenched teeth.

"Why, brother?" Neville asked angrily. "Why do you fly into a rage whenever someone mentions Lauriette's name affectionately or even inquires about her?

Any other time you do not seem to give her a second thought.''

''Neville, stay out of things which don't concern you!''

''She does concern me, Dev!'' he shouted. ''She is being put through her own private hell and you just turn your head!''

''Nev—''

''Do you even realize how many sleepless nights she has had since we buried father?'' he went on, cutting off Devlin's reply. ''A hell of a lot! Almost every night! How do I know? Because we sit up until daybreak together . . . playing chess or piquet . . . anything to relieve the hellish torment that is tearing her apart inside.''

Devlin's eyes bore into his brother's. ''How long?''

Neville gazed down at the ground. ''Since the night you left for Cornwall,'' he answered sullenly. ''Whether we hear it or not, she truly does. Only when she was so concerned about father did she not hear it, but the nightmares were still there.''

''Why did she not—''

''Not tell you?'' Neville finished for him. ''Though Lauriette has not come right out and said so, she does not want to depend upon you for anything, does not want to bother you with her fears. Any fool could see that! Why, Dev? Why should your wife feel that way? Are you tired of her already! Is that why you treat her this way, why you sleep in your old room?''

Devlin exploded, grabbing Neville by the front of his shirt. ''Damn you, Neville!''

Neville's eyes were as angry as Devlin's. ''So that is it.'' his eyes widened with surprise. ''I've found your Achilles' heel! You are afraid—''

A blood-curdling scream of horror pierced the quiet evening and startled, Devlin let his brother go.

"What was that?"

"Laurie—it was Laurie!" Devlin exclaimed and headed in the direction of the scream with Neville close behind.

They found her where she had fallen, her body limp, her face a deathly pale white color. Devlin surveyed the area, searching . . . searching.

"Oh, little one!" Neville cried, kneeling beside her. Very gently he lifted the upper half of her body into his arm, her head resting against his chest.

Devlin turned and was taken aback by the tender scene. Memories of ten years before of Neville and Theresa flashed through his mind. Surely Neville could not be forming an attachment to Lauriette!

"Nev, find Judd and have these woods scoured," he said curtly. 'I'm not sure what to look for . . . something or someone who could have terrified Lauriette."

Bending, he possessively removed Lauriette from his brother's embrace. Lauriette sobbed a moan. Without another word, Devlin turned toward the house.

"Oh, my lady! My lady!" Dolly cried as the door to the bedroom burst open.

"A basin of cool water and cloth," he ordered, and the little maid ran to fetch it.

Carefully, he laid her on the bed, feverishly working with the top buttons of her dress. He stroked her cheek lovingly, his lips brushing her forehead.

"If only you could understand my torment, cherub," he fiercely whispered. "I'm a very independent man who vowed long ago to keep my freedom. It is for your own good that I chose to sleep in another room. I have to get you out of my blood and the only way is to cut you out! I'm not the kind of man who belongs to one woman, a man to believe in love. I'm Lucifer the devil, the pirate, the rogue . . . the taker of woman's bodies!''

Angrily he got up and strode to the window. ''I have vowed to protect you, to keep you but I will do no more . . . I will give you no more! I care for you because you are my wife, my obligation. Outside of this there is nothing!''

''Milord?'' Dolly spoke from the door.

Taking the basin of water and cloth, he dismissed her. He would care for Lauriette himself. This little act of kindness, he could not deny himself.

''N-no . . . n-no . . .'' she moaned returning to consciousness. ''N-no . . .''

Lauriette's eyes gradually opened and there Devlin was, sitting so close to her, his face filled with concern. It had been so long, so very long since he had been in this room with her. The night of Lord David's death!

''The . . . the thing!'' she whispered, remembering in detail the gruesome horror. ''Oh, my God, my God!''

''What frightened you so?'' he asked gruffly. ''Was it Branscombe? Did he encounter you in the woods?''

Her mouth flew open in anger. ''Do you think I am so spineless I would be afraid of Henry?'' she pushed Devlin away from her. ''Go away! You'd never believe me anyway.''

''Cherub—''

The coldness in her now green eyes stopped him. ''I found the voice,'' she told him in a very even tone. ''It followed me back from my walk. At first I was afraid and ran but it became so soft—almost pleading. I turned—oh, Dev, it was terrible! This—this man standing only as far from me as you are now—his face so badly burned and—and bleeding. . . .'' Her voice trailed off.

Taking a deep breath she continued, ''He . . . was covered with blood . . . everywhere. He reached out for me . . . I remember nothing after that.''

''Well, we'll find him, whoever he is,'' Devlin scowled.

Lauriette looked at him, a bit startled. ''Then . . . then you do believe me?''

Devlin nodded. ''Judd and Neville are combing the woods at the moment,'' he informed her.

''They won't find him.'' Lauriette eased her way off the bed. She moved to the window, gazing out at the deserted courtyard. ''For some reason I know they won't find any trace of him.''

''I don't want you going into the woods anymore,'' he said flatly.

''Why?''

''You stand there and ask me why, knowing somewhere out there a madman is on the loose?'' he questioned insolently.

''But, Dev, he didn't want to hurt me,'' she explained quickly. ''He was trying to tell me something—something important. I know that now.''

''I want you here in this house where I can keep an eye on you!'' he flung at her.

''I understand clearly now,'' she shouted at him. ''But I will not be treated as a prisoner or a child, sir! You have no right—''

Before Lauriette knew what was happening, Devlin grabbed her wrist and jerked her into his arms. ''Rights, wife?'' he mocked. ''You would debate rights with me? When we married, you gave up all rights!''

Lauriette struggled in his steel-like embrace. ''Ours was a marriage of convenience,'' she reminded him. ''I forfeited none of my rights, sir! I am my own person and I always will be.''

Grabbing both her wrists, Devlin gently brought them to the small of her back, pulling her tightly against him. ''My wishes shall be obeyed no matter how many of your damn rights get trampled upon."

"You are a cruel devil!" she spat at him. "It is not that—that poor man in the woods that bothers you so. You're more bothered by this afternoon—and Henry!"

He looked down at her, anger rising within him. She was coming too close to the truth. He smiled cruelly. "Your Henry is too wise to cross me, madam," he said through clenched teeth. "he knows of my reputation. You are mine, Laurie, never forget that!"

Blinking back tears, she leveled her eyes with his. "Let me go, Devlin," she murmured softly, trying to control the tremor in her voice. "I am no use to you now. Let me leave. I'll go back to Philadelphia and need never bother you again."

Devlin was so furious, he could barely control his wrath. "*No!*" he roared.

"But why?" she went on dangerously. "Lord David is dead and he is the only reason you married me."

He released her wrists and walked to the door, keeping his back to her. Lauriette brushed away the tears, feeling hurt inside now that she had spoken the obvious truth.

"It . . . it is obvious to me that you've . . . you've tired of me," she said in a small voice.

"What?" Devlin whirled about.

Lauriette blushed deeply. "You've tired of me—I don't blame you. You warned me it would happen."

He closed the distance between them in an instant. Softly, he tilted her chin upward with his hand. "No matter what, cherub, you belong to me and I'll never let you go," he whispered. "And you will not go into the woods again!"

"Devlin!" she stormed.

"If I find you disobeyed me" he warned, "I'll lock you away in your room!"

"Do you think so little of me that you see me cuckolding you at every turn?" she cried.

"I've known enough women in my life to know one cannot trust any of them!" he returned smartly.

"I hate you!" she wrenched away from Devlin.

He walked to the door. "Do that, cherub," he raged. " 'Twill be better for you in the end."

Thirty-Five

The days were lazily drifting by, April was left behind as May brought about the world of blooming. It had been a quiet time for Lauriette, a time for her to look within herself for answers.

She had taken to heart Devlin's words and had not ventured any further than the gardens. After she was over her anger, she calmly looked at her unusual situation. Devlin was right. She was a fool if she continued to put herself in a dangerous situation. Also his threat to her caused a shudder in her when she thought of it, and she decided not to provoke him.

Sitting in the garden she absently stared at the forbidden woods. Judd and Neville had found no trace of the tortured man. There were not even footprints where she'd fainted—only her own. She was adamant about seeing the man—it was definitely no dream—but she could not ignore the fact the neither of them could find anything.

Devlin was off to Ravenswell, Lord Bottomsley's country home, a few hours ride from Essex Hall. Since their last heated encounter, he had remained more than civil to her but continued to sleep in a separate bedroom.

Lauriette bowed her head. It was hard to keep up the pretense of indifference when she ached so longingly inside. He was only a few rooms away but to her it might as well have been a million rooms. How could he have tired of her so quickly, when she was still a novice desiring to know more!

She sighed thoughtfully. The days had become increasingly long. Judd usually accompanied Devlin wherever he went. Neville was spending a great deal of time in the huge library. Even Muriel was hardly seen until supper, riding off on mysterious jaunts. Again, she was alone.

Lauriette thought of Henry. He had returned to visit her many times, but she had refused to see him. Her worry with him was twofold: She feared another argument with him, and she feared what Devlin would do.

"It must be a gloomy place you're thinking of."

She looked up to see Neville strolling toward her, a beaming smile upon his face.

"What brings you out of the library?" she inquired.

"A fair!" he announced.

"What?"

He sat himself on the ground at her feet. "Seth Gordon told me there is a county fair going on in the village." He smiled. "I came to ask for your company."

Lauriette thought of Devlin. "Well, I'm not—"

"Come with me, little one," he pleaded. "We'll dress as country folk and stay just long enough to see the sights. We'll be back long before Dev returns—I know that is what's bothering you."

Neville stood and grasped Lauriette's hand, pulling her up. "It has been a long time since you laughed," he said softly. "We'll forget everything today. Say you'll come!''

Giving his hand a squeeze, Lauriette laughed impishly. ''I'll come.''

Lauriette, dressed in a dark skirt, peasant blouse and green shawl, and Neville, dressed in blue knee breeches and homespun shirt, walked around the fair like two children off on an adventure. The day was calm and lovely, fluffy white clouds were drifting in the blue sky. The grounds were filled with people of all classes enjoying the delights of the fair.

There were many merchants who set up tents and were now calling in a singsong voice to the people who wandered about to come buy their wares. Lauriette smiled as Neville led her to many different tents and gazed in wonder at the freak animals the farmers had on exhibit.

''Are you hungry yet?'' he asked.

Lauriette laughed. ''I've hardly thought about it.''

He led her to a clearing, away from the throng of people and tents, down to a small pond.

''Wait here,'' he said. ''I'll be but a moment.''

Lauriette knelt down and taking a handful of water, splashed her face then dabbed it with the edge of her shawl. It was a most perfect day and she was enjoying it immensely.

''Lauriette!''

Henry was standing over her as she rose. He was superbly dressed and Lauriette found it odd he dressed so fancy for a county fair. His eyes moved slowly from her old straw bonnet to the faded skirt she wore.

''Hello Henry.''

''Why haven't you seen me?'' he demanded right off.

''Henry, there was no reason to have another scene,'' she answered gently.

"I only want to know one thing," he said. "Are you happy with Lord Devlin at Essex Hall?"

Lauriette managed a beguiling smile. "I am very happy, Henry," she answered. "I've never regretted my decision."

Henry looked at her squarely, his blue eyes searching her face. "I don't believe you," he said firmly. "But I will accept that answer for now."

"Here is something to eat," Neville cut in, casting a wary eye on Henry.

"Neville, this is my sister's husband, Sir Henry Branscombe," she reluctantly introduced. "Henry, Devlin's brother, Neville."

Henry's eyes raked over Neville, resting on the missing arm and Neville turned red with irritation.

"Your servant," Henry muttered, then turned to Lauriette. "I will see you again soon." He then made his way back to the fair and disappeared into the crowd.

Neville handed her some bread and cheese. "Did he insult you?" he angrily asked.

"No," she replied. "Please, let's forget about Henry and enjoy this day."

Instantly he broke into a smile. "Your're right, little one, let's not waste one moment."

It was almost dusk when they arrived back at Essex Hall. The day could not have been more perfect and nothing could erase the smile from Lauriette's lips. It had been so long since she had been anywhere—since the Winter Ball.

"Did you notice that fat woman faint at the sight of the cow with two mouths?" Neville laughed as they entered the drawing room.

"Poor things," she said softly, "to be put on display like that!"

"You should have had your fortune told."

Lauriette laughed. "Ah, but I do not believe in such things." She smiled. "When I was small, my brother used to threaten me. He would sell me to gypsies and have with me! Then I would have such dr—"

"So, you've been to the fair,"

Lauriette's voice faded as Devlin rose from the far chair, his face sullen, his eyes an icy black. Never before had she seen him so furious; even his stance expressed anger.

"You have been to the fair," he repeated.

"Yes, Dev," she bravely whispered. "Only for a few hours."

"He needs no explanation, Lauriette," Neville said angrily. "You are not his slave or prisoner and the tension he puts you under is cruel."

"Neville, stay out of this," he warned through clenched teeth, his hands doubled into fists.

"Like hell I will!" Neville returned heatedly, taking a step forward. "*I* pleaded with her to go! 'Twas something you wouldn't think of doing!"

"Go to your room, Lauriette," he ordered vehemently. "We'll talk later."

"You can—"

"It's all right, Nev, really," she reassured him. Lauriette turned back to Devlin. "I await your company, my lord."

Neville slammed the door after her and turned on Devlin, his face livid with rage. "So, are you going to do what you told her?" he demanded. "Are you going to kill me?"

"Do you realize how frantic I was to return home and find her gone?" Devlin demanded furiously. "Not letting anyone know where you were, no note—nothing!"

Neville smiled cruelly. "Lauriette is precious, brother." His eyes took on the blackness of the Essexes, his jaw set firm. "Her face took on a glow and she laughed . . . oh, how she enjoyed herself with me—*me* Dev! Just the simple things of the outdoors and nature that two people can share!"

"I've heard enough!" Devlin stormed, his temper becoming blacker.

Neville stood rigid, defying his brother. "She is a remarkable woman, you know," he continued. "So full of life, so much to give, so willing to share—"

"Damnation, man, hold your tongue!"

"Any man would be lucky to have her . . . never need to even look at another woman," he pushed goadingly. "Such a passionate little thing—"

"Damn you to hell!" He flew at Neville, savagely grabbing his homespun shirt and shaking him. "If you've touched her, I'll kill you!"

Neville laughed in his brother's face, a cold hard laugh. "I wish to God I had!" he flung in his face. "I would take her far, far away from your evil clutches!"

Devlin looked at Neville with a startled expression. Gradually, he let go, pushing Neville from him.

"You do not love her!" Neville accused. "You only desired what belonged to Brimley—just as you once did mine!"

Neville rushed at Devlin with such hatred, his fist catching Devlin squarely on the jaw. Devlin staggered back, his hand touching the corner of his mouth and finding blood.

"I'll take her from you!" Neville hissed. "Do you hear me, Dev? Right from under your nose. I'll seduce your wife and carry her off!"

Devlin's control snapped as he lunged for Neville, all the frustration and hurt from the past ten years drowning him.

Suddenly, there was another pair of hands prying his away. "Let go, Dev, let go!" Judd shouted. "You're killing him! Let go!"

Coming to his senses, Devlin released Neville and backed away as his brother collapsed to the floor. Neville was gasping, his hands clutching his throat.

Devlin moved unsteadily from the room and gradually made the stairs. He flung the bedroom door open with such force, Lauriette cried out in surprise.

"Dev, your face!" She rushed to him without a moment's thought of his brutal anger.

He easily caught both her wrists in a viselike grip and she gasped as his fingers cruelly bit into her skin. "Cherish this day the rest of your life, my lady," he sneered, his black eyes boring into hers. "It will be the last time you will act the part of a harlot!"

Uttering a cry of outrage, Lauriette managed to get a hand free and slapped him smartly. "How dare you!" she seethed, her face hot with hurt and anger.

Devlin caught her hand and jerked her to him, his cheek reddening with her handprint. "Did Neville touch you?" he said roughly. "Damn it, tell me!"

She grew stiff against him, her eyes dangerously flashing green. "Think what you like," she replied coldly. "You know women so well!"

Devlin gazed into her eyes and immediately knew the truth. He drew a heavy sigh of relief.

"You should not have gone," he snapped.

"What are you going to do now, my lord?" she returned harshly.

He eyed her angrily. "I should do what I threatened," he growled.

Suddenly she paled. "No!" she cried. "You'll not lock me in here! I won't be a prisoner again—ever! Do you hear?"

"Your threats fall on deaf ears, madam," he laughed bitterly.

Lying upon the table was a knife used in peeling

fruit. Before Devlin knew what was happening, Lauriette grasped it, turning the point until it touched the tender place between her breasts. Her eyes were glistening with tears.

"I will kill myself before I'd go through that hell again!" she vowed earnestly.

Devlin took a step toward her, his eyes frozen to the knife. "I would not do that, cherub," he said softly. "I remember your captivity, too."

Shutting her eyes tightly, tears streamed down her cheeks. Devlin moved swiftly, knocking the knife from her hand and pulling her into his arms in the same moment. He crushed her to him, one hand stroking her hair. The scent of honeysuckle filled him.

"I couldn't find you," he murmured. "I became frantic."

Lauriette pushed away from him, her eyes still showing anger. "Frantic at the thought of someone touching your harlot!" she threw at him.

He stiffened at her words, his eyes turning black. "If you dare disobey me, we'll find another form of punishment," he countered savagely.

"You cannot treat me like a child!" she cried.

Devlin smiled sardonically. "I can treat you any way I desire, wife."

"I do hate you!" Her voice shook with emotion.

"I believe you've told me that before." He laughed.

Lauriette was awake and dressed by the time the sun filled the sky. She had spent a restless night more awake than sleeping. Such a battle with Devlin, so much said that could not be forgotten. She sat in the drawing room, absently sipping on hot chocolate.

The door opened and Lauriette looked up with an expression of surprise. Neville entered dressed in elegant traveling clothes.

"Neville—"

"I've only a few minutes," he said quickly.

"What is happening? Where are you going?"

"To London," he grimly replied, crossing the room, "to the townhouse."

"It's my fault, isn't it?" she muttered.

"No, little one, no!" Neville protested. "Devlin and I have always been at odds. This parting was bound to come." Softly, he smiled. "We may look alike but that is where it ends."

"I shall miss you," she whispered.

Neville grasped her hand, pressing it passionately to his lips. "Then come with me, Lauriette," he begged, his eyes caressing her face. "Come with me to London."

For a moment she was speechless. Neville was offering her a way out of Essex Hall. Slowly her eyes beheld the whole of the drawing room, as if weighing it against the townhouse.

Withdrawing her hand, she rose and walked around the Chippendale sofa. "Neville, you're very kind to offer, but I can't."

Neville frowned. "You mean you won't."

"Won't—can't. It's all the same," she replied, looking down at her wedding band. "My place is here."

He looked at her with disbelief. "You cannot be serious!"

"But I am," she answered sternly.

Neville moved around to where she stood. "Lauriette, there is nothing for you here but loneliness and hurt," he argued.

"No matter what you say, my place is here."

His face was crestfallen. "It's me, isn't it," he declared. "Without this arm, I'm only half a man!"

"Oh, no, no," she protested. "How can you say that after all the time we've spent together? You know it

doesn't matter to me."
"Then why?"
She looked away from him. "I pledged my loyalty to Devlin," she sighed.
Neville's bitter laugh startled her. "You are too innocent for your own good, Lauriette," he said roughly. "My brother only knows how to use people. He is a proud, arrogant man who constantly needs to be assured he still has that magnetic charm he was born with."
"I'm only as good as my word," she defended.
Neville grabbed Lauriette's arm, forcing her to face him. "Your word means about as much to him as your feelings!" he snapped. "He will never love you. He is incapable of love!" He smiled lazily. "The devil has no heart."
Lauriette gazed at him steadily. "I will not desert him," she said firmly. "I gave my word."
He released her arm and shrugged silently. He slowly walked to the door, then turned.
"If you change you mind, little one, you will know where to find me" His voice was soft. "Good-bye." And blowing Lauriette a kiss, Neville disappeared out the door.

Thirty-Six

Four days drifted by since Neville's departure from Essex Hall. Devlin had become much more attentive to her since the day of the fair, his smile soft and gentle, his eyes that passionate brown that always set desire rising within her.

It was such a difficult situation, being man and wife in name only, at times she had to hold back the impulse to rush into his room and throw herself upon him! How she hated him at night when the dream would wake her and no one was there to comfort. How she hated him when her mind would drift and she could feel him lying beside her, caressing her, making her hot with desire. . . .

"Damn him!" she swore aloud, throwing a satin pillow at the door. Cradling her stomach, Lauriette rocked back and forth. Faith! Yearning for his touch caused her to ache inside so, it almost doubled her over. What was wrong with her? Didn't Devlin realize what he had done to her by teaching her the pleasures of love? "Damn him! Damn him!"

A gentle knock on the door brought Dolly inside.

"Beg pardon, yer ladyship," she bobbed a curtsey. "Lady Muriel requests yer in th' drawin' room. She says it's important."

"Thank you, Dolly." Lauriette smiled. "Tell her I'll be right down."

Coming down the stairs Lauriette frowned. Muriel had been absent every day for weeks now. She deliberately ignored any questions as to her whereabouts or about with whom she was keeping company. Now out of the blue, she needed to see Lauriette? For some reason, Lauriette felt all was not right.

At the door she stopped. "Dolly, where is his lordship?"

Dolly thought for a moment, then grinned. " 'Is lordship is at Myers' cottage a'checkin' repairs."

"I was just curious," Lauriette replied, and opened the door to the drawing room.

Muriel was lounging on the sofa, slowly fanning herself. As Lauriette closed the door, she smiled sweetly and got to her feet.

"You wanted to see me, Muriel?"

"Why, yes, I did," she said coyly. "I have brought an acquaintance back to Essex Hall and I am anxious for you to feast your eyes on him!" Muriel motioned graciously with her hand.

Lauriette went deathly pale, holding onto the back of a chair for support. "Evan!" It came out more like a gasp than a whisper.

Evan Brimley stood only a few feet from her, hands clasped behind his back, his inscrutable gaze resting on her face. He smiled slowly, silently nodding. "Hello, my dear."

This cannot be happening! she thought frantically. But it truly was, here and now, and Devlin was miles away!

"Well, Evan, I will leave you and Lauriette to reminisce," Muriel said sarcastically. "I am so happy I could help you surprise her."

"Muriel—"

"Don't thank me, Lauriette," she cut in hastily. "I was only too happy to help. And don't worry about the servants, darling girl, I'll tell them you are not to be disturbed."

The door closed quietly leaving Lauriette and Evan alone. He was still the same man that had humiliated her.

"I only arrived from Scotland a few days ago," he said. "I came as soon as I could."

"But why?" she asked. "Why?"

"I would have thought it obvious to you," he smiled. "I've come to take you home."

Lauriette stared at him completely dumbfounded. "You—you can't be serious!" she exclaimed.

"But I am. You are betrothed to me."

"Evan, listen to me," she tried to keep her voice calm. "I ended our betrothal the night of the Winter Ball. Remember?"

Evan nodded. "But you were only angry with me, my dear."

"Stop calling me that!" she cried, her nerves growing taut. "My name is Lauriette—Lauriette!" Distraught, she paced back and forth. "Surely Marie-Claire told you—sent you word—Evan, I married Lord Devlin Essex months ago!"

" 'Tis only an obstacle to be overcome," he shrugged. "We will just have it annulled."

He appeared so calm, so fully in control. "I won't leave here!" she declared stubbornly. "This is my home and here I stay!"

"You will leave here with me today," he said firmly, quietly.

Lauriette was infuriated by his calm manner. "I am no longer frightened by you, Evan!" she cried angrily.

"You cannot bully me like before."

In two easy strides he was beside her. Wrenching her arm behind her, Evan roughly pulled her to him. Only the set of his jaw betrayed his anger.

"You could not wait to climb into another man's bed!" he hissed. "You are mine! You always will be mine!"

"Let me go!" she gasped in pain as he applied pressure to her wrists. "Evan, you're hurting me!"

Judd spent a leisurely morning in the Boar's Head Tavern in the village and was now lazily galloping back to Essex Hall. The skies promised a rainless day and he smiled at the thought of sneaking a quiet nap under some leafy oak tree.

Then his thoughts drifted to Lauriette. Perhaps he would challenge her to a game of chess or piquet. In the past month he had learned the hard way that she was quite an opponent! And not only in games—as Devlin was rapidly finding out.

Judd reined in his horse as he came into view of the house. An elegant coach with four matching grays was waiting in the courtyard. Silently, he dismounted and made his way nearer the coach. A gold insignia almost blinded him as the sun emerged from behind a cloud.

"My God!" he muttered. "Brimley!" Making his way back to his horse, in an instant he was off; digging his heels into the horse's side.

Devlin was just finishing the inspection of the cottage and mounting his horse, when Judd appeared at the top of the hill. He hurriedly motioned for Devlin to join him.

"What's wrong?"

"'It's Brimley," he stated breathlessly. "He's here."

* * *

"I've never been yours, never!" Lauriette cried furiously.

"We were betrothed!"

"You severed that when you slept with Marie-Claire!" Her voice raised a degree.

Grabbing her chin viciously, Evan forced her to look up at him. "I own you!"

"I am another man's wife!"

"You slut!" he spat. "You little whore! You give a man a come-hither look, wanting to end up in bed with anyone, *anyone* but me! I'll have you, my dear Lauriette, one way or another. I'll have you!"

"Then you shall be with a corpse, Evan!" she countered. "For I'll kill myself first!"

"Tramp!" he sneered. He savagely backhanded her with such force, she hit the wall and slid down to the floor.

"Brimley!"

Lauriette barely heard the low growl. It sounded like Devlin's voice. Could it really be? She was so stunned, she was not quite certain what was going on about her.

Evan whirled around to squarely face the devil himself. Devlin's form filled the doorway, his face dark, his eyes dangerously black. Devlin's eyes strayed for a brief moment to Lauriette as Judd tenderly helped her up, tending her cut lip.

"It has been a long time, Essex," he said cordially.

Devlin nodded. "What brings you to Essex Hall?"

Evan glanced at Lauriette. "Lauriette, my betrothed."

Slow and easy, he half-smiled. "Then you've come for naught, for Lauriette is my wife."

"She will come with me." Evan shrugged casually.

Devlin's gaze rested on her, his face never altering, never showing the rage he felt as she nursed her already bruised cheek and swollen lip.

"We shall see," he declared. "Well, Laurie, make your choice. Whom do you prefer?"

Did he actually believe she had a choice? Why must he infuriate her so? A choice?

Gradually, Lauriette released Judd's arm and moved to Devlin's side. He smiled down at her, that odd crooked smile of his, and gingerly stroked her cheek.

"There! You see, Brimley? The choice has been made," he told him firmly. "She does not wish to go—and I would not let her go."

"I see she has you bewitched also."

Devlin looked at Evan closely.

"Tell me. When you bedded her, were you very disappointed she was not a virgin?" he asked harshly. "How did it feel to wed used merchandise?"

Devlin stepped forward, black fury enveloping him but felt Lauriette's hand restraining him.

" 'Tis not true, Evan," she said softly. "You have never touched me."

"Does she not lie well?" he asked Devlin. "Think back—your first night. No stain, no proof."

"Damn you!" Devlin growled and lunged for him. "I'll kill you!"

Devlin hit him squarely, knocking Evan to his knees. He stood over Evan, panting, his anger not abating. Slowly, Evan got to his feet.

"I demand satisfaction."

"This time I will not turn you away," Devlin replied savagely.

"The appointed time and place?"

"Vesner's Glen at dawn," he answered stiffly. "My second shall be Walter Armsby. Your choice of weapons?"

Devlin smiled sardonically. "Rapiers."

"No! Oh, no!" Lauriette cried, clutching Devlin's

arm.

Evan nodded curtly. "I will see you at dawn—if you are man enough to appear!"

Without further ceremony, Evan walked past them and out to his awaiting coach.

"How the devil did he get in here!" Devlin demanded.

"He—Muriel—" she stammered.

"I could certainly use a drink, Judd," he said. "How about you?"

Judd reached up, wiping his brow. "I will gladly join you, cousin," he half laughed. "I must say, he carries himself well."

"That is the secret to his reputation," Devlin confided. "He always gives the appearance of utter calm which usually completely intimidates his opponent."

"Amazing," he commented. "Does he ever lose his temper?"

Devlin smiled. "We shall see at dawn."

Lauriette stood back, her gaze moving back and forth from one man to the other, unable to believe this casual conversation going on!

"Are you both insane?" she exclaimed. "How can you stand here so casually and converse as if nothing has happened!"

"You are making too much of this, Laurie," Devlin said harshly.

"You can't be serious!" she returned crossly. "Dev, Evan is an expert with a rapier!"

He gazed down at her, his eyes a warm brown. Tenderly, he tilted her chin. "Could it be my lady cares about my safety?"

Lauriette brushed away his hand. "Please, Dev, be serious!" she urged. "Judd, say something! Tell him how foolish he is being!"

Judd looked at Devlin, his blue eyes twinkling with

amusement. "Dev, this is foolish," he repeated, then smiled. "I can hardly wait till dawn!"

"Damn you!" she swore out of frustration. "Damn you both! By all means, go out to Vesner's Glen at dawn and get yourselves killed! It'll serve you right!" With a choked sob she fled the drawing room, leaving behind a much subdued Devlin and Judd.

It was long into the night, a warm breeze billowing out the curtains as she lay upon her bed wide awake. Angrily, she brushed away tears which continued to plague her. This was so insane! Duelling, for what reason? Was it because of her or was it because of revenge which was planted ten years before?

No use. Sleep would never come this night! Donning her thin wrapper, Lauriette ventured out into the hall. How she wished Neville was here, perhaps he would have been able to talk some sense to his brother.

She stopped at Devlin's closed door, noting the light under it. So, she was not the only one who could not sleep!

Devlin lay there, hands clasped behind his head, staring a hole into the canopy. Since his coming to bed, he had lost most of his anger and had sobered completely. Brimley would never know how close he came to dying that first moment he entered the drawing room.

He could not erase the sight of Lauriette collapsed on the floor and Brimley standing over her. God! He should have killed him then and there, but something inside of him whispered *revenge . . . revenge . . .*

Devlin rolled onto his side, Brimley's words haunting him. *No stain . . . no proof!* There had been no blood staining his sheets that night so long ago, but that was not uncommon. Many women lost their maidenheads riding horses or falling. The lack of it could be easily explained . . . but damnation! How could Brimley have possibly known, unless—

A light knock on the door broke his thoughts. "Enter!"

Lauriette opened the door, a tray in her hand. She quietly closed the door behind her and glided across the room.

"I brought you a hot buttered rum, my lord," she whispered, sitting the tray and steaming mug on the nightstand.

Devlin was thoroughly enchanted at the sight of her in her thin blue silk wrapper. The night was extremely warm, the light from the candles outlining her naked body beneath the material. She sat down beside him.

"I see you could not sleep either," she sighed, folding her hands in her lap.

His eyes beheld her face, a frown covering his as the bruise on her cheek and her swollen bottom lip became quite prominent in his eyes. Without hesitation, he reached up, cupping her wound with the palm of his hand.

She smiled gently, placing her hand over his. It was such a magical moment, quiet and serene, if it could only go on forever!

"Please, Devlin," she murmured, "don't go at dawn."

He smiled crookedly. "Have you so little faith in my ability, cherub?" his voice was tender.

"I wish no one's death on my hands," she said simply.

Devlin withdrew his hand and leaned up on his elbow. "Brimley slurred your reputation!" he said raising his voice a degree. "And he made certain intolerable accusations . . ."

"But they are not true!" she defended. "You know that!"

Devlin looked away from her and her eyes grew

wide.

"You—you believed him," she whispered, unable to control her voice. "You actually believe I would let him touch me!"

"No—"

"Yes, you do!" she cried, jumping to her feet. "I can see it in your eyes." Lauriette gave out with a sobbing laugh. "How you must hate yourself, my lord, being saddled with a harlot for a wife!"

Lauriette fled the room, soundly slamming the door behind her.

"Lauriette!" he angrily shouted, but all he heard were her receding footsteps.

Thirty-Seven

The day broke with a gloomy touch of fog rising from the ground, a fine mist galling as Devlin and Judd mounted their horses.

"Some hellish day," Judd muttered, turning up the collar of his greatcoat.

Devlin's expression was black. "Fine day for a funeral," came his hard reply.

Lauriette, curled up in the windowseat, watched as the two horsemen rode out of sight. She leaned her bruised cheek against the coolness of the pane. A crystal tear rolled down as she once again felt the humiliation and hurt Devlin dealt her. How could he believe the worst of her? If so, why had he married her in the first place?

Revenge! Even the word stabbed her heart. The only way to avenge Theresa Whitley's death and the loss of Neville's arm! Devlin knew she was Evan's betrothed when he approached her. What a fool she had been! Devlin knowingly used her as an instrument of revenge and look at the length he went to accomplish what was going to happen now! He married her—merely to enrage Evan! There was no other reason. His concern for her well-being had been only a ruse! The realization struck her with such force, her heart felt as if it had been ripped out of her chest.

How could she have been such a fool—how?

Sir Martin Boyce stood between the cloaked figures, his voice was low and melodious. "This duel has been agreed upon by both of you. You will continue until honor has been satisfied."

Devlin and Evan nodded in agreement to Sir Martin's last officiating words. Vesner's Glen had a few guests invited to watch the duel, and they stood very quietly off to the side. This duel would be a fine one to witness, and some of the bystanders knew of the long-standing feud between the two.

Both men removed their greatcoats and Evan removed his jacket as well, but felt more secure in wearing his waistcoat. Devlin, on the other hand, was simply dressed in black breeches and a white linen shirt opened to the waist.

Devlin turned and nodded. Sir Walter Armsby presented the rapiers to him and taking much time, Devlin chose. Then Judd stepped forward, carefully grasping both swords and placed the tips together. This was the signal. The duel was to begin.

The sound of clashing steel pierced the early morning air as the small crowd formed a circle around the duelists. Brimley was quick to the attack, his lunges quick and solid but Devlin conceded him little ground, parrying his movement with ease. The rapiers flashed in the dull morning sunlight.

Devlin smiled sardonically at his opponent as Evan's breathing became somewhat labored at the onslaught of his thrusts. They circled slow and cautiously, each aware of the other's swordsmanship. They were very well matched.

It began misting once more as the sun hid behind a cloud. The clamor of steel rang out again and again as they thrusted and parried. Devlin carried himself well with pantherlike grace, his determination to best Brimley foremost in his mind.

Then suddenly Devlin lunged, as if tired of the game. He pressed forward, their swords locked near the hilt.

Devlin's black eyes bored into Evan's, his mouth set grimly.

"You will pay," he muttered.

They disengaged quickly but Brimley could not moved fast enough and Devlin's sword pierced his right shoulder, spurting blood. The sword clattered from his hand as he clasped the wound.

"You have drawn blood, Essex," Sir Martin stated swiftly. "Have you been satisfied?"

"I am most satisfied, Sir Martin," came his strong reply. He then turned to Evan. "I pray you will do the honorable, Brimley, and leave *my wife* in peace. She is mine and I share with no man. Remember that."

Devlin turned to walk off the dueling ground, when Brimley vehemently whispered, "Little whore!"

With a cry of rage Devlin whirled about, striking him with the flat of his sword. Brimley screamed in pain as he fell to the ground covering his now mutilated face.

Devlin seethed with fury. "You foul her good name by merely saying it, you bastard!" he whispered furiously. "If ever I see you again, I shall finish what I have started!"

Then it was over as Judd placed Devlin's greatcoat on his broad shoulders. They both quietly watched as a few of the onlookers helped carry Brimley off the field and into an awaiting coach.

" 'Tis over, cousin," Judd sighed with a smile,

"and quite admirably done I might add."

Devlin laughed bitterly. "He no doubt assumed I was a poor hand with a rapier."

"Glad I am this dastardly business is over!" he declared, gazing up at the ever-darkening sky. "A few more minutes here and you would have been dueling in a downpour."

"Well, then, come on," Devlin urged goodnaturedly.

"Let's show Lauriette the glad tidings!"

Devlin grimaced. "After last night's scene, I doubt if she'll be happy to see me alive."

Thirty-Eight

Lauriette sat alone in the windowseat staring intently at the courtyard and road leading from the Hall, her hands nervously shredding her lace handkerchief. On the mantel a clock slowly ticked away the minutes, the sound becoming more exaggerated as time dragged by.

She could not get her mind off the duel. Out there somewhere a duel was taking place and she sat here, her stomach painfully tied in knots, not knowing what was coming about!

As the thought came to her, Lauriette jumped to her feet. She had to go somewhere. Had to get out of the quiet house or go out of her mind!

Leaving word with Barton that she was going to take a walk, she collected her green cloak and, pulling the hood over her curls, started off through the garden.

Lauriette silently entered the forbidden forest thinking not at all of her last ordeal there but instead her mind filled with worry and dread over the duel. All at once she thought of the tiny little tower room which housed memories and treasures of days past. Her eyes became filled with such sadness and disappointment. It could have been so wonderful, so beautiful. . . .

Plunging deeper into the woods, the little rocking horse came to her mind, and a strange smile graced her lips. In her heart of hearts she had secretly hoped to some day use that faithful yellow steed. Her smile faded. No—no children would come from her womb, to sleep securely in the tiny cradle or laugh with joy on that noble animal's back. Never would she hold her child to her breast, a warm beautiful child with dark curling hair—a child of Devlin's.

The duel! The thought of it hastened her steps. Had they started or was it over already? How could they duel on the slippery ground caused by this hateful mist? It could possibly end in death. And whose death? Evan's? Devlin's?

Stop this! her sensible mind demanded. Devlin would be just fine. He was a man who thrived on danger and adventure. He would not choose the rapier unless he was an excellent swordsman. One thing she knew for certain, Devlin Essex never blundered into anything!

But what if something went amiss? What if Evan did defeat him? How could she live without him?

No, no, no! She thoroughly rebelled against the idea. "I do not love him!" she spoke aloud, but yet her words sounded hollow and without the ring of conviction.

No, Lauriette could not afford to let herself love him. It would be so easy to do, so easy to throw her arms around him, to give herself so wholly. Immediately, she took hold of herself. It was senseless to go on about what might have been! He could never love her, he had told her as much. He did not believe in love, to him it was a mere delusion. Even Neville told her as much. Devlin was not capable of that rapturous emotion.

Lauriette decided to keep her own emotions in check, never to let him know of the constant turmoil raging inside. To show Devlin Essex her strange devotion would only repel him and drive the wedge between them deeper. In the end he would only come to resent her and think her a clinging vine.

Resolutely, she made up her mind. She would take from him only what he decided to give—a kind word, a brief kiss—whatever. She would never ask of him, never give him the opportunity to resent her in any way. And *never* would she let him touch her heart or glimpse any trace of deep affection in her manner!

Lauriette looked up, startled to find herself at Clara's neat little cottage. So deep in her troubles was she, Lauriette never thought how far she had journeyed. Suddenly, she was not sure it had been wise to come.

She knocked timidly, trying to mentally form what to say. The door opened and Clara gave out a cry of pleasure, her arms enveloping her favorite girl.

"Come in, come in," she urged, pulling Lauriette into the cozy room.

Lauriette felt relief immediately, the warmth from Clara's kitchen filling her. She looked to the dear woman and smiled lovingly, hugging Clara tightly.

"Sit down, child." She motioned to the chair. "We've much to talk about! Well, Seth usually keeps me informed but you know him—so vague about everything."

"Do you like it here, Clara?" she asked, taking a seat.

Her smile radiated her entire face. "It's my first home," Clara said gently, then quickly added, "since Philadelphia, that is. We're happy here, dearest. His lordship is very generous."

"Yes, he can be," Lauriette returned faintly.

"Oh, honey, I'm sorry," she said sadly. "Seth told me of the duel."

Lauriette looked up at her pleadingly. "Clara, I have

to know how to get to Vesner's Glen," she blurted out. "Please, I can't sit at the Hall pacing back and forth and wait for some word! I need to be there! I have to!"

"Now, now, child," Clara soothed. "Just calm yourself a bit."

Lauriette irritably rubbed her forehead. "I'm sorry, Clara. It's so hard to sit and wait and wonder what is taking place. I can't bear to react like some refined young lady and sit and sew while Devlin—"

"Of course, child," Clara said softly, "it is hard to be a woman at times—most of the time. But his lordship would be very angry if you suddenly appeared at the dueling ground."

"I'm at my wits' end with *his lordship!*" Lauriette replied harshly. "Men! Vain, prideful and arrogant! I care not what the man thinks!"

Clara smiled slowly, her gray eyes deepening. " 'Tis so hard to love such a vital, powerful man," she mused.

Lauriette slowly raised her eyes to Clara's kind face. "I do not love Devlin!" she insisted.

Clara eyed her knowingly. "My sweet, I hear your words but your face and eyes betray you."

The green in her eyes became dominant as subtle anger shook her. "Are you going to give me the directions or no!"

The old woman lowered her eyes, her voice soft but underlying firmness. "No, Lauriette, I will not tell you how to get there. I realize you are upset and waiting is very difficult, but this time I'm certain I'm right."

Lauriette lifted her chin stiffly. "Very well," she said. "I'll find someone else to tell me. . . ."

"Lauriette—"

"No, it's all right, Clara, really," she reassured. "I know when I'm beaten."

Lauriette stood and walked to the door. "Don't worry about me," she told her quietly. "I shan't do anything rash. Thank you for your company."

She closed the door behind a tight-lipped Clara. She loved the old woman dearly and Clara did indulge her quite often, but when she felt something was wrong, she would not budge even an inch.

Disheartened, she strode along the path that led further away from the hall. Such was her lot, she mused, to be treated like a child in all matters. Even Clara forgot from time to time she was a grown woman almost twenty-two years old.

She followed the path as it veered to the right and into a small clearing. A fallen log lay in her path and with a sigh Lauriette seated herself. It was a lovely place with the misty rain making everything glimmer.

Lauriette noted she had no apprehension at being alone in these woods. The mere thought of the gruesome man she had seen caused an involuntary shudder, but in this small clearing, she felt safe.

It was nearing noon, she was certain, and her thoughts were drifting back to Devlin. Lauriette gazed down at her muddy slippers. What was love? How could one be sure there was such a thing? She felt obligation, loyalty, warmth, even pride in Devlin, but love?

She thought back to a book she once read where the heroine threw herself in front of a sword to save her beloved. Love was sacrificing oneself to keep the other from harm or suffering. Love was feeling the same hurt the other felt and wanting to take it from him, spare him. Love was seeing him smiling softly at you and feeling warmth flood through your being.

"I love him," she said aloud, her heart grieving. "I love a man who can never love me." It sounded so achingly empty. He would never know. He would hate her if he knew. The devil has no heart.

Her head came up as she felt a sudden tingling of her

senses, as if eyes were upon her. Reluctantly, she turned, a smile crossing her face.

It was Devlin . . . Devlin!

Thirty-Nine

Lauriette jumped up, running towards him, her face glowing with joy that he was all right. She stopped suddenly only inches away, her smile fading. Devlin's face was a mask of controlled fury, his black eyes were glistening and focused upon her.

A feeling of dread came over her. "You didn't—"

"No, madam, though he no doubt wishes he were," his mouth barely moved to form the words. "I gallantly bowed to your wishes and your lover lives!"

She was stunned by his words and his unreasonable anger at her.

"Are you not relieved, *my dear*?" he asked sarcastically, using Evan's pet phrase for her.

Her hand lashed out catching him on the jaw. His eyes glittered like ice, the imprint of her hand reddening more with each passing moment. Slowly, a twisted grin spread across his lips.

"Liar!" she stormed at him, hammering her small fists against his chest. "Liar!"

With an easy sweep, Devlin caught both hands and roughly pulled her against him. Their faces were only inches apart, she could feel his hot breath upon her.

"He was your lover!" he hissed, his fingers cruelly biting into her skin. "Admit it!"

"No! No!" she cried, wincing at his grip. "No one has ever touched me but you!"

With a low growl, Devlin released her, pushing her away from him. He could not control his black temper a moment longer. Over and over came Brimley's words, his accusations, his knowledge of Lauriette before he found her.

"Then, madam, I wish you to explain to me how in the hell Brimley knew there was no mark of a virgin upon my sheets!"

Lauriette's anger rose to a fevered pitch, her breasts heaving to hold back her scalding tears. With a trembling hand, she pointed to the pistol at his belt. "Kill me! For God's sake get it over with and have done!" she flung at him. "For I swear upon everything I hold most dear, I pledged my loyalty to you. I will not speak of this—this subject again and you, *sir,* will not question me further!"

He was struck speechless by her own anger. Even in his rage he could not suppress the feeling of admiration at her courage. Most women would have cowed but not this one, not his Lauriette!

The soft rustling of silk brought him out of his thoughts and he saw Lauriette quickly moving away from him.

"Where do you think you're going?"

She turned for just a moment, her eyes sparkling with unshed tears. "Home!" she stated hotly. "Back to Claymoor, where my word is accepted as truth—away from you!" Lauriette turned back and began to walk faster. She heard his boots hurrying to catch up with her and she broke into a run.

Lauriette gave out a startled cry as a steel arm encircled her waist, raising her completely off the ground.

"Let go of me!" she demanded.

Before she could move out of his grasp, Devlin planted her feet on the ground and whirled her around to face him. He stared down at her, his eyes like chips of glistening coal.

"Your home is Essex Hall, my lady," he sneered, his hands holding her firm.

"I'll not let you treat me like some piece of property!" she returned just as heatedly.

"Ah-h, but you are, cherub," he retorted cooly. "You are mine and mine alone. You will stay at the Hall, with me, at my beck and call, day or night. No, lovely Lauriette, there is nothing I cannot do if I desire. You are my wife, my property, my chattel if I so wish it! I will never let you go—never. . ."

His lips came down to claim hers and with eager anticipation, even though angered and hurt, Lauriette slightly parted her lips. The thrill of his deepening kiss caused her knees to go weak and unconsciously she pressed herself against him. Then suddenly it was over. She opened her eyes to find him staring down at her, a triumphant smile on his lips.

She raised her hand but Devlin caught it in midair. "Don't think this battle over yet, sir!" she spat.

Gripping her waist, he began pulling her toward the center of the woods. "This is a shortcut to the Hall," he said quietly. "Come on! Keep up or I'll sling you over my shoulder."

Even though his mood had lightened somewhat, her anger had not abated one whit and Devlin literally dragged her along. He was still upset, but his confrontation with Lauriette had exhilarated him. If she feared him, she did not show it and he admired her for it.

Suddenly Lauriette stopped and could not be moved. Devlin turned to give her a scathing but the sheer terror on her face brought him to a halt.

"What is it, cherub?"

Her eyes, wide and frightened, scoured the tiny clearing they had come to. Her face was drained of color, her body shook violently.

"Laurie?"

"I . . . I don't know," her voice shook. Suddenly, she grabbed his arm, desperately trying to pull him away from the clearing. "Please, Dev, if you have any feeling for me, please don't make me walk through there. Please! I can't, I just can't!"

Devlin's brows drew down in concern. "Laurie, tell me what it is," he urged. "Let me help!"

She was breathing rapidly, her nails digging into his arm. "I'm frightened and I don't know why. This—this place is evil! I know it! Please don't make me cross there!"

He gripped her shoulders hard, making her look up to him. "Think for a moment, Laurie, think! Why are you afraid of this place?"

Her wide eyes wandered over the quiet surroundings until they came to rest on the ground by a huge elm tree. Muffling an agonized cry, Lauriette wildly tried to twist away from Devlin's steel grasp.

He shook her roughly. "Tell me! Tell me what you see!"

"My God, my God!" she moaned. "There's—there's someone buried there—right there!"

Devlin arched a brow and stared at the hardened earth beside the elm.

"You must believe me!" she whispered, on the verge of hysteria. "I know it, I just know it!"

Lauriette felt a weakness rapidly spread through her, flashes of memory or dream kept turning around and around. Letting out a tiny, startled cry, she slumped in Devlin's arms.

* * *

The servants at Essex Hall were in an uproar since the afternoon before when his lordship had carried the poor mistress upstairs. Barton handled the servants strictly, during the late afternoon and evening, not giving them any time for speculation on what might have happened.

Barton could not help but admit he was also thoroughly intrigued. He had never seen his lordship so distraught. He had given strict orders concerning her ladyship and then closeted himself for a long time in the library with Master Judd. When they had emerged, both men headed toward the stables, their faces grimly set.

Now morning came and he, as well as the other servants, walked quickly and quietly, their faces reflecting their curiosity.

Devlin was slumped in an overstuffed chair, his dirty boots propped on the night table. His clothing was disheveled and dirty, his face held a full day's growth of beard, his hair was tousled. He stared intently at the silent figure in the bed.

It had been quite a twenty-four hours. Tiredly, he rubbed his eyes. Sometime in the middle of the night Dolly softly woke him. Lauriette, though given a strong sleeping potion, was having violent nightmares.

He spent the night at her side trying to calm her outcries, her sobbing. Whatever was locked inside her was pushing her towards the edge. He was suddenly afraid for her, afraid he would lose her. There was something in her past that was tearing her apart, trying to get out, but what?

It had to do with the remains he found in the woods. Devlin scowled. Who was it? How did she know of the unmarked grave? Perhaps—a lover? The man who took her virginity? Took what should have been his?

Unreasonable anger filled him once more. The mere

speculation of another man's hands upon her, another man seeing her as he had—he was filled once more with rage.

Lauriette's eyes began to flutter, then opened. She stared at the ceiling for a long moment, trying to gather her thoughts. Suddenly the afternoon flooded over her and she cried out, covering her eyes.

"Laurie, Laurie," Devlin's voice caressed her name as he gathered her into his arms. "It's over. A bad dream. That's all, just a bad dream."

Lauriette pulled away from him. "The grave?"

Devlin's face darkened, his hands fell away. "There is a grave."

She gasped. "I prayed it was just one of my nightmares."

"Lauriette, who was he?"

The bluntness of his words stunned her. "I . . . don't know."

Devlin gripped her shoulders. "You know," he accused. "You have to know!"

"B-but I don't! I swear!"

"Madam, no one knew that unmarked grave even existed, save you!" he said harshly. "Who is it that's buried there? A friend? A lover? Who, Lauriette!"

"I don't know!" she cried. "I don't know!"

Devlin shoved Lauriette away and stood, pacing the floor. He never before felt such frustration and anger. She sounded so convincing, yet—

He stood over her, scowling. Lauriette raised her eyes to meet his, green defiance glistening in them. Even in his anger, he desired her more than anything and his ire increased at the thought of her affecting him so!

Devlin's voice came in a low hiss. "Then tell me, madam, how it is you know so much, yet know nothing at all! Someone's remains are in that grave out there, a grave you knew of, but you want me to believe you have no knowledge of who it is or what became of him!" He retreated to the foot of the bed. "You swear no man has ever touched you, yet I almost killed a man yesterday who said differently. You appeared quite the virgin that night, but no blood stained my bed! Just what, madam, am I to believe?"

Her eyes narrowed and at that moment Lauriette came close to hating him. "You can believe what you like," she replied tartly. "In your eyes I have been nothing but an instrument of revenge, the perfect lure to settle a hate that began to fester long before I stepped foot on these shores. Do not speak of treachery or deceitfulness to me! 'Twas you who invented the words!" Stubbornly, she settled back in bed.

With an angered groan, Devlin flew to the door. Lauriette flinched as it violently slammed shut. An agonized sob shook her. What was happening? Was she going insane?

The grave! How did she know? Lauriette slowly shook her head. Everything that was coming about had to do with her summer here four years before. She was not certain how, she just knew; as she had known of the cottage, the gruesome man, and yes, the unmarked grave.

She quietly dressed herself in her green riding habit, not bothering to ring for Dolly. She bit her lip as Devlin crept into her mind. If only he had a trace of trust in her. No, he felt better in believing Evan's rantings about her. And as far as the grave—why would she refuse to tell him if she knew? And she desperately longed to know all the mysteries which besieged her soul.

Forty

"And what was her reply?"

Devlin slammed his fist down against the mantel. His face was dark with anger. "She had no answers," he replied hotly. "She *says* she doesn't know *how* she knows, she just does!"

Judd shrugged easily. "Perhaps she's right."

"What?" Devlin exclaimed. "My dear Judd, that just isn't possible!"

He looked evenly at his cousin. "Have you ever known Lauriette to lie?"

Devlin was silent.

A flash of green caught the corner of his eye and he moved to the drawing room door just in time to see Lauriette close the main door. She was at the bottom step as he opened it.

"Where are you going?"

She slowly turned, her face very sober, her eyes like glittering chips of green ice. "I am going to take Caesar for some exercise," she answered stiffly. "If you are afraid I am to meet a secret lover somewhere along the road, you are free to accompany me—to be certain your *property* arrives back here *intact!*''

Devlin stood on the top step clenching and unclenching his hands. At that moment he longed to turn her over his knee and thrash her good and proper!

He smiled sardonically. ''I am certain you will return intact without my presence, my sweet,'' he calmly told her. ''After all, you know too well how bloodthirsty I can be when aroused.''

Lauriette presented her back to him as she walked away from the courtyard toward the stables. The arrogant gall of that man! First he denies her the privilege of her horse, then in almost the same breath lets her go!

''Perhaps I should ride with her.'' Judd started off down the steps when Devlin stopped him.

''Leave her,'' he said bluntly. ''I know where she is going.''

Judd looked at him. ''How could you? Where is she going?''

''She's going to the family tomb.''

''What?''

Devlin nodded. ''Unbeknownst to her ladyship, I've followed her a number of times—to assure her safety—and when she is troubled or angered, she goes to the family crypt and visits Father. Don't worry,'' he urged, ''she'll return within the next hour.''

Lauriette rode easily, giving Caesar a full rein, enjoying the breeze against her hair and face. She had gone to Lord David's tomb to think and to feel near the old man, but this time she felt no comfort, no lifting of her spirits. She sat pensively for over an hour, her tangled mind unsettling her to the point of tears.

Finally, she mounted Caesar and galloped across the fields. She put everything from her mind and let her senses take over. Right now she felt as free as any gypsy, with the wind teasing the fair from under her hat. She slowed Caesar to a trot and grimaced at the thought that it was time to return to the Hall. The sky was beginning to cloud and the air smelled of rain.

As Lauriette entered the bridle path which led back to the Hall, her thoughts returned to her troubles.

"Doesn't he realize if I knew a way to remember about that grave I would?" she asked herself. "He doesn't believe a word I've said. I can see it in his eyes. And I have no way to convince him I speak the truth!"

So preoccupied in her thoughts was she that she was oblivious to the darkening of the sky or the misty rain that was already dampening her habit. She was not sure what to do or say anymore. She asked to be sent to Philadelphia; he adamantly refused. He seemed not to want her yet he would not let her go.

A crash of thunder brought her out of her reverie just in time to see a black cloaked rider galloping towards her at a breakneck speed from the hill. Lauriette was stunned and could not seem to move. Suddenly, the dark rider was upon her, his horse rearing up.

With a terrified cry, Lauriette covered her face as Caesar, himself in a fright, reared back in retaliation and Lauriette was thrown from the saddle. She lay crumpled in the path, face down in the mud.

The dark rider stared down at the unconscious woman then reined the black horse and galloped back toward the hill. At the top the rider turned back and stared for a long moment at the prone figure lying on the path. She had never moved, not a sound came from her lips after that startled scream.

"Good-bye, Lauriette," Muriel's husky voice whispered. "I promise I will comfort Devlin when they find your body. I will make him very happy."

Forty-One

The rain beat heavily against the French doors as Judd peered out at the drenched flower garden. Three hours had passed since Lauriette had left and with each passing moment, he was becoming increasingly alarmed. He rebuked himself for not going with her. After all that had happened in the past weeks, he did not deem it logical to let her ride off alone.

Devlin sat in an overstuffed chair lazily sipping brandy. His calm demeanor infuriated Judd, but underneath it all, he was churning inside. A clap of thunder boomed overhead followed by a zigzag of lightning in the black sky.

"Dev, I fear something has happened to her," Judd said quickly.

Devlin shook his head, still angry with her from the morning's confrontation. "Her ladyship is no doubt somewhere under a roof waiting out the storm."

Lightning streaked across the sky once more and Judd turned to Devlin, his face drawn in stubborn determination. "And what if she isn't?" he countered. "Dev, it has been three hours! The past hour out in that damnable storm!"

Devlin gazed over Judd's shoulder at the rain-streaked window. She had never been gone this long from the house before, but knowing Lauriette, she could be doing it merely to agitate him. Suddenly he frowned. But what if something happened? What if she met Branscombe on the road—or worse yet, Brimley!

He was out of the chair in an instant, silently cursing himself. He had allowed his anger to cloud his thinking! "Come on," Devlin said briskly. "No harm in checking."

They had been out in the rain for almost an hour, both searching frantically for Lauriette, calling out her name above the maddening downpour. There was no trace of her.

"Judd!" Devlin shouted. "Ride to Claymoor and check there. I'll ride out to the tomb again."

Judd nodded and wheeled his horse around, heading in the opposite direction. Devlin once again rounded the forest, his eyes searching for anything, *anything* that would lead him to her.

It was at the Essex Tomb he discovered the seldom used bridle path, which was a shortcut to Essex Hall. Giving Nomad a knee, he slowly started down the path. The rain pouring down made it extremely difficult to see and part way down the path he almost turned back.

But something down the way caught his eye. Devlin dismounted and led Nomad. A horse snorted in the distance and Devlin quickened his step.

"Caesar!" he called.

Caesar snorted again and nervously pawed the ground, nuzzling a heap of green in the mud.

"My God!" Devlin cried, breaking into a run. "Laurie!"

He sunk to his knees beside the crumpled figure. Tenderly, he turned her over, cradling her head.

Lauriette was unconscious, her face bruised by the fall. Devlin felt something warm and sticky in his hand and withdrew it, supporting her head with his knee. Blood! She was badly hurt! He must get her back to the Hall immediately!

He lifted her up onto Nomad's back, and then mounted himself. Cradling her in his arms, he rode back to Essex Hall, trailing Caesar behind. He cursed himself for letting her ride alone. He must have been insane! He would never forgive himself if anything happened to her!

Pauley had been summoned to fetch Dr. Quade, an order that sent the young man flying to the stables. Dolly stood at the foot of the bed, her hands gripping the post while Devlin undressed Lauriette. She was not sure what to do, her mind still shocked by the sight of her mistress so quiet, so lifeless. His lordship had ignored her cries and mumbled something about "taking care of Laurie," and all but pushed her aside.

"Towels, Dolly," he demanded softly.

With loving tenderness, Devlin dried her, his eyes drinking in the sight of her nude body. She was so lovely, so desirable to him. The past weeks of sleeping away from her rose in his mind and a hard lump formed in his throat.

Forcing himself to think logically, Devlin covered her and demanded more blankets of Dolly. Lauriette had not moved, not batted an eye since he found her. He could not tear his eyes away from her still form.

"Yer lordship, Dr. Quade is a-waitin'," Dolly said in a half whisper.

"What? Aye, aye, send him in immediately." His usual powerful voice sounded quite subdued.

Dr. Quade looked down through his spectacles at Lauriette's motionless body. He drew his eyes downward in thought.

"Perhaps, your lordship, 'twould be best for you to wait outside in the hall," he whispered.

"What? Aye, I'll be waiting . . . just outside the door," he answered distractedly, his eyes still upon Lauriette. Slowly, he backed to the door.

In the hall Devlin paced back and forth, his head bowed, eyes riveted to the floor. His mind kept returning to Lauriette lying helpless on the ground, the rain pouring down upon her. She had to be all right!

"M'lord," Dolly's dignified voice broke through his tortured thoughts, "while yer a-waitin' Dr. Quade, perhaps ye might like ta slip out o'them wet clothes. We don't want ye to git down sick."

He mumbled something Dolly did not quite catch and headed for his room. He pulled off the wet garments and toweled himself mechanically. He dressed quickly in fresh fawn breeches and a simple white shirt, then immediately was out his door.

Dr. Quade met him at the stairs, the old man's face very sober. "Her ladyship has a slight concussion," he quietly informed Devlin and indicated with his hand to the back of Devlin's head. "Right about here. She'll be a-coming round soon. But there's more. She's fevered." Devlin's eyes met the doctor's. " 'Tis not uncommon what with her ladyship being in the rain for so long, but she'll need close watch."

"I understand," Devlin said flatly.

"I'll return on the morrow," he said. "Keep her attended at all times."

Lauriette felt as if she were emerging from the depths of a monstrous cave. She became faintly aware of familiar sounds around her and struggled to open her eyes. Cold, so very cold! Where was she? Was that Dolly's hushed voice?

Her head was throbbing and everything appeared quite blurred. What was happening? Valiantly she tried to sit up but found she had no control over her arms. They felt like lead weights. Why was she so cold?

She tried calling out to Dolly but all that came was a weak moan. She heard booted feet suddenly cross the floor and a blurred face loomed above her.

"Laurie," Devlin's voice sounded so distant but so tender, "Laurie, my love."

She tried to form words to ask him what was happening to her, but all that came forth were tiny, helpless moans. She was seized by violent shaking, her teeth chattering.

"Dolly! More blankets!" Devlin bellowed. "Quickly!"

Why was she so cold? She was so tired and her eyes closed of their own will. Just to sleep, she thought, sleep.

Devlin placed blanket upon blanket, Lauriette still trembling uncontrollably. At least she woke, if only for a few brief moments, but she was so weak!

He slumped on the chair near the bed, his soft brown eyes riveted to the bed. In the unusual quietness of the room, his eyes gradually closed as he slipped off into exhausted sleep.

It was hours later when a thrashing sound from the bed abruptly woke him. Night had fallen and he quickly lit the candles, illuminating the room. Lauriette lay tossing and turning, the blankets thrown back from her nude body, her flesh a cherry pink. Devlin placed his hand upon her forehead. She was burning up with fever.

"Too . . . hot!" she moaned as Devlin covered her. She flung her arm, sending the covers away from her once again.

Devlin covered her, then sat down beside her, hands

on each side of her shoulders holding the blankets in place. Lauriette's face was crimson, beads of perspiration on her forehead and upper lip. She settled back into a restless sleep and Devlin returned to the chair.

It was almost dawn when cries from the bed brought Devlin to his feet. Reaching the bed, he gently pushed her back against the pillows and covered her again. Wringing a cloth out in the basin, he pressed the coolness to her burning brow, sponging her face lovingly. She was so sick!

Her eyes were opened, glazed with fever. "Come look! Come look!" she pleaded urgently. "There's something under my bed!"

Her fever so high, Lauriette was becoming delirious. Rinsing out the cloth, Devlin bathed her face and neck.

"Please don't jest," she whimpered. "Come make certain. I'm afraid!"

Devlin smiled crookedly. So at one time she was afraid of the dark. She grew quiet for a long moment, then her lips began to tremble.

"She was the one he wanted," she murmured. "Please don't worry, James, 'tis for the best."

His eyes narrowed as he listened to her ramblings. What man was she speaking of—and to whom was she speaking? Branscombe? The mysterious skeleton in the grave?

Lauriette's eyes grew wide with terror. "Who are you? What do you want?" she demanded frantically. "Give them what they want, Peter!"

The name she blurted out brought Devlin's head up with a start. She had cried his name before.

"Please, please!" she cried, writhing. "Don't hurt me, I beg you!"

Suddenly, Lauriette cried out half rising out of the bed. Devlin struggled to get her back down.

"Don't touch me!" she rasped, so hatefully, so murderously. "Don't touch me!"

She moaned deep in her throat, a sound of unbearable pain. "Oh-h, Peter!" she breathlessly whispered. "Sweet, gentle Peter! My love, oh my love!"

She had had a lover! The revelation rocked Devlin hard. But why had she lied? Why had she pretended the part of a chastened virgin? How many had there been?

Another spasm seized Lauriette and she cried out mournfully, "I hurt, Jamie." Then she sobbed out in a childlike voice, "Make it go away! Peter! Peter!" Suddenly, she shuddered. Her voice came like a reverent whisper. "Gone . . . gone . . ."

The sun was just appearing above the trees, the storm perished sometime during the night. Devlin watched as she finally slept; he was drained to the very center of his being. Peter, Jamie, Branscombe, Brimley—how many more were there?

"Yer lordship? Yer lordship?" Dolly's voice whispered. "Let me set with th' mistress for a time. Ye go git a bite o' breakfast."

Numbly he consented and in a trancelike moved to the door. He was filled with mixed emotions so strong he felt suffocated. He wanted to hate her at that very moment but he could not.

"Dev!" Judd's anxious voice called from the drawing room. He rushed out. "How is she? Will she be all right?"

Devlin slowly shook his head. "I pray to God she will, but I don't know." His eyes narrowed as he looked over Judd's shoulder to the white face of Henry Branscombe. "What the devil is he doing here?"

Judd glanced over his shoulder. "Branscombe offered his assistance in searching for Lauriette," he explained. "He was with me when we ran into Dr. Quade. He insisted on waiting here for word."

Henry stared at Devlin and Judd could feel the tension between the two men. Devlin's eyes turned a smoky black, his face was cool and unreadable.

"She has the fever," he answered lowly. "She spent a rather bad night."

"Where did you find her?"

"On that unused bridle path leading from the cemetery," he answered. "She was unconscious. Caesar was standing guard over her. Never left her side."

"She should never have been unaccompanied, sir!" Henry said stiffly. "Your negligence has brought this misfortune to her!"

Devlin froze, his sardonic gaze boring into Henry. "I suggest you take your leave now, Branscombe," he said in an irritable voice.

Henry's face became a livid red. "I will not be intimidated, Essex!" he exploded. "You have no right to order me about!"

Devlin sidestepped Judd to face Henry squarely. He was exhausted and angered and this man was the last straw. "I am very capable of caring for *my wife,* Branscombe," he said through clenched teeth. "What goes on inside my house is none of your affair!" He turned to Judd. "Kindly see him out!"

Devlin brushed past Henry, headed for the dining room down the hallway.

"She fell by your hands, Essex!" he shouted, stopping Devlin cold. "She wanted to have done with you and you could not accept her wishes!"

Devlin turned, his face masked with fury straining to be released.

Henry sneered. "I love her, Essex, I've always loved her!" he shouted. "You cannot abide the idea that she returns my love!"

With a savage growl, Devlin ran for him. One hand closed around Henry's flawless cravat, while the other clashed with the man's jaw. Henry crumpled to the floor.

"Understand this, Branscombe," he heaved, "what is mine *I keep!* Lauriette is mine and I share with no one . . . *no one!*" He turned to a startled Judd. "Get him out of here!"

Forty-Two

Devlin sat at the lonely table, absently playing with the food on his plate. It was utterly useless. He could not bring himself to eat. He could not get Lauriette out of his mind. Henry had been right. He caused her accident just as surely as if he had pushed her! If he hadn't been so angry, if he hadn't been so damn stubborn—if, if, if!

With a groan he rose and slowly walked into the hall and started up the stairs. A commotion at the door brought his attention around. Barton was arguing with someone at the door.

"Sir! I protest!" he flustered. "Ye cannot barge—"

With a stream of wild oaths, the intruder pushed passed the frustrated Barton but stopped dead in front of the stairs. Blue eyes boldly locked with ever-darkening brown, each man appraising the other.

Devlin scowled. This man was a rugged sort dressed in sailor's clothes, captain's clothes. His face was a weatherbeaten brown, his blue eyes striking something familiar, a chestnut beard covered the rest of his features.

"Yer lordship! I tried to stop—"

"It is all right, Barton," he waved the butler away and retreated down the steps until he faced the stranger. "What is it you want?"

"Where is Mistress Claymoor? I demand to see her!" the man blurted out.

Devlin's scowl deepened, his brows drew downward. "And just what is your business with Mistress Claymoor?" he growled. "Another of her lovers perhaps?"

With a rage startling Devlin, the stranger slammed his huge fist into him. He staggered back, falling against the stairs. The man stood over him, legs parted, his fists clenched.

"You insolent cur!" he hissed. "I am James Claymoor, captain of the *U.S.S. Intrepid* . . . and Lauriette's older brother!"

Brother! The word bursted inside his brain as he gazed wonderingly. The eyes! It was the same color blue that Lauriette's sometimes turned.

"Then give me a hand," Devlin held up his arm, "for I happen to be Lauriette's husband!"

James sat quietly, a brandy in his hands. "How serious is it?"

Devlin took a chair opposite him. "Serious enough," he answered. "She regained consciousness for only a few moments before drifting away again."

"I don't understand it," James shook his head. "Lauriette has always been an excellent horsewoman. You say the horse was not violent?"

"Caesar is gently spirited, somewhat like Laurie," he said quietly. "He was beside her when I found her."

James leaned back. "I've been so worried," he responded. "I tried my damnedest to talk her out of coming here."

Devlin's laugh was gentle. "She can certainly be

stubborn.''

James returned the smile. ''Has always been that way.''

''And afraid of the dark?''

James gazed at him. ''Why, she was! The only thing she was frightened of.''

Devlin leaned forward. ''James, who is Peter?'' Devlin noticed the color drain from the man's face.

''Why?''

''Because Laurie has been calling for him,'' he answered quietly. ''She became delirious at dawn. Who is he?''

James's eyes met Devlin's and filled with tears. ''Peter was her brother.''

Devlin was shocked and placed his brandy on the table before he dropped it. Brother! That thought never crossed his mind. Suitor, aye! Lover, aye! But brother?

James sighed, wiping his eyes. ''Perhaps 'twould be best to start at the beginning,'' he said. ''Peter was Lauriette's twin, only a few minutes older than she. And no brother and sister were ever more devoted to each other.'' He faintly smiled. ''I watched those two grow into lovely youngsters and no other brother could have been as proud!''

His face darkened. ''Four years ago we came to London to see our Uncle, Sir James Claymoor. It was a happy time for all of us, especially Lauriette who was at such a romantic age. She met Henry Branscombe and immediately became enamored of him. At the time it seemed he returned her affections, but that was short-lived when Lauriette came upon Henry and Marie-Claire, her sister, in a very compromising position.''

''So, she really did love Branscombe,'' Devlin murmured.

''Love? I think not,'' James replied. ''Merely infatuation. A girl's first romance. Henry was not a suitable choice, by my standards. He was too weak-willed. But nevertheless, her heart was broken though she tried to keep up a brave front. We left her mostly to herself for the stubborn wench could not tolerate pity, especially from those she loved! But Peter would not let it be. He was devoted to her and could hardly bear the hurt she was going through."

James took a burning gulp of brandy. "One hot afternoon in May, Peter's devilish temper got the best of him and he vowed to ride to Elmsford, Henry's father's estate, and have a round with him. So beside himself with anger, he swore to tear the man's heart out. Lauriette overheard him from the balcony upstairs and ran down to stop him. But by the time she reached the courtyard, he was already galloping off. There was no way to deter Lauriette and she mounted her horse to give chase."

He stood and began to pace restlessly. "I was in the village and returned late in the afternoon to find them both gone. Elliott told me what came about and I sorely cursed him for not pursuing them, but he shrugged, telling me they were no longer children."

He ceased his pacing and faced Devlin, his blue eyes stormy. "They did not return to Claymoor," he whispered sullenly. "Search parties were sent out but could find no trace of them. Finally, two days later, I came upon a delapidated cottage on the edge of some woods. It was there I found Lauriette . . ." He paused a moment, choking back a sob. James' face darkened with rage. "I hardly recognized her! She had been beaten senseless, her eyes were wide and vacant. She was huddled in the far corner of that place clutching a filthy blanket to her. I slowly moved towards her, then kneeled before her. Her eyes rose to meet mine and she choked back a whimper. "I hurt, Jamie," she murmured and her eyes filled with tears. She fainted and I picked her up in my arms.''

He returned to the chair, burying his face in his hands. ''She had been starved and beaten. We almost lost her to the arms of death. The doctor was summoned and while I kept vigil over her, the search went on for Peter. He was never found.'' James gazed for a long moment, as if contemplating whether to go on. ''Lauriette was delirious. My lord—Lauriette had been raped, not once but many times in those two days by the same man!''

Devlin jumped to his feet, the gruesome story almost too much to bear.

James went on quietly. ''In her delirium the whole horrid story came out. Four men stopped them in the woods and when one of them attempted to touch Lauriette, Peter flew at them. She begged them to take their valuables and not harm them but the leader had other things in mind,'' he said harshly. ''Peter was held by two of the men and forced to watch while the leader ravished his sister! Lauriette fought the man but could not stop him. Then while Lauriette was tied up by her own clothing, she watched horrified as they tortured Peter, slowly killing him. A strapping youth of seventeen!

''Then as her brother lay dead at her feet, the leader once again forced himself on her. The bitter humiliation took place again and again! She was forced to dig her brother's grave! Can you imagine what that must have done to her? Having to bury her her twin like that? Then that evil bastard took her again . . . throwing her on top of Peter's grave.''

James slammed his fist on the arm of the chair. ''The bastard left her for dead! Another day in the hellhole, she would have been!'' he growled. ''By the grace of God, Lauriette recovered and by some sweet miracle, she did not remember that incident at all. She didn't even recall having a brother named Peter. We thought it a blessing that her memory was gone and made arrangements to leave for Philadelphia. Since that time she had fears she couldn't understand and vague nightmares, but she was safe from the degradation that had befallen her."

"And Brimley," Devlin said slowly, "did he know what happened?"

James looked up at him. "Of course! Elliott had to tell him!" he snapped. "He was to wed her, he had to know why there would be no blood on the bridal bed. Even though her maidenhead was not intact, she was still as much a virgin as any virtuous maid."

So she had spoken the truth! Branscombe had never touched her, neither had Brimley.

He extended his hand to James. "Thank you for telling me this painful story. I welcome you to Essex Hall, James," he said sincerely. "I am so full of gratitude, I do not know where to begin."

James arched a brow. "You can start by filling me in on the past six months."

Devlin quietly gave James a slightly abridged account of his meeting Lauriette, his rescue of her and finally leading up to the accident.

"Damnation!" James cursed. "I knew Brimley to be a scoundrel! I tried to dissuade her."

" 'Tis all past now," Devlin reminded him, placing an affectionate hand on the man's shoulder. "At the moment that bastard is no doubt recovering poorly from two serious wounds."

"That you gave him?"

Devlin's smile was grim. "Aye!"

James' laughter burst forth. "Good man!"

Dolly's excited cry brought both men into the alcove. "Yer lordship! Yer lordship!" she cried. "It's th' mistress! She's a-ravin' again!"

Devlin took the steps two at a time with James following. He burst into the room and rushed to the bed.

"Marie, let me out! Please let me out!" she cried. "I can't marry him! I won't!"

Devlin glanced at James' solemn face. The brother's eyes were full of love and concern. Silently, he knelt on the opposite side of the bed.

Lauriette moaned. "I'm frightened, Dev, I'm frightened!"

"Hush, cherub," he whispered, sponging her forehead.

She thrashed about. "I am his wife!" Her voice strengthened. "I'll not desert him!"

James looked at Devlin's tortured face.

"Dev, Dev," she murmured, "I'm afire!"

Slowly, James grinned.

"Oh, Laurie, Laurie," he whispered, oblivious to James.

"If only there was love," she moaned, "if only . . ." Her voice trailed off.

Forty-Three

Lauriette woke very slowly, savoring the smell of fresh spring air that seemed to caress her face. She felt drained of strength and the back of her head was aching. It was night and she was snug in her bed—but why was she buried beneath a stack of blankets in the middle of May? And why was the bed drenched?

She lay there trying to think. Had Devlin been in the room with her? She vaguely remembered him calling to her. "Laurie love." Yes, those had been his words . . . so full of tenderness. Had he really called to her or had she been dreaming?

Weakly, she struggled to sit up, a soft groan escaping her lips. A movement from the chair caught her attention.

"Dolly?" her voice sounded strained. "Is that you?"

A candle was lit and Lauriette was surprised to see Devlin standing beside the bed. He looked so drawn and haggard, with dark circles under his eyes, his face unshaven. Devlin smiled at her, a smile which softened his face.

Gently, he placed a hand on her forehead. It was wonderfully cool.

"You look so tired," she smiled.

His eyes were a warm brown. "And you . . . you never looked lovelier," he whispered.

"Dev, I'm all wet! What is happening?"

"You've been sick, cherub." Going to her bureau he chose a blue nightgown. He rang for Dolly, then proceeded to dress Lauriette as if she were a babe, ignoring her weak protests.

"Oh, mistress," Dolly cried, entering the room. "Yer all right! Thank God! Thank God!"

Devlin gathered her into his arms as if she weighed nothing.

"Change the linens on her ladyship's bed," he told the maid, then sat down on a chair, cradling Lauriette against him. It was as if he was afraid to let her go, afraid he would lose her.

"How long," she asked, "have I been ill?"

"Three days," he answered softly. "You certainly had us worried."

Lauriette frowned thoughtfully. Three days gone out of her life in the blinking of an eye. Her head jerked up as that stormy afternoon came to mind.

"Cherub, what is it?"

She trembled and snuggled against him. Her hand crept up and rested on his shoulder. "Who . . . found me?"

Devlin lifted her chin. "I found you, Laurie. Evidently, you fell and struck your head."

Her horizon blue eyes were now sparkling clear, no haze of the fever marred them. Abruptly, she turned away. Again he brought her chin around and she had to face him.

"Tell me," he murmured.

She bit her lip, unsure of how he would react.

" 'Twas not an accident," she said hastily and felt him tense. "Dev, please I'm not insane, you must believe me!"

His eyes held hers steadily for a long, endearing moment. "I believe you, Laurie," he nodded. "Go on."

"I was returning home," she recalled, then blushed prettily. "I had been to Lord David's tomb. A man, dressed in a dark greatcoat came crashing down upon us! He—he reared the horse and Caesar, loving Caesar reared to protect me. That is when I fell."

"Do you remember anything about the rider?"

Lauriette shook her head. "Only that he wore a dark greatcoat, either black or brown, and a scarf or cloth pulled over his face. Oh, Devlin, it was horrible!"

"Hush, love," he soothed, pulling her face to his shoulder. "Nothing will ever hurt you again, I promise."

"Th' bed is ready, m'lord," Dolly interrupted.

"See cook," he told her, "and have some broth sent up."

With a brief curtsey, Dolly disappeared to fetch the broth and Devlin gently placed Lauriette in the freshly made bed. He was being so careful of her, she had to smile at the feeling.

"I really don't think I'm ready to eat," she said quietly, then raised her eyes to meet his. "I would give just about anything for a warm bath at this moment."

He smiled down at her. "The first thing is to get your strength back," he advised. "We'll see in the morn about getting you that warm bath . . . if you'll consume most of that broth Dolly is bringing."

He was being so nice to her, so kind, her courage rose enough to ask, "Dev, you're no longer angry with me?''

"No, cherub," he replied. "I've no more anger left in me . . . at least not for you." Devlin gazed down at the small white hands he held. Lauriette's eyes never wavered from his face. He grinned. "But I will say this, there will be no more willful jaunts across the fields without someone with you." His face grew serious, his eyes darkened.

"I am sorry," she whispered softly. "I would never worry you intentionally. But—but there is so much happening that I cannot understand and it frightens me!"

Devlin gripped her hands tighter. "No more, cherub," he said urgently. "You will not be alone to face it!"

His voice sounded so confident, so strong. Lauriette quickly looked uo at him. Did he know something she did not?

"The grave—"

He placed a finger against her lips. "That can wait. Getting you well cannot."

A light knock on the door announced Dolly carrying a bowl of steaming chicken broth. "When cook hear ye was awake, there was a a-fixin' like she was makin' a grand feast!" she laughed brightly.

"Goodnight, Dolly," he said simply, taking the bowl from her hands.

"Aye, s-sir, as ye say, sir." she curtsied, a light smile upon her lips, and left quietly.

"Really, Dev," Lauriette protested. "I'm quite capable of feeding myself."

He grinned. "That may be, but for tonight you shall indulge me and open your mouth."

Lauriette suppressed a giggle and opened her mouth. She was surprised and very pleased at the taste of cook's special broth and finished it completely.

"Now I think it's time you went back to sleep," he sighed, tucking her in.

"I do feel a bit tired," she reluctantly admitted. "But I'm afraid to close my eyes."

Devlin brushed a stray curl away from her pale cheek. His eyes were soft, dreamy, a look about them she had never seen before. "Cherub, I shall only be a few feet away," he whispered. "All you need do is call out."

"B-but—" She bit back her words as he snuffed out the candle. No, she would never ask of him. She would only take what he decided to give. Disappointment flooded her as tears stung the back of her eyes.

"G-goodnight, Dev," she murmured.

"Sleep well, cherub."

It was almost dawn when Devlin was aroused by sobbing. Slowly he made his way to the bed. "Another dream?" he asked gently.

Lauriette's bottom lip quivered. "Y-yes."

Lying down beside her, he tenderly pulled her into his arms. Lauriette snuggled closer, her head resting upon his chest. Devlin stroked her hair, hushing her, driving her fears away. Gradually, her trembling abated and her low, even breathing told him she finally slept.

Devlin held her even closer, his heart filling with contentment. It suddenly dawned on him how utterly happy he felt holding her in his arms and was totally confused by it.

"It is because I'm relieved she's out of danger," he mused. "It is because I no longer suspect her loyalty."

A frown settled upon his face. *The dark rider. Why would anyone wish to harm Lauriette? Unless . . .* Devlin shook his head. That thought was almost impossible to accept. After all, four years had passed and no doubt the bastard that ravished her was far from here.

A name popped into his mind. "Brimley?" No, he was in no physical condition to ride down upon her. Someone had done so, but who?

Forty-Four

"What?" James literally jumped out of his chair, his eyes a stormy blue.

Devlin eyed him keenly and held back an affectionate smile. The Claymoors were certainly a tightly knit clan.

Judd stared at him in disbelief. "But—but who would deliberately want to harm her?" he asked amazed. "Brimley is not in any condition to do anything, and Branscombe claims too much affection to hurt her!"

James leaned over the table. "What has Henry to do with this?"

Judd suddenly felt guilty. "Nothing, really," he stammered, "he just confessed to Dev his—er—affection for Lauriette."

"Affection, indeed!" he muttered. "Damn the bastard, that weak-willed ass!"

"No need to worry, James," Judd said quickly. "Dev took care of him proper."

"Enough talk of Branscombe," Devlin stated, looking down at his half-finished breakfast. "You're spoiling my appetite. James, sit and finish eating. I swear to you I'll get to the bottom of this.'' He turned to Judd. ''And if you're finished, cousin, why don't you visit with Laurie a bit. But, mind you, don't mention James. He is a surprise.''

Judd smiled boyishly. ''Trust me, cousin,'' and was up and out in an instant.

James laughed heartily. ''I see your cousin is taken with the little imp.''

Devlin nodded his agreement. ''I'm afraid the entire Hall is quite taken with her,'' he smiled. ''My staff cannot seem to do enough for her.''

James stared into space, a forlorn look upon his face. ''Aye,'' he said quietly, ''she is such an easy one to love.''

His sentence came out more like a caress, startling Devlin. His mind kept turning over and over; *No such thing . . . no such thing . . . no such thing . . .*

''I needed to talk with you privately before you see Laurie,'' he said seriously. ''Certain things are happening to her right now you should be made aware of.''

Quietly and evenly, Devlin proceeded to tell James of Lauriette's frequent nightmares, the cottage, the mysterious voice, everything. James listened with interest, his eyes growing wide with anger.

''The grave—''

''Is no doubt Peter's,'' Devlin finished grimly. ''It is slowly coming back to her, but she has no idea why. It is more what she senses rather than what she knows. Either way, she becomes terrified.''

''My poor sweet pet,'' he groaned.

''Was there anything about—about that animal she mentioned?'' Devlin asked hopefully.

James sadly shook his head. ''I belive she totally destroyed any images she might have had of him.'' Then his face brightened. ''Wait! She was ranting, mind you, but she mentioned black eyes . . . black beady eyes were her very words. And something else—a star, that's it! She kept repeating blue star over and over."

Devlin frowned. "Not much," he said, half to himself.

"We scoured the woods and surrounding area for weeks afterward but found no trace of him or his band."

"Perhaps he wasn't English." He toyed with the idea. "But then, the bastard could have been anything—even French!"

"I'd sell my soul to the Devil himself just to find him!" James swore savagely. "He almost destroyed a woman he never saw before that unfortunate day!"

Devlin rose. "Come. It's time for Laurie to feast her eyes upon you," he smiled. "You'll no doubt be the very best medicine for her!"

They stood in the partially opened doorway for a time watching Judd maintain a one-sided conversation. Lauriette had been carefully bathed and dressed by Dolly's loving hands and placed back in her bed, her freshly brushed hair fanning across the plumped pillows.

She looks so lovely, James thought lovingly. Even though the fever had taken its toll, her sweetness and beauty showed through her pale cheeks.

Devlin felt it too, as a stirring in his loins threatened to shatter his composure. Would he never be able to get this enchantress out of his blood?

Lauriette caught the movement and looked toward the door. "Jamie!" she gasped.

James rushed to her open arms, crushing her to him. Tears spilled over her cheeks and onto his shirt sleeve. Devlin and Judd stood silent, witnessing the touching scene. Devlin felt overcome with confusing emotions—

happiness and jealousy combined—and withdrew from the room motioning for Judd to join him.

Lauriette pulled back from James to take a long hard look at her dearest brother. "Look at you!" she laughed through tears. "A long beard no less. Oh, Jamie, I thought you would never return!"

He laughed and kissed her forehead. "Ah-h, forgive me, pet," he sighed. "The seas are becoming more dangerous with each passing month. There is many a privateering ship lurking in the waters now. But I came to see about you. Expecting you to be married to Brimley and reluctantly waiting to hear my 'I told you so'!"

Lauriette blushed prettily and lowered her eyes. "Please, Jamie, don't tease!" she pleaded. "I couldn't bear that right now."

He hugged her tenderly. "There is no need, pet," he said happily. "I heartily approve of your choice of husband."

"You—you do?"

James nodded. "Just the kind of man you need!" he smiled. "Intelligent, strong, good head on his shoulders and not bad to the eyes."

"Oh, Jamie!" she cried in exasperation.

His eyes grew serious. "Devlin has explained everything, pet."

Lauriette blushed deeply. "I seem to make a mess of everything."

"You cannot direct fate, Lauriette," he said. "What is going to happen will happen."

She grinned impishly. "You are so philosophical this morn!"

Placing a hand underneath her chin, he forced her to look at him. His eyes were full of love and understanding. "Do you love him, pet?" he asked softly. "Do you love Devlin?"

Tears glistened in her eyes. Her answer came out

mournfully. "Yes, Jamie, oh yes!" she whispered.

He smiled a knowing smile. "Then I will be able to leave you without reservation."

"Leave! When?"

"At the end of the week, pet," he replied. "My ship is being overhauled and then loaded and then I will be bound for Virginia."

Lauriette grabbed his shoulders. "But, Jamie, you don't understand!" she cried. "He doesn't love me! He doesn't even believe in love!"

James smiled wickedly. "Lauriette, that man searched for hours in the pouring rain for you," he argued. "He never left your side when you came down with the fever, he pulled you through. I know! I saw it with my own eyes."

"No, Jamie," she protested. " 'Twas only out of obligation."

"Obligation be damned!" he ground out. "You did not see the anguish on his face, the raw pain in his eyes! You did not see his mouth tremble when you were at your worst!" James pulled her into his arms. "He may not believe in love at this very moment, but I swear to you, my sweet, Devlin Essex is hopelessly in love with you. Trust me. I know."

"Oh, Jamie," she moaned. "If only that were true!"

Lauriette was up and about by the time James's visit came to an end. The four days went by too swiftly, there was so much left unsaid, so much she wanted to say but could not find the words.

It had been a wonderful four days and she smiled inwardly, thinking of how well Dev and Jamie got along. They laughed, joked, argued—and even got drunk together one night. It was as if they had known each other all their lives.

Then came the morning when he had to leave. He had delayed his journey as long as he dared and now he waited to say his good-byes. Judd warmly shook hands with Lauriette's brother, wishing him farewell.

Devlin hugged James affectionately, feeling much closer to this man than to his own brother. "Our home will always be yours, my friend," he said gruffly.

James' face clouded. "I leave without any reservations, Devlin," he said with much feeling. "Keep her safe."

"I will," he answered.

James turned to Lauriette. A catch escaped her lips as she ran into his outstretched arms. "Must you go?" she whimpered.

He laughed gently. "The sea is my life. Remember, pet?" he asked, his eyes dreamy. "That sunrise on deck?"

Lauriette returned his smile sadly. "I've thought of it often," she sighed. "Return soon, Jamie."

"I will, love."

"God speed," came Devlin's voice directly behind her. She felt his hands upon her shoulders.

James was mounting his horse, but Lauriette could not bring herself to watch him leave and buried her face in Devlin's chest. His arms encircled her like steel bands, his lips pressed a kiss on the top of her head.

"He'll return soon, Laurie," he soothed. "The months will pass swiftly."

Their eyes met, lingering on the expression each held and slowly their lips touched and stayed for a bittersweet moment.

Forty-Five

He stood in the doorway gazing pensively at his lovely wife. The weeks since her illness were well put to use and gradually Lauriette regained the pink in her cheeks and the healthy fullness in her figure. But she was so saddened by James's departure, to see him suddenly after all those months and then to have him leave again, she could not accept the emptiness that surrounded his leaving.

"You know, I became rather fond of him, too," Devlin's soft voice entered her faraway thoughts.

He towered over her and she caught her breath. His eyes gazed at her so warm and brown, the slashed dimples deepened as he smiled.

"I'm sorry," she weakly returned his smile. "He is just so special to me."

Devlin pulled the chair opposite the sofa and sat down, their knees gradually touching. Electrified, she anxiously glanced up. Must he affect me like this?

He looked deeply into her blue-green eyes and immediately Lauriette looked away. He must never see what her eyes would reflect, he must never know.

"Tell me about Captain James Claymoor," he urged. "Tell me why he means so much to you."

Lauriette blushed deeply. "Please don't tease."

Devlin took her hands. "I never tease, cherub."

Her heart leaped. He was making an effort, he truly wanted to know about her special brother.

She smiled in such a way, it caused Devlin's heart to lurch. "Ever since I can remember there has only been one love for Jamie—the sea! When I was seven and he was seventeen, he would tell me stories of ships and famous captains. His one aim in life had always been to build his own ship and sail her. And he did!" She beamed. "Jamie knows every piece of wood, every yard of sail, every nail that holds the *Intrepid* together."

"That must have been quite a feat," Devlin said with open admiration.

Lauriette nodded. "It took him years to build it," she proudly replied. "My father had been a successful master shipbuilder and that same kind of force is in Jamie." Devlin saw the pain in her eyes before she lowered her head.

"He died in the War?"

"Yes," she answered quietly. "He was killed at Yorktown. I know very little of my father. The War took all the good men away from their loved ones." She thought for a moment then sighed. " 'Twas better he died in battle for if he would have survived, what the British did to his shipyard would have killed him. At least he died thinking he left his family a future."

Devlin squeezed her hands sympathetically. There was so much he did not know about his strange young wife.

"Jamie allowed me to spend my free time with him and his workers in the shipyard." Her eyes sparkled at the happy childhood memory. "I was ten and he was twenty when he made his first run. He was so proud—

and so was I! He christened her the *Intrepid* because she was a brave and unshakable piece of love.''

''And you, cherub,'' he smiled, ''did you take after James and acquire a taste for the sea?''

Lauriette gripped his hands, excitement flooding over her. ''Many times!'' she whispered breathlessly. ''I fear there were many times Elliott and James almost came to blows because they disagreed on how I should be reared.''

Devlin could not suppress his laughter and Lauriette joined him. ''Elliott thought I should be reared like any gently born lady and to be protected from life, but Jamie disagreed. He thought a woman should learn about life and be protected from only things that could do injury or harm. To him I was an equal—a whole person with a mind to develop. Elliott demanded I go to a proper girl's school and Jamie scooted me off to sea with him as my teacher!''

Devlin could picture Lauriette standing on deck of the *Intrepid,* the wind billowing through her golden brown curls and whipping madly at her gown, molding it to her curvaceous frame. . . .

''But when we returned from Jamaica, Elliott had his way and I was sent to Boston to learn the ways of ladies,'' she sighed. ''Three years in that dismal school! But Jamie came for me and he was pleased with my newfound maturity and begrudgingly admitted that perhaps Elliott did know what he was doing! It was so wonderful to be home again with Elliott, James, Ben, and Peter. . . .''

Devlin held his breath watching Lauriette's face pale, her eyes look at him in confusion. ''Did I tell you that James hit me?'' he was trying desperately to lure her away from that name.

Presently, she looked at him only half hearing what he had said.

Devlin nodded. "I mistook him for a troublemaker, perhaps an acquaintance of Brimley," he hurried on, relieved to see her interested. "I called on him and he knocked me to the floor!"

Lauriette laughed gaily, her laughter like the tinkling of chimes.

"Madam, are there any more brothers you have neglected to tell me of?" he arched a brow.

"Only one, my lord," she replied. "One Benjamin Franklin Claymoor but I doubt you will ever have an occasion to see him. Last we heard he was in New Orleans seeking his fortune."

"Ah-h!" he exclaimed. "So the Claymoors have a black sheep!"

She smiled impishly. "Doesn't every family?"

"Touché, madam."

Spring drifted lazily into summer and Essex Hall came alive with the preparations for going to Lord Craigmore Bottomsley's ball. There was an easy truce between Devlin and Lauriette and with each passing day their relationship was becoming deeper.

Devlin stood at the foot of the stairs, his legs slightly parted, a sardonic smile uoon his rugged features. He was impeccably dressed in dark blue; a flawless white cravat at his throat only succeeded in calling attention to his deep tan.

Dolly hurriedly trounced down the stairs, Lauriette's overnight valise in hand. Devlin watched as she disappeared out the door, then turned back to the stairs and was held transfixed at the vision of beauty who stood poised midway down the steps.

There was no other word for Lauriette but *vision*. He caught his breath, his heart pounded in his ears. She smiled radiantly down at him. Her dress was a pale blue silk styled in the latest Parisian mode: small puffed sleeves, the waist just underneath her breasts, the neckline cut square and very low, exposing the deep cleft of her creamy breasts. Her golden brown hair had been swept up and Grecian curls framed her face.

She seemed to float down the remaining stairs rather than walk and Devlin's heart gave a lunge as she placed her hand upon his arm. "You will be the loveliest woman there!"

Ambrose House was only an hour's drive from Essex Hall and Lauriette became a nervous knot of anticipation as they neared the huge mansion. This would be her first ball as Devlin's wife; she would be open for inspection tonight and a shudder passed through her at the thought.

"Dev, I'm frightened," she whispered, gripping his hand. "I'm not a titled miss nor a graceful lady! I'll—"

He gently touched her shoulders, turning her around to meet him. "Laurie, you are as much a lady as any woman there tonight," he stated, "moreso than most. You are my wife and I am not ashamed of you. Remember that. Now, are we ready?"

She nodded, her eyes reflecting devotion.

After they were announced by the footman, an elderly woman dressed in deep purple descended upon them. "Devlin, you rogue," she cried, extending her hand to him. "I see you finally decided to grace us with your presence and now we have a chance to meet your bride." Her gray eyes moved over Lauriette from head to toe. "My, she is lovely! I'm afraid you will not see a great deal of her tonight, my boy," she teased lightly. "All the young bucks in the ballroom will be besotted with her."

Devlin smiled warmly. "Next to Laurie, Mattie, you have my heart" he laughed, kissing her hand. "My wife, Lauriette. Laurie, my father's oldest friend, Lady Mathilda Bottomsley."

Mathilda hugged Lauriette affectionately. "Now, Devlin, I am not quite that old!" She laughed, her arm around Lauriette's shoulder. "Now, you go find Fitz and talk about whatever it is you do talk about while I take Lauriette to your room."

As they moved up the stairs, Lauriette smiled back at Devlin to let him know she was not afraid any longer.

Once inside the lavish bedroom that was to be theirs for the night, Dolly immediately began fussing over her.

"You have a lovely house, Lady Mathilda."

"What—this monstrosity?" she laughed. "And my close friends call me Mattie."

Lauriette nodded happily. "I would like that."

"I must admit, Lauriette, we were all very curious about you," the old woman said bluntly, then took Lauriette's hands. "But I can see now why Devlin married you. American or no, my sweet, that man would have been insane to let you go!"

"Mattie—"

"Hush, child! No need to feel embarrassed around me, goodness no!" she laughed. "Anyone can see you are in love with the handsome rake . . . and he with you."

"Mattie, I—"

"Well, I must tend to my other guests." She flounced to the door, cutting off Lauriette's words. "Come downstairs as soon as you are ready. I imagine Devlin will pace about nervously until you are securely at his side!"

The maid fussed with a few stray curls and muttered as she brushed away a fleck of dirt from Lauriette's hem.

"Dolly," Lauriette said, her mood thoughtful, "what is your impression of Lady Mathilda?" She always valued Dolly's sensitivity to people.

"Well, missie, I thin' Lady Mathilda is a gentle soul and a romantic at heart," she explained. "A straightforward lady for certain, but she has a kind heart . . . especially towards his lordship . . . and ye!"

The orchestra was already playing as Lauriette moved down the huge winding staircase, her heart joining with the gaiety of the night. Devlin held out his arm to her and Lauriette gratefully accepted it.

People dressed in their finest were sneaking glances and murmuring about the notorious Devlin Essex and his lovely American bride. Why, everyone at the ball knew of her broken betrothal to Sir Evan Brimley and many a romantic story was passed of how the devil swept her away from him!

Most of the women sighed as they went over the different rumors again and again. It was one thing to hear about their story but another to be able to see them together! Even the gentlemen were not above speculating about the marquess and marchioness. He must have been either thoroughly entranced by the American or a complete fool, they mused, but after catching a glimpse of the fair Lauriette, they smiled knowingly. But even so to duel with Brimley, a renowned swordsman . . .

The musicians began to play a waltz, a new dance which was taking the world by storm. Lauriette heard the melodious tune and gazed hopefully at Devlin. He smiled wickedly and nodded.

Devlin's hand was warm upon her waist; Lauriette could feel the heat of his flesh searing through her thin silk. Shyly, her eyes lifted to meet his and his warm brown eyes reflected her own thoughts. Guiltily, she blushed and Devlin laughed. Good God! she thought desperately. Am I that transparent?

Devlin was burning with desire for her. It was beginning to flow through him, consuming all in its path downward toward his manhood. Tonight, his brain shouted, tonight she will be mine! Oh God, he could not wait another day! Here, in his arms, faithfulness, loyalty, passion, desire, sorrow, joy—how could he have been such a damn fool?

Tonight, after their sweet reunion, he would ask her. She would say yes, she would follow him wherever he traveled; she was that kind of woman. Together they would board the *Horizon Queen* and sail to America. He would take her to all the places that were special to him. Have her see the new nation through his eyes and finally settle on his homestead in Kentucky.

Was it love? He did not even know if there truly was such a thing, but he knew how this bride-child made him feel and no other woman had ever affected him in such a way. If there was such a thing as love, then this little enchantress could be capable of unlocking that door to him!

"Dev, why didn't Judd attend tonight?" she asked.

He smiled at her innocence. "My love, even though Judd and I are related, he doesn't happen to be titled."

" 'Tis cruel and unfair," she replied. "I have no title—"

"But my dear Marchioness, you do!" he countered gently. "I assure you Judd doesn't miss this in the least. He's probably at the tavern, wenching this very moment."

"Devlin!" she gasped.

His hand squeezed her waist intimately and Lauriette beamed.

The waltz ended and Lauriette was besieged with admirers requesting a place on her dance card. A young man, Sir Nathan Longsworth, claimed her hand for the quadrille and brightened at the thought that he was the first to claim the marchioness's attention. There came countless young dandies after Sir Nathan, each anxious for those few precious moments when dancing with the devil's bride. All were curious as to how this quiet beauty captured the uncapturable and came away with a feeling of respect and liking for Lauriette and envy of Lord Devlin.

"Gossip!" Sir Jocelyn Pettigrew smirked. "Should have known better than to think that rare pearl was a fortune huntress."

Sir Nathan Longsworth agreed heartily. "Seems her ladyship is not without funds . . . plain to see she is gently bred."

Sir Edwin Goodbody laughed. " 'Tis a pity Marie-Claire is not here to witness her sister's triumphant presentation to the cream of society." He winked. "I see ol' Henry's taking advantage of his wife being gone."

The three admirers turned and watched as Sir Henry engaged the marchioness in a waltz. They were not the only ones who were drawn to the couple. Black glistening eyes watched as they joined the dancers.

Lauriette felt very self-conscious as Henry's eyes stared into hers. "Please, Henry," she said quickly, "must you stare at me so?"

"You are so lovely this evening," he whispered. "Far lovelier than I have ever seen you."

She blushed and looked away. "You are embarrassing me."

Henry only laughed, tightening his grip on her hand. With expert maneuvering, he guided her through the many couples and out into the night air. Lord Bottomsley's terrace was illuminated by a full moon accompanied by a handful of twinkling stars.

He waltzed with Lauriette slowly, oblivious to the tempo of the music or Lauriette's immediate discomfort.

"Henry, this is not proper," she sternly told him. "Please take me back in."

"Do you not enjoy the fragrant night air?" he asked softly. "This night was made for lovers."

Lauriette looked at him sharply. "Then we will leave this night for lovers," she answered plainly. They had ceased dancing, but Henry still held her.

He stared at her, his gray eyes smoldering. "The lovers have yet to take advantage of this night."

She pulled away, shaking her head. "No, Henry."

Henry grasped one of her hands, holding it tightly so she could not retreat further. "You still care," he whispered. "I know you do. There is no need for you to deny it any longer, Lauriette."

"Henry, why can you not believe that I'm very happy and content at Essex Hall," she said passionately. "There is nothing between us now—or ever!"

"You are wrong, my sweet," he protested. "Soon there will be nothing to stand in our way."

Lauriette snatched her hand away, her eyes a stormy green. Henry took a step forward. "You loved me once—"

"Lauriette!" Devlin's voice growled as he stepped out of the shadows.

Henry stiffened as Devlin stood by Lauriette's side, possessively securing his arm around her waist. Bowing curtly, and without another word, he abruptly took his leave.

Devlin turned his fiery gaze upon Lauriette. "I suggest in the future, madam, you be more discreet as to whom you walk in the moonlight with," he snapped.

"Are you insinuating that I—"

"That I will not tolerate that bastard wooing you!" he sharply cut in. "You are *mine,* Laurie! Don't let me have to remind you of that again!"

Forcefully holding her hand in the crook of his arm, he pulled her along with him into the ballroom and over to the abundant buffet Lady Bottomsley had prepared.

Devlin's manner had changed quickly and as he placed a glass of wine in Lauriette's trembling fingers, he honored her with the most passionate of smiles.

Still burning from his harsh words, Lauriette returned his smile. "You overbearing monster," she whispered through her smile.

Devlin brought her hand to his lips, his dark eyes boldly caressing her. "Yes, I am," he replied lightly. "I am many things when it comes to you."

Before Lauriette could think of a stinging reply, Lady Bottomsley was calling to them both. Trailing behind her was a rotund, elegantly dressed man in his early fifties and on his arm a stunning blond woman clothed in a thin silver gown.

"Good heavens, I missed you two when I was making introductions," she laughed, her eyes twinkling. "Late arrivals, I'm afraid. May I introduce the Marquis and Marchioness of Sutherford, Lord Charles Emory and his lovely companion Lady Salene Thompson—"

Lauriette was stunned, not hearing the rest of Mattie's formal introduction. So this was Lady Thompson. This is the woman Devlin was with when she sent word of Lord David.

It was evident to Mattie and Devlin that the two women were carefully measuring the other. The difference between the two was startling, different as night and day. Where one was small, the other was tall; one was dark, the other fair; one with unusual blue-green eyes, the other pale gray.

" 'Tis quite an event meeting you at last," Salene said, her eyes raking over Lauriette.

Lauriette nodded gracefully, her eyes now a deep blue, accepted the challenge. "I, too, have long wanted to meet you," she half smiled. "Dev has told me a great deal about you."

Salene's eyes openly moved to Devlin and passionately moved over him. He felt Lauriette stiffen as she linked her arm with his. He was very amused.

"Lord Emory, Lady Thompson, if you will excuse us—"

Devlin waltzed Lauriette out onto the dance floor, suddenly feeling elated at the obvious jealousy that appeared on Lauriette's face.

"I didn't realize you were acquainted with Lady Thompson."

Her eyes, a cold emerald green, met his. "You mean Salene?" she contemptuously drawled out the woman's name. Devlin was surprised in the coldness of her soft voice. "I only know of her. Perhaps it is you, my lord, who should learn to be more discreet!"

The shock of her words faltered his step and a rending sound stopped them in mid-dance.

"Laurie, your dress—"

Lauriette gazed down at the torn lace. "I shall have Dolly repair it," she said stiffly. "If you'll excuse me. . . ."

She hurried from the ballroom and half ran up the winding staircase. She was too close to tears and by the time she reached the safety of their room, they were steadily falling down her cheeks.

Devlin accepted another glass of bourbon, his spirits soaring. Jealous! Lauriette had actually showed jealousy and he felt gloriously happy about it.

"Devlin!" the husky urgent voice came from behind him. "I have only a moment. Meet me in the library. I *must* talk with you! It is most important."

Before he could reply, she stepped away. It was Salene. Devlin grimaced. What in the devil could she possibly have to say to him? For a brief moment he decided against meeting her, then thought differently. When it came to Salene, he could leave nothing to chance.

Salene turned quickly as Devlin entered the library, his face void of expression. She leaned against Lord Bottomsley's desk, a seductive smile upon her face.

"Well, get to it, Salene," he said impatiently. "What is all the mystery?"

She moved slowly toward him. "I just had to see you, that is all," she said huskily.

He started to turn towards the door, but her hand stopped him. "I congratulate you, Devlin," she said. "I did not realize your wife was so lovely."

Devlin glared at her. "Is that why your brought me in here?" he questioned. "To tell me you think my wife lovely?"

Salene laughed, her hand touching his shoulder. "No, not exactly. I just wished you to know," she replied. "I wanted to see you alone for a few moments. I wanted to apologize for my burst of temper the last time we saw each other."

"Salene, there is no need—"

She placed her fingertips over his lips. "But there is, darling," she murmured. "We are alike, Devlin, we need each other. I only wanted to tell you when you return to London, I will be waiting for you."

"What?"

Salene laughed. "Come now, darling, do not tell me you can stand this close and not want to bed me!"

Devlin's eyes hardened as his gaze raked over her. How could he have ever been attracted to—to this! He felt sick inside.

Her arms lightly slithered around his neck. "I've always belonged to you, Devlin," she sighed. "I can never be you wife—but I shall always be your mistress—"

"Oh!" A gasp from the door brought Devlin around as he violently wrenched Salene's arms from his neck.

Lauriette slammed the open library door, gripping her fan so tightly her gloves grew taut across her knuckles. Her face bore no trace of the raging emotions tearing her apart. Only her eyes, a fiery green, betrayed the anger inside.

"My dear Marchioness—"

"Shut up!" Lauriette snapped at Salene, who stopped, her mouth still open. "I need no explanations from you—either of you!"

"Laurie—"

Lauriette stiffened at the sound of Devlin's voice. "As of now you owe me nothing, my lord," she said so coldly, Devlin was stunned. "As I understand it, this ends our . . . *understanding.* Please, do not let me stop this—this *touching* little scene. I would never wish to come between *lovers!*" She spat the last words at him before wrenching open the door and flying out.

"Laurie!" he called.

Salene laughed gaily. "You see, my love?" she said sarcastically. "Revenge is always sweet, is it not? Especially when one waits patiently for it."

"Salene—" he hissed.

"I warned you!" she screamed at him. "I warned you that someday I would destroy any happiness you might find in another's arms!"

Devlin was beside himself with controlled fury. Salene was laughing. . . .

"Lady Thompson!" Mattie's booming voice, full of disapproval, ceased Salene's laughter. She stood in the doorway, her face full of disgust.

"Never have I been more disgusted by such cruel and disgraceful conduct," she hissed. "You will leave my house, never again to be welcomed here."

Salene left, humiliated beyond words by Lady Bottomsley. There was no need to stay any longer at any rate; she had successfully destroyed Devlin's marriage.

"You wait!" she sternly told Devlin as the door closed behind Salene. "Give Lauriette time to compose herself."

" 'Tis not what you think. . . ."

Mattie arched a brow. "How do you know what I think?" she countered. "If I had any sense, I would toss you out on your noble . . . It does not matter. If I did not recognize how much you love your wife, I would throw you out!"

"Now, Mattie—"

"Don't you argue with me, you rogue!" she admonished. "And do not give me that gibberish of not believing in love! It is written all over you! And you, my handsome devil, are an utter fool if you keep up this childish pretense! You are about to lose the most precious thing in your life because of your blasted arrogance! Now, you sit here and think about what I said for at least an hour. Then you go up to your room and make love to that beautiful wife of yours! Do I make myself clear?"

Devlin grabbed Mattie, placing a kiss upon her startled lips. "Yes, dearest Mattie," he laughed, "perfectly, wonderfully clear!"

He sat alone watching the clock gradually ticking off the minutes. The gay sound of the ball was muted against the closed door. All his thoughts were one thing only—Lauriette!

What a fool! he cursed himself. All the months behind and he never thought, never let himself think—he was in love! All the signs were there, even from the beginning, and he did not realize it, would not let himself consider it. What a fool!

The proposed hour was almost up but Devlin could stand it no longer. She had to be told and now! He would convince her and if it took all night, by morning there would be no doubt left in her mind.

She loved him, he knew this, but even if she did not, he would make her love him. Somehow, some way.

He took the stairs two at a time, oblivious to the stares of Lady Bottomsley's guests. His heart was bursting with its glorious revelation.

"Laurie!" he burst in the room. He stopped cold, the eerie stillness encompassing him.

The room was empty. Laurie, Dolly, everything—gone.

Forty-Six

Early morning hours found Lauriette already dressed for the day in a blue muslin gown, pacing the library floor like a caged lioness. She and Dolly arrived at the Hall sometime in the wee hours of the morning and somehow managed not to wake the entire household.

She had dismissed Dolly and sought the comfort of her bed, but sleep would not come. Tears flowed freely. She could not erase the picture of Devlin and Lady Thompson together, her face lifted awaiting his kiss, her arms possessively around his neck. . . .

With an enraged groan, she flew from the bed only to tirelessly pace the floor. At dawn she stood at the window to witness the beautiful sunrise, only to have it marred as Devlin's face floated before her eyes. Would she ever be able to forget this hurt inside?

And now she stood at the open French doors gazing at the lovely gardens that gave her so much pleasure. What was Devlin doing at this very moment? Was he beside himself with worry? Was he erupting with anger because she took his coach? Suddenly, she frowned. Or was he asleep . . . with Lady Thompson in his arms. . . .

"Lauriette!" Judd exclaimed. "What the deuce are you doing here! Where is Dev?"

She turned, impatiently brushing away a tear. "Gone to the devil for all I care!" she stormed and flew out of the room.

Judd slowly ran a hand through his hair and grimaced. He thought at least last night all would go well for them, away from the Hall and all of the memories, good and bad. Evidently all had not gone well.

Lauriette wiped her eyes once more and stared at her reflection for a long time.

"Oh, Lauriette," she said aloud, "what are you to do now? You should pack your trunk, you know, and leave before he returns. You can go to London and—what?" She lowered her head. "No, no you won't do that. You can't leave him, can you!" She glared at her reflection. "You are hopelessly in love with a man who cannot or will not love you."

Tears stung her eyes. "Am I doomed for the rest of my life to live like this?" she choked back a sob.

A light tap on the door silenced her. "Lauriette? Are you all right?"

"I'm fine, Judd," she managed to calm her voice. "I'm resting right now."

"If you want to talk, I will be in the library," he said quietly. "Are you sure you're all right?"

"I'm sure."

She heard his retreating footsteps and with another sudden burst of tears, threw herself onto the bed.

It was well into the afternoon that sleep finally came, but it was a troubled sleep filled with Devlin and Lady Thompson. A sounding rap on the door woke Lauriette with a start.

"Sorry to trouble ye, missie." Dolly popped into the

room, a worried expression on her face.

"What is it, Dolly?"

"A messenger from Claymoor, mum."

"From Claymoor? You're sure?"

Dolly nodded. "Direct from Sir Henry. He has ta see ye right 'way. 'Tis very urgent th' messenger says. He's ta await yer convenience an' take ye back ta Claymoor wi' him."

"Dolly, straighten my hair."

"But—but, missie, yer not a-goin' alone!"

"My hair, Dolly!"

A few moments later, Lauriette emerged from her bedroom and headed down the stairs to the awaiting messenger. Lauriette stopped suddenly. Why it was just a young boy shabbily dressed and very thin. Her heart went out to him as the boy self-consciously bowed.

"What is your name?"

Reluctantly, he raised his blue eyes. "Joseph, milady."

"Joseph, how old are you?"

"Jus' turned sixteen, milady."

"Have you been in Sir Henry's service very long?"

Joseph gulped nervously. "All me life, milady."

Lauriette arched a brow. How could Henry treat his servants thusly? This young man looked as if he hadn't eaten in days.

"Sir Henry sent you?"

"Aye, milady . . . well, Mr. Jonas, he sen' me."

Lauriette tied her bonnet. "Then come, Joseph," she said over her shoulder.

An open carriage awaited her and though Joseph opened the door for her, Lauriette refused to get in. "If you don't mind, I would rather ride up front with you."

Joseph blushed as he nodded. This lady was very different from the ones he had infrequently come in contact with. Could this truly be Lady Marie-Claire's sister?

With a snap of the whip, they were off. They had been traveling for some time before Lauriette spoke.

"Have you a family, Joseph?"

"Nay, milady, I'm orphaned."

She laid her hand upon the boy's thin arm in sympathy. "I'm sorry."

Joseph shrugged. "No need ta be sorry, milady, never knew ma folks."

Joseph turned off the main road and it was only a matter of minutes before Claymoor came into view. Lauriette stared in awe. It was the first time she had seen it since that horrible nightmare with Marie-Claire. But it was so different now! The gardens had been repaired and the house had been transformed back to its elegant beauty.

Joseph helped Lauriette down and led her up the stone steps. He rapped several times with the brass knocker. "I'll leave yer now, milady." He bowed neatly. "Mr. Jonas will be a-answerin' th' door."

"Thank you, Joseph." She smiled.

The young man murmured something she could not quite understand then ran down the steps and around the corner of the house. The door slowly opened and a cry of joy escaped old Jonas as he pulled Lauriette inside.

"Jonas, how well you look!" she remarked, giving the old man a hug.

"And you, missie," he said, smiling brightly. "Or should I say my lady!"

Lauriette blushed. "Do you know why Henry sent for me?" she asked, quickly changing the subject.

Jonas' smile faded. "I do, missie, but 'twould be best for Sir Henry to tell you." He gently took her arm. "You're to wait in the sitting room until he returns."

The serene stillness of late afternoon at the Hall was shattered as the great door burst open and Devlin stormed in looking more like Lucifer than the rumors stated.

"Laurie!" he shouted fiercely. "Damn you, Laurie, get down here this instant!"

Judd came running from the library then came to a skidding halt as Devlin's black eyes bore into him. He did not know what to say or even if it would be wise to speak. Devlin was the worse for wear, his clothing wrinkled, no doubt slept in.

"Dev—"

"Lauriette!" his voice boomed. "Where the devil is she! We've got a bit of unfinished business to settle and damn her soul, she's going to sit and listen. Laurie!"

"Dev, what's going on?"

"Going on!" he exclaimed, pacing back and forth. "She left me stranded, *stranded* at Mattie's last night. No word, no way to get home! I had to suffer the attentions and questions of Lady Bottomsley till I thought I would go mad! Then I had to wait until this afternoon before she would lend me a horse! Just desserts, is what she said. Laurie! Either you come down or—"

"She is not here."

Startled, Devlin stared at Judd a long moment. "What do you mean not here?"

"Dolly told me less than an hour ago."

"B-but, where?"

"Where do you think, Devlin?" Muriel's husky voice cut through their conversation. As they both watched, she slowly descended the stairs.

"She went to Claymoor," she informed them both. "I overheard her talking to her maid. I must say, it was rather nice of Henry—he even sent his own carriage for her."

Devlin's stone face was unreadable but Judd knew instantly the fury within him. Turning on his heel, Devlin stalked into the sitting room, immediately going to where the liquor was kept. Without a word, he poured himself a healthy glass.

"Dev, please, it is too early."

He killed the glass in one burning gulp. "Leave me be, cousin."

"Then if you must drink, drink bourbon or brandy but not whiskey," Judd reasoned. "You are not accountable for your actions when you drink whiskey."

He downed another glass and poured one more. "Judd, just get out and leave me," he growled. "I just want to be left alone."

Lauriette drank the tea Jonas had prepared and sat for a long time staring into space. Somewhere in the huge house a clock fatefully ticked off the minutes. She stood and restlessly began to pace. No one had come into the room since Jonas had brought her tea. The silence was beginning to grate upon her nerves.

Leaning against the window frame, she thought of Essex Hall. Had Devlin returned yet? Sadly, she lowered her head. There was a chance he wouldn't return. Perhaps since it was known to her now, he could very well decide to go back to London with Lady Thompson.

When she last saw him, hurt caused her to lash back at him. She had told him their agreement had been dissolved. She did not mean it, only hurt made her want to hit back. But he could have taken her at her word. At this very moment he could be lying in her arms . . .

"Lauriette! Thank heavens you came!" Henry's urgent voice brought her around.

"Henry, what was so important to send a messenger for me?" she questioned. ""I have been waiting hours for you!"

His face was very sober as he took her hand. "Come over here, my love, and sit," he said gently.

Confused, Lauriette sat down, her mind racing. "Henry, what on earth—"

"Lauriette," he interrupted, "I received words today from Vienna. Marie-Claire . . . your sister . . . she's dead."

The onslaught of his words stunned her. "W-what?"

"I'm sorry, Lauriette. She died in an accident—on a boat—she fell overboard and drowned."

"B-but, Henry, she—" The rest of her words were lost in a sob.

Henry held her tenderly against him. "It is all right, dear," he soothed, stroking her hair.

His news had been so unexpected, she was numb from shock. All her pent-up anger, all her fears, all fell upon her as she sobbed uncontrollably. She cried for Marie-Claire, the sister who never loved her. She cried for all the long forgotten childhood memories.

"We will talk of our future later," he said gently, as Lauriette dried her eyes. "I will have Jonas take you to your room."

A pang of alarm went off inside her head. Confused, Lauriette met Henry's gaze. "My . . . room?"

"Of course! There are so many things that have to be said, Lauriette. We have many plans to make."

Her eyes grew wide. She stood and backed away from him. "I'm going home."

He laughed easily. "But, my sweet, you are home. Claymoor has always been your home. Are you not pleased at its appearance?" He moved towards her. "I did it for you. Everything . . . for you . . . for us!"

"Stop it, Henry!" she cried angrily. "Are you mad?

Do you realize what you are implying?"

Henry grasped her hand and greedily pressed it to his lips. "You told me once there could never be anything between us because I was your sister's husband," he reminded her. "Well, I am no longer your sister's husband."

She violently shook her head. She must not panic. By sheer will Lauriette forced her voice to remain calm and steady. "Henry, that was so long ago. A great deal has happened since then. I am married now. Remember?"

Henry's face grew dark at the mention of her status. "I lost you once, Lauriette. I swore I would never let you go again."

"You cannot lose something you never possessed."

Henry gave a start. "You love me."

"No, Henry, I'm sorry but I don't," she whispered.

He grabbed her shoulders, wrenching a gasp from her. "No!" he protested. "You loved me once—"

"*Thought* I loved you!" she cried, twisting free. "I never realized what love was until I met Devlin!" Her hand was on the sitting room door. "What a fool I have been—such a fool!"

She was out in the foyer before Henry caught up to her. His steely grip found her wrist and he ruthlessly jerked her against him. His eyes were a cold, unrelenting blue.

"You will stay because I wish it!" he snapped.

"Let me go, Henry."

"You will stay!"

"Let me go or I'll scream this house down around your ears!"

He laughed curtly. "Do you think my servants will interfere with my wishes?"

"Be pleased ta let th' lady go." The young voice never wavered, never cracked.

Young Joseph, the messenger, emerged from the

shadows, a cocked pistol in his hand. Lauriette felt Henry's grip loosen and she wriggled free. Cautiously, she moved to Joseph's side.

"Put that down, boy!" Henry ordered. "I'll have you whipped!"

"I think not, Henry," Lauriette cut in. "Joseph is in the employ of Lord Devlin now and my lord would look very unkindly upon you touching one of his servants."

"Come, milady." Joseph was backing towards the door.

Outside awaited a closed carriage, the side lamps lit for night travel. Without a moment's hesitation, Lauriette climbed up to the driver's bench then held the pistol as Joseph climbed up beside her. With a loud crack of the whip they were off, leaving a stupefied Henry at the open door shouting like a madman.

The cool night air brought a flush to her cheeks as she sank back against the back of the bench, weakness flooding over her. The horror of Henry's advances and the shattering news of Marie-Claire's death encompassed her. Stubbornly, she brushed a tear away, refusing to give in to hysteria.

"Are ye all right, milady?"

Lauriette smiled wearily. "That I am, thanks to you, Joseph," she said. "You saved my life tonight and I am in your debt."

"Ye owe me nothin'."

They were silent the rest of the way to Essex Hall. Joseph brought the carriage to an easy halt in front of the steps and jumped down. He accompanied Lauriette to the door and made a bow to leave.

"No, Joseph," she said softly. "I meant what I said to Sir Henry. From this moment on you are part of our world."

"Milady," he stammered, embarrassed at her generosity, "ye needn't—"

"Come along," she ordered, one hand on the door, "no servants entrance for you either."

Once inside the foyer, Joseph gazed in awe at the elegance of Essex Hall. He felt very self-conscious and ashamed at his present condition.

"Lauriette! You've come back!" Judd rushed toward her, his face full of concern.

"Of course I've come back!" she retorted, then looked at him curiously. "Why are we whispering?"

He glanced nervously at the closed library door. "Devlin's here. He came in shortly after you departed for Claymoor."

Lauriette paled a shade at the mention of Devlin's name. Immediately, she looked at Joseph. "Judd, this is Joseph," she introduced. "He's going to be a permanent fixture at the Hall. Could you see to it he has suitable clothing . . . and a good meal?"

Judd eyed the boy suspiciously.

"I'll explain everything later," she added quickly. "Right now I—"

"No, Lauriette," he cut in. "Now is not a good time to see Dev."

"But I don't understand."

"He came home and found you gone. . ." his voice trailed off.

Lauriette blushed furiously. "It was urgent," she told him quietly. "Henry received news—Judd, my sister died some days ago in Vienna. That was why I was summoned to Claymoor."

Relief flooded over his face. "Still, it would be wise to wait until morning," he advised. "He has been drinking quite heavily."

Lauriette nodded. "I see. You're right, of course," she agreed. "And I am tired."

"You go on," he said gently. "I'll take young Joseph here under my wing. He can bunk in with

Pauley.''

She smiled gratefully. ''I will retire then.''

''Milady . . .'' Joseph stammered. He could not find the right words to express his feelings.

''Good night, Joseph,'' she whispered. ''Sleep well.''

Lauriette quietly walked up the stairs, the rigidness with which she carried herself was gone as she collapsed on her bed feeling safe and secured within the walls of Essex Hall.

Quietly, she slipped out of her dress and chemise, shrugging into a light, airy nightgown. The night had grown increasingly warm as she lay atop her bed.

Defeatedly, she flung one arm across her eyes. Was her entire world going mad? She was filled with remorse and sadness uoon hearing the news of Marie-Claire's death, but she felt no loss, for to feel loss there had to be some form of attachment. There was none between the sisters.

She involuntarily shuddered at the thought of Henry. She was filled with disgust by him, his cold attitude of his wife's death. How callous and unfeeling he was. How could she ever have thought herself in love with him!

And last, Devlin had returned home and from the look on Judd's face, in very black spirits. Lauriette felt her chest constrict as Devlin's face flashed before her. How could she have allowed herself to fall in love with him? To fall in love with a man who discards women as easily as some men discard cravats!

Lauriette tossed and turned for hours, but sleep just would not come. With a frustrated groan, she swung her legs off the bed and reached for her blue satin wrapper. Tying it at the waist, she headed for the door. Perhaps a dull book from the library would put her to sleep.

The stairway was faintly illuminated by a long, tapering candle perched midway on the banister. Quietly, Lauriette descended the stairs, the stillness relaxing her.

Opening the library door gradually, she stopped breathing and stood frozen as her gaze rested on Devlin. He appeared to be asleep, his head resting on the wing of the chair. She felt a stab of anguish. Devlin hardly looked like himself, a black curl rested carelessly on his forehead, a day's growth of beard on his face, his white shirt soiled and wrinkled.

Silently, on tiptoe, Lauriette crossed the room and plucked the first book within her grasp.

"I see you decided to return."

Forty-Seven

Lauriette cried out in genuine shock and turned quickly, her heart pounding murderously. Devlin had not moved a muscle, his dark head still resting on the wing of the chair. Only his eyes, cold and very remote, pierced through the dim light of the library.

She could barely breathe; her back was against the bookcase and fervently Lauriette wished she could render herself invisible and blend into the wood.

Devlin stood, his movements pantherlike smooth, and strode silently to the open door. He closed it with such raw violence, it shook on its hinges. Lauriette winced, involuntarily holding her breath. Devlin leaned against the desk, legs carelessly crossed, arms folded across his broad chest.

His entire being was tensed and as his hard gaze raked over her, she felt her own muscles tense in a haze of impending doom. His face looked as if it had been carved out of granite as he contemplated her. His eyes, now a glistening black, were unreadable, but his usually full sensuous mouth was drawn downward in a tight line. She gulped nervously.

"I—I did not mean to wake you," she stammered, her courage badly faltering under his scrutinizing stare. "Only I—I couldn't sleep, so I—I came for a book."

Devlin's laugh was hard and bitter. "I have to admit I'm rather shocked you're here. Did you forget something perhaps?"

Lauriette stiffened at his sneering tone, so unlike him. What had she done that was so horrible?

"Perhaps dear old Henry decided he'd rather not have used goods. Is that what happened?"

Her head jerked up defiantly. "There is no reason to explain myself to you, my lord," she returned coldly. "You have already formed your own verdict and have declared me guilty as charged!"

Devlin's dark eyes wandered over her once again. Her golden brown curls hung carelessly over one breast almost to her waist, her cherub face was held up proudly, her chin thrust outward in indignation. He felt a maddening throb in his loins at the sight of her in that revealing satin wrapper.

Angrily, he poured himself another glass of whiskey and gulped the burning liquid down; the heat of it brought stinging tears to his eyes. He longed to touch her, to erase everything that had happened in the past twenty-four hours. Silently, he swore. Henry's leering face brought savage pain to his chest.

His brooding gaze fell once again upon her and Lauriette caught her breath. She could not tear her eyes away from his, and for a fleeting moment he let his guard down and Lauriette saw the naked hurt in his eyes.

Lauriette managed to draw upon her courage. She moved slowly away from the bookcase, the book clutched against her breast. "I wish no argument with you tonight, Dev," she said cooly. "I'll return to my room and let you get back to your liquor."

Devlin's hand enclosed upon her wrist as he lazily pulled her to face him.

"What a damn crazy fool I was! How you must have enjoyed your part as the innocent, shy Mistress Claymoor, using me all the while to get back at dear old Henry. Tell me, was it worth suffering my attentions?"

Lauriette could not have felt more pain than if he had struck her. She glared at him with a mixture of hurt and contempt.

"You speak of use, my lord. I learned from the master how to use people," she answered hotly. "And, indeed, *you* taught me well."

"Me!" he exclaimed, deliberately grinding his fingers into her tender wrist. "You sought to humiliate me by deserting me at Lady Bottomsley's and to run to your lover's arms the moment my back was turned. How many times have you met him while I was gone?"

Lauriette cried out against his cruel grip, but she could not twist free.

"You, madam, are a cursed thorn in my side!" he hissed furiously. "You are no better than a bitch in heat, chasing after one man then another! Brimley, Branscombe, Neville—does the list never cease? A whore, madam, I gave my name to a whore! Thank God there was no issue from our brief union—they would have been bastards, every one of them!"

Wildly, Lauriette struck out at him with her free hand. She beat against his chest wanting to hurt him, maim him, leave him as nakedly vulnerable as he had her.

She saw him through a haze of tears, his face cold and ruthless. Was this the man she had swooned with unfaltering love for? This man who had just heaped upon her insults and humiliation?

"An instrument of revenge is what you married me for!" she viciously flung at him, tears streaming down her face. " 'Twas *you* who left me alone, *you* who stayed with Lady Thompson in London, *you* who deserted my bed! It was *you* who held that—that woman in your arms last night! I give you in return what you've given me—nothing! Yes, thank God you never got me with child—you've never been man enough to!"

Too late, Lauriette realized her anger had pushed Devlin too far. "Please, please, Devlin, let me go!" she pleaded, shrinking from the smoldering look in his eyes. She knew in that split second what was going to happen. "No, Devlin, please no!"

"Aye, Lauriette, *my dear,*" he drawled cruelly, his hand roughly tugging at her wrapper belt. "I wish to taste the delights which Henry thought so desirable."

Struggling against him, Lauriette managed to free one hand. With a terrified cry, she raked her nails across his cheek and blood flew from the wound. Growling, Devlin violently shoved her away and Lauriette slammed against the wall, her breath knocked from her.

His hands forced her to the floor as she fought him bitterly. "Oh God, no, Dev!" she cried, pummeling her fists against his shoulder blades. "Please, not like this! Not like this!"

Devlin's free hand feverishly tore at her nightgown, his drunken mind deaf to her cries. All he thought of was to hurt her as she had done him. Make her pay for the pain he endured.

His hands cruel upon her shoulders, he restrained Lauriette, cursing her, calling her every degrading name he could think of.

"No-o!" Her scream died in a wail as he brutally entered her.

"Peter!" she moaned. "Peter . . . Peter . . . Peter . . ."

She lay stiff and unyielding underneath him, her

sobs breaking the stillness of the room. The brutal invasion of her body was over.

Wearily, Devlin rolled away from her, the fogginess of the whiskey giving way to sober thought. He became horrified, staring down at the hysterically sobbing woman curled up in a ball. What had he done to her! Oh God, he had hurt her! His brain cleared at an amazing rate.

Numbed and dazed by Devlin's brutal rape, Lauriette struggled to her feet. A pain from her loins brought an anguished moan from her swollen lips. Unconsciously, she pulled the tattered wrapper across the badly torn gown, her eyes staring blankly ahead.

Within the few violent minutes, Lauriette Essex had reverted back to Lauriette Claymoor, seventeen, ravished by an unknown assailant. It was real, it was true, it was happening now.

Devlin was so filled with self-loathing, he had to force himself to look at the precious jewel he may have destroyed. There was no way to go back, to undo the hideous crime he had just committed. His eyes were filled with shame. She stood near the desk, her back towards him, her shoulders sagged in surrender. Had he truly destroyed what he loved most?

He slowly stood, his eyes resting on her back. "Laurie . . . forgive me," he begged, his hand outstretched in supplication. "I . . . just went crazy . . . you were gone . . . to him . . ."

Lauriette slowly turned, her blank eyes spilling over with tears, a pistol rested in her trembling, bruised hand. "My brother dead." Her voice was void of emotion, her eyes stared right through him. "You killed Peter . . . my Peter!"

He realized instantly what his brutal assault had done to Lauriette. He had ruthlessly pushed her over the edge. Now she saw him as the man who had ravished her and killed her twin . . .

"No—no, Laurie," he said tenderly, gradually moving towards her. "Oh, my love, it's me—Dev! It's Devlin . . . Devlin!"

"Murderer!" she cried shrilly, the pistol held firmly in her hands.

"My God! What have I done to you!" he groaned. "Laurie, honey, it's Dev . . . Dev . . ." Devlin held his hand out in front of him, his eyes glued to the pistol.

Suddenly, his hand came up hitting the pistol. The weapon discharged and Devlin sucked in his breath as the ball slammed into his shoulder. Blood quickly spread across the white shirt. The pistol clattered to the floor as Devlin crushed Lauriette against him. His eyes were clouded with pain and sadness.

"Forgive me . . . cherub," he rasped. "I never . . . meant to . . . hurt you." The last words rushed out like a fierce sigh as he crumpled to the floor.

The door burst open as Judd came onto the scene, followed only by Barton. His face grew livid with rage as his eyes took in Lauriette's pitiful state but stopped as he spied the pistol.

"Dev!" he cried bending down. "Barton, hurry! Send for Dr. Quade at once!"

Barton urgently disappeared out the door as Judd protectively turned Lauriette away from Devlin's unconscious body.

"Oh, Lauriette," he murmured, his voice so full of shock and sympathy. "What did he do to you?"

His words rushed past her as she looked at him with her blank expression. Her lips opened to speak and at that moment, her legs decided to fail her and Lauriette felt herself being pulled into a pit of darkness.

Forty-Eight

Lauriette was slowly rising out of a fog, a sea of faces swimming before her. She was faintly aware of the rushing past her door and of distant whispers.

Insistently, her eyelids fluttered, then opened. Without moving, she willed her eyes to explore the room she was in. Presently, she sighed. It was her own.

"Devlin!" the loud cry involuntarily escaped her lips. She tried to sit up but was gently pushed back by loving hands.

"Rest yeself, missie," Dolly whispered. "I'm here to care for ye."

"But . . . Devlin!"

Dolly's face grew dark. "Dr. Quade's wi' him now. Ye lay quiet like. Ye need yer rest."

Alarm consumed her. "I have to go to him, Dolly!" she insisted, pushing away the maid's restraining hands. "Let me up, I say!"

With an exasperated sigh, Dolly turned away from the bed. It was a painful struggle, but Lauriette finally managed to stand. She had to go to him, be with him. Memories of what she'd done washed over her.

"Dolly, please help me dress," she begged, conscious of her appearance.

Dolly grudgingly helped her into a light muslin gown, gasping at the bruises that peppered her breasts and shoulders. Stiffly, Lauriette ignored Dolly's soothing words and hurried out into the hall.

"Lauriette! You should not be out of bed!" Judd's gruff voice stopped her in front of Devlin's door. "You should be resting."

"I can't." Her voice broke as she fought to hold back the tears. "Is Devlin . . . alive?"

Judd nodded grimly. "Dr. Quade just left."

"Is . . . he going to be all right?"

"Your concern is quite admirable, but under the circumstances, you have every right to despise him." His voice was harsh, bitter.

"No, Judd, it was my fault—all of it," she fiercely gripped his arm. She had to make him understand. "I . . . provoked what happened."

"Lauriette—"

"What did Dr. Quade say?" Judd hesitated. "Judd, please!"

"The ball went through the side of his chest and out through his shoulder," he told her. "A few inches more to the left and he would have died. He is going to need constant care for some time, but he is young and healthy. He should be able to recover completely."

"Oh, thank God!" she murmured gratefully. "Let me go into him now."

Judd barred her way. "Lauriette, you are under no obligation . . .

"For heaven's sake, Judd," she cried, "*I* am the one who put him there!"

"Dev absolved you of any wrongdoing," he said. "He told me he drove you to it. You need not go in that sickroom under any sense of obligation. I don't think the bastard deserves any!"

"'Judd," she said quietly, tears falling. "Judd, I love him. No matter what's happened, I can't change my feelings for him."

There! She had finally said it and it came out so easily. Judd's resolve melted away under the intense gaze of Lauriette and lowering his eyes, he stepped aside.

The heavy draperies were drawn against the bright sunlight; the room was deathly quiet. Slowly, she walked toward the bed, her heart pounding in her ears.

Devlin's face was terribly pale. A sheet was pulled up to his waist, his bare chest partially covered with bandages already beginning to show the pinkish stain of his blood. Numbly, she sank to the chair near the bed and gazed longingly at Devlin's still face.

She bit down on her bottom lip so hard she tasted her own blood. *How could I?* she questioned herself bitterly. *How could I have done . . . this!*

Guilt swept over her like a hot breath from hell. All the forgotten moments that continually eluded her came to a slithering halt in one violent gush.

Devlin had been right. She was not what she pretended to be. He had not been the first man to touch her and that thought left an icy coldness in the pit of her stomach. No, she had been a sacrificial lamb at seventeen, bent to the depraved lusts of a madman whose entire being was only a blur to her even now.

And Peter—beloved Peter had died trying to save her honor and she had been powerless to help him. She had been forced to watch as her twin brother died at *their* hands. She remembered—oh, *how* she remembered. Every depraved moment, every degrading detail.

Devlin moved slightly and moaned. Lauriette flew to his side instantly, her voice soothing, her hands administering a cool cloth to his face and forehead.

"Cherub," he moaned. "Laurie . . ."

"Hush, darling," she whispered tenderly. "I'm here—I'll always be here. As long as you need me."

"Laurie . . . Laurie . . ." He drifted off once again.

The day wore on, but Lauriette refused to leave his side. Judd, Dolly and Barton came and went but Lauriette was oblivious to everyone around her. Only Devlin mattered, Devlin whom she loved.

Night gradually fell and Judd entered the room and tried to persuade Lauriette to rest for at least the night. She adamantly refused to leave Devlin's side and rudely ignored anyone who tried to take her place. Finally, in total surrender, Judd stormed out of the room and Lauriette snuggled into the overstuffed chair.

Soon Lauriette lost track of the days as Devlin hovered on that thin line between life and death. She stubbornly refused to give up her claim on him, talking to him even though he was unconscious, stating he would not dare to die and leave their argument unfinished.

She went on tirelessly, bathing him as best she could, changing the dressing on the wound; every ministration was done by her for she would not let anyone else near him. She was on the verge of exhaustion but stubbornly refused to give in.

By the tenth day his restlessness increased. He ranted incoherently, striking out with his good arm at invisible assailants. Lauriette covered him again, whispering loving words of comfort and at the sound of her voice, he grew still. She began to withdraw and stopped as she felt his hand possessively tangled in her hair. A sob caught in her throat as she tenderly pressed his hand to her cheek.

On the eleventh day, Lauriette grew increasingly concerned as Devlin began to grow feverish. By nightfall, his temperature skyrocketed as he thrashed about.

It was all she could do to hold him down, piling blankets on top of him.

Devlin began to rant, hurling curses that echoed down the corridor. Lauriette gently pushed him back down but this time he flung her from him and struggled valiantly to get up.

"I'll kill you, Brimley!" he screamed. "I'll kill you!"

"Judd!" she shouted. "Judd!"

It was some time before she and Judd finally got him calmed down. Lauriette was drained completely of any strength but still refused to leave him.

Near morning his fever pitched even higher. "Laurie, where are you?" His voice sounded as if he was going to cry. "Laurie . . . "

She sponged his face again, her eyes filling with tears. "I'm here, my love," she sobbed. "Open your eyes and see. I'm right here."

Lauriette felt as if she just closed her eyes when he cried out again. "Don't leave me!" he said hoarsely. "Don't leave me!"

Her arms went around his neck as she lay down beside him, turning him on his side to face her. She held him gently, his head against her breasts and cried with him until sleep overcame them both.

Sunlight filtered in through the heavy draperies, a bluebird sang merrily just outside the window. Lauriette woke with a start, feeling guilty of her restful sleep.

She looked down and was overjoyed as Devlin's warm brown eyes, void of fever, gazed wonderingly at her.

"Laurie." His voice was weak, barely above a whisper.

"Hush," she pressed her fingers to his lips. "We'll talk later."

Exhaustion overcame him as he drifted back to sleep.

Gently, Lauriette lifted herself from the bed and hurried out of the room. Her heart was joyous.

"Judd!" she called. "Judd, hurry!"

Lauriette ran down the stairs to meet him, tears of happiness streaming down her pale cheeks. Judd's face was set heavy, expecting to hear the worst.

Her arms went around his neck as she hugged him tightly. "The fever's done!" she cried. "He'll live! He'll live!"

Judd joined in her celebrating, laughing and twirling her around. He loved Devlin dearly, more than he could have any brother.

"See him," she urged. "See for yourself. He's going to be all right. I just know it."

Judd kissed both of her hands and took the stairs two at a time.

"Don't tire him," she called out, then tiredly walked into the sitting room. She was suddenly very much aware of her own dwindling strength. Devlin was going to live and that was all that mattered.

"Well, I see you finally left his side," Muriel's husky voice came from behind her. "You must be very relieved to know you will not be branded a murderess."

Lauriette's head jerked up as she whirled about to face Muriel. "I am in no mood to spar with you."

"Perhaps not, precious, but at any rate you will hear me out," she demanded. "To begin with, I must commend you on your unwavering nursing of Devlin. But then, keeping in mind your pretty neck could very well be stretched otherwise—"

"Stop this at once!"

"Not this time, Lauriette," she sneered, "not until I am finished! You nearly destroyed the only man I have ever loved—and he returned that love. Ah, yes, I see you are disbelieving. Nevertheless, it is true! Devlin did not realize I was free when he married you—or he never would have gone through with this absurd arrangement.''

Lauriette gripped the sofa for suppoort. ''You are lying.''

Muriel laughed cruelly. ''You think so? Tell me, do you think a virile man like Devlin has been sleeping alone in his room every night?''

''N-no, Dev would never—never do that,'' she stammered, dazed by Muriel's words. ''Not a few doors from . . . me.''

''If you would only have died from the fall!'' Muriel hissed. ''I did my best—''

''You? You were that rider?'' Lauriette questioned. ''Why—why?''

''I had to get rid of you so Dev and I could have a life together. He knew it was me who ran into you. He was quite angry, but he did understand.''

''No!'' she cried. ''Dev would never be a party to murder!''

''You little goose!'' Muriel's smile was sadistic. ''How do you think Devlin will feel when he regains his strength and sees you every day, knowing you tried to kill him!''

''No, no! It wasn't like that!'' Lauriette cried. ''I didn't know . . . I didn't realize . . .''

''Do you think he'll believe you?'' she continued relentlessly. ''He'll grow to despise you, if he hasn't already, and it will grow worse with every passing day. Because soon, everyone will know that I am to have his child. Did you hear me, Lauriette? Devlin's child.''

''Muriel, I don't—''

''I do not care what you believe!'' she spat. ''Can you really stand the humiliation of seeing me day after day, my belly growing with life, knowing that Devlin will love me all the more because I carry his child?'' Muriel stood by the open door. ''I suggest you leave,

Lauriette. Leave before Devlin remembers and begins to hate. Especially since you could not give him what he desired most—a child."

With the dignity of a gently bred lady, Lauriette quietly informed Dolly of their leaving and bound her to secrecy. She wished only one trunk packed and they would leave before dawn.

"B-but, milady," Dolly exclaimed, "where'll we go?"

"To London," her reply was crisp. "I leave all the details of our leaving to you."

In the early morning hours, just as the sky was beginning to lighten, Lauriette silently creeped into Devlin's room. Just once more she had to behold his face and brand it upon her memory. If only he could have loved her, if only she could have done something to make him love her. But it was too late now. He would forget her almost immediately and within months be holding his own child. Lauriette bit hard on her lip to keep from crying. A child that was not hers!

Devlin's eyes flickered open and he tried to bring the blur before him into focus. The faint scent of honeysuckle was present and he smiled crookedly.

"Laurie . . ." he murmured.

Her voice was soft, gentle, yet saddened. "Hush, my darling, you must sleep."

"Laurie . . ." He felt so tired; the drug that they had given him had not worn off. Why was her voice so laced with tears?

"Forgive me, my love," she whispered. He felt her gently hand touch his cheek. In his present state, though, he could not even raise his head. "If only we could have loved each other."

What was she saying? Why was she talking that way? But he was so tired, so very sleepy. Gradually, his eyes closed, secure in the feeling of her hand still upon his cheek.

When he was once again asleep, Lauriette placed a final kiss upon his lips then quietly made her way out the door. The Hall was not yet stirring, but time was now important. In the courtyard awaited an open carriage and Lauriette stopped immediately upon seeing a tall young man dressed in clean clothing, holding the door open. The man's eyes were a clear blue and his sandy-colored hair was being whipped madly by the wind.

" 'Tis Joseph, milady," Dolly said quickly. "Caught me at th' stables, he did. Says he's a-goin' wi' us."

Lauriette smiled sadly. "I welcome your company, Joseph."

With Joseph's assistance, Lauriette and Dolly seated themselves and they were off to London just as the sun began to shine. Lauriette gazed straight ahead, vowing not to look back. If she did, she might weaken and return, no matter what the consequences.

Along toward dark, they stopped at a small inn along the London road and Lauriette found out just how valuable Joseph really was by seeing to their rooms and to dinner.

"And where are you going to sleep?"

He smiled sheepishly. "In th' stable, milady."

"You will not!" she snapped, grabbing his arm. "Come with me."

The portly innkeeper was surprised as the well-dressed young woman came towards him with a red-faced young man in tow. No doubt the young man had offended her.

"Sir, do you have any more rooms available?" she inquired.

"Why, that I do, mum," he told her curiously.

"Then please be good enough to see that my brother has one of the best you have." The innkeeper was openly surprised. "You must forgive Joseph's appearance. It's his age, sir! Very rebellious. Now, thank the innkeeper, you ingrate, and let us go to our rooms!"

Joseph, still embarrassed, bowed and followed Lauriette and Dolly up the stairs. Never had he met anyone like this woman.

"Milady, ye didn't—"

"Joseph, for what you have done for me, I've come to regard you as a brother." She smiled affectionately. "Good night."

He felt choked inside. No one had ever been so kind and generous to him before. He felt so much warmth swell up inside him. "Good night, mum."

Forty-Nine

After two full days of traveling on the London road, they would be in London by nightfall. Joseph and Dolly paced restlessly beside the carriage as they waited for Lauriette to emerge from the inn.

"I don' like it," Dolly grumbled to Joseph. "She looks bad, she does. Hardly's ate anythin' an' she can't sleep at night!"

"Once we get her to Sir Neville's, she'll be all right." Dolly's eyes widened at the sound of Joseph's refined words. Why, he almost sounded like a male Lauriette! Joseph noted Dolly's surprise and blushed. "Her ladyship's helping me."

Dolly smiled. "She's a fine teacher, lad."

Lauriette came out from the inn, her face very white, her frame like fine china. "Well, are we ready?"

"I think ye should rest for a day, missie," Dolly said critically. "Ye don' look well."

"Don't fuss, Dolly," she returned, trying to give a smile she did not feel. "The sooner we arrive in London, the sooner you'll see Mr. Bonnar!"

Lauriette suffered the bouncing, jostling trip in silence, trying to keep up the pretense of feeling just fine. But she wasn't fine at all. She could not eat, sleep just would not come, her whole being, her whole reason for being seemed to vanish into thin air and she was left with nothing.

She had to make some effort to get out of this depression that was dragging her lower and lower each day. *Home,* she thought. *Philadelphia, the sea, the farm!* Yes, she would center all her powers on these thoughts. She would survive and live a quiet existence on the land she loved.

Shortly before dark, Joseph brought the carriage to a halt in front of an impressive townhouse. Lauriette's heart twisted painfully. She did not know if she could go through with it. Bittersweet memories were smothering her, her legs were gradually turning to water. She was aware of being assisted up the steps by Joseph and hearing his heavy knock.

Panic rose inside as the door opened, and a very sober-looking valet eyed them. She moved her mouth but no words would come.

"This is the Marchioness of Sutherford." Joseph's strong voice held a ring of authority. "Open this door wider, I say! Her ladyship is not feeling well."

The valet opened the door and Joseph helped Lauriette inside.

"What is going on!" Neville stared as his eyes found Lauriette's pale face. "Lauriette!"

It was too much to bear. Neville stood before her in a black satin dressing robe, looking so much like Devlin she could hardly breathe. His face began to swim before her.

"Lauriette!" he cried as she fell against him.

Swiftly, Joseph was beside Neville, gathering Lauriette into his arms. Concern covered his young face, his mouth set grim.

"Follow me upstairs," Neville told him.

Joseoh tenderly laid her on the bed while Dolly fussed over her.

"Exhaustion's what it is, sir," Dolly explained. "She's been so full of worry for his lordship."

Neville eyed the young man curiously. "And who might you be?"

Joseph returned his gaze. "Joseph, sir."

Neville extended his hand to him. "Let us go downstairs and become acquainted."

Joseph followed Neville down to the drawing room. He offered the young man a drink, but he refused.

"The last time I saw Lauriette she was just fine," Neville said evenly. "Would you mind telling me what's amiss?"

Joseph looked down at his hands. If Lauriette trusted this man, so would he. "I can't tell you very much." In his manner of speaking, he told of his first meeting with the marchioness, his rescue of her and all that he knew of the shooting, which was not too clear.

Neville's face grew very sober as he listened to the boy's words. His eyes became black, his mind conjuring up all sorts of torturous pictures of what provoked Lauriette into shooting Devlin.

"And you have become an adopted brother to her ladyship?"

Joseph nodded, blushing. "Yes, sir, in a manner of speaking."

"Well, then, I welcome you to my home, Mr. Claymoor."

Joseph smiled brightly. He had always been known as just 'Joseph,' never another name to go with it. Now he had one—Claymoor. "Thank you, sir."

"Sir Neville," Dolly spoke, "her ladyship wishes ta see ye."

"Is she all right?"

Dolly nodded. "She's just tired, sir," she sighed. "Ain't had a decent night's sleep in weeks."

"What happened at the Hall?"

Dolly lowered her head. "I think she wants ta tell ye."

Neville stared down at Lauriette for a long moment, a mixture of emotions bubbling inside. Two months before she would not come with him and now here she was, looking so fragile, so vulnerable.

"Neville," she whispered.

"I'm here, little one," he replied, sitting down on the bed.

Her eyes were glistening with tears. "I should have never come here!"

"Nonsense." He smiled. "Where else would you go?'"

"I need to ask a favor," she said quietly.

"I would do anything for you."

"Neville, I want to go home," she blurted out. "I want to go back to Philadelphia."

Neville's eyes burned into hers. "Lauriette, what happened at the Hall? Why did you shoot Devlin?"

"Oh, Nev, I never meant—I didn't know—" She began to sob.

Neville embraced her, murmuring soothing sounds.

"I went crazy," she cried. "I thought he was someone—from my past—"

"It's all right, little one," he whispered, stroking her hair. "Nothing can harm you here."

"I want to go home, Neville," she sniffed. "Please, I beg of you, make the arrangements, please!"

"There is nothing I wouldn't do for you, Lauriette," he said huskily. "I'll take care of it on the morrow."

Cupping her face in his hand, Neville kissed Lauriette tenderly. "You know you can stay here as long as you like,'' he whispered. ''I'll give you love.''

She gazed up into his eyes. ''But I cannot return your love,'' she said sadly.

Gently, he touched her cheek, his voice warm. ''It is Devlin, isn't it?''

She began to cry again. ''I'm sorry, Neville. I suppose it has always been Devlin, though I didn't realize it. God forgive me, I love him and I always will.''

''Then why are you running away?''

Lauriette placed her hand over his. ''Because you were right, Nev,'' she answered bitterly. ''The devil has no heart—at least not for me!''

''Because of my feelings for you, I will take care of everything,'' he said evenly. ''And how many will board the ship?''

''Just me.''

''What?''

''I have given Dolly a generous dowry and she'll be marrying her Mr. Bonnar.''

''And what of Master Joseph?''

''Joseph?''

''Joseph!'' Neville bellowed.

In a moment or two Joseph appeared in the doorway, anxious concern written upon his face. Neville motioned him toward the bed.

''Are you all right, milady?''

''Milady!'' Neville laughed. ''That is no way for a brother to address his sister—especially if he is accompanying her to Philadelphia.''

Joseph smiled happily, understanding what Neville was leading up to. ''Of course, *Lauriette,*'' he grinned. '' 'Twould be uncivil for me to leave my sister unprotected.''

''Quite right, Master Joseph,'' Neville joined in. ''You will go with me tomorrow to make the arrangements. Best get some sleep.''

Lauriette reached out and grabbed his hand. "Thank you, Joseph."

"Goodnight . . . Lauriette," he said slowly and left the room.

"The boy is devoted to you."

"And I to him," she replied. "He saved my life, you know."

Neville smiled. "That is strange. To hear him tell it, 'twas the other way around."

Her eyes grew serious. "There is one thing more," she said. "Neville, could I possibly, legally make Joseph my ward?"

A light came into his eyes. "You are truly an amazing woman," he said. "I will see what I can do. And now, little one, I expect you to get plenty of rest and food. If you do this for me, I'll book passage."

"It is done then," she sighed. "All I want now is to go home."

Two weeks flew by quickly as Neville went to the docks each day in search of a proper ship. There were many leaving for America yet he would not book passage on any of them as fears for her safety rose inside.

Lauriette was gradually regaining her strength. Tearfully, she parted from Dolly on her wedding day, but still the little maid returned faithfully each day to care for her mistress for as long as possible.

Using his influence, Neville managed to have Joseph legally adopted into the Claymoor family and Lauriette was filled with love for this new brother. They both had been orphaned but now they had each other. Each day was spent on his English and manners and within that time even Neville was startled at how much of a Yankee the boy was becoming.

It was early July when Neville came bounding in, an

elated smile upon his face. "Well, I found your ship!" he announced. "You and Master Joseph will sail on the morning tide on the *Elizabeth Todd* under Captain Rodell, a very good friend of mine."

Lauriette's heart pounded with excitement. "Tomorrow!" she breathed, then looked at him anxiously. "What did you tell him?"

Neville grinned. "I told him *my wife* was dying of homesickness and though I could not make the trip myself, that her young brother was accompanying her."

"Neville!"

He placed a kiss on her hand. "At least let me dream, little one," he said sadly. "I did it to protect you and Joseph. I do have some influence and I know Augustus Rodell will keep you safe."

The next morning Lauriette and Neville stood on the dock watching the beautiful sunrise. She had been so anxious to go and now that the time had finally come, she hesitated leaving him.

"How will I ever be able to repay you!" she smiled faintly, tears glistening in her blue-green eyes. "You've done so much."

Neville placed his hand on her shoulder. "The captain and crew are watching, my love," he said. "You can repay me by showing those aboard how much you will miss *your husband.*"

In an instant she was in his arm, kissing him with much warmth and passion. Neville's arm came around her waist, underneath her shawl, as he pressed her closer to him. It was he who broke away trembling.

" 'Tis done, little one," he said.

Lauriette was shaken herself by the way she had kissed him.

"I almost forgot," she said shakily. "Would you give this letter and package to Dolly? I . . . couldn't bear to say good-bye to her."

"I will make certain she has this before the end of the day."

Joseph came up quickly. "Time to sail, Lauriette," he said excitedly. How handsome he looked in his new clothes.

"Take care of your sister, Master Joseph, she is very precious to me."

"I will, sir."

Neville turned to Lauriette, kissing her one last time. "Perhaps if we were not twins," he sighed, "if I didn't look like Devlin, I could have stolen your heart."

"I love you in my own way, Neville," she smiled through tears. "Like the dear, wonderful friend you are."

"Lauriette, it's time," came Joseph's urgent voice.

"Take care, Neville."

"God speed, my love," he shouted. "I'll wait for your letters."

Lauriette, with Joseph at her side, stood at the railing of the *Elizabeth Todd*, waving at Neville until he was nothing more than a blur on the docks. Slowly she dried her eyes, refusing to move until England sank out of sight.

It was the end of her life as Marchioness of Sutherford, the end of her life in England. She was going home to the place of her birth, where love and security waited for her. Joseph placed a possessive hand on her arm and she smiled up at him. It would be a new life for them both.

Devlin. His name escaped in a breathless sigh. No more would she feel the sweetness of his kiss, the passionate strength of his arms. Even if it was only lust on his part, the memories would carry her throughout her life. *Devlin.* Her only love!

Fifty

Devlin woke, the early morning sun in his sleep-swollen eyes. For a long time he silently tried to put things together. Where was he? What happened? He was so disoriented. A sudden rustle of skirts caught his ears.

"Laurie?"

The room filled with the scent of heavy musky perfume. "No, it is Muriel."

Devlin's eyes focused on the woman who now sat beside the bed. "Where's Laurie?" he said evenly. "I want to see her now."

Muriel laid her hand upon his arm. "She is not here, Devlin."

"Where in the hell is she?"

"I do not know," came her calm reply.

"She was here!"

Muriel shook her head. "Devlin, we will talk of this now and then you will decide what to do," she moved to the bed. "Lauriette fled this house as soon as she shot you."

"No!"

"Please listen," she entreated. "I must tell you now. It is better for you to know. She wanted you dead—she told me so and anyone else who would listen. That morning, when you were so critical, she fled taking her maid and that—that urchin she brought from Sir Henry's. She left and never once looked back."

"But—but I remember her hands—"

"Mine, Devlin, mine!" she cut in. "I have been at your side constantly since that fateful night. 'Twas my hands that cared for you."

The deadly silence was broken only by the ticking of the clock on the mantel.

"There was one more thing you should know," Muriel said quickly for fear of losing her courage. "She told me, and proudly, that she was returning to the only man she ever loved—and the father of her unborn child."

Devlin's face grew dark, his eyes black and wild. Then in one savage tone he growled. "Get out! I wish to see no one—*no one!*"

"But, Devlin, I only told you because—"

"Out!" came his agonized scream.

Muriel was quick to obey as the night stand came crashing to the floor. Outside she leaned against the door, a satisfied smile on her face. The lie had worked with ease and soon, very soon *she* would be mistress of Essex Hall!

Two days later Judd came in from his journey to Cornwall. With Devlin laid up, he had taken over his cousin's many duties and as a favor to Devlin, went to check on the *Horizon Queen*. At his arrival, Muriel informed him that Devlin was fully conscious and was sitting up in bed.

Judd grimaced. He now had the unpleasant duty to tell Devlin of Lauriette's disappearance. In the past weeks he had grown increasingly concerned for her welfare. He had paid a visit to Henry's that first morning they found her gone, but even after a thorough search of Claymoor Judd was convinced he knew nothing of her. But where had she gone and why? No doubt she left because of the shooting, but God knows she was absolved of it—even Devlin claimed full fault. And she had been so overjoyed when Devlin's fever broke and he had been conscious for a few moments.

Lauriette never had to tell him, he could tell each time she mentioned Dev—She was hopelessly in love with him. How could his cousin have been such a deuced fool to think her involved with Henry! Jealousy . . . the jealousy of a man in love had caused it. Did Dev have any inkling he was in love?

But how to tell him Lauriette was missing. Taking a deep breath, Judd turned the doorknob and plunged in.

The draperies were still drawn against the July sunlight. His eyes adjusted to the dimness and he moved to the bed.

"Glad to see you awake," Judd said cheerfully.

"Took your own sweet time getting here," he growled. "Sit."

Judd eyed him curiously for a long moment, then took a chair beside the bed. "I took the liberty of checking out the *Horizon Queen,* Dev. I must say old Simon is taking good care of her."

"Good," he said briskly, the scowl was still upon his face.

Judd was beginning to feel uncomfortable. He left explicit instructions that no one was to mention Lauriette's disappearance.

"Dev, there's something we have to talk about—"

"I do not wish to discuss *her!*"

Judd was taken aback by the fierceness in Devlin's voice. His eyes were blazing black, cold and hard.

"Dev, I know you've been through a bad time, but Lauriette—"

An enraged growl bursted forth as Devlin's hands savagely grabbed his coat, pulling him from the chair.

"I warn you, cousin," he snarled through clenched teeth, "if you value your life, never mention her name again—ever!"

Judd held his breath, his entire body was shaking. Devlin was so full of fury, his fingers digging into Judd's jacket.

"Fine, fine, Dev," he murmured hastily. "Anything you say."

Holding him for a moment longer, Devlin gave out a hard groan and shoved Judd from him. "Now get out of my sight!"

Weeks slowly dragged by. Devlin grew stronger and began to move about. But he was not the same endearing cousin Judd had known all his life but rather a moody, brooding man who rarely said anything.

It was not long before Devlin once again took over his duties, going about it mechanically. No longer was there any joy or happiness in tending the estate and riding across the land.

The servants walked quietly around his lordship, knowing of his black moods and fits of temper. Never did they mention Lauriette's name, though their faces reflected sorrow. Everything was quite a mystery to them—especially to Barton who had become taken with the young mistress.

Muriel had stepped into the role of mistress of Essex Hall with relish. She would make herself indispensable to Devlin in the running of the house then soon, very soon, she would be sharing his bed.

She stood, arms akimbo, glaring at the sitting room. Of the entire house, she disliked this room most of all—

perhaps there was too much of Lauriette's influence here.

"Barton," she called. "I need you."

Barton appeared momentarily, a frown on his face. "Yes, milady?"

"I wish to move the sofa around to where it faces away from the fireplace," she ordered. "Then I want some of these ridiculous landscape paintings removed and return them to the tower." Muriel turned, picking up a sketch pad and thrusting it into the valet's hands. "And destroy this at once."

Barton stood his ground, his passive face revealing nothing of the anger and contempt he felt within.

"Well? What are you waiting for!" she demanded impatiently.

"Milady, the mistress, she—"

"*I* am the mistress of Essex Hall!" she reminded him haughtily. "I order you to do as you are told!"

"But she preferred—"

"Are you deaf, man?" she spat.

"What is going on in here," Devlin questioned angrily as he entered the sitting room. "Muriel, I could hear you all the way upstairs."

"This—this man," she sputtered, "refuses to do as I ask!"

Devlin arched a brow. "Is this true, Barton?"

The valet had his head bowed but immediately his eyes lifted. " 'Tis true enough, your lordship."

"He refused to move this furniture as I requested!" she sniffed.

"I'm sorry, your lordship, but the little mistress—" His words broke off before he spoke her name. Stiffening his back he bravely continued, holding out the sketch pad. "She tells me to destroy this! Forgive me, your lordship, and at the risk of incurring your wrath . . . this I cannot do! *She* used the pad lovingly. Aye!

Many a time I watched her, the hours she spent . . . Nay, sir, I cannot destroy this!''

Devlin's eyes were a glistening black, his chin set firm, yet he did not lose control. Instead, he spoke in a very hushed tone. ''Then place it somewhere out of my sight.'' He turned and started to leave but at the last moment turned around. ''Barton, for the time being the room will stay as it is.''

Reaching the sanctuary of his bedroom, Devlin sunk down on the bed, his head in his hands. After all the weeks he could still not put her out of his mind! He must be going mad. He could not stop thinking about her, dreaming of her . . .

He took a deep breath. Honeysuckle! The room seemed filled with the sweet fragrance. *She* always smelled of honeysuckle.

Dejectedly he shook his head. He could have forgiven her anything . . . *anything* except bearing another man's child. Love? Hah! He had been right at the beginning. No such thing—never was!

''Lauriette.'' Her name escaped his lips before he realized it and instantly, an agonizing pain swept through him. Oh God, would he ever learn to live without her? *But I must, I must!* he told himself. He had given her his loyalty, his trust and she betrayed him with another man, living with him all the while. Over and over he told himself he hated her, despised her. He had to learn to hate her, how else would he learn to survive?

Violently wrenching open the door he shouted, ''Barton! Bring me a bottle!''

It was nearing the end of August, and Essex Hall was sadly quiet. Lately, Devlin had begun to drink heavily, locking himself in the library, sometimes sleeping there all night. With each passing day it became worse and worse. No one knew how much longer the situation could go on.

Devlin was awakened from a drunken sleep by the sound of voices raised in anger. He lay there for a few minutes trying to ease the pounding in his head, hoping the two at odds would end their disagreement. He sighed heavily as the voices grew louder. Finally, out of desperation, he slung his legs over the side of the bed then stood, swaying slightly at first.

"Go away, I tell you!" Muriel stormed. "You are not welcomed here."

"I stay," Dolly argued stubbornly, "until I see his lordship. 'Tis important!"

"His lordship will not see you!"

"Then I'll wait 'til he does!" she returned angrily.

"What the devil's—" Devlin stopped short upon seeing Dolly.

Dolly dropped a hasty curtsey. "Yer lordship!" she exclaimed. "Came soon's I could."

Devlin scowled. "Go away."

"Yer lordship, please!" Dolly cried. "Ye must see me, ye must!"

"For God's sake, Dev," Judd's voice came from behind, "for all our sakes . . . let Dolly speak."

Devlin looked down at the little maid's tearstained face, then glanced at Muriel who had paled greatly.

"Please, yer lordship, I beg ye."

"Then let us all retire to the drawing room," he said sullenly, motioning with his hand.

Muriel started forward when a hand roughly gripped her elbow. "I have a feeling you should join us, my lady," Judd informed her.

Devlin lounged in an overstuffed chair, his feet stretched out before him. He did not like this one bit, but for some reason, he could not refuse her. God, did he need a drink!

Dolly gulped nervously. It was Judd who came to her

rescue.

"You can beat me to death if you have that desire," he said, "but first you will hear me out. Then if Dolly regains her courage, she may make her speech."

"Make it brief," Devlin snapped, rubbing his forehead.

"I realize you do not wish to talk of Lauriette, but there are things which have to be said," Judd began. "The first thing you must know is that Lauriette went to Branscombe's house that night because of an urgent message."

"Hah!"

"Please, milord, 'tis true!" Dolly cried.

"Branscombe received word that Marie-Claire was dead," he informed Devlin. "She died in an accident in Vienna."

Devlin sat very still, his face a mask of stone. Only a small muscle twitched in the cheek that belied his cool demeanor.

"When Lauriette disappeared that morning you regained consciousness, I took it upon myself to try and find her—"

"Wait!" Devlin cried, sitting forward in the chair. "What do you mean the day I regained consciousness?"

Judd looked at him strangely. "Why, the next morning is when I discovered she was gone."

Devlin's mouth flew open. This news was not registering. "You—do you mean she—"

"Yes, yes, Dev," Judd cut in, "Lauriette cared for you from the very beginning."

" 'Tis true, yer lordship," Dolly joined in. 'Th' missie would'na let any o' us near ye. She would'na leave yer room—all those days an' nights a-waitin'."

"She's telling the truth, Dev. Lauriette stayed with you through it all."

Devlin shook his head to clear it. "But why, why did you not tell me, why?"

Judd laughed bitterly. "After the way you threatened me when I returned from Cornwall?"

All the times he had heard her voice angrily urging him back from death, all the times he thought the tender words spoken were nothing but dreams. . . . His hard gaze fell upon Muriel. "Go on."

"I went to see Branscombe, hoping he would know of her whereabouts," Judd said. "He knew nothing. I thoroughly checked Claymoor and she was nowhere to be found."

Devlin's dark eyes bore into Muriel until she could stand it no longer.

"Muriel, what have you done?" he demanded. In two easy strides he was out of the chair and at her, hurtfully gripping her wrists. "In God's name why? Why did you lie to me?"

"Because I love you!" she screamed at him. "She is not good enough for you, She was nothing but an American nobody. She was not for you—never for you!"

"How many other lies have you told!" he said bitterly, shaking her.

"You are hurting me!"

"How many!" he roared. "And the part about her running off with her lover—and carrying another's child—another lie, wasn't it?"

"Yes, yes!" she screamed.

Devlin flung her hands away from him. "Get out!" he hissed through clenched teeth. "Be gone from Essex Hall by the time I leave this room!"

Jerking the hysterical Muriel from her seat, he savagely shoved her toward the open door, slamming it after her. He then turned on Dolly and Judd, his eyes sparkling with anticipation.

"Where is she?"

Dolly glanced from Devlin to Judd and back to Devn. "I do not know."

Devlin stood towering over the little maid. "What do ou mean you don't know! You were with her, weren't ou?"

"Aye," she nodded, "until I married." Dolly withrew a small satin box from underneath her shawl. She asked I give this to ye, milord, an' wrote me this etter . . . but I canna read so well."

Devlin could not tear his eyes away from the small hite box he held. Judd held out his hand for the letter. If you will permit me." He glanced from the letter to Devlin, then began.

Dearest Friend,

Forgive me for not saying good-bye in person, but I fear I am too much a coward. I pray your life with Mr. Bonnar will be long and filled with happiness. Faithful Dolly, I am entrusting this small package to you in hopes that you will return it to his lordship. Tell him that in months to come he will see I made the right decision in leaving. I pray, in time, he will forgive me for what has come to pass and that he will remember me fondly. It is my dearest hope that he will find another much more worthy of what is in the package.

Your loving friend, Lauriette.

Judd refolded the letter and stared out at the cloudless sky, afraid to trust his voice.

With trembling hands Devlin opened the small satin box. Nestled in layers of velvet, he found his mother's ring.

There was a set determination to his face and a strange glint in his eyes that made Judd smile. "Where was she when you last saw her?''

"In London," Dolly replied, "at th' Essex Town house, milord."

Devlin's brows shot upward. "With Neville." Jeal ousy consumed him.

"Her ladyship collapsed on arrivin' on Sir Neville' doorstep," she said gravely. "Exhaustion from all tha happened. Spent days abed, she did. I was a good chap erone!"

"What are you going to do?"

Devlin smiled for the first time in weeks. "Do?" h exclaimed. "I'll tell you what I'm going to do. Sen Barton with words to the *Horizon Queen.* Have Simon se sail for London. We'll meet him there."

"Then, we're going after her?"

Devlin smiled ruefully. "Aye, that we are!"

Neville was resting quietly in the drawing room, glass of bourbon in hand. Lauriette had sailed on th *Elizabeth Todd* weeks ago and even now he could no come to grips with her leaving. She had been like breath of spring, something warm and beautiful, tha passed through his hand and out of his life forever.

Wearily, he shook his head. Devlin was such a fool A passionate woman for the asking, yet he had let he go.

A commotion in the foyer brought him to his feet an he stood wide-eyed and silent as Devlin and Judd's ap pearance intruded upon his peaceful solitude.

"What the devil do you want here!" Neville de manded.

"Your welcome leaves much to be desired, broth er," Devlin returned in the same tone.

Neville sullenly poured himself another drink. "Di you think I would welcome you with open arms?"

Devlin moved toward his brother, his face dis

traught. "Nev, I didn't come to fight with you. 'Tis time we laid our differences to rest."

Neville eyed him coldly. "Is that why you are here? To settle our differences at long last? Forgive me if I do not believe you."

Devlin's brown eyes met his. "I came for Lauriette," he said bluntly.

"She is not here."

"I realize that. Dolly told me. But, Nev, where is she?

His face bore no trace of sympathy for his brother. "What kept you from coming after her sooner? Were she mine I would have been hot on her heels from the moment she disappeared."

"There—there were extenuating circumstances, Nev. Now, where have you hidden her!"

Neville turned on him, his eyes black with cold fury. "Exactly what gives you the right to demand this!"

Devlin was becoming increasingly perturbed at his brother. "Because she is my wife!" he exclaimed.

"You are a fool, Devlin, if you think I will tell you anything on that bit of rot!" he growled. "I know she is your wife. That was always a fact which could not be overlooked, but you do not deserve her—you never have! You have caused her unspeakable pain—so much of it that she arrived on my doorstep faint with nervous exhaustion! What happened at the Hall, brother? Why did Lauriette shoot you?"

"Now is not the time—"

"Now *is* the time, Devlin!" he cut in sharply. "Though to be sure, I know most of the facts. Don't look so stricken. Lauriette mentioned nothing of it to me, she is far too generous to do such a thing. But I saw the marks on her neck and arms. It does not take much of an imagination to figure out what happened!" Forcefully, he slammed down the bourbon glass. "So if you will excuse me, I'll retire for the night."

"Neville—" Devlin caught up with him in the foyer.

"I am not crazy enough to set you upon her!" he spat at him. "Give me one—*one* good reason why I should tell you!"

Devlin slowly looked up at Neville, his face pale and sad, unshed tears glistening in his brown eyes. "For God's sake, Nev!" he groaned, Then with much anguish in his voice he said, "Because . . . because I love her!"

Neville looked at Devlin for a long hard moment, then plopped himself on the stairs and ran a hand through his dark curly hair. He was defeated. Any other words Devlin might have said would never have swayed him but those words had done him in. Devlin sat down beside him.

"I arranged passage for her and Joseph," he said quietly. "They're on their way to Philadelphia."

"Philadelphia!"

Neville nodded. "She wanted to go home."

"What ship did she sail on?"

"The *Elizabeth Todd,*" he replied. "Captain Rodell is a good friend. I would not trust her life with just anyone."

"I know that, Nev."

"What will you do now?"

Devlin stared thoughtfully down at his folded hands. "At dawn I leave for Philadelphia."

"I will tell you now, Dev, I asked Lauriette to stay with me," he said sadly. "I offered her my love."

Devlin said nothing, feeling a mixture of jealousy and compassion for his estranged brother.

"She refused me," he finished simply. "Do you know why? Because she could never return my love—because you had already captured her heart."

Devlin tenderly clasped his brother's shoulder. "I

give you my word, Nev, I'll never hurt her again."

Neville looked at him steadily. "I honestly believe you mean that."

Fifty-One

Devlin. His name was no more than a breathless sigh upon her lips. Tears stung the back of her eyes. *Stop this!* she told herself. *You must stop thinking about him! What good does it do you? You cannot go back to what was before . . . Any love you might have had for him is gone . . . It died that horrible night.* Lauriette stared longingly out at the choppy waters, her heart heavy.

You have to forget . . . you just have to! she thought. *Think, Laurie, let your mind dwell on what he said to you, did to you! No sane woman could love a man who was capable of that. He insulted you cruelly, his body used yours worse than one would a whore . . . and he was sleeping with Muriel when only a few doors away you lay awake wanting him, longing for his touch. . . .*

"It is over," she said aloud. "I will learn to live again, to find some kind of purpose to my life."

"There you are," Joseph's soft voice brought her out of her thoughts. Gently, he took Lauriette's arm. " 'Tis time for supper, dear sister. Captain Rodell refuses to sit until you are seated."

She smiled up at him. "Then by all means, Joseph,

let us not keep the captain waiting."

Aboard the *Elizabeth Todd,* days lazily drifted into weeks as Lauriette and Joseph quietly settled into a routine. Weather permitting, Lauriette spent as much time as possible on deck, to the amazement and admiration of the crew. The *Elizabeth Todd* was a commercial vessel not in the habit of carrying passengers and this young woman was a credit to the crew, for she was as sturdy a sailor as any of the seamen.

Supper was a quiet affair that night; Captain Rodell and his officers conversed with Joseph in an amiable fashion, but the entire meal was subdued as Lauriette maintained silence, only speaking when someone addressed her. By the time dessert was served, she was close to tears.

"If you gentlemen will excuse me—" She fled the room with Joseph close on her heels.

He caught her as she opened her cabin door, his hand gently holding her arm. "Lauriette, what is amiss?" he questioned softly. "You haven't been yourself all evening."

Tears streaked her cheeks. "I . . . don't know," she cried. "I'm just not myself today. Please, express my apologies to the captain. I'll be fine tomorrow."

Joseph held her hand in his own, his blue eyes searching her face. "You are not ill again, are you?"

Lauriette managed a smile. "No, dear brother, 'tis just a case of melancholy. I shall be just fine. You return to the captain and enjoy your evening."

"Are you sure?"

She nodded. "I will see you in the morning."

Joseph raised her hand to his lips. "Sleep well, sister."

Lauriette entered the darkened cabin and upon closing the door, leaned heavily against it. She sobbed openly, without restraint, letting all her sorrow, all her frustration come to the surface. She would cry Devlin Essex out of her system, completely drown his memory and cleanse her soul and heart at the same time.

It was near dawn when Lauriette woke from a deep, dreamless sleep. She lay there silently staring out the tiny porthole at the ever brightening sky. The ship rocked gently, creaking as the sea rolled against it.

The silence consumed her, her heart quickened as alarm overtook her. Something was happening or going to happen. Suddenly, there was a coarse shout and the sound of running feet. The roar of a cannon deafened her and she screamed as the ship rocked violently.

Gathering her wits about her, Lauriette managed to slide from her bed and quickly dressed in a simple blue muslin gown. She was just finishing the buttons when her door burst open and Joseph stood there, his face flushed from running.

"We are being boarded by a privateer!" he said urgently. "The captain orders you to stay here. 'Twould not be wise to let them suspect a woman aboard."

Lauriette nodded numbly. "Are there any hurt?"

"We were lucky," he replied. "Their cannon split the top mast but none was injured. They boarded us before we knew what was happening."

"What is Captain Rodell going to do?"

"Give him what he wants, I suppose," Joseph shrugged. "The *Elizabeth Todd* is not equipped for sea battles. There is naught the captain can do."

Joseph hushed her as the shuffling of feet and scraping of crates were heard overhead. Lauriette gazed fearfully at the ceiling, unconsciously holding her breath. Joseph silently moved away from the closed door and sat down beside her.

Suddenly there was an exchange of gunfire and more

loud shouting. Lauriette stiffened as there was a loud movement of pounding and scraping. What was happening?

A loud crash rocked the cabin as the heavy wooden door flew back. Joseph jumped to his feet, placing himself in front of Lauriette. Shakily, she got to her feet and peered over his shoulder.

A tall man with raven black hair stood in the shattered doorway, hands on hips. His intense black eyes gazed past Joseph to Lauriette and a mocking smile curved his full lips.

"Who are you and what do you want?" Joseph demanded evenly, his fists clenched.

"I am captain of the *Fateful Lady,*" he announced. "As to what I want, I should think the answer is obvious."

The realization of the pirate's words struck him with such force, Joseph paled. "No-o!" he cried and rushed headlong for the man.

"Joseph!" Lauriette screamed.

The young man was no match for the powerful man as the pirate grabbed him by the shoulders and flung him away as if he were a rag doll. Joseph slammed savagely into the far wall and crumpled to the floor, stunned by the blow.

Lauriette ran to her brother, pulling his head onto her lap. Her eyes glowed icy green. "You are a cruel monster!" she spat. "He was trying to protect me!"

"If you will come with me, *señorita?*"

She stood as Joseph came around, her small hands clenched. "Not without my brother."

The pirate arched a dark brow as if contemplating. "Very well, *señorita,* with your brother."

His dark eyes took in the young man's rugged form. He was ready to fight to the death for his lovely sister. It would not be wise at this time to have him harmed.

"Aldo! Vasquez, *venga aquí,*" he roughly shouted. Two burly looking seamen appeared behind him. He nodded to Joseph. "See that he does not hurt himself—nor anyone else."

Before Joseph could even strike out the men were beside him, restraining him.

"Now, if you will, *señorita?*" he bowed graciously.

Head held high, Lauriette raised her skirt and slid past him. On deck she stifled a gasp as her eyes beheld the damage done to the *Elizabeth Todd*, her crew lined up single file, muskets leveled at the men.

"What are you going to do?"

The pirate eyed her intensely. "What do you think I will do?"

"No!" she cried, grabbing his arm. "Please, they cannot harm you now. Let them go—please!"

His face was still hard and cold, even as he smiled. "Does this mean so much to you?"

She nodded silently.

"Then for you I will let the ship go," he said simply. "It is a favor—but it will put you in my debt. *Comprende?*"

"I . . . understand," she slowly replied.

"*Muy bien,*" he said curtly. "It is time to depart."

"My lady!" Captain Rodell cried out. "You cannot—I gave my word to Sir Neville!"

"Everything will be all right, captain," she said.

"There is no time for pleasant conversation, *señorita.* We go!"

Lauriette restlessly paced back and forth in the tiny airless cabin the pirate had locked her in. Two days had slowly dragged by and she was becoming increasingly alarmed. She saw no one but a cabin boy who silently brought her food and saw to her needs. She had questioned him about Joseph, but the boy merely left the food without a word.

What was going to happen? She had fully expected to be ravished as soon as they boarded the *Fateful Lady* but no one, save the cabin boy, came near her. For that Lauriette should have been grateful, but the constant thought of when it was going to happen kept her as taut as a bowstring.

The door opened and Lauriette jumped from fright. The pirate stood there in the door and carelessly slung over his arm was a green silk gown. His black eyes found Lauriette in the far corner of the room and immediately he smiled sardonically. Silently, he closed the door.

"We are having a guest dining with us tonight," he broke the silence. "It is my wish you join us."

"But I'm not presentable—"

"I have brought you a gown to wear."

"No doubt found among the booty," she returned tartly.

His teeth flashed white and even. "This is so." He laughed. "I have also brought you a brush and gold pins for your hair. Fresh water will be brought to you presently."

Lauriette looked at him anxiously. "My brother, Joseph, is he all right?"

The pirate nodded. "Jose is fine and will continue in good health as long as you do as you are told," he said quietly. "And right at the moment I wish you to grace my table. Here."

She took the gown and accessories from him then moved toward the bunk.

"What is your name?" he asked softly.

Lauriette returned his gaze, defiantly lifting her chin. "What is yours?"

"I am Captain Esteban Cordero, your servant, *señorita,*" he bowed. "And you?"

"I am Lauriette . . ." She hesitated for a moment. "Lauriette Claymoor."

"A very beautiful name," he complimented, "for a beautiful woman."

His words plunged into her heart as a familiar voice inside echoed, *A beautiful name, little cherub, and well suited to you.*

"And now, Lauriette, I will leave you to dress," he said and closed the door, locking it after him.

Captain Esteban Cordero swiftly walked to his own lavish quarters, his stride confident. Señorita Lauriette was a striking wench, no doubt about that! The image of her supple form filled his head and he smiled. There was a time not long ago when he did not know how to treat women but now . . . he had grown wise in the ways of the flesh and soon enough he would add this little trinket to his bracelet.

Shutting the door behind him, Cordero came up short as he spied someone sitting at his desk, boots resting on the top.

"Clay! My honor, I did not expect you for another hour, *mi amigo.*"

The man smiled ruefully, removing his boots from the desk top. He was dressed in tight leather breeches which fitted into his dark boots. A white, open throat shirt of lawn clashed greatly with the reddish brown skin of the man. His blue eyes were cold as he stared at Cordero, the smile he wore showed even white teeth. Impatiently, he ran his hand through his golden brown hair.

"I believe you were preoccupied," he said easily.

"It is good to see you," he motioned the deep leather chair.

"And you," Clay replied. "I heard this trip was quite profitable."

Cordero smiled. "Soon you will see just how profitable.''

''I understand she's beautiful.''

''Truly a prize, Clay,'' his eyes grew warm. ''The moment I saw her behind her brother—''

''Brother?''

Cordero nodded. ''I brought him, too, a brave conquistador. I would have brought her entire family to have her.''

''Well, then, bring this beauty here so I may congratulate you on your excellent taste.''

''Manuel!'' he shouted and almost instantly a swarthy little man appeared at his back. ''Bring the *señorita.*'' He turned back to Clay. ''And you, amigo, how was your fishing this voyage?''

''I'm afraid King George will find less gold in his coffers,'' He grinned. ''We didn't leave anything except the clothes the crew wore.''

Cordero laughed boisterously. ''I can see I was wise in going into partnership with you.''

A sharp rap on the door brought the conversation to a halt. Manuel opened the cabin door and lightly pushed Lauriette ahead of him. She stood silently in the shadows, her eyes staring at the floor.

She felt Cordero's hand on her elbow, urging her forward. ''Let Captain Clay have a look at you.''

Their eyes met, blue on blue, and Clay jumped to his feet as Lauriette cried out.

Her eyes filled with tears and she began to feel lightheaded. ''Ben? Oh faith! It is you! Ben!''

Before she could take a step towards him, her head began to swim. Cordero caught her as she began to fall.

''Lolly!'' Ben cried running forward. ''My God, it's Lolly!''

Gently, Cordero laid her upon his huge bed as Ben wet a cloth and placed it on her forehead. He sat down beside her, distraughtly patting her hand.

"Who is she, Clay?" he asked. "How do you know her?"

"She is my sister, Cord," he said grimly.

"Your—what?" Cordero exclaimed. "But—but her name is Claymoor!"

"Aye, mine is, too, but I haven't used my name since coming to New Orleans." Softly, he looked down at his sister. "Last I heard she was on her way to England to—" He turned to Cordero, his face gray with sudden anger. "Did you hurt her? By God, if you did, I'll—"

"No, no, Clay," he protested. "I have not laid a hand upon her, I swear!"

Lauriette began to come around, her eyes fluttering. "Ben," she whispered.

"Lie still, Lolly," he smiled gently. "As soon as you're able, we'll dine and then you'll board the *Sorcerer.*"

"The *Sorcerer?*"

"Aye." He nodded proudly. "My ship."

Fifty-Two

Lauriette was once again on board a ship owned and captained by a Claymoor and she felt overwhelmingly proud. She turned, looking to Joseph, who was confidently handling the *Sorcerer*'s wheel as if he had been born to it. Ben stood beside him, instructing and advising him. She smiled recalling when she took to task the complicated matter of explaining Joseph to Ben. But they had taken to one another immediately and now after weeks of close quarters, they could not have been more suited if they had been blood brothers.

Not far ahead of them, the *Fateful Lady* cut through the choppy waters with ease. It, too, was a beautiful ship, its white sails billowing in the salty breeze.

"Well, how do you like her?"

"She's quite impressive," Lauriette complimented handsomely. "But then, so is her captain."

Ben flushed from the high praise of his sister. "Well, she is definitely not the *Intrepid*."

"Jamie would be pleased, Ben," she placed a hand upon his arm. "I am proud of you—even though I do not agree with your—unorthodox way of doing it."

"Desperate times demand desperate means," Ben's expression hardened.

"But why piracy?"

"Not piracy, Lolly, privateering," he argued. "What I do is completely legal. I carry a letter of marque signed by Mr. Madison himself!"

"That silly piece of paper still doesn't give you the right to kill innocent people and sink ships!" she retorted.

Impatiently, he shook his head. "I will not discuss my criminal activities with you any longer." He turned Lauriette to face him. "What I would like to talk about is you. I've asked Joseph several times, but apart from stating you saved his life, he will tell me nothing. What's wrong, Lolly? Why, last I heard you were on your way to England to marry a nobleman . . . Brimley was his name—" He paused, noticing the pained expression on her face. "Why won't you share with me? I was easy to talk to before when we were children. Lolly, I haven't changed."

Lauriette gripped Ben's hand tightly, her eyes filling with tears. "Well, I certainly *didn't* marry Brimley!" her voice was tinged with bitterness. "Ben, please, not right now. I just cannot bring myself to talk about it yet."

He gently held her shoulders. "But if you cannot tell me, who can you tell?" His eyes gazed intently into hers and saw the raw pain there. "Who is it that has hurt you so badly? Damnation, I'll kill—"

"Stop it! Stop it!"

She shoved a bewildered Ben from her and fled to the cabin. She hurled herself onto the bed and sobbed deeply. No, she would not even *think* his name! Because of him, she fled England! Because of him she could barely eat or sleep! Lauriette drew a heavy sigh. Because of him she could never love another, for only he filled her dreams and could awaken her passions with his fiery touch. Wearily, she dried her swollen eyes. The only way she would ever be rid of him would be in death!

The weeks that followed, Lauriette spent most of her time in the cabin despite strong protests from Ben and Joseph. No matter what they did in amusement, nothing seemed to shake Lauriette's feeling of depression. The brothers grew increasingly concerned over her welfare as her trays came back hardly touched and dark circles appeared under her eyes.

"I am quite worred about her, Joseph," Ben confided one afternoon. "Do you know what ails Lolly? Can you not tell me so I can help?"

Joseph lowered his head. "Would that I could, Ben," he whispered sadly. "Lauriette has done so much for me . . . but I gave her my word I would not speak of it. I have her trust. I cannot betray her no matter how much I wish to tell you."

Ben smiled affectionately at his adopted brother. "Lolly did well by bringing you into our family."

Joseph blushed hotly. "What will you do?"

"We should dock tonight and first thing tomorrow I'll take her to Jean Bourget's home. He's a a close friend of our family. Jean will be able to talk some sense to her! It seems that when none of us could budge her, Jean could do wonders.'

The *Sorcerer* docked in New Orleans during the early morning hours. Ben secured Cordero to the supervising of the unloading of the ship, and then as Lauriette readied herself for her first entrance to New Orleans Ben hired a coach.

Lauriette smiled at her first sight of the docks with its bustling, teeming life. Although the days in England and while at sea were very warm, she had not anticipated such humid weather.

She folded her shawl and placed her gloved hand on Joseph's awaiting arm.

"Are you feeling better?" he asked anxiously.

"There is nothing wrong with me!" she snapped irritably.

Joseph merely shrugged off her bad temper. "You might be able to convince the crew that you're all right but not someone who has been at your side for months," he reminded.

Lauriette flushed. "I tell you I'm fine. You'll just have to accept that!"

Ben was waiting for them at the docks and Lauriette gave out a cry of exclamation at the sight of such an elegant coach.

"Well, Joseph, have a care," Ben advised. "Stay with Cordero. I'll be back by nightfall."

"You can count on me, Ben," he smiled.

"Joseph, aren't you coming with us?"

Quickly, he looked to Ben. "I promised Joseph he could watch the unloading of the ship, Lolly," Ben explained.

"B-but . . . but—"

"Come along, sweet." He hurriedly handed her into the coach. "Joseph will be just fine." The coach lurched forward giving Lauriette no time to disagree.

They were not away from the docks too long before Lauriette became fascinated with the beautiful city. She was truly surprised by the elegant beauty of the townhouses as they cantered down the avenues, the lovely homes framed by black wrought-iron fences.

The people of this strange city entranced Lauriette. In the humid climate the women wore light dresses of every color in the rainbow, and the gentlemen dressed quite elegantly. Lauriette was quite impressed by the whole of it.

Soon the coach came to a halt in front of a huge brick

house guarded by the same kind of black wrought iron she had seen so many other places. Flowers of every color and variety bloomed there and in the middle of the green lawn was a huge fountain.

"Ben, is this Jean's house?" she asked. "I thought he lived on a plantation."

"He does," Ben answered, "but like Englishmen, Creoles have a house in the country and in the city, too."

Lauriette felt lighthearted as Ben helped her down, and stiffening her spine she clung to his arm as they were led inside the courtyard into the house and announced by a black butler.

Jean came into the foyer, a huge welcoming smile greeting her. He hugged Lauriette tightly, then held her at arm's length to look at her. Immediately, a frown wrinkled his brow.

"What is this, Lolly? Have you been ill?"

"No, not really—"

"Tell him the truth, brat!" Ben interrupted, not unkindly. "Aye, she has been, Jean. Hasn't been eating or sleeping."

"Come," he motioned, urging them into the sitting room, "you will sit, *oui?* We have so very much to talk about. I have not seen Ben for so long. *Mon Dieu!* I cannot believe it is really you!"

"Jean, I need a favor," Ben asked.

"But of course, *mon ami.*"

"Until I can secure a house for Lolly—"

"Say no more, Ben, I would not have her stay anywhere but here," he smiled warmly. "When I left you in England, you were so *désolée* but yet I had to leave. Tell, *ma petite,* did M'sieu Essex finally get to see you? Perhaps you could enlighten me as to why he felt it so . . . so *urgent* to see you."

Lauriette felt as if she would stop breathing. Suddenly Ben was curiously looking at her, too. Her head began to ache and the lightheadedness returned.

"Jean!"

Both men turned as a tall, elegantly dressed woman came into the room. Lauriette looked up but was unable to stand. The woman was very beautiful. Her hair was raven black and styled in the latest French mode, her eyes were almond color, her olive skin flattered the lovely peach-colored silk dress she wore. Lauriette smiled but that smile froze as she caught the coldness in her eyes and the severeness about her mouth.

"Fleur, a surprise," Jean turned toward his wife. "Ben's sister, remember I've spoken of her, is visiting New Orleans for a time. She has graciously consented to stay as our guest. Forgive my manners. Lauriette, may I present my wife, Fleur."

"*Enchantée*, madam—"

"How dare you!" Lauriette's polite words were drowned out by Fleur's hissing voice. "I will not have this—this woman in my house! Do you hear me, Jean? Your precious 'Lolly' will not stay here!"

"Fleur!" he said hotly, his face red with anger and embarrassment.

"I will not have any of your—your business associates nor their families under my respectable roof!" Fleur cried jealously. "They are murderers, rogues and highwaymen—and sisters are no better!"

"I am master here—"

The pain was becoming worse. "Jean, please!" Lauriette managed to stand. Every voice sounded so far away. "I do not wish to stay here—"

"Lolly!" Ben cried as she weakly collapsed against him.

With deft sureness Jean caught Lauriette up in his arms, much to the amazement of his wife. "Ben, tell Amos to send my carriage around," His voice was laced with controlled anger.

"Where are you going!" Fleur demanded, stamping her foot.

Jean turned on her, his gray eyes cold and hard. "I am going to take my little friend to someone who will not turn her away," he spat at her. "For what you have done this night, madam, I will never forgive you."

"Jean—"

"*Assez!*" he shouted. "Deem yourself lucky if I should step foot here again!"

Jean swept past Fleur, carrying Lauriette out to Ben and the awaiting carriage.

"Jean, we'll return to the ship."

"No. It would not be wise to take her back there," Jean tenderly placed her on the seat and drew a coverlet over her. "She needs tender care, *mon ami,* and another woman with whom to talk."

"Where?"

"I shall take her to Celeste Dubois," he said simply.

"To your mistress?"

"She is a kind, considerate widow that has my attention and is socially accepted in New Orleans," he argued. "I can think of no one more capable to care for Lauriette. Can you?"

Ben sat back in the seat, a sullen look on his face. From his upbringing he knew it was highly improper to take Lauriette to the home of a woman that he knew was seeing a married man and Lord knows what their Puritan mother would have said! Nervously, he gulped. Tomorrow he would start hunting for a place for her —a home of her own. That was what she needed. A place to care for, a place to entertain callers—

The carriage slowed to a halt on a fashionable street lined with stately townhouses. Lauriette moaned softly as Jean lifted her into his arms once again. Ben swung open the wrought-iron gate and they entered the garden.

The door was opened by a butler and they entered.

"Jean! I did not expect you—" The young woman stopped on the stairs as Jean moved past her. Quickly, she turned and followed him up the stairs.

"Sorry to put you out, Mrs. Dubois," Ben murmured.

"Who is the girl?"

"My sister. I'm afraid the journey was too much for her," he said sullenly.

Celeste placed a reassuring hand on his arm. "She is most welcome here, Ben."

They both looked up to see Jean at the head of the stairs.

"She woke for a few moments," Jean informed them. "She is so . . . so *fatiguée,* she slipped back to sleep."

"I will take care of her," Celeste said kindly.

"Where did you find her?" Jean inquired.

Ben grinned. "That is a long story, my friend," he sighed.

"Then you may accommodate me tonight at the *Sorcerer.*"

Ben glanced at his timepiece. "It is time for me to return to my ship. I'll give you a full accounting then." Then he checked himself a moment. "If you'll return the favor by enlightening me on this M'sieu Essex!"

Jean nodded. "I shall be most happy to."

"Jean, tell Lolly I'll return in the morning."

"Take my carriage, Ben," he waved. "I will see you soon."

As soon as the door closed behind Ben, Jean turned to Celeste and took her in his arms. "I am so grateful, *ma cherie,* that you are here."

"I will always be here for you," she said softly, kissing his chin. "Now come and sit. Tell me of all that has happened."

Jean tiredly rubbed his eyes. "I could have killed her today, Celeste!" he blurted out heatedly. "It would have been nothing to strangle her! I would have felt nothing."

"You must not say such things!"

"Ben brought Lolly to me for help and protection!" he argued. "I extended her the hospitality of my home and Fleur threw it back in my face! And with Lolly sick. I tell you I could have killed her! She knows my feelings for Lolly . . . Lolly is the little sister I never had. When she was so small, she caught my heart with that enchanting smile of hers. There was a time long ago when I was as one of her brothers. I still care . . . I always will care."

"But of course, Jean," she replied softly. "It will always be so. But are you certain that you wish to leave her here? I mean, she may be quite insulted when she finds out that we love each other."

"Nonsense, my Celeste." His gentle smile was warm. "She will love you as I do."

"Jean," Celeste whispered, as his mouth touched hers.

"Why could I not have met you first . . ."

"Jean," Lauriette's voice roused them both. "Jean?"

Both hurried up the stairs to her.

"I am here, *ma petite.*"

"Where am I?" she asked. "What happened? Where is Ben?"

"Not so fast, Lolly," he laughed, sitting down beside her. "Are you feeling better? Perhaps I should send for a doctor."

"Please, no," she protested. "I am fine."

"No, you are not!" he argued. "Ben told me you have not been acting right or eating or sleeping. Is this true?"

"Yes, Jean," she bowed her head.

"Such nonsense!" he shook his head. "It is no wonder you faint! Now, you will rest and regain your strength here where I can keep my eye on you."

"But where am I?"

"You are in the house of a very special friend of mine," he explained. "Celeste will take good care of you."

"Did I hear my name?"

The woman who entered the room was not much older than she. Celeste was a beautiful woman, her eyes a velvety brown, her hair the color of sunlight and her skin flawless alabaster.

"I brought you tea, *mademoiselle,*" she smiled warmly and Lauriette liked her immediately.

"I will be honest with you, Lolly," Jean said slowly. "Celeste is a widow and socially respected in New Orleans . . . but she is also my mistress."

"Jean!" Celeste exclaimed.

"It is all right," Lauriette reassured her. "Thank you for taking me into your home. Please call me Lauriette or Lolly, if you prefer."

Celeste nodded, feeling herself already beginning to take to the young woman. Most ladies in her predicament would have been outraged to find out of her love for a married man. Perhaps Jean was right about this special one.

"Ben has gone back to his ship." Jean informed her. "He will see you in the morning."

"I'm afraid I've become a burden to him."

"I do not believe Ben thinks that at all," Jean returned. "In fact, he is most happy to have you here with him."

Lauriette accepted the tea from Celeste. "As always, you are too kind."

"I would like to hear what has been happening in

London,'' he pressed. ''Did Sir Henry recover from his wound?''

Lauriette shifted uncomfortably. ''Yes, he was well last I saw him.''

''And I take it you did not wed Sir Evan. I imagine James is quite pleased, no?'' he grinned. ''Then what have you been up to, Lolly? From the expression you wore upon your face when I asked before, I presume Devlin Essex was able to see you.''

The teacup clattered on the saucer.

''Lolly, what is it? Did I say something wrong?''

Before she could stop herself, her entire life at Essex Hall came tumbling out. At first it was difficult to speak of Devlin but as Lauriette continued, it became easier until she spoke of that horrible night when everything exploded in her face. She sobbed brokenly as she told of her departure and Neville's kindness. On and on she continued, tears steadily falling, until she could go no further, exhaustion leaving her limp.

Moved greatly by her story, Celeste moved to her side and cradled Lauriette in her arms. Jean sat silent, his brows drawn downward in thought.

''So, you have run away from Dev.''

Even the sound of his name pained her heart. ''I couldn't stay any longer, Jean, surely you can see that!'' she cried indignantly. ''It wouldn't have mattered anyway. Devlin barely knew I was alive. He sought to humiliate me, to hurt me beyond reason, and in fact, he did so!''

''Forgive me, *cherie,* but knowing Essex as I do, I did not think him capable—''

''But he is!'' she vowed hysterically. ''I thought to change him with my love—yes, Jean, *love*! But Muriel pointed out the error of my ways. There is only so much a heart can take!''

He placed a comforting hand on her shoulder. ''But,

Lolly, he could not be near you all those months and not grow to love you," he commented softly, then smiled. "I am afraid you are unaware of your charms, *ma petite.*"

Lauriette choked back a sob. "But he has no heart through which to see me!"

Celeste soothed her tenderly. "I think it is time to let her rest," she said sternly.

"You are right."

"Jean!" Lauriette clutched at his hand. "You must promise not to tell Ben. Please!"

Jean looked from Celeste to Lauriette. "*Très bien,* Lolly, at least for now. But soon he must know. What would he do if Essex came for you?"

Lauriette laughed bitterly. "If I had shot you, would you follow me?"

"That I would, *ma petite,*" he seriously replied, "if only for revenge."

Fifty-Three

Weeks passed swiftly as Lauriette regained her health and vigor in the house of Madam Celeste Dubois. Ben had been at her to go house-hunting, but Celeste seemed so pleased to have her stay she just kept putting off the chore. Lauriette felt at home in this private sanctuary Celeste called home.

Shortly after her recovery, Captain Esteban Cordero came to call on her quite regularly. She began to look forward to his visits; his manner was very free and easy with her as though she were a lifelong friend whose company he immensely enjoyed.

This particular morning Lauriette was readying herself for a tour of the city and outlying countryside. She dressed in a simple blue muslin gown, and a fashionable bonnet swung from her arm. Her spirits were soaring as this was her first venture from the house.

"Where are you going?" Celeste asked as Lauriette picked up her parasol.

"Esteban has promised to show me the wonders of New Orleans—the cathedrals, the market place, the beautiful park in the square—I look forward to it so!"

"It is Esteban now, Lolly?" Celeste arched a brow. "Highly improper, no?"

"Oh, Celeste, please don't worry so," Lauriette smiled, grasping her friend's hand. " 'Twas Ben's idea for him to visit. He has become a good friend."

"Indeed? Perhaps at the beginning, his guilt for abducting you, but now?" she frowned. "*Capitaine* Cordero is a passionate man—I see it in his eyes when he looks at you."

"No, Celeste," Lauriette corrected. "He has become a great friend, nothing more I assure you."

"Not for you, maybe—"

"He has always been a gentleman, truly."

"Lolly, it would not be wrong to look upon him as a man," Celeste said slowly.

Her eyes widened as she determinedly shook her head. "There can never be anything romantic for me again," she murmured.

"It is difficult, *cherie,*" Celeste sighed, "to be the kind of woman destined to love only one man."

Lauriette gazed at her and Celeste smiled knowingly. "Yes, Celeste, truly difficult."

Lauriette was filled with the sights and sounds of New Orleans as she rode beside Esteban in a fashionable carriage—complete with chaperone provided by a protective Celeste. Cordero smiled lazily, enjoying Lauriette's excitement, the flush in her cheeks making her an even more lovely sight. . . .

"Where are we now?" Lauriette asked anxiously.

"We are at the Vieux Carré," he explained. "This is one of the oldest parts of the city."

"It is so lovely," she breathed. "And the exquisitely ornamented ironwork of those balconies and railings—French or Spanish?"

"Perhaps a little of both," he shrugged and looked

back at Dimity, Celeste's black maid. "Do you think she minds being along?"

Lauriette looked from him to the maid and laughed. "She's the kind of chaperone who is there for propriety's sake but otherwise than that . . ."

Esteban joined in her laughter. "At least Celeste is properly taking care of you."

It was mid-afternoon before Lauriette realized how long they had been sightseeing and how famished she was.

Cordero smiled. "We will eat at a small inn not too far from here," he told her. "It is a most reputable establishment, I assure you." He then looked again at Dimity. "What do we do with her?"

"Celeste said that we were to bring her plenty to eat when we are done and she will be very happy." Lauriette smiled impishly.

The inn was very quiet and most decidedly French and, as Cordero had assured her, most respectable. It seemed many of the gentry dined there frequently.

Cordero took the liberty of ordering for Lauriette and both seemed to enjoy the silence of the other as they ate.

"Do you still wish a drive in the country, Lolly?" he asked, pushing his chair away from the table. "If you are tired, we can go—"

"Oh, no, Esteban, please," she begged prettily. "Truly, I am not a bit weary. Can we not go driving?"

Cordero laughed. "How could I refuse you? Come, let us be on our way."

Taking his arm, they strolled through the center of the crowded inn. They were stopped suddenly as a tall burly looking man blocked the door. Lauriette could not suppress a gasp as she stared at him. Though he was dressed quite fashionably, the man seemed to radiate an all-consuming power. His thinning hair was a brown color, his face was distorted by pox scars but it was his eyes that disconcerted Lauriette so. His eyes were a cold, hard black that peered out from beneath bushy black brows. The man smiled a smile so cold, she shuddered involuntarily.

"Captain Cordero, is it?" the man's voice had a strange rasp to it.

Cordero arched a brow, his face a strained mask of aloofness. "You know it is, *señor,*" he returned evenly. "And now, Fourier, you will excuse us . . ."

"But you have yet to introduce the lovely *mademoiselle,*" he interrupted, his black eyes boldly roaming over Lauriette.

Lauriette felt Cordero stiffen. "M'sieu Fourier, allow me to introduce Mademoiselle Lolly Clay," he gritted his teeth "Lolly, M'sieu Alexandre Fourier."

"*Enchanté, mademoiselle,*" he raised her hand to his dry lips. "*Trés charmante, vraiment.*"

"*Merci,*" Lauriette managed cooly, withdrawing her hand.

"Are you perhaps related to M'sieu Benjamin Clay?"

"He is my brother, m'sieu."

Alexandre Fourier seemed to ponder this for a moment, then stiffly moved aside. "*Bonjour.*"

Cordero propelling her arm, he escorted her out of the inn and to their awaiting carriage. After placing the basket of food they brought back into Dimity's lap, Lauriette felt confused and kept looking back over her shoulder. Never had she felt such dread before. But who was he and why should she feel thusly? Yet something in the back of her mind nagged at her. Something about him was familiar, but why?

Cordero handed her into the carriage and noticed how pale she had become. "Lolly! Are you all right?"

"Yes, Esteban. It's just that—that man!" Against her will, she shuddered again. "Who is he?"

"An agent for the French Government." He nodded to the driver and the carriage jolted forward. "He is a most dangerous man."

"Why did he ask about Ben?"

Cordero frowned. "I am afraid your brother and I have our disagreements with the illustrious m'sieu. You see, it is not only English ships we are in a habit of boarding, *querida.*"

Her eyes grew wide at his admission. "You—you mean M'sieu Fourier—"

Cordero nodded gravely. "He has been trying to catch us in privateering for over two years."

"But Ben says you have a letter of marque—"

"An American letter of marque cannot save us here," he enlightened her. "We are out of the jurisdiction of the American government, *comprende?*"

"But—but, Esteban—" He could see the fear in her eyes.

"*Silencio,* Lolly," he impatiently interrupted, "We will speak of this no more. Just stay as far away as you can from Fourier. He is evil!"

Lauriette stood poised atop a green hill overlooking a valley of wildflowers. The October breeze gently teased tendrils of golden brown hair from beneath her bonnet. With a swift tug of the ribbons, the hat was removed and the wind was free to whip and caress her tresses.

Cordero sat near Lauriette, watching her with amusement. She made an enchanting picture for him; his heart began to pound furiously and a lump formed in his throat. No woman had ever affected him so.

"It is lovely here, no?" His breath was warm against her shoulder. Lauriette blushed. "Lolly."

"Isn't it time we started back, Esteban?" she turned suddenly and began to walk away.

"Lolly, stay," he commanded softly, his hand holding her arm.

She turned and faced him, eyes brimming with tears. "P-please," she murmured as his hands brought her closer, "please let us go."

"Look at me." Reluctantly, she leveled her gaze. His eyes were warm and generous, gazing lovingly into her own. "Can you not see what is there, *querida,* what I am going to say? My eyes are a mirror to my heart. *Te amo,* Lolly, I love you."

"No, please," She turned her face away unable to bear his tender words, but Cordero would not relinquish his hold upon her. "You must not say these things to me, Esteban, please!"

His eyes grew cloudy. "Is it because I am a privateer, Lolly?" he questioned. "Are you afraid I cannot provide for you? Because if that is it, there is no obstacle."

"Esteban—"

"Lolly, I am a wealthy man. It is true, I swear!" he smiled. "I have a fine plantation downriver. You will never have a worry, *querida.*"

"Esteban, please listen!" she pleaded. "I cannot!" Sadly, she bowed her head. "I am not free to love—I am already married."

His mouth set firm, Cordero stood frozen for several agonizing moments. Then gently he lifted her chin, his dark eyes taking in her tear streaked face.

"You . . . ran away from your husband?" he asked curtly.

She gazed directly into his eyes. "I did," she whispered, then checked herself. "I just left. There was nothing more to be done. He didn't want me any longer."

Cordero softly stroked her cheek. "Then he is a fool!" He drew her into his arms. "Your being married does not change my mind or my heart, *querida.* I still desire you.''

Lauriette pulled away from his grasp. ''You do not understand, Esteban,'' she retorted firmly. ''I cannot love you in return. It is impossible.''

''Impossible?'' he mocked lightly. ''I know not such a word.''

''Please,'' she pressed. ''Please do not ask of me any more than I can give!''

''Very well,'' he conceded, ''We will continue on this way for a time—but I warn you, Lolly, I will not give in!'' He offered her his arm. ''Come. It is time I returned you to Celeste.''

It was a silent journey back to New Orleans, much of the glamor and excitement colored by their mixed emotions. The carriage came to an easy stop in front of the iron fence; Cordero alighted first then assisted Lauriette, his hands warm on her small waist. He walked her to the door without a word spoken.

Lauriette turned. ''Thank you for today, Esteban.'' She smiled softly. ''It was one of the most lovely days I have spent in a long time.''

His huge hands enclosed hers. ''You make it sound as if we will never see each other again,'' he said quietly. ''I told you I do not give in so easily. Will you permit me to call again?''

''Of course,'' she answered. ''We are friends, are we not?''

''Then allow me to escort you to the coming masquerade ball next week.''

''Ball?''

He nodded. ''Ben will have your invitation with him tonight. Will you allow me the honor?''

'' 'Tis I who would be honored.''

He made a courtly bow and started to leave when Lauriette stopped him.

''Esteban, would you say nothing of our talk to

Ben?'' she asked. ''He does not know that I am wed. I would rather put that discussion off for the time being.''

Cordero grinned conspiratorially. ''Rest assured, Lolly, your secret is safe with me.''

Fifty-Four

The night of M'sieu and Madame Jourdane's masquerade ball blossomed with a symphony of stars twinkling overhead in a sapphire blue sky. It was to be quite an elegant affair with nothing but the *crème de sociètè* attending. A night to remember!

Jean Bourget sat at his desk pondering some important business. He was deep in thought, his brows drawn. Word had reached his ears that Fourier was making inquiries about Ben's activities again. Normally he would not have been so concerned. Fourier could inquire all he wished about Ben, for dock people were a loyal bunch, but this time he was including Lolly in his investigation. They would have to take more precaution in protecting her. Fourier was an evil bastard!

"Massa Jean," The old black butler's face was anxious. "Massa Jean . . . someone's a-waitin' ya."

"Tell them tomorrow," he growled. "I am occupied and already I am late for the ball!"

"B-but, massa, sir!"

"Never mind, man," a deep husky voice drawled. "I'll announce myself."

"*Mon Dieu!*" Jean cursed. "I said—" The words died in his throat.

Standing before him was Devlin Essex, an arrogant half-smile on his bearded face. He was attired in a luminous black cloak pushed back at the shoulders. Underneath he wore leather breeches tucked into soft leather boots. His lawn shirt was opened almost to the waist exposing the mat of curly dark hair on his chest. He was far from the elegantly dressed gentleman he had last seen almost an entire year ago.

"Devlin!" Jean jumped to his feet and Devlin laughed boisterously. Jean was dressed as a musketeer.

"Masquerade ball," he muttered self-consciously. "I am quite surprised to see you, *mon ami.*"

Devlin gazed at him shrewdly. "Are you? I think not," he returned quietly. "I believe you know why I'm here."

Jean nervously gulped. Calming his trembling hands he poured two brandys and handed one to Devlin. "Would it not be better to tell me rather than have me guess?"

His expression was placid, his eyes jet black. "I came for Lauriette." It was a statement of fact, not a question.

Jean cleared his throat in a feeble attempt to cover his nervousness. "Lolly?" Here? What brought you to the conclusion that she is here—and what concern is it of yours?"

Jean jumped as Devlin's glass came slamming down on the desk, shattering into thousands of tiny slivers. His face was contorted with anger, his eyes glistening black. In an effort to control his fierce emotions, he clenched his fists. "Damnation, man, you sorely try my patience!" he said savagely. "It doesn't matter how I know, only that I *do* know! Jean, let's not play games! We've been friends far too long for this."

Jean looked at him quite soberly. "The man I once knew—*oui,* we were good friends but the man who stands before me now, I am not so certain."

Devlin sighed heavily and sank into the nearest chair. The stoic expression he had been wearing fell away, revealing his raw feeling. "So—you know," he said wearily. "I deserved that remark—but a man filled with jealousy and uncertainty, a man who had never . . ." His voice faltered and trailed away.

Jean's heart went out to Devlin. Never had he seen him in such a state. Cool, insolent, aloof Devlin was no more. It was a huge responsibility. He held this man's fate in the palm of his hands to do with as he chose. It was entirely up to him to decide . . .

"*Mon ami,* I wish you to join me at the masquerade ball tonight," he said suddenly, a twinkle in his eyes. "There is something you may find interesting."

The numerous French doors were open wide to increase the ventilation of the crisp night air. The elaborate Jourdane ballroom was ablaze with light, and soft melodious music filled the air.

Lauriette instantly became belle of the masquerade. A flurry of excitement tensed the air as she appeared on the Spanish Captain's arm. The mysterious Lolly Clay, sister of the wealthy Benjamin Clay, an enigmatic man in his own right—she was beautiful and witty, always gracious and charming but holding herself with an air of refinement. "The Unobtainable" is what the Creole bucks began calling her and her number of available dancing partners all but secured her position in New Orleans society.

Cordero possessively claimed her for another waltz, smiling as his eyes caressed her over and over. Lauriette was a beautiful vision; her gown was white silk trimmed in tiny red satin hearts beneath the breasts and around the deep plunged neck and puffed sleeves. Her golden brown hair hung loosely to her waist, a crocheted cap with hearts crowned it. She returned Cordero's smile, her eyes a cerulean blue through the red satin half-mask.

"I am most grateful you have not joined in the laughter, *querida,*" he commented drily.

"Laughter?"

He glanced down at himself and grimaced. "This—this court jester's costume is almost too much for me to endure!"

The costume was bright orange and green set off by yellow stockings and apple green shoes which curled up at the toes. The hat he wore was of various colors looking more as if he had grown horns, and to top it all there were tiny bells jingling from it. Cordero did present quite a humorous picture.

Quickly Lauriette stifled an urge to laugh. That would humiliate her escort painfully. "Well," she managed, "it does seem out of character."

He reluctantly laughed. "I should have come as a highwayman or perhaps a dashing pirate."

"Ah, but then people would have recognized you instantly," she teased. " 'Twould have been too close to the truth."

"*Señorita!* You have wounded me deeply!"

The waltz was soon over and Lauriette was pulled this way and that by her admirers. It was a wondrous evening, a night to remember and she was loathe to think of it ever ending.

Celeste, dressed as a shepherdess, stood near the door and watched Lauriette gaily enjoying herself. She smiled as she felt Jean stand beside her.

"Lauriette is having an evening to remember," she whispered in an amused voice.

Jean returned her smile. "More than you will ever

know," he replied mysteriously.

Lauriette and one M'sieu Bayard were partaking of some wine when the next waltz began. The young man smiled appreciatively. "I believe, *mademoiselle,* this is our waltz."

He bowed graciously and started to offer her his arm when a dark shadow fell across them. Lauriette looked up, her eyes widening at the sight of M'sieu Fourier, for though he was dressed as a Roman soldier, the scarred face and broad shoulders could belong to no one else.

"I wish this dance with Mademoiselle Lolly," he stated coldly, ignoring M'sieu Bayard. "I am certain you will not mind."

Bayard flushed angrily but held his temper. "As you wish, M'sieu Fourier," He bowed out without further ado.

Lauriette was shocked speechless as Fourier maneuvered her out onto the floor as if she were only a mere puppet to do his bidding. Her mind ordered her to resist, but she was powerless to do so. She was in awe of this man and fear left her numb.

"You are very lovely tonight," he spoke in a low voice. "You have the air of a lady. I wonder . . ."

"I dislike your rudeness, *m'sieu!*" she said crisply, finding her tongue at last. "It would make one think that perhaps you are no gentleman."

"I have never given the appearance of being one," he returned sarcastically. "I am what I am. Can you say the same?"

"How dare you!" she hissed. "You've no right—"

"France gives me the right to do anything I choose." He spoke the words softly, but his eyes—his eyes gleamed lustily.

Lauriette was afraid. She could not pull her eyes away from him, as if the power he radiated was draining her will. She was utterly helpless. With the craftiness of a sly fox, Fourier waltzed Lauriette out onto the veranda and over to a corner at the far end in shadow and far enough away from the open doors.

The night was unseasonably warm for December but in spite of it Lauriette shivered. Trembling, she leaned against the stone fence surrounding the veranda. Fourier stood forbiddingly, blocking the way.

"What do you want?" she barely whispered.

"I told you I would see you again, *ma petite,*" he rasped arrogantly. "I wish you to fill in some missing pieces for me."

"*Je ne comprends pas,*" she murmured breathlessly.

"You will understand," he declared ruthlessly. "Mademoiselle Clay, where is your brother tonight?"

She blinked at him in confusion. "I don't know."

"Come now!" he mocked. "You are close to him, are you not? Surely he would tell you so you would not worry."

Lauriette drew herself up, pushing aside her fear of the man. "*M'sieu,* my brother is well over twenty years old and I do not keep an eye on him! You cannot keep me here against my will. That would be quite foolish on your part. You thrive on fear, *m'sieu,* but I for one am not afraid of you!" Lauriette prayed fervently that he believed her.

Fourier arched a bushy brown. "You are not frightened, *ma petite?*" He took a step closer and Lauriette held her breath. "It is you who should not be foolish. You have no idea what I am capable of. *N'est-ce pas?*"

"I wish to go back inside!" she summoned bravely, her chin tilted upward defiantly. She moved forward but Fourier mockingly barred the way.

"*Pardon.*" Another huge shadow now joined them. The man engineered past Fourier easily. "*Mademoiselle* has promised this dance to me, *m'sieu.*" The stranger gallantly offered Lauriette his arm. With trembling hand she engaged it and they moved past a startled Fourier.

At the doors, the gentleman took Lauriette into his arms and moved her out onto the floor. This was the first opportunity she had to look up at him and was surprised beyond words. The gentleman was dressed as a highwayman, complete with pistols tucked neatly into his belt. His hair was dark and curly and an equally dark beard gave him the air of a rogue. Soft brown eyes gazed out from the black mask and Lauriette felt an odd sensation in the pit of her stomach, her heart began to quiver strangely.

"Am I so atrocious-looking, *mademoiselle*?" his voice was husky with a slight French accent.

Lauriette's eyes widened. "My apologies, *m'sieu,*" her legs trembled as she smiled. "It is only that you— 'Tis not important." She was being quite silly. "I am very grateful for your intervention. To say thank you seems very insignificant—you might have saved my life!"

The highwayman's eyes sparkled with a sensuous light all their own. "Allow me to escort you into the buffet, Mademoiselle Queen of Hearts."

The words echoed in her ears, her heart began to hammer. "I-I've already been engaged this evening." Her words sounded so faint. It was as if reliving a scene from the past.

The highwayman smiled, a crooked half-smile, revealing slashed dimples. "Then perhaps we can even the score—"

His words were lost to her as the color drained from Lauriette's face. This could not be happening! "No-o!" she cried and twisted out of his arms.

"Laurie!" he shouted over the music but he could not make his way through the throng of people. By the time he reached the entrance she was gone.

Fifty-Five

"What? Lolly, make sense!" Celeste urged. "You are talking foolishly."

Lauriette wrung her hands, her eyes brimming with unshed tears. "It was Devlin, I tell you!" she exclaimed.

"It was only someone who looked like him," Celeste logically pointed out. "Did you not tell me this man wears a beard?"

"Yes."

"You see?" she smiled. "That evil M'sieu Fourier has your wits confused. And how could he find you, Lolly? You are supposed to be in Philadelphia."

"But his words, Celeste—"

"*Cherie,* it was coincidence. That is all," she interrupted. "Lie down and rest. Tomorrow your head will be clear and you will see I was right."

"I'm sorry you had to come home so early from the ball."

"Do not let it worry your pretty head," she replied, patting her hand. "Jean was not able to come here tonight and when he left early, all the joy went with him.

I sacrificed nothing, dear."

"You are so good to me, my dearest friend," Lauriette sighed. "What would I do without you?"

"*Agréables rêves, ma petite,*" Celeste whispered. "Tomorrow will be brighter."

Lauriette lay down upon the bed and Celeste dropped the netting in place. "Sweet dreams, Lolly."

Lauriette lay quietly, listening to the night sounds in the distance. As always, she was at peace in this room. Gradually, her eyes began to close, and within the hour, she was sound asleep.

Much later the sound of angry voices and the tramping of feet woke Lauriette. She remained still listening to the muffled voices that were coming closer and closer. She gave out an involuntary cry as her bedroom door shattered open, and silhouetted against the hallway light stood the highwayman as imposing as ever.

Celeste was behind him, ranting and raving in French and behind her a number of servants who looked on in shock. Lauriette snatched the covers to her chin as he entered the room. Gone was the dark cloak and mask. The beard did not disguise the enigmatic features of Devlin Essex.

"Devlin!" she whispered hoarsely.

"So we meet again, Mademoiselle Clay," he said insolently.

Before she knew what was happening, Devlin swept back the netting and scooped her up in his arms.

"*M'sieu,* please, what are you doing?" Celeste cried indignantly, powerless to stop the man. "You brute! You rogue! This is kidnapping . . . kidnapping!"

Celeste ran after Devlin screaming for him to stop but he continued as if he heard nothing. Lauriette was too numb to move. She could not believe this was really happening. The front door banged closed with a violent sound and out he went to an awaiting carriage. Roughly, he plopped Lauriette on the leather seat.

"Ben!" Celeste frantically cried out from the open window. "Stop him! He has Lolly!"

Devlin had one foot on the carriage step when a hand clamped on her shoulder.

"Lolly! What's going—"

Devlin twisted free, backhanding the intruder. He had been many months in his quest, he was not about to let anyone interfere.

"No-o!" Lauriette shrieked as she saw Ben lunge for him. "Ben, no!"

One savage right and Ben crumpled beside the carriage. Devlin stood over him, his fists clenched. Too long his temper had been held in check.

"Dev, please!" she cried, scrambling from the carriage. She stood between the two as Ben shakily got to his feet. She looked directly into his eyes. "This is Ben, my brother. Ben, may I introduce Lord Devlin Essex, Marquess of Sutherford. My husband."

Ben violently shook his head to clear it. *Did she say husband?* Confused, he looked from Lauriette to Devlin, then back to Lauriette.

"Have Celeste tend your face," she said softly. "Ben, I must go with him." She laid a restraining hand on his arm. "Please?"

Devlin took her arm and handed her into the carriage. With a nod from him the carriage jerked forward. Lauriette gazed longingly over her shoulder and saw Ben still standing there, this mouth open in bewilderment.

With a sigh she turned back around. Her breath caught in her throat as, in the darkness, she could feel Devlin's eyes intently upon her. What was to be her fate? Anxiously she swallowed hard. Was it hate that propelled him to search her out? Yes, she thought sadly, come to have done with me! She prayed the end would be swift, that he would at least be that compassionate. Fervently, she hoped to have courage enough not to beg for her life. It would only disgust him further.

The carriage turned down a quiet avenue lined with trees and at the end of the avenue, turned in to a lovely French house surrounded by a brick wall and exquisite gardens. The sun was just beginning to rise as they alighted from the carriage.

Devlin swept Lauriette into his arms as they entered the house. Two black servants, a man and a woman, awaited them as they entered the house. Devlin brushed past them and mounted the stairs.

"You will hold breakfast until I call," he ordered over his shoulder.

Devlin did not set Lauriette on her feet until they were safely inside a luxurious bedroom. Lauriette silently moved away as he closed the door. The time had come. She was ready.

He turned and stared at her, his brown eyes taking in all of her from her disheveled mane to the soft curves underneath the silk bedgown.

Lauriette had seen the pistol lying on the bureau as they entered. It was as if fate pushed her hand. Slowly her hand grasped the weapon as she pulled it from its place.

Devlin's eyes widened at the sight of it but he made no attempt to move. Almost shyly, she moved toward him, one bare foot in front of the other. Now she was only an arm's length away.

"Here." The word came out in a breathless whisper as she thrust the pistol in his hands. Hesitantly, she took a step backward. Lauriette closed her eyes tightly, squeezing out the tears as she did so. "I cannot take the apprehension any longer. Shoot when you are ready."

Little fool! he thought, shocked. *She thinks I came for re-*

venge, With a huge sigh, he placed the pistol behind him on the night stand.

In one movement he had her in his arms hugging her fiercely, his heart singing. "I can't believe I found you!"

Lauriette was torn between her desire to stay in his arms and the bitter memory of her last days at the Hall. She moved out of his arms.

"How . . . how did you find me?"

Devlin was disappointed by her coolness. "I must admit you led me a merry chase, Mistress Clay," he laughed bitterly, his eyes glaring at her. "Let me see . . . I suppose you could say I began at Neville's. He told me of your arranged passage to Philadelphia and the adoption of one brother."

"Joseph," she murmured.

"I believe that is the name I was told" he said scornfully. "We sailed to Philadelphia and sought out Captain Rodell of the *Elizabeth Todd*. You can imagine my surprise to find you'd not reached Philadelphia at all but had been kidnapped! Then came the final jolt—to find you went willingly!"

"Captain Rodell told you that?" she cried, stunned by his words.

"He said you did not fight the bastard!" he flung at her. "He said the pirate's ship was called *Fateful Lady*. I took a chance in coming to New Orleans. Luck was with me! I paid my respects to Jean, by the way."

"He told you?"

Devlin shook his head. "He didn't have to. I knew as soon as I walked into that ballroom it was you."

"Esteban!" His name came out before she could stop it. She had forgotten all about him!

He eyed her darkly, his mouth drawn. "Captain Cordero was your escort. Commander of the *Fateful Lady*," he said it almost savagely. "How touching!

Everyone was commenting on what a striking couple you made."

Her eyes narrowed in anger. "You have no right—"

"Rights!" he exploded. "Madam, do not speak to me of rights! After what you have done?"

"After what I—" Her head jerked up as she glared at him through icy green eyes.

He reached for her, his hands hurtfully digging into her shoulders. His black eyes glittered dangerously. "How cozy, madam," he hissed. "The two of you tonight. Did you enjoy his touch while on ship? Was he a tender lover?"

Lauriette could not believe what he was saying. All those months with her and he could still not sift out her character through all the lies and deceit.

Now her anger matched his own as she stubbornly fought the tears that threatened to fall. "But of course! I am the most artful courtesan in New Orleans!" she spat at him. "I bedded Captain Cordero as well as every one of his crew—in one night! And when I boarded the *Sorcerer*, I did the same thing. Why, my stay in New Orleans has been one affair after another and—"

"Stop it, damn you!" he shook her roughly, jealousy coursing through him. "If I thought for one blessed moment it was true, I'd—"

"What?" she demanded hotly. "Do what you are so noted for—rape?"

The word cut him like a knife. Lauriette saw the naked pain in his eyes but it was too late. His hands fell to his sides.

Swiftly he turned and walked out of the room, the door slamming behind him.

Lauriette stood there for several long moments, the turbulent emotions swirling inside. Suddenly she flung herself on the bed and sobbed deeply. Nothing had changed. She remembered his words the night she shot him. A cursed thorn in his side. A bitch in heat. A whore! His words—his very words.

"If he only knew," she murmured. "If he knew he was definitely not the first man to—touch me. Dear God! But it was against my will! I was innocent in the cruel debauchery!" Sniffing, she looked around the comfortable room. "Is this to be my fate, my punishment for what I did wrong? To love a man to whom I am only a piece of property? I cannot live this way—I simply cannot! To die of jealousy and humiliation when he is with another woman and to die of wanting him when he takes residence down the hall! To love him and never have it returned—to have him throw Muriel and her child in my face! Perhaps 'twould be better to end it all right now."

With false courage, she picked up the pistol and cocked it. Tears fell unchecked as she choked back a sob. "Faith!" she cried. "And it wasn't even loaded!"

Fifty-Six

Joseph sat on an empty barrel and concentrated studiously on mending the sail in his workworn hands. He stopped for a moment to ease the pain in his back and gazed proudly across the deck of the *Sorcerer*. In the past months since coming to New Orleans, he had an insatiable desire to learn to sail. Cordero and Ben had immediately taken him under their wings and now, after hard work, he could best any sailor on the high seas!

"Young Joe!" Zeb Hanks shouted from the docks. "Young Joe!"

"Aye!" he shouted back, leaning over the railing.

"There's someone a-waitin' to see ya," the old man motioned with his thumb, "at th' tavern yonder."

"Who be it?"

Zeb shrugged. "If me source be right, he be th' cap'n of th' *Horizon Queen*."

Joseph drew his brows downward. Now, why would a captain . . . Placing the sail on the vacated barrel, he hurriedly moved down the gangplank. The only way to find out was to go see.

He entered the darkened dock tavern and asked for

the captain of the *Horizon Queen*. As his eyes adjusted to the dim light, the tavernkeeper pointed to the table in the far corner. Joseph made his way over to it. His blue eyes widened in recognition.

"Sir Neville!" he smiled. "I—" His eyes fell to the hands that held a mug. The man had both. Joseph's face fell.

" 'Tis all right, Joseph," Devlin grinned. "You're not the first to make that mistake. I am Neville's twin."

"I . . . I can see that, sir," he said slowly.

"Please, sit down," he motioned. "I took the liberty of ordering you an ale."

"Thank you, sir," he mumbled. He could not take his eyes from the man's face. He frowned. "You are his lordship."

Devlin nodded. "Though I'd prefer it if you would call me Devlin." He smiled.

If he didn't know of this man's nature, he would have sworn he liked him. "I don't see why I should call you anything, *your lordship*."

Devlin took a gulp of the ale and quietly set the mug back down. "I deserve that, Joseph," he said plainly. "God knows I deserve a hell of a lot more than that. I want to make things right with Laurie. I never want to hurt her again. You must believe that!"

"Give me one good reason why I should believe anything you say!" he sneered. "Why I shouldn't walk right out that door!"

Devlin looked Joseph directly in the eye. "Because Laurie is my wife!" he said sternly. Then he lowered his head and in a tortured voice whispered, "Because I love her."

Joseph was quite taken back by Devlin's open admission. Stunned, he sat back in the rickety chair and took a big slug of ale. He thought back over the months with Lauriette and sighed. So, he was what she pined for!

The hidden pain in her eyes, the days of depression, the sudden outburst of tears, the lonely night she had just barely murmured his name. . . .

He looked up at Devlin and studied his face for a long moment. "What do you want to know."

Devlin leaned forward. "Laurie is with me now. I bought a house and she is there now . . . no doubt sleeping," he told Joseph. "I wish to know everything that has taken place since she left the Hall." Joseph could see the pain and uncertainty in his eyes. "For my own peace of mind . . . please!"

Joseph told him about the trip to London, Neville's arrangements for passage to America, and Lauriette's melancholy the whole time.

"Then came the morning we were boarded by the *Fateful Lady*. I was scared but more so for Lauriette. I stayed in the cabin with her. Cordero began to search the ship and it wasn't long before the door shattered open and we had been found."

"About Cordero," Devlin interrupted. "Captain Rodell stated Laurie went willingly."

Joseph glared back, his lips tightly white trying to control the angry feelings inside. "Lauriette went willingly—in order to save his ship from being scuttled! Damn his hide! The man doesn't know how fortunate he is!"

"Then what happened?" he asked impatiently.

Joseph sighed heavily. "We were aboard two days, then Ben's ship was beside us and we finished our journey on the *Sorcerer*. She wasn't well when we docked and ended up for days abed. The way hasn't been easy for her, let me tell you. Last night she was to go to a masquerade ball—her first social event since arriving."

Devlin was uncomfortably silent. He had wanted to know everything that happened since she left his life and that is exactly what Joseph told him, but he wanted to know more—more!

"I know what it is," Joseph snarled, his eyes narrowing. "You want to know all about the men! Isn't that right?" Devlin opened his mouth to speak, but Joseph cut him off short bringing down his mug of ale violently. "Well, I'm the one what can tell you! I can name every one of them, where it happened and what time of day or night it was." He felt some satisfaction in seeing Devlin's face pale. The bastard deserved it, yet when he thought of Lauriette . . .

"There weren't any," he said in a strong, calm voice. "That's right, your lordship, not a blessed single one! Oh, aye, it was on Cordero's mind, to be sure, but when he found out she was Ben Clay's sister, well . . . And, here, in New Orleans, who is going to be crazy enough to bother a young lady with two brothers looking after her?"

Devlin smiled ruefully, remembering Ben Clay's face hours before. His heart was lifted to the heavens with joy.

Joseph slowly shook his head. "For a man married to Lauriette, you don't know her very well!" he scoffed. "When she loves someone, it is forever."

He stared at the boy for a long moment. "And you seem to think she's in love with me."

"Look, I don't know what happened that night at Essex Hall; I don't want to know!" he returned hotly. "Whatever it was it almost destroyed the best person in my life! If she hadn't cared, she would not have run. I'm not saying it'll be easy to win her over, she's a wildcat at times. But if you weren't lying to me, if you really love her, then whatever you have to do it will be worth it."

Devlin smiled. "You're very wise, my friend."

"Only let me give you this warning," Joseph said seriously. "Don't ever cause her pain again, for if you do, you'll answer to me! She's all I got and I fiercely love her!"

He looked at the boy through different eyes, combined with admiration and respect. "I can see you do."

When Lauriette woke from an exhausted sleep it was midday, and the sun was streaming through the windows. Lazily she rose, rubbing her eyes. It wasn't a dream. She was still in the same room and Devlin had found her.

She frowned as her eyes found a trunk. It looked like the one she had carried across the Atlantic. Quietly, she padded across the floor and lifted the lid. It was her trunk; all her clothing had been neatly folded and put there. Gentle Celeste! She must have packed it herself. So! Devlin went back and fetched her belongings. *How generous!* she thought sarcastically.

Without bothering to ring for the maid, Lauriette quickly shed her nightgown and donned undergarments, then chose a creamy yellow daygown with matching slippers. Vigorously she brushed her hair to a golden sheen and tied it at the nape of her neck with a yellow ribbon.

Her gaze anxiously raked the closed door. Perhaps Devlin locked it—perhaps he planned to keep her a prisoner! Her mind conjured up the nightmare she experienced at the hands of Marie-Claire, and Lauriette flew to the door. She breathed a sigh of relief as the knob turned in her trembling hands. Swiftly, she was out in the hallway and immediately smiled. When Devlin brought her in earlier, she'd had no time to survey her surroundings. From where she stood, the house was truly lovely.

The stairway curved subtlely; its black wrought-iron banister gave it a French charm. Dreamily, Lauriette leaned over the banister. The foyer below was quite large with various chairs and tables tastefully placed, and above a crystal chandelier hung from its domelike ceiling, sparkling in the sunlight.

"I'm glad you're up. I was just going to wake you," The deep, melodious voice made her jump.

Devlin relaxed behind her, a towel resting on his naked shoulders. Lauriette blushed deeply.

"You shaved off your beard."

His dark eyes twinkled and he grinned. "I am flattered you noticed."

"I would have to be blind not to," she remarked irritably.

"My, my! We've a sharp tongue this afternoon," he rebuked gently. "Are you hungry?"

"Famished," she replied heartily.

He nodded to the open doors below. "The servants are Belda and Cheney. Tell Cheney I will join you for dinner in a few moments," Lauriette hesitated. "What is wrong?"

"It's only that I'm not certain—certain of my—"

"You're my wife, Laurie," he said to her as if she were a misbehaved child. "No matter how you wish it otherwise, it is a fact. You're not a prisoner here. You are Madame Essex, mistress of this house. Now, see to it our dinner is ready when I come down."

"Yes, Dev," she barely whispered as she headed down the stairs.

Devlin smiled warmly and watched as she gracefully moved. How lovely she was and how much he loved her!

Lauriette sat across from Devlin at a small round table, eyeing all the mouth-watering food. Belda was an excellent cook! Though she was hungry, she knew within moments after partaking of a bit of food, her appetite would fail her. Devlin watched her closely as she put barely a spoonful of everything on her plate. She was much thinner than he remembered.

The dinner was a quiet affair, Lauriette hardly eating, fully aware of Devlin's intense gaze upon her. Sliding his empty plate away from him, he leaned back in his chair.

"You've hardly touched your food," he commented.

Lauriette looked down at her plate. "I'm not as hungry as I thought."

"You'll need your strength." His eyes gleamed wickedly.

His remark fell on Lauriette and she blushed hotly. "I am not the same gullible girl that was in England."

Devlin rose and quietly walked to the back of her chair. Lauriette stiffened as she felt his hand gently caress her shoulder. "No, madam, I think not."

"No, Dev," she said coldly, "I'll not be seduced."

Expertly his hand moved to lightly touch her throat where her frantic pulse beat. Devlin smiled triumphantly. "No, Laurie, That is not my intention at all."

She was finding it increasingly difficult to control the emotions burning inside. Why was he doing this to her, the cruel heartless beast! Devlin laughed lightly, then moved away.

The smoky look in his brown eyes made her pulse race. "Enjoy your house, Laurie," he smiled sardonically. "I am going to take a much needed nap and I do not wish to be disturbed." Turning on his heel, he left Lauriette sitting quietly, a pretty pink flush to her cheeks. Absently, she took a bite of her food, then another . . . and another . . .

Lauriette explored the adjoining rooms on the ground floor and became thoroughly enchanted with the little house. Outside, bushes and trees blotted out the surrounding fence which secured the house, and the well-kept gardens were delicately lovely. The gardens reminded her of the Hall and immediately she was saddened. How she missed Lord David, even after all these months!

Well, Devlin bluntly told her she was not a prisoner here, but why would he trust her? Dejectedly, she sighed. Why not trust her! Where could she go? He found her here, he would find her anywhere!

She decided to write a note to Celeste and tell her all was as well as could be expected. It would give her something to do while she waited for Devlin to wake. Her wooden secretary was upstairs, still packed with the rest of her things.

Lauriette opened the door to her room and padded across the floor to her trunk. Pulling away the folded clothing, she found it at the very bottom. Bringing it out, she sat on the floor, her legs tucked underneath her, and opened the lid. She smiled mistily as she withdrew several pencil sketches on the parchment. They had been done in the quietness of her cabin aboard the *Sorcerer* and in her room at Celeste's.

They were poor, shakily done sketches that warmed her heart. One was a half-hearted attempt at Essex Hall, another was a detailed sketch of Lord David—it brought tears to her eyes. The one she held now was of Devlin, his black brows drawn downward, a satanic smile that, as she gazed longingly at it, wrenched painfully at her heart. Why on earth had she kept them!

"You make a lovely vision, cherub." His voice sounded warm and lazy from sleep.

Lauriette gasped, her hand dramatically clutching her chest. Devlin was lying the full length of the bed, his head cradled by a pillow. He smiled arrogantly at her.

"You startled me!" she accused, dropping the sketches and jumping to her feet. "What are you doing in here?"

"Why, I had been sleeping."

"Forgive me, then, for disturbing your sleep!"

As she headed for the closed door, his hand clamped around her waist and slowly he pulled her toward him. Before she knew what was happening, she was sitting on the bed, Devlin's hands holding the upper portion of her arms. Her heart began to pound as she felt his eyes devour her.

"No, Dev," she said through clenched teeth. "I will not be taken against my will—not ever again!"

His hand gently massaged the side of her neck. "And I agree. No woman should ever be taken against her will."

She was in turmoil. "Dev, you—you said you had no—no intention of—seducing me!" She could barely breathe, her traitorous body beginning to melt.

"*Tu as raison, ma chèrie*," he said softly, one finger tacing the decolletage of her gown. "At least, not against your will. I said I would not seduce you—but I cannot stop myself from at least touching you."

His hands cupped her face, bringing her down to meet his parted lips. His kiss was moist, gentle . . . Suddenly after long grueling months of dreaming, longing, she was alive with desire. His touch—the only touch that could bring her fulfillment. Devlin groaned as Lauriette returned his kiss; his arms encircled her waist as he pulled her over him to rest next to him on the bed.

Devlin muttered curses as he fumbled with the buttons down the back of her gown. Finally out of desperation, he gave the material a yank and tiny yellow buttons flew every which way.

He kissed her again passionately, hands tugging at the sleeves of her dress. Lauriette was filled with such longing, she ached. She moaned softly as her dress and chemise floated to the floor. Frantically, she pulled at

Devlin's clothing until soon nothing but air separated them.

Devlin leaned on one elbow and gazed down at her, his hand caressing her thigh. "You are beautiful, my wife," he whispered huskily, his words sounded wonderfully possessive.

He kissed her forehead, eyes, nose and tenderly plundered her mouth. Her hands moved from his neck to caress his broad shoulders, muscles rippling under her warm touch.

His lips blazed a path across her neck and down to her full, quivering breasts. She moaned deep within her throat as she cupped her left breast, feeding it into his sensuous mouth. He had awakened in her that which was asleep and the force of her passion urged her on. He moved downward, his lips burning her as he made her tingle with want.

Lauriette was on fire. Her nails dug into his back as she tried to pull him up, but he would not move. She gasped aloud as his mouth touched her treasure. Her fingers entwined themselves in his curly hair, tears of joy streaked her face.

Suddenly he was up and poised over her. His eyes were heavy with desire. "Tell me, Laurie, do you want me?"

Lauriette gazed up at him through half-closed eyes. "Yes, Dev, oh yes!" she panted. "Take me—take me now!"

As he entered, Lauriette cried out, raking her nails across his back. Even if he hadn't talked with Joseph he would have known there had been no one else save him. She was still so small, a woman who had briefly known only one man's touch. Devlin smiled joyously.

He moved evenly with long, sure strokes, his hands caressing her taut breasts, his lips burning hers. She moved in a natural rhythm with him, surprised by her own sensuality. She belonged with this man no matter what. She could never belong to anyone else.

"Dev, oh Dev!" she moaned in his ear.

It was happening again as it did at the Hall. A thrilling heady sensation began at her loins and gradually, ecstatically, painfully, spread through her until she was clinging to Devlin, arching her body upward, not able to get enough of him.

"Laurie!" Devlin groaned as his body began to shake and he held her fiercely to him. It was ecstasy, a feeling he never had experienced with another.

He was still lying on top of her, his breath uneven and deep. Shyly, her hand moved up to caress his neck. Lauriette smiled. He was so big yet he did not crush her. How strange!

Finally he rolled away but brought her close to him, her head on his shoulder. They were both quiet, both content in the aftermath of what they shared. With a gentle hand, he reached over and brushed a stray curl away from her face.

He would always love her, protect her, and be with her. How could he have been so blind for so long?

"Laurie—"

She was sound asleep, one hand draped across his chest. He smiled that strange half-smile of his and lightly kissed the top of her head.

Fifty-Seven

In the weeks that followed the Essexes settled comfortably into the little French house. Their days went swiftly by, Lauriette and Devlin amiable toward each other and their nights filled with the madness of love.

Lauriette's appetite was almost back to normal; she added a few pounds here and there, and was transformed into a well-rounded woman. She became almost radiant since Devlin had come for her. Celeste, Jean and her brothers had been to visit and each commented on the fact.

Celeste and Lauriette sat together in the gardens, their shawls tightly around them. It had begun as a small dinner party with family and friends. While the men relaxed with their cheroots and brandy, Lauriette and Celeste relaxed in the serene garden.

"I have never seen you so beautiful, ma petite," Celeste smiled. "Are you happy?"

"Oh, Celeste, if I only knew all this was real!" she sighed heavily.

"The way of love is not easy, no?"

"No!" she exclaimed. "I'm afraid to be happy, to

feel secure in him. So much has happened between us, bad and good.''

''But he treats you good, no?''

''Very good. He is kind and generous and passionate,'' She bowed her head, embarrassed by her words. ''Am I wrong, Celeste, to want more?''

''How lucky you are, *ma chèrie,*'' Celeste whispered sadly, ''to be able to call your man husband. To have his name.''

''Celeste, forgive me. I'm a greedy, selfish woman who feels sorry for herself,'' she admitted. ''I know it is difficult for you and Jean.''

''It is all right.'' She hugged Lauriette. ''We did not meet each other until I was already widowed and he had been married for some time. Jean loves me, he spends as much time as he can with me. I am as happy as I can be, Lolly. Perhaps someday we will be able to tell the world of our love.''

Tears filled Lauriette's eyes. ''If I could have his love, I would be the happiest of women! But that—that woman is constantly between us. I can't help wondering about her.''

''Could you not tell Devlin what is in your mind?'' Celeste asked. ''Could he not put you at rest over this hussy?''

''Ask him?'' she said in astonishment. ''I am afraid of the answer. Don't you see? She was with child when I left—*his* child!''

''Oh, *chèrie*—''

''I think that was the worst hurt of all,'' she angrily brushed the tears away. ''Did I tell you about that tiny room I discovered at the Hall? A room full of childhood. A lovely little cradle, a faded yellow rocking horse . . .'' Her voice trailed off. She sniffed. ''I had secretly hoped . . . prayed that I would . . . but I didn't!''

"Sometimes, Lolly, it is better—"

"I know, I know," she murmured. "He hasn't mentioned her at all . . . or her condition. I left him to her—she said it was what he wanted. Oh, Celeste, I fear I'm only a possession to him! He only came after me because his pride wouldn't permit him to let me go!"

"Everything will work out for you, Lolly," Celeste soothed. "You will find a way to pierce his heart. I know you will."

Lauriette smiled at her through her tears. "I think it is time we joined the gentlemen."

Arm in arm they strolled to the house. The deep sound of laughter filled the sitting room as they entered.

"So there you are," Ben smiled. "What on earth were you two doing out there in the dark?"

"Taking advantage of a lovely evening—away from a stuffy smoke-filled room," Lauriette replied tartly, taking his arm. "I do wish you'd find a nice girl to make an honest man out of you."

"Here now! We'll have none of that tonight!" he gently rebuked, embarrassed to be the center of attention. With a graceful hand Ben placed Lauriette on the sofa. "I prefer my life as it is—single!"

Lauriette gave out an exaggerated sigh. "It seems I shall never be blessed with dozens of nieces and nephews. You, Jamie, and Joseph at sea and Elliott deep in politics, I suppose I'll never become a doting aunt!"

Joseph laughed heartily, slapping his knee. "Well, Ben, what have you got to say?"

Ben grimaced, a teasing gleam in his eyes. "Well, perhaps you'll not be an aunt in the near future, but it is possible that I could become an uncle, my sweet!"

The words were spoken lovingly in jest, but they struck her with such force she paled considerably. The rest laughed and she numbly forced a smile.

Suddenly Devlin stood behind Lauriette. He placed a warm hand upon her shoulder and gave it a reassuring squeeze.

"So you will be leaving us in the morning, Ben?" he sympathetically changed the subject.

"I've laid around shamelessly these past months. This will be young Joe's first voyage and he's going as second mate."

"The waters are quite dangerous now," Devlin said seriously. "We had quite a run in with one hellish British privateer, the *Iron Mistress*."

"But—but you're British," Joseph exclaimed.

"Dev!" Lauriette cried. "You could have been killed!"

Devlin smiled down at her, his thumb lightly brushing her chin. "The colors I waved were American," he informed them. "I've been a declared American for years."

"Was it quite a battle, Dev?" He smiled hearing Joseph call him by his first name.

"I'm afraid there was some damage done to the ship," he said. "When we put into port, the work began. My cousin, Judd, is still on her making sure it's done right."

"Judd is here?" Lauriette cried.

"He'll be visiting us as soon as the ship is finished," he replied. "He is most anxious to see you."

"Well, I am afraid we must bring this delightful evening to an end," Jean said, rising and offering his hand to Celeste.

"He's right, Lolly," Ben stretched. "We leave at dawn."

Lauriette rose and embraced Ben. "Please be careful."

"You know I will, brat," he returned affectionately.

She turned to Joseph, hugging him tightly. "And you, my young brother, I could box your ears for your choice of occupation!" she smiled through tears.

"Your love'll bring me back, Lauriette," he whispered, then turned away.

Devlin placed an arm around her. They said farewell from the porch as Jean and Celeste left. Joseph waited for Ben in the carriage.

"I need a favor," Ben whispered to Devlin. "Tell no one of our journey. I wouldn't ask this of you if it were not important. When I return, I'll explain everything."

Lauriette hurried upstairs as Devlin put out the candles in the sitting room. Mechanically, she shrugged out of her gown and into her nightgown. She could not shake Ben's words. It was as if he knew her very thoughts, the very thing she spoke with Celeste about.

Before she knew what was happening, she dissolved into tears. Her body wracked with sobs. If she just wasn't so unsure of Devlin!

"Laurie, what's wrong?" his tender voice reached her at the same time his hands did.

He turned her around but she could not look up at him. Gently, Devlin folded her into his arms.

"Ben and Joseph will be back before you know it," he reassured. "There is no need for tears, cherub, they're capable of taking care of themselves."

Lauriette was enveloped by his warmth and stole her arms around his waist. She would make him love her—she would drive away any thoughts of another woman!

Lauriette's moist lips parted as she placed a brief kiss upon his chin. Devlin gazed down at her with a confused expression. Her face seemed to glow; he caught his breath. Her hands moved to cup his face. Another kiss on one cheek then the other, his eyes, nose . . . he encircled her waist, his fingers sensually kneading the soft flesh along the way.

Lauriette's capable hands worked at the tiny buttons of his shirt then pushed it off his shoulders. Devlin smiled wickedly, a smile that had given him the nickname, the Devil. Soon they were both free of clothing. Only the magical light beamed from the full moon enabled them to see one another.

"So beautiful," he murmured thickly, "so damned beautiful . . ."

His hands moved over her back and buttocks with so light a touch it left Lauriette breathless. The next moment she was caught up in his arms.

She felt the bed beneath her and watched with amazement as Devlin shed his breeches, cursing soundly. Then he was with her, his hot hands playfully teasing her aroused breasts. Her hands glided across the rippling muscles of his back, sliding downward across his hip until it found his manhood. He groaned aloud, his mouth finding hers, his hands returning the pleasure she was giving him.

He kissed her brutally, possessively as he rolled her onto her back. His flesh became one with Lauriette's and she moved with him as one possessed. A wild, uninhibited abandon was loosed in her that challenged him and Devlin took has as the tide rose higher and higher. Their love became complete in that last single moment then all reason failed.

"Oh, love!" she cried in his ear. "Oh, my love!"

It was so rapturous, so beautiful! He held her tenderly, still warm from their lovemaking. How could this one enchanting woman do so much to his heart and soul? It was something no other woman had ever accomplished.

"Dev?" she whispered dreamily. "Have you known many women?"

Devlin chuckled, his arm tightening around her. "I've had my share of them."

She shyly stroked his chest. "Did . . . did you love any of them?"

There was a long moment of silence. He answered in a reverent tone of voice. "There has been only one woman in my life I've ever loved, cherub."

Lauriette closed her eyes feigning sleep, disappointment filling her. Tears blurred the back of her eyes as she rolled away from him, presenting her back. His arm clamped about her waist like a vise as he pulled her against him, his hand cupping her breast. Lightly, Devlin placed a kiss on one soft shoulder then nuzzled his face into the pillow. It was not long before he was sound asleep.

Hot tears spilled from her eyes onto the pillow. Muriel! The only woman he ever loved! How could she have been so foolish as to ask him a question like that! Would she ever learn?

Fifty-Eight

The days continued on. Devlin began to leave more and more; business was his explanation. The depressed state Lauriette found herself in became more obvious in the days that passed.

She brooded, her thoughts and feelings carefully hidden behind a mask of calm acceptance of her life with Devlin. He was troubled and worried about her but did not know exactly how to deal with it. Females! If he lived a hundred years it would still not be long enough to understand their peculiar ways!

Still, there was something very wrong though he could not quite put his finger on it. Their lovemaking had always been ardent, flaming, but as of late she began to hold a part of herself away from him. No matter how passionate and tender he was, he could never reach that separate part of her. Why? That question haunted him! His mind drifted back to the night of Ben's leaving. What a night that had been! Lauriette held nothing away from him then and it had been the sweetest night of nights!

Devlin stared out the window at the busy cobbled

street. He was in the modest shop of Pierre Voland, a most honest and respectable jeweler in New Orleans. He had come here with the express wish of buying Lauriette something to raise her spirits.

"M'sieu Essex! How honored I am to have you in my humble shop!" Pierre Voland was a small, rather delicate-looking man with silver hair and huge round blue eyes that watered miserably.

Devlin smiled amiably and nodded. " 'Tis I who am honored, *m'sieu*, that you so readily know of me."

M'sieu Voland's eyes sparkled. "All of New Orleans speaks of how you romantically spirited away the lovely Mistress Clay—"

"Who happens to be my wife," he added cooly.

"But of course," Voland stammered, his face turning a bright red. "I meant no disrespect, *m'sieu*!"

"I wish to see some of your best work," Devlin said in a much softer tone. "Something very special for my wife."

"At once, *m'sieu,*" Voland breathed a sigh of relief. It would not be wise to anger this young giant!

He returned with two trays covered in red velvet. The smile he wore brightened his aged face. The two trays held his very best work.

The first tray was exposed to Devlin. He carefully examined each beautifully created piece. Jewels of all sizes and colors glittered like raindrops on a moonlit sky. He was dissatisfied. He could not picture Lauriette in any of these! They were far too ostentatious for a soft woman.

"Have you anything else?" he inquired. "Something very simple yet exquisite?"

Voland unveiled the other tray. "This is the finest in all of New Orleans," he boasted proudly. "Each piece is one of a kind. I have made them myself."

Devlin's dark eyes fell on a lovely, delicately made

heart suspended on a fine gold chain. Yes, that was it! He could picture it around Lauriette's slender white neck.

"I have selected this." He held it up, a satisfied smile on his lips.

"A very wise choice, *m'sieu*" Voland agreed. "I am rather partial to that particular piece."

"I wish it engraved."

"It can be done immediately, *m'sieu*."

Lauriette held onto the banister for support until the dizziness passed. Eyes closed tightly, she mentally began to think back to her last monthly flow. January! Her head jerked up in recognition, her face paled a shade. This was the beginning of March. She was with child—Dev's child!

The dizziness vanished and she hurried into the sitting room and gazed at herself in the large mirror. Yes, she was different, she could see a difference already! Slowly, she ran her hand down across her flat belly. The change was not there—not yet. It was in her face; her cheeks were flushed, her blue-green eyes sparkled brilliantly and her skin glowed under the change that was gradually beginning to take place. Her eyes traveled downward to her belly and she smiled. A child! A beautiful child!

Suddenly she turned away from her reflection. Devlin! What would he do when she told him? Would he be overjoyed or angry? She frowned. He already had a child over there! He had given a child to the woman he loved. And now when he was faced with fatherhood from her, how would he react? Would he love the baby that came from her womb? Would that child perhaps soften him to love her? There was a chance he would be repulsed by her and the baby.

Absently, Lauriette brushed a tear aside. He had

been so kind and loving towards her since he found her, she could almost swear he loved her maybe just a little. But she knew better! She knew about his affair with Muriel under the same roof with her. Sleeping with her, planting his seed inside her when all the while she was down the hall aching for his hands, his lips, his . . .

She could go no further. She must wait. Wait just a bit longer to tell him. Perhaps if she were to wait just a while, he would tell her he loved her!

"Laurie!" Devlin's voice came from the foyer.

Quickly, she dried her eyes and put on a smile. "I'm in here, Dev," she called back.

As he came into the room, Lauriette brightened at the sight of his handsome face. Would she ever be able to tell him how much she loved him?

His hands gently touched her shoulders. "Turn around and close your eyes," he said. "Don't argue with me, cherub!"

With a half-hearted groan she turned, closing her eyes. She felt something cool touch her chest but remained as Devlin asked. His capable hands now turned her in another direction.

"Now open them."

Lauriette opened her eyes then blinked several times. A locket in the shape of a heart nestled comfortably just above her breasts. It was truly the most lovely necklace she had ever seen.

"Oh, Dev . . ."

"You're not going to tell me you cannot accept it, are you?" His deep voice held a note of warning.

"It is beautiful, Dev," she whispered, her mouth trembling just a little. "I shall treasure it always and shall never take it off."

He held her at arms' length and grinned softly. "Here now! We can't have you crying over a trinket! It was meant to cheer you up, not make you cry."

Again, the nausea and dizziness struck her as she stumbled against Devlin.

"Damn!" he cursed, sweeping her up into his arms. "I should have remembered your health."

She glowed with his concern. Maybe there was a chance for happiness together. Contentedly, she snuggled against his neck.

"There's nothing wrong with my health!"

"A nap wouldn't do you any harm," he gruffly told her. The bedroom door was opened and Devlin tenderly laid her on the bed. "I am going to be out for a few hours and I want you to rest until I return."

She stared up at him, annoyance clearly written on her face. "But . . . but, Dev, you were gone all morning!"

"As much as I would like to stay and romp with you, milady, I have business to attend to."

Inside she seethed. So that's all she was! A good romp! "If my company displeases you so much, milord, that you cannot wait to be out of my sight, perhaps I can remedy that!"

Immediately his hands pinned her shoulders to the bed, his soft brown eyes turned to sparkling black. "Do not tempt fate, Laurie," he hissed through clenched teeth. "You belong to me body and soul. Never forget that! We are bonded together and that bond can never be broken!"

"Part of that bond was 'and keep only unto her,' " she said, unreasonable jealousy filling her, "or is it only the vows that I made that have to be kept!"

His hands closed tighter, bruising her shoulders. His face was a hard mask of anger. So, she wanted to hurt did she! "I own you, mistress, just as I own this house and all the furnishings. To run away again would be foolish because I would follow you no matter where!

And I would take great pleasure in hunting you down . . . indeed I would!" His words were like tiny daggers stabbing at her heart. "I will use you until I tire of you and then"—he crisply snapped his fingers—"then I will cast you off as I did the others!"

Her head was turned away from him. With an angered growl, he flung himself from her and slammed the door in the process.

Lauriette jumped as the door viciously banged shut. She gave out with a strained sob, throwing a pillow towards the door. Exhausted from her anger, she cried herself to sleep.

Devlin leaned against the closed front door ferociously rubbing his eyes. As soon as he left their room, he felt regret. He should never have said those cruel things to her, but there were times when she could drive him close to the brink of insanity. Wouldn't it have been easier just to tell her he was going down to the docks to see if the *Horizon Queen* had been spotted yet? Of course, it would have been easier but he was not accustomed to explaining his every move to a woman!

He smiled absently. Could it be that the amiable Madame Essex caught the green-eyed monster? The idea of it delighted him. Only women who love are jealous! And there was that time last summer at Lady Bottomsley's—it was the same look! By God, she was jealous, the little minx!

There would be time when he returned, plenty of time for making up . . . making love . . .

"Madame . . . madame," Belda was gently shaking her.

"Yes, yes, Belda," she covered a yawn. "I am awake."

"You have a visitor, madame, in the sitting room," she whispered rapidly. "It is a gentleman, madame, very *joli!* He is *espagnol!*''

''A Spaniard?'' she questioned, jumping out of bed. ''Did he give you his name?''

''*Oui*, madame,'' Belda replied, unbuttoning Lauriette's wrinkled gown. ''Señor Esteban Cordero.''

''Hurry, Belda,'' she cried anxiously. ''The green evening frock.''

Cordero was standing in front of the full length windows, legs slightly parted, hands clasped behind his back.

''Esteban.''

He turned and smiled, taking in the loveliness of her. She was more beautiful than he remembered; her face was radiant.

''Lolly!'' he said softly, pressing both her hands to his lips. ''I just returned from sea last night. I could not wait a moment longer to see you!''

Lauriette blushed under his intense gaze.

''That last night, *querida*, Ben explained everything to me,'' he said in a harsh tone. ''*Dios*! What a monster to follow you here!''

''Not a monster, Esteban. Just a man who doesn't relish the idea of giving up something he possesses.'' Her reply was filled with bitterness. ''Let's not talk of it. Tell me about your latest adventure.''

Cordero escorted her to the sofa, then began a colorful account of the past two months. He beamed with pride as he told of the boarding of several French and English vessels—and of the booty brought back. Lauriette clapped her hands joyfully at his adventures.

Suddenly without warning, Cordero knelt beside her and took her hand. ''Dearest one, I cannot bear to see you live as this with one who hurts you so!'' he declared. ''Come with me! We can leave now, this very moment. The *Fateful Lady* is waiting. I can take you away from all this. Be mine, Lolly!''

She was touched deeply by Cordero, but she was already committed. "Oh, Esteban!" she said softly. "I cannot go with you, now or ever."

He was bewildered. "But—but you say he treats you as a possession! That he does not love you! You ran from him!"

"I know, I know," she sighed. "That is all true."

"Then why, Lolly?"

She lowered her head. "Because I love him," she sadly replied. " 'Tis but a simple fact. I've never loved anyone else. Not as I love him. I'm sorry, Esteban, but it would have been unfair of me not to tell you."

He stood, looking down at her with a confused, horrified expression. "But how can you love one such as he!" he scoffed. "An old, fat titled gentleman. Surely, it is pity and you have mistaken it for love."

"Esteban!" she cried, outraged at his words.

He came to her side as she stood. "Come with me, *cara!*" he urged. "Together, we will see the wonders of the world! I will give you everything that you desire. I am a wealthy man and—" His voice faltered as his eyes fell on the man casually leaning against the door frame, his face dark and inscrutable.

"I see you didn't expect me back so soon," he said evenly, but his eyes were like black pearls.

"I'm pleased you arrived when you did," her voice trembled slightly as she moved forward to take his arm. She felt it tense under her touch.

"I have the honor to present Captain Esteban Cordero," she introduced. "Captain, my husband, Devlin Essex."

Cordero's eyes widened in surprise as they acknowledged each other. Why, this was no old man at all! They were both the same height and build and as far as he could guess, he perceived they were around the same age.

"Thank you for entertaining my wife in my absence, Captain," the possessiveness in his voice was unmistakable. "But now that I am home, there is no need of your staying."

"Devlin!" Lauriette gasped.

"It is all right," Cordero replied tensely, picking up his hat. "I have many things I have to attend to—"

"And many more conquests to make," Devlin rudely cut in.

Cordero felt Lauriette's hand restraining him. "Please go, Esteban," she gently pleaded. "I will be fine. Don't worry."

"Lolly, if—"

"Just please go. Everything will be fine."

He glared at Devlin for a long moment, then nodded to Lauriette and hurriedly left.

Never had Lauriette been so embarrassed. "How could you!" she demanded, standing right in front of him. Her eyes were green fire.

Devlin grinned crookedly. "The incomparable Captain Cordero!"

"Dev, he is a friend."

"Friend! Hah!" he flung at her. "Madam, I am not a halfwit! I saw how he looked at you . . . making love to you with his eyes!"

"Devlin!" she exclaimed. "I'll hear no more of it!"

He grabbed her wrist, pulling her back to face him. "How long has this been going on?" he demanded, then his face became gray as a thought viciously struck him. "He's the reason you've held part of yourself away from me! He's your lover!"

Tears began to fall. "Lover! You are crazy!" she screamed.

"Crazy am I! I've got eyes! I can see what is before me!" he countered. "He was begging you to go away with him when I came in. You were going to, weren't you? Answer me!''

''Get out!'' she cried, wrenching free. ''You've no right to even question my faithfulness after what you've done!''

''Don't you for one moment—''

''Out!'' she shrieked, hurling a vase at him.

''Gladly,'' he said curtly, slamming the door closed.

Lauriette's eyes darted around the room until it fell upon another vase and with an oath that would shame a sailor, she hurled it against the closed door.

Fifty-Nine

The explosive anger had stopped hours before and now an empty coldness settled upon her. How could she continue to live with a crazy man! Would he constantly accuse her of adultery every time a man walked through the door? Did he truly think her capable of sleeping with another man?

How she hated him! Lauriette sighed. Hated him yet loved him. Why did life have to be so confusing—and so painful!

Belda slipped into the sitting room, a dinner tray in hand. "Madame, *s'il vous plait,* you must eat," she murmured.

Lauriette rubbed her throbbing forehead, managing a weak smile. "Just set it down, Belda, perhaps in a little while."

The maid's hand softly squeezed Lauriette's wrist. "It will be all right, madame," she consoled. "My Cheney and I, we have *beaucoup de discussion* and then we make up. *N'est-ce pas?*"

Her blue eyes filled with tears. "I hope you are right, Belda."

"You will see!" she smiled and disappeared out the door.

Night was falling as Lauriette paced irritably. Perhaps he would not return at all. Perhaps he would board a ship and sail right back to the waiting arms of Muriel! Lauriette drew a sigh. She probably pushed Devlin to that point when she told him to get out.

Lauriette was so preoccupied she did not hear the firm rap on the door. Quietly, Cheney entered the room interrupting her thoughts.

"Madame, there is a messenger at the door." There was a trace of alarm in his voice. "He wishes you to come."

Lauriette felt fear well up inside as she ran to the door.

"Madame, your husband has been hurt in an accident," the huge man dressed as livery told her.

"Oh, no!"

"Please, madame, he is asking for you!"

"Yes, right away," she cried frantically. "Cheney, my cloak . . . hurry!"

"Perhaps I should accompany you," he advised, concerned with her welfare.

"It would be best for you to stay here," she said quickly. "I will bring Devlin home immediately."

"My coach is waiting." The livery took her arm. Lauriette ran to keep up with him.

Swiftly, he opened the coach door and helped her inside. Lauriette was unaware of the dinginess of the darkened coach or of the rank odor. All her energy was centered on Devlin. He had to be all right! She would never forgive herself if he died! Her love, her only love!

From the darkness of the coach came an evil laugh. "So, mistress, we meet again."

Lauriette froze, terror paralyzing her limbs, her voice. Fourier! It was Fourier! Before she could think to move, something was blown in her face and she gasped as her head began to swim. Suddenly all was lost and she slumped against the seat.

Alexandre Fourier casually sat back, his hands folded comfortably across his stomach. His eyes were riveted on the dark unconscious form before him. Grinning evilly, he licked his lips. What a reunion it would be!

It was only a few days past as he sat drinking alone in his room that it came to him. Ever since he first set eyes on Mistress Clay, she struck a familiar chord in him. There was something about her, the way she carried herself, the expression in those strange eyes . . . yes, she was quite familiar to him. Then it struck him with such clarity, he laughed heartily. Clay . . . Claymoor . . . Claymoor Estate, Dorset!

Funny that he should remember that incident. There were so many others before her. Perhaps it was because she was no scullery maid or farmer's daughter. This one held herself in the saddle like a queen!

That particular day he had been cast out of his home, and his guardian, Lord Jocelyn Walsh, had disowned and disinherited him, stating that he should go back to France, to his mother's family and survive the best way he could. Lord Walsh had learned of his unsavory loving of innocent lower class maids and was repulsed by it. The thought of his guardian even now, after five years, made him seethe with anger. No one had a right to dictate the way he would conduct his life!

It was only a matter of having a few friends and being in the right place at the right time. Her and that upstart with her! He smiled dreamily, remembering that strange day. The two thought he and his three companions were highwaymen! But after seeing the girl, there was only one thing that would cure the aching in his loins—her! Oh, she was a tigress all right. Fought him every step of the way and he rejoiced in that memory. She had been quite a challenge and to beat her to submission had been only the beginning.

'Twas a pity about the boy, though. He had only meant for them to beat him unconscious, not to kill him. Pity, but after the boy died, the girl fought that much harder. Alexandre licked his lips greedily. For two days he enjoyed her charms. When he left her in the flea-bitten cottage on Essex land, he assumed she was dead or soon to be at least. What a shock to find her here in New Orleans!

It was strange that she had not recognized him, for surely he thought he would have been imprinted on her mind. She had not remembered him at all, but soon, very soon she would!

The *Horizon Queen* docked in New Orleans just as the sun was setting. Judd, feeling quite satisfied with the repairs made, was most anxious to have the ship secured and get on his way to Lauriette's. The thought of her brought a smile to his lips. Hopefully now they were spending their days and nights professing their love for one another!

"Mr. Morton," he shouted and from out of the darkness came Kelly Morton, who had been with Devlin many years.

"Aye, sir?"

"I'm off for the captain's house," he informed the seaman. "I leave the *Queen* in your capable hands."

Judd knew the way to the elegant little townhouse. Devlin bought it years before, their last visit to New Orleans. Judd chuckled lightly. He could not help but wonder if Dev had thought of acquiring a wife when he bought it!

It was a clear, breezy moonlit night and just right for walking. Judd surmised he was only several blocks from the house and a stimulating walk would do him a world of good. Impressive horses and carriages were out on such a night, the cobblestones echoing through the wind.

He stopped short as a worn coach sped around the corner, almost running over him. It came to an abrupt halt in front of a huge stone house in which only a few lights glared out from the windows. This was rather a seedy avenue and the great house appeared no better with its weatherbeaten paint partially stripped away, its grounds neglected pitifully, even the fence that once protected it was gone.

Quietly, Judd lingered in the shadows and watched with interest as a tall man dressed in elegant clothes emerged. As if suspecting someone lurking about, the man carefully looked around. As he gazed toward the darkness that hid Judd, the light from the street caught his features.

Judd sucked in his breath. The notorious Alexandre Fourier! He had heard sometime back the man had been disowned by the English side of his family when they learned of his sadistic ways with men as well as women. Four or five years ago he was all anyone talked about in the taverns he frequented. He also heard it rumored that Fourier was now an acting agent for the French in these parts.

He shrewdly watched as Alexandre Fourier leaned into the coach and produced a young woman in a green velvet cloak, the hood covering the face. As he passed the street light, the girl's hood fell away. He saw something shiny drop and for a brief second a brown curl which glistened gold under the light. Swiftly, Fourier carried her up the walk and into the unfriendly house.

Poor thing, he thought with a tinge of anger, doesn't know what she's in for! Well, it's none of my business!

He trotted off but came to a stop underneath the

light. Something glistened in the dirt. Judd bent down and picked it up. A stunning gold heart on a delicate chain. The clasp had broken. His finger could feel engraving of some sort. He held it up closer to the light. In Florentine script was engraved the letter *L* with the letter *D* entwining it. Quite a lovely piece of craftsmanship and very expensive by the looks of it. He would keep it for now and perhaps on the morrow stop by and drop it off—now was not the time to return anything!

Devlin was sullenly going from one private club to the next in the process of getting disgustingly drunk. He was in no mood to return home and face Lauriette's wrath nor admit to her his unreasonable jealousy.

Upon entering the Ace Deuce Club, he proceeded to secure a quiet table in the corner away from the loud talking and gaming. He nodded his approval as the valet placed a bottle of bourbon and a glass before him. Carelessly, he poured himself a healthy glass and quickly drank it down.

Jealousy. Devlin Essex's downfall! Never before had he ever been jealous over a woman. In fact, he had always been quite easygoing when it came to his paramours—until Lauriette. How do you tell a woman you're terrified you'll lose her? That she is so precious to you that you hate every man that looks her way. How could love be so complex?

"Señor Essex, may I join you?

Devlin's eyes slowly traveled upward, widening at the sight of Esteban Cordero. With a wave of his hand, he motioned the chair across from him.

They sat for a long time in silence watching the people at the gaming tables and others making their way up to the private rooms to play cards. They each had a bottle and both drank quite freely.

"*Señor,*" Cordero broke their silence, "I feel you owe

me an apology."

Devlin cocked a dark brow and glared at the man across the table. He filled his glass spilling most of the bourbon over the table. "Why?"

"Why?" he repeated, leaning across the table. "Because you humiliated me in the presence of your wife! I have honor, too, just as you, *señor!*"

"Is—is it honorable to desire another man's wife?" his words came out a bit slurred.

Cordero downed another glass of whiskey. "But that was before I met you, Essex! When I thought she ran from a husband who was old and fat . . . *Dios*!"

Devlin drained another glass and motioned for two more bottles to be brought. "You have a point, Cordero," he conceded. "My apology."

"Apology accepted," Cordero hiccuped loudly. "But I would have, you know."

"Would . . . would have what?" he slurred.

"Taken her away," he said simply, pouring another glass.

Devlin smiled foolishly. "So would I," he mumbled. " 'Fact, that's what I did. Took her right away."

Cordero grinned back. "Very smart, *amigo*!" His elbow missed the table. "A woman deserves a decisive man."

"Women!" Devlin growled. "They're as changeable as the weather! Can't ever do enough for 'em. Can't ever please 'em."

"Right you are!" Cordero joined in. "Women are never satisfied, no? My last woman? Nag, nag, nag!" He began to laugh boisterously. "I sent her back to her family *pronto!*"

Devlin laughed with him. "You're better off, my friend, to bed 'em and disappear!" he sobered a bit, a scowl appearing. "Or else you end up losing your heart."

"I know . . . I know . . ." Cordero replied.

"I love her, Cordero," he confessed. "God help me, I've never been smitten before! Been with so many women, thought I was safe and I was—until the first night on the waterfront." His eyes held a faraway look. "I've never been the same."

"That . . . that is why she would not leave with me," Cordero pushed his empty glass away. "Because of her great love for you. She never would leave you."

Devlin leaned over the table. "She loves me?"

"You find that hard to believe, Essex?" he offhandedly asked. "She thinks you do not love her."

"What? That's insane! 'Course I love her!"

"Did you tell her that?"

Devlin ran an irritated hand through his dark hair. "Cordero, I'm new to this . . . game!"

"Essex, there is more to love than showing!" he flashed a drunken grin. "You must tell a woman you love her, *comprende?*"

"You're right—absolutely right!" he stood up, wavering a bit. "And you . . . you come with me to see I do it right."

Judd paced back and forth in the foyer, his hands nervously behind him. He had hurried to the townhouse and found no one there but the servants.

"Are you absolutely sure what the gentleman said?"

"*Oui, m'sieu,*" Belda answered, "He say M'sieu Essex was hurt and asked for madame."

"And how long ago was that?"

"Hours, *m'sieu*, hours ago!" Cheney cried. "Madame said she would bring him back."

He did not like the sound of it, not at all! If Dev were in an accident, they would have brought him to her! Something was wrong.

The shuffling of feet and loud, brawling voices

brought Judd to the door. Wrenching it open, he stared in consternation at the two drunkards as they stumbled in.

"Belda, strong black coffee and hurry!" Judd ordered, then faced Devlin and his companion.

"Cousin! I see you've made it. And th' *Queen*?"

"Devlin, where is Lauriette?"

Dev blinked his eyes several times trying to focus. His head was beginning to throb.

"Let's go into the sitting room—both of you," Judd said gruffly. "Belda! Hurry with that coffee!"

After four cups apiece of Belda's special coffee, Devlin and Cordero sobered up. They both were plagued with uneasy stomachs and hammering heads.

"Dev, I repeat, where is Lauriette?"

"What the devil are you ranting about!" he growled. "Have you checked upstairs?"

"Damn you!" Judd cursed, grabbing him by the shoulders. "Look at me! A livery came for her hours ago! He told her you'd been hurt in an accident and she went willingly because she thought you needed her!"

Judd's words finally soaked in. "But I'm fine, save for a huge head."

"Then who came for her and why?"

Cordero was deep in thought. "There is no one who would do her harm," he replied.

The scene hours before came to him. "What about Alexandre Fourier?"

Devlin eyed him curiously. "Fourier . . . the man at the masquerade ball. He was the one who'd taken her out on the terrace—"

"Aye," Cordero joined in. "He forced an introduction from me weeks ago. He knows she is Ben's sister."

"Why Fourier, Judd?" he asked quickly. "Surely you have a sound reason for suspecting him."

Judd nodded grimly. "Something I just happened

upon earlier this evening. Dev, have you ever seen this?'' He withdrew the broken necklace.

''My God!'' he cried, snatching it up. ''Laurie's! Where did you—''

''Hurry, there's no time to waste!''

Lauriette sighed deeply, the effects of the strange drug gradually wearing off. She woke as if from a deep sleep, her head feeling quite heavy. Her eyes began to flutter, then opened, and she lay quietly, completely disoriented.

She struggled to sit up, easing her way to the edge of the bed. The room was unknown to her and everything appeared oddly formal, from the ornately carved mahogany bed to the heavy red velvet draperies.

Closing her eyes, she gently rubbed her forehead. Her thoughts and actions were still very lax, as if in slow motion. Alexandre Fourier! Her hand protectively moved to her chest. She remembered the coach, her punishing guilt over Devlin's accident, then that sinister voice.

Fear began to heighten her senses as Lauriette found she could move faster and think much more clearly. More questions crowded her mind. Why? Why did he abduct her?

As if sensing his captive was awake, Alexandre Fourier swung the door open and filled the doorway, looking more ominous than before. Seeing Lauriette awake and perched upon the edge of the bed, he smiled a cruel, lecherous smile.

''I can see by the sparkle in your eyes you had a most restful nap.''

Lauriette jumped to her feet, the offhand tone of the man making her leery. ''Why have your brought me here?'' she bravely demanded. ''Why have you done this?''

He moved easily into the room, closing the door behind him. "I promised you we would see each other again," he reminded her. "Only this time there will be no interruptions."

Cold fear settled upon her but she vowed not to show it. Defiantly, she lifted her chin. "It would be wise for you to release me, sir!"

He glanced at her with such a lustful eye, Lauriette took a step backward. "Mistress Clay, your threat rings hollow."

Lauriette glared back at him. "Think you so?" she scoffed. "My husband will tear New Orleans apart to find me. I would loathe to be in your boots when he does!"

"Ah, yes, the impressive Lord Essex!" he laughed. "I'm afraid your husband is in no condition to look for you tonight and by the time he is, we'll be far from here."

Lauriette paled, her heart pounding furiously. She could not afford to show her fear. "It is plain to see you do not know my husband at all," she returned.

His lips curled contemptuously. "His lordship will not want you at all . . . after I am through with you." His eyes slowly raking over her, Fourier began to unbutton his waistcoat. "You have no idea who I am, do you?"

In an instant Lauriette broke for the door. Hands like steel bands clamped around her waist as her fingers barely touched the knob. An enraged cry was torn from her as Fourier dragged her back to the center of the room. His hands were on her shoulders, cruelly digging into her tender flesh, tearing the fabric of her gown.

Her hands pushed against his chest in a valiant effort to get away. "No-o-o!" she screamed as her knee came up, grazing his groin.

Fourier yelped as his hands went down to cover his

crotch and Lauriette sidled away from him.

Fourier glared at her with such hate and contempt, Lauriette froze in her steps. He was wild, his eyes like evil black slits, welts rose from his pox-scarred cheek where her nails had dug in, and his shirt was torn from neck to waist.

Lauriette gasped as he turned toward her. A tattoo in the shape of a blue star was openly displayed on his chest. The past came rising up before her like a whirlwind, the nightmare of that summer so long ago stood before her.

"You!" The word came out in a hoarse gasp. She was trembling violently.

"So, you remember now!" he sneered. "What days we shared!"

"My brother . . . you killed my brother!"

"Your brother?" he laughed. "So that's who he was. He didn't quite take to my bedding you, did he?"

Tears burned the back of her eyes as she relived the unbelievable hell over in her mind. "For what you've done may God commend you to everlasting hell!" she cursed.

Before Lauriette knew what was happening, Fourier's steely fingers grabbed her arm and viciously jerked her to him. His free hand grabbed her other hand, cruelly wrenching it behind her before she could do him any harm.

"And once again I shall possess you," he whispered lustfully, his hand moving over her breast.

She struggled fiercely, lashing out with her feet but Fourier only laughed at her efforts. Her fighting him only tended to arouse him further.

"I'll die first," she cried. "You'll rape a corpse!"

"We shall see, spitfire," he hissed, his hand savagely entwined in her hair. "There will be no death until *I* wish it!"

As his lips buried themselves in her neck, Lauriette gave out a high piercing scream.

Fourier laughed arrogantly. "There is no one to come to your aid. Scream all you like."

His fingers hooked into the neckline and gave it a sadistic tug. Lauriette felt the fabric fall away from her breasts. She screamed again, tears blinding her.

Somewhere in the back of her mind she could faintly hear Dev's voice. She cried out pitifully, calling his name over and over. How totally ironic life was. She was in the hands of the madman who scarred her soul four years before. To die this way, away from her beloved Devlin, never able to tell him she loved him.

It was then that the door shattered under the weight of three men and Fourier was momentarily stunned by the interruption. Devlin's presence filled the doorway.

Fourier whirled Lauriette around, his arm viciously biting into her neck. She gave out a strangled cry as her eyes fell on Devlin. He stood several feet from them, his body rigid, his eyes glistening black. Behind him emerged Judd and Cordero. Upon seeing them Lauriette began to struggle until Fourier tightened his arm, cutting off her wind.

"Stay still, Laurie," Devlin urged.

"You're wise, your lordship," he spat, "and better at holding your spirits than I thought."

"Let my wife go, Fourier." His voice was low and deadly.

"The man's crazy," Judd whispered behind him. "Look at his eyes." Devlin nodded slowly.

"Your wife's got my brand on her," he said with an ugly laugh. "Quite a little tigress."

He took a calculated step forward. "You hurt her, you'll die a slow, miserable death."

"I have first claim!" he snorted righteously. "She was mine first!"

"Let her go, Fourier," his voice demanded, taking another step forward.

"First claim, first claim!" Fourier ranted.

Judd moved sideways, catching Fourier's crazed attention. In that exact second Devlin's hand flashed, grabbing Lauriette's arm, twisting her away from Fourier's startled grasp, and spinning her into Cordero's arms.

Fourier was helpless to do anything but defend himself. Devlin's eyes caught sight of the tattoo and recognition rung a bell. Unbridled fury gripped him.

"Get her out of here!" he ordered harshly, barely able to get the words out.

"Dev!" she cried hoarsely. "He's—"

"I know!" he cut in coldly. "Get her out of here!"

She was stunned by the blunt coldness in his voice and silently propelled her feet as Cordero and Judd shuffled her out. It was out in the open, her dreaded secret. Devlin knew now he was not the first. Their life together, what there was of it, was over.

Judd found her velvet cloak at the foot of the stairs and protectively covered her.

"It'll be all right, Lauriette," he comforted. "Dev has to do what he has to do."

They handed her into Devlin's coach. The ride to the house was silent, the two men too concerned to converse. Judd was grim. He knew what was happening back at the evil house. Devlin would kill that brutal bastard without a moment's hesitation. When he saw Lauriette imprisoned in his grisly arms, he felt that same murderous rage.

Belda hovered over Lauriette like a mother hen, tenderly bathing her, tending several bruises Fourier had put on her, then dressing her in a soft nightgown and tucking her into bed. Lauriette had not murmured one word during the entire time.

Now she was alone in the secure comfort of their bedroom. Tears welled up and spilled over. Alexandre Fourier, the man who had cruelly beat and raped her years before. In the entire world to live, she had managed to cross his path. Now any happiness she might have had with Devlin was gone.

"Laurie?"

Devlin stood at the side of the bed. He had quietly come in while she was in thought. His hair was badly tousled, his shirt torn and dirty. There was a darkening bruise by his mouth and his left cheekbone was blue and swollen.

"Dev!"

Suddenly she was in his arms crying silently. "It's all right, cherub," he whispered placing a kiss on the crown of her head. "He will never hurt you again."

He lay down beside her, drawing her closer.

"Dev, he—"

"Sh-h," he gently silenced her with a kiss. "Put it from your mind. He was an evil man who preyed on young women. It's over, Laurie."

Then he didn't know! Fourier never got the chance to tell him everything! "I want to go home," she whispered brokenly. Safe, secure Philadelphia.

"And so we shall," he replied, sensing her thoughts. "I'm taking you where no one will ever hurt you again. Home—my home."

England—Muriel! Lauriette stiffened. Never! The bitterest blow of the night. She had been foolish to hope for his love. She was only his possession. Taking her back to England proved it. He was obsessed with her only because she failed to bow to his every whim. Perhaps Fourier did tell him! That could be why he was taking her back to England—and the child! What of *their* child?

Sixty

The day had gone quite well, and as Devlin alighted from the carriage he whistled happily. He had been gone from the house since sunup making preparations for their journey. They would board the *Horizon Queen* tonight and on the morning tide sail for Virginia. Then from there he would sign the ship over to Judd and he and Lauriette would travel overland to Kentucky and his plantation, Even Tide.

Devlin placed his hat and cane on the highly polished table in the foyer. "Laurie!" he called. "Laurie, I'm back!"

The house was strangely quiet. He glanced up at the stairs and found Judd coming towards him, his face grim.

"Everything is in readiness," he said. "Where's Laurie?"

"Gone."

Devlin's head jerked up in surprise. "What do you mean gone!"

"Dev, listen to me. I returned an hour ago and found her gone. All her clothes are missing, her trunk

—she's gone!"

"No!" he bellowed, slamming his fist down. Anger flooded over him. "She wouldn't—"

"Dev, damn it, listen!" Judd growled. "A messenger gave me this shortly before you arrived." He handed him the letter.

Devlin crushed it in his huge hand, unable to believe what was happening.

"Read it," he urged, "Please, Dev."

Frantically, Devlin tore the envelope open. His eyes greedily scanned the hastily scribbled note. "From Cordero," his voice was hard. "He has taken Laurie to Philadelphia because she asked him to. He asks us to give them time—a few days start, then follow. He will meet us at Pelican's Inn when we dock. Says it is urgent he talks with me first."

"What are you going to do?"

"Do?" he repeated angrily. "Follow Laurie to Philadelphia. I swore I'd never let her go—and I won't! I'll follow her to hell if need be!"

The *Horizon Queen* set sail a week later on dawn's outgoing tide. The captain stood at the wheel, his face set with grim determination. His days and nights were filled with want of Lauriette. He would find her in Philadelphia and there would be many questions in need of answers!

It was mid-May by the time the *Horizon Queen* reached Philadelphia. Devlin could barely contain himself as the ship weighed anchor. He jumped ship before the mates had time to lower the gangplank and was already hailing a sailor to get directions to the Pelican's Inn.

Cordero relaxed in the dark coolness of the inn, his eyes set on the door across the room. For six days he sat at the same table and waited for Essex to walk through that door. After all this time his patience was beginning to wear thin. Distractedly, he poured himself another drink.

"Cordero." Devlin stood over him, looking as dark and foreboding as Satan himself. His face bore no trace of a smile or greeting. "Where is she?" It was more of a command than a question.

"Take a seat."

"I have neither the time nor the patience—"

Cordero roughly grabbed his arm. "You are calling attention to yourself!" he hissed. "You have waited this long, you can wait a little longer."

He looked at the man for a long moment then grudgingly sat down.

"That is much better, *amigo*." He nodded. "Lolly is at Claymoor Farm, an hour's ride out of Philadelphia by horseback."

"That's all I wanted to know—"

"Wait!" he argued, grabbing Devlin's arm again. "You must not be hasty. Let me tell you of our voyage. There are things—"

"I haven't time," Devlin growled. "Thank you for sending me the note. I am in your debt."

"Essex!" he called, but Devlin had already swept out of the inn. Cordero sighed defeatedly. The man never even gave him a chance to tell him how much Lauriette had changed. Well, with a man like Essex, it was just as well he find out for himself.

Devlin rode towards Claymoor Farm with all the determination of a man possessed. He pushed his horse faster with an overwhelming need to see Lauriette, to know she was all right.

As he had arranged for a horse, he had glanced at a scar-faced man across the stable from him. It was only a fleeting glance, but something in the man's manner reminded him of Brimley. At the thought of that revelation, a cold, bitter knot formed in his stomach.

As Claymoor Farms came into view Devlin was impressed by the huge place which looked more like a London manor misplaced.

"I wish to see Lauriette Essex," he formally told the servant girl who answered the door and walked past her.

"B-but, sir!" she protested. "You can't come—"

"I wish to see her now!"

"What is this, Naomi?"

Devlin gazed up at the man who emerged from the sitting room. He was tall and thin, but the hair and eyes clearly showed him related to Lauriette.

"Where is Lauriette?" Devlin shouted, ignoring the servant girl.

"Devlin!" James came from behind the older man.

Eventually, Devlin's face broke into a grin. "By God, James! I thought never to see another friendly face." The two heartily shook hands.

"Elliott, Lauriette's husband, Devlin," James introduced. "Devlin, our brother Elliott."

"Won't you join us, Mr. Essex?" Elliott asked cooly.

"Where is she, James?" he could hardly contain his impatience. "I know Laurie's here and I have to see her!"

"Calm down a bit first," James advised. "You're going to need a clear, even head when you see her."

Devlin slumped back against the chair.

"I do not think it wise for you to see her."

He looked over at Elliott whose face still held that cold expression. "Sir, she is my wife!"

"And my sister!" he countered. "Though to be sure, she is no longer the delightful little creature whose sunshine filled this house!"

"Elliott, there is no need to vent your frustration on Dev!" James growled, then turned to Devlin. "Lauriette told me that she remembers everything."

Devlin ran a tired hand across his eyes. "She told you about Fourier?"

James nodded woodenly.

"I hope to God his soul rots in hell!" he ground out. "And now Brimley."

"What?"

Devlin's voice was controlled but his eyes were furiously black. "I'm not certain, but I saw a scar-faced man across from the stable. For a moment I would have sworn it was Brimley."

James turned his anger toward his brother. "God help you, Elliott, if it's Brimley! Every time I even think about that betrothal I become angry all over again!"

"James, where is Laurie?" he interrupted.

"Out past the orchard near the pond," James replied. "She spends most of her time there. Good luck to you."

Lauriette sat near the edge of the pond, her knees drawn up underneath her chin. A most unladylike position but quite comfortable for thought. Lazily, she tossed a handful of pebbles into the water and stared at the endless circles they made.

Home. She had managed the voyage alone, returning to the only place that represented love and security to her. Elliott had been quite shocked at her rather sudden appearance but welcomed her with open arms. Then James appeared and an onslaught of neverending questions began.

She sighed deeply. If James kept at her much longer, she would end up telling all. The only thing James knew was that she remembered everything and her nightmarish encounter with Alexandre Fourier. Now he was at her constantly wanting to know why she left Devlin, what had he done that was so unforgivable.

Lauriette heard the sound of a cracking twig behind her as she stood. She turned and gasped at the deformed man standing only a few feet from her. He had a deep crease that began in the middle of his forehead angling down across his left eye and ending below his ear. The scar caused his left eye to pucker until he could just barely see out of it. The stranger was dressed in elegant clothes, a gentleman one would think.

"You startled me!" she stammered nervously. "Have you lost your way, sir?"

The man's grin caused a shiver to go through her. "I know my way around here quite well," he replied. "You are looking quite well, my dear."

"Evan!" his name emerged from her lips like a horrible whisper.

"Yes, Evan," he mocked, stepping closer. "I have waited a long time for you to return home. We have a score to settle, you and I."

"Evan, please, what happened—" She struggled for words.

"Essex did this to me," he sneered. "Because of you, who belonged to me in the first place!"

"I'm sorry! I didn't know!" she cried.

"Where is he?"

"In New Orleans," she quickly replied.

"You lie!"

"No, it's true I tell you!"

"I saw him . . . in Philadelphia."

"It can't be!" she protested.

He grabbed her arm dragging her to him. Frightened, she looked up into his eyes. He was crazy, his eyes were glazed and wild looking.

"Evan, please," she begged.

"I cannot hear your pleas this time, whore," he spa
"Essex came for you, the only one that means anythin
to him and he shall have you—dead!"

Before she could move, could begin to fight him
Evan's hands fitted themselves around her slende
neck. Frantically, she reached up, her hands helplessl
trying to fend off his. Her air was slowly being shut of
She would die here by the pond and it wouldn't b
hours before they would find her. *Devlin!* her heart crie
out. *Dev!*

She stopped struggling, her strength evaporating
Tears wet her face. She cried for the love she never ha
and the child who would die with her.

Just before the blackness consumed her, Lauriett
could have sworn she heard the crack of a pistol.

Sixty-One

Devlin paced the sitting room, his nerves worn to a razzle. He could not shake the memory of Lauriette lyng there on the ground like a broken doll. Rage filled him—hopeless rage that he failed to protect her. But he was alive, and Dr. Jacobs was upstairs attending er at this very moment.

"Dev, sit down," James said gently. "There is nothng you can do."

"I killed him too fast," Devlin cried through lenched teeth. "He should have died a slow agonizing leath over and over and—"

"Devlin, man, get hold of yourself!" James roughly grabbed him by the shoulders. "You've nothing to reproach yourself for. You got there in time, that is what counts! Now, for heaven's sake, sit down! Elliott will ell us as soon as Jacobs is finished with her."

It was at that time Elliott and the good Dr. Jacobs entered the sitting room. Both Devlin and James jumped o their feet.

"She's going to be fine," the doctor told them. It was the first time Devlin saw Elliott smile.

"Her throat will be somewhat tender for several days," he said crisply. "The bruises on her neck will disappear in time."

"Thank God," sighed James.

"Lauriette is a very lucky girl," he added. There's no chance that the baby was harmed either."

Devlin was stunned. "Ba-baby? You—you said baby!"

Dr. Jacobs was amused. "Yes, I did say baby."

"This is wonderful!" he laughed, slapping James on the back. "A baby! I'm going to be a father—and you an uncle!"

James laughed, too. "Imagine! Our Lauriette a mother!"

"I'll go to her now." The joy of fatherhood lit up his face.

Elliott blocked the way to the stairs. "I'm sorry, Essex, Lauriette doesn't want to see you."

"That's insane!" he argued. "Of course she wants to see me. She has to!"

Before Elliott could stop him, he was up the stairs and at Lauriette's door. He started after him, but James laid a quieting hand on his shoulder.

"It would be far wiser to let them settle it privately."

Lauriette was sitting in a wicker chair by the open French doors leading out to her balcony. She looked so lovely and fragile sitting there in a lavender dressing gown, the lace neck gently folding under her chin to cover the dark bruises. She turned as the door slammed shut, her eyes widening at the sight of Devlin.

"The doctor says you're all right."

Absently, Lauriette pressed her hand to her throat. "Please go," her voice was much huskier than usual.

"Not without you."

"I can't live with you, Devlin, I just can't."

"You're my wife!" he reasoned, anger mounting. "I told you—"

"I know what you've told me!" she cut him off. "You've forced my hand! You won't leave me in peace without having a scene, then so be it! But this time it is you who will listen!" Lauriette stood but kept her back to him.

"I cannot live with a man who stays with me out of obligation. I cannot live with a man to whom I am merely an obsession. We cannot base our lives on lies, whether they were told to protect or told unknowingly." She sighed dejectedly. "Please, Dev, don't make me go any further with explanations which would be painful to both of us. Leave me now."

Devlin shook his head unable to accept her words. "Laurie, you're not being fair."

"Fair!" she cried, turning on him. "Don't you *dare* talk to me about fairness! There is nothing—nothing left between us. We both have lived a lie and I refuse to be used again!"

"But I never—"

"You did, you did!" she accused. "I'm a woman with needs and desires . . . and I have my pride, too! You rejected me! You did! The nights . . . all those terrible endless nights when I lay there needing . . . aching—"

"Laurie—"

The look she threw at him left him stunned. There was so much hurt and raw pain in those huge eyes of hers.

"To want something so dearly and know that it is hopeless . . ." Her voice was filled with anguish. "I ran from Essex Hall so there would be no barriers between you two. I couldn't bear to stay a moment longer when I found out . . ." Her voice broke. "Please, Dev, please go."

"No, I can't go without—"

"I am not the virtuous woman I thought I was!" she screamed at him. "You were right, you know, that night. You weren't the first! That man, Fourier? He . . . knew me four years ago . . . at Claymoor."

"Stop it, Laurie!"

"Go back to Muriel!" she cried. "I know all about your affair with her and I absolve you of your obligation to me. I can't go on like this, wanting something that can never be mine!"

"But—the baby!"

She glared at him for a long moment. "*My* baby!" she answered. "Only mine! How could you think for one moment I could return to the Hall and live under the same roof with her and her child—knowing that at any given moment she might decide to try and end my life again—or worse, maybe that of my child? Go, Dev, go back to the only woman you've ever loved! I'm out of the way for good. Why you chose to follow me I don't know. Perhaps out of pride or revenge. Whatever the reason it will do you no good here. I'm at home and here I stay!"

His mind refused to listen. She was ranting like a lunatic! Muriel? He never even *liked* Muriel!

"Laurie . . . my wife. You're mine!"

"No, no, no!" she cried, tears falling now. "Admit defeat! Let me go! Leave now or I'll call my brothers!"

"Laurie, no!"

"James! Elliott!" she shouted brokenly.

The door burst open and both stood there speechless at the strange pair.

"There's no need," Devlin murmured. "I'm leaving now."

His boots echoed against the tiled floor, the sound

becoming fainter and fainter. Downstairs the door slammed shut and Lauriette dissolved to the floor, a mass of sobs.

Sixty-Two

What a lovely sunset, all yellow, orange, red, and gold. And the sky that unusual shade of blue . . . Lauriette stood, shoulders squared, back straight, on the balcony until it was dark. Pride had kept her head erect, tears in check and somehow she had managed to get through the rest of the day.

She could not forget the look in his eyes as she sent him away. It was a look of insurmountable pain as in the loss of a loved one. But it had to be done, she had to do it for herself as well as the child she carried.

"Lauriette, climb into bed now," James's paternal voice softly prodded.

"Did you see the sunset, Jamie?" she faintly asked. "Not as awesome as that sunrise aboard ship. Remember, Jamie?"

"Aye, that I do, pet." Tender hands took her by the shoulders and easily moved her towards the bed.

James bent over, lovingly tucking her in. "Here." He handed her a mug. "It's a sleeping draught. Dr. Jacobs left it for you. Go on now, it won't hurt. Only help you to sleep."

Obediently, Lauriette drank all of it then lay back against the pillows. "I did right sending him away, didn't I, Jamie?" Her eyes filled with unwanted tears. "I couldn't spend my life with a man who doesn't love me, could I?"

"Oh, pet!" he groaned, but Lauriette was already drifting off to sleep. Somehow they would be together, they had to be!

Lauriette awoke with the sudden apprehension of feeling the presence of someone towering over her. She could feel someone staring down at her, she could hear the person's breathing, but the sleeping draught she had taken hours before was still working and her limbs had lost their will to move.

A cry from her lips was muffled as hands tenderly rolled her up into the bed covers, her hands conveniently held at her sides. She was then gathered into strong capable arms and felt the man move to the French doors. Lauriette could not shake the drug, could not even manage a weak scream.

"And now, cherub, I'm going to lift you over the rail of the balcony and down to the waiting arms of Judd," Devlin whispered against her hair. "One scream and he has orders to drop you, so take care."

She felt herself being lowered by Devlin's strong hands, then felt Judd take her by the waist. She was unable to struggle in the heavy bedclothes. The night air pierced her senses and her head began to clear. She heard Devlin jump, landing on his feet and suddenly she was swept up in his arms.

She lay helplessly against his chest during the dark coach ride, a mixture of emotions tearing her apart. Though she was dismayed by his abduction of her, she could not ignore the warm feeling of being in his arms or even summon a little bit of the anger she had felt earlier.

During the drive, Lauriette managed to drift back to sleep and did not wake until the coach came to a stop. Once again she was carried out of the coach and up the gangplank to the captain's cabin on board the *Horizon Queen*.

There was a small lantern hanging overhead as they entered the cabin. Gently, Devlin laid her on the large bunk and with nimble fingers, divested her of the hindering covers.

Lauriette took a deep breath. She wanted to rant and rave at him, to demand he take her home, but the anger was not there any longer. Only a deep sadness for what could never be.

Devlin sat on the edge of the bunk, his arms on either side of her waist. "It seems we have done this before," he sighed, a crooked smile appeared. "I'm becoming rather an expert at removing you from bedrooms. What hell I go through to keep you near me!"

Lauriette closed her eyes as his hand gently stroked her cheek. "Why do you insist on prolonging this torture?"

"As I am aboard your ship, sir, you hardly leave me any choice."

His voice was grim. "I'm glad you are going to be sensible." He stood, hands clasped behind his back and slowly paced. "I want to tell you a story about a foolish—damn foolish man! He was reasonably good looking, intelligent, wealthy and quite arrogant. Women came easily to him and he enjoyed whoever took his fancy without regret or fondness. They were his to use merely for the asking.

"He felt himself immune to love," he continued, "for none of those women ever affected his heart. Until one day—one day he encountered an unusual young woman with eyes the color of the sea and sky and from that day forward he was never the same. Of course, at the time he assumed it was a physical attraction. Later, he called it protection and almost too late he realized it was love.''

Tears glistened in her eyes, her throat fought to hold down the sobs. He returned to her, catching her hands in his.

''I love you, Laurie,'' he said softly, ''more than life itself. That is why I will never let you go. Love—the emotion poets write of—I've been stung and I can't live without you. I refuse to live without you.''

''But—but, Dev, I'm not,'' she stammered.'' Alexandre Fourier . . .''

''I know,'' he cut in. ''I've known since last summer.''

''How?''

''You were delirious after your accident. You ranted about Peter, about what happened. Then James arrived and he explained everything. That was why Brimley made those slanderous comments. He knew also! Had to know because he was marrying you.''

''You don't understand—''

''I do, Laurie, I do! That doesn't matter. Don't you see? You were powerless to prevent it. It wasn't your fault. That night so long ago, you were a virgin, Laurie. The fact that there was no blood has nothing to do with it. I taught you how to love—no one else.''

''But—but that night at Lady Bottomsley's . . .''

''It was a set up ingeniously carried out,'' he replied. ''Mattie advised me to stay away for a time in order to give you time to calm down. I waited almost an hour, but when I got to our room, you had vanished.''

Lauriette was grasping at straws, afraid to believe in him. ''But afterward, in the library.''

''I was consumed with jealousy,'' he said in a low voice, reliving that night. ''A man in love torn apart by jealousy. Laurie, I'd give my life to relive that night. What I did to you, said to you—'' As a thought struck him, he gazed intently into her eyes. ''How long have you known about the child?''

Her cheeks grew red. ''Three months,'' she whispered.

''Why? Why were you afraid to tell me?''

She lowered her head. ''Because I was afraid you wouldn't believe it was yours.'' Tears glistened down her cheeks. ''You called me a whore. You said one time that any issue would no doubt be a bastard! Then, in New Orleans, you accused me of sleeping with Esteban Cordero. How could you expect me to tell you?''

''Again, my damnable jealousy,'' he conceded. ''I loved you so much I was afraid I'd lose you at every turn. Then Cordero was there asking you to run away with him . . . Laurie, that baby is mine! I know beyond a doubt because I know the kind of woman you are. The kind who belongs to only one man.'' He smiled at her. ''That's why I wanted to take you away from New Orleans. To protect you—''

''Protect me!'' she shouted. ''To take me back to England? To subject me and my child to the ridicule of a society that rejects our kind? To establish me once again in the same house as your paramour? To perhaps fall victim of Muriel's rage again? A rage that could even harm my baby? How can you want to put me through the humiliation of living under the same roof with your mistress and your illegitimate child?''

Devlin grabbed her by the shoulders and held her tightly. ''That's enough!'' he said sternly. ''Muriel led you a merry chase I see! There was never an affair between us and there *is no child!*''

''But—but that night—you said you loved her!''

''Again you misunderstood,'' he said gently. ''You asked me if I ever loved a woman and I told you only one. Remember? And that one, cherub, is you. Only you."

"I am so confused," she groaned.

"Muriel caused your fall?"

"Yes. She said you both needed me out of the way. She said you did not know about it until it happened and when you found out you were quite angry at her attempt. I thought that was why you were so kind to me."

"We have both been duped proper!"

"But, to want to go back to England—"

"Not England to live, ever again!" he said harshly. "I never meant you to think we were going there. We were going to Kentucky. I have a place there where I raise thoroughbred horses. That was going to be our new start."

She looked away from him. He was telling her he loved her. So many misunderstandings, so much pain . . .

"I love you Laurie," he quietly stated. "I never said it before because I thought you would know by the way we made love. How totally ignorant I was, and now perhaps I've said it too late. Is it too late, cherub, for us?"

She held the key that could open the door to love and happiness. Was she strong enough to take the chance that Devlin was speaking the truth? Could she really live her life without him?

She gazed up at his soft brown eyes, her lips trembling. "It will never be too late," she whispered.

Her arms encircled his neck as she pulled him down to her. Their lips met, warmth flooded through them.

Devlin's head jerked up quickly. "The child?"

Her laugh was soft and gentle. Taking his hand she placed it upon her slightly rounded stomach. "You can do him no harm for several more months."

Her husky words convinced him as his hands began to sensuously undress her. His hands began to massage and caress her, ever so gently teasing her breasts, down to the rounded stomach and down even further to her parted thighs.

Devlin's lips devoured hers, his kisses hungry and searing. His hands continued to explore, pressing her closer and closer to him. He had been so long without her!

He moved against her, passion overruling anything else. She belonged to him, body and soul, a merging of both which would end in oneness. He touched her, caressed and loved every part of her until she was breathless with want.

"Now, my love, now!" she cried as he plunged into her.

Desire mounted as he took her away with him. She was riding on a sea of never-ending rapture, wholly surrendering herself to the only man she ever loved. The urgency was born out of having been apart for two agonizing months, and as she clung to him, arching herself against him, she moved faster nearing that point of no return.

Her being exploded at the onslaught of passion, her arms and legs holding him tightly. Never before had it been this right, this perfect! Devlin shuddered against her and moaned, planting kisses on her shoulders.

Lauriette lay in the circle of his arms, happiness covering them like a blanket.

"There is something I almost forgot." Devlin leaned over the bunk and began to fumble in a drawer. "Two things." He held up the gold heart. "I had the clasp fixed." He securely placed it around her neck. "And, last of all, this. . . ."

Lauriette's eyes filled with tears as he placed the wedding ring once again on her finger. "That ring is proof you were destined to be mine.''

''Oh, Dev! she whispered joyously. ''I love you with all my heart! You are my life!''

''As you are mine,'' he returned huskily. ''Everything I have is yours.''

An impish smile lit her features, and Devlin grinned, placing a kiss on the tip of her nose. ''What is it, my love?''

''Well,'' she began, her arms winding their way around his neck, ''there is the most wonderful rocking horse . . .''

BESTSELLING ROMANCES BY JANELLE TAYLOR

SAVAGE ECSTASY (824, $3.50)
It was like lightning striking, the first time the Indian brave Gray Eagle looked into the eyes of the beautiful young settler Alisha. And from the moment he saw her, he knew that he must possess her—and make her his slave!

DEFIANT ECSTASY (931, $3.50)
When Gray Eagle returned to Fort Pierre's gates with his hundred warriors behind him, Alisha's heart skipped a beat: would Gray Eagle destroy her—or make his destiny her own?

FORBIDDEN ECSTASY (1014, $3.50)
Gray Eagle had promised Alisha his heart forever—nothing could keep him from her. But when Alisha woke to find her red-skinned lover gone, she felt abandoned and alone. Lost between two worlds, desperate and fearful of betrayal, Alisha hungered for the return of her FORBIDDEN ECSTASY.

BRAZEN ECSTASY (1133, $3.50)
When Alisha is swept down a raging river and out of her savage brave's life, Gray Eagle must rescue his love again. But Alisha has no memory of him at all. And as she fights to recall a past love, another white slave woman in their camp is fighting for Gray Eagle!

TENDER ECSTASY (1212, $3.75)
Bright Arrow is committed to kill every white he sees—until he sets his eyes on ravishing Rebecca. And fate demands that he capture her, torment her . . . and soar with her to the dizzying heights of TENDER ECSTASY!

Available wherever paperbacks are sold, or order direct from the Publisher. Send cover price plus 50¢ per copy for mailing and handling to Zebra Books, 475 Park Avenue South, New York, N.Y. 10016. DO NOT SEND CASH.